Educating
Simon

Books by Robin Reardon

A SECRET EDGE
THINKING STRAIGHT
A QUESTION OF MANHOOD
THE EVOLUTION OF ETHAN POE
THE REVELATIONS OF JUDE CONNOR
EDUCATING SIMON

Published by Kensington Publishing Corporation

Educating Simon

Robin Reardon

KENSINGTON BOOKS
www.kensingtonbooks.com

Cinderella At The Grave
From INTO THE WOODS
Words and Music by Stephen Sondheim
© 1988 RILTING MUSIC, INC.
All Rights Administered by WB MUSIC CORP.
All Rights Reserved. Used by Permission
Reprinted by Permission of Hal Leonard Corporation

KENSINGTON BOOKS are published by

Kensington Publishing Corp.
119 West 40th Street
New York, NY 10018

All Kensington titles, imprints, and distributed lines are available at
special quantity discounts for bulk purchases for sales promotion, pre-
miums, fund-raising, and educational or institutional use.

Special book excerpts or customized printings can also be created to fit
specific needs. For details, write or phone the office of the Kensington
Special Sales Manager: Kensington Publishing Corp., 119 West 40th
Street, New York, NY 10018. Attn. Special Sales Department. Phone:
1-800-221-2647.

Kensington and the K logo Reg. U.S. Pat. & TM Off.

eISBN-13: 978-0-7582-8477-8
eISBN-10: 0-7582-8477-2
First Kensington Electronic Edition: August 2014

ISBN-13: 978-0-7582-8476-1
ISBN-10: 0-7582-8476-4
First Kensington Trade Paperback Printing: August 2014

10 9 8 7 6 5 4 3 2 1

Printed in the United States of America

*Dedicated to the City of Boston
and to everyone whose life was changed
by the Boston Marathon bombing
on April 15, 2013*

Do you know what you wish?
Are you certain what you wish is what you want?
If you know what you want, then make a wish.

—Cinderella's mother, *Into the Woods* (Stephen Sondheim)

Your silence will not protect you.

—Audre Lorde, poet, writer, activist (1934–1992)

Part I

Worlds Destroyed

Terra Cotta, Coral, Lilac

Yeah, I know. I have to colour it out for you. I'll do it a few times, but after that you can refer to the chart I've provided for you in the appendix of this journal.

Terra cotta = *O*; Coral = *N*; Lilac = *E*

ONE. As in entry number one.

And you might ask, "Why are you bothering to number the entries at all when you're lying in hospital with your wrists tied up in bandages? Will there even *be* a Two? And whom do you think you're writing to, anyway?"

Good questions.

Bright Blue, Navy, Terra Cotta (Two)

That first one was a short entry. Lots of reasons why. For one, I don't feel much like telling anybody anything right now, so when the hospital shrink comes in and does his best to make me talk, it's exhausting, so I also don't much feel like going on about anything afterwards.

For another, all I have is my mobile phone, and whilst I'm great at texting, it's a lot more trouble than typing. Which is what I'll have to do with this . . . this composition when I get home. If I ever get home. And if I ever feel like continuing this journal.

Bright Blue, Cream, Bright Red, Lilac, Lilac (Three)

I'm home. For now. And whilst I've finished typing the notes from my mobile into my laptop, I can see that they look pretty pathetic on a full screen. Not much there. Rather like my life.

Didn't use to be that way. I'm fairly sure I remember a time when life was good, when my mum and dad and my cat and I were a family, when I was doing really well at Swithin Academy. In fact, I was doing so well that Dad once told me, "Not too early to be setting your cap at Oxford, Simon. Oxford is blue, you know. Blue for wide open skies."

To which I replied, tongue-in-cheek, because this was a kind of running joke with us, "It's terra cotta. But that's fine, because that's an earth colour, and I'll need a good foundation."

I think I was maybe fourteen when he said that. A couple of years ago now. And a few months before he died.

Sorry; can't really talk about that. Needed a break.

Maybe I can talk about the good parts. There were a lot of them between my father and me. For one thing, I have Tinker Bell because of him. When I was thirteen I said I wanted a pet, and Mum suggested a corgi, probably because she likes dogs better than she likes cats. But Dad smiled at me and shook his head. He knew. And he took me to pick out a kitten, a British shorthair, with thick, plush fur and a round, wise head and big eyes that miss nothing. She's a sweet, intelligent cat. I named her Tinker Bell.

My dad and I used to go to church together. Mum was never that interested, but Dad and I would go almost every week, either to our usual (St. Cyprian's) or, if we wanted something special and planned ahead, we'd go into town to Westminster or St. Paul's. Dad used to tease me that if he'd gone into the priesthood as he'd planned, I wouldn't be around. As an Anglican priest he could still marry, of course, but my mother wouldn't have married him.

I took the church quite seriously when I was younger, and over Sunday dinners Dad and I would sometimes go over the sermon we'd heard that morning, teasing apart the Holy Word in a way that brought it into real life, our own lives. But I had begun to question my faith not long before my father died. I was starting to ask questions to which there are no good answers, and the more people I asked, the more disparate, fumbling answers I heard. Dad at least admitted that we don't have all the answers, but it seems to me that if God wanted us to take Him seriously, He would have made things clearer. It also seems to me that if the message of Jesus was so all-fired important, it should have been clear from the very start. What about all those people who lived before Jesus was born? If Jesus was really the one true Path, then why the hell didn't the Jews hear from him sooner? Why didn't everyone? For that matter, what about all the people who never heard about Jesus, through no fault of their own, because they lived in—I don't know—northern Germany in 75 C.E.? Or in ignorance in Iceland centuries after Jesus was supposedly resurrected? And those are just the most obvious questions.

There I go, capitalising the pronouns. It's automatic. I'll stop, because after I lost my faith I realised I might be an atheist. And when my father was killed—that's right, he didn't just die—well, that was it. Quite obviously there was no God of mercy looking out for him, or for me or Mum, on that day.

As for how he died—well, I'm not going into that right now.

Bad enough *that* he died. But then to have one of my idiot class-mates ask if maybe the reason was that God was punishing me for my lack of faith . . . I nearly flattened him. I admit to a certain amount of arrogance, but I'm not self-centred enough to think God would kill anyone, let alone someone like my father, to pun-ish me. No God worth worshipping would do such a thing.

But enough of that.

One of the best things about being with my father was this con-dition we share. I almost certainly got it from him, along with my red hair. The special condition is synaesthesia. Most people don't even know what it is. And people who have it don't all experience it the same. My dad and I see letters as having colours. Each letter always has the same colour, but my terra cotta *O* is . . . was . . . blue to my dad. His sister, my Aunt Phillippa, sees colours when she hears music. I don't much like Aunt Phillippa, but I kind of wish I could see colours with music, too.

I wouldn't give up being a synaesthete for anything. I'm actually very smart—IQ of one-sixty-three and the vocabulary of an intelligent adult twice my age—but when I was younger, what impressed the other kids in school was that I could spell anything I'd seen at least once. The whole word takes on the colour of the first letter, really, but the other letters retain some of their own colour too. In the case of *Oxford*—with two terra cottas, a dove grey *x*, a pale green *f*, a bright red *r*, and a dark brown *d*—the other letters don't do much to modify the first letter. But take another word, and the effect is different. *England*, for example, is lilac, coral, fuchsia, bright orange, pale yellow, coral, dark brown. The whole word takes on a lilac tint, but I can still see the orange and yellow and brown. If you changed one of the letters—say, bright blue for *t* instead of brown for *d*—I'd know it was wrong right away, and my fabulous memory would tell me why.

I can hear you say, "So what? If I saw *England* spelled *Englant*, I'd know it was wrong right away, too."

But consider this. Would you know immediately that *Nuefchatell* is misspelled, and why? Or *Cairphilly?*

Caerphilly. Don't get me started. Don't talk to me about anything having to do with Wales.

Pale Green, Terra Cotta, Pale Pink, Bright Red (Four)

Simon. Blood red, bright yellow, brick red, terra cotta, coral.

Blood red, overall. I think maybe that's why slitting my wrists would have been my method of choice.

True confession time. That was not a typo, to say "would have been." I didn't actually do it. I was sitting on the closed toilet seat, contemplating how warm the water should be when—if—I turned it on, and I was staring at the razor blade I held between the thumbs and forefingers of both hands. I stared and stared until my vision got a little blurry and I began to feel faint. I slid to the floor and leaned against the wall for—I don't know, maybe ten minutes? And then I set the blade down. To be honest, I don't really know why I didn't go through with it. I do remember thinking that there would always be razor blades.

I'd sat there, giving myself a little time, drawing a mental picture. I remember thinking there would be rather a lot of blood. Red. Bright red blood. The bathwater would be full of it, swirling in beautiful shapes that I expected would be the last thing I would see. I pictured my mother finding me there. She'd scream, perhaps call my name a few times, maybe even try to lift me out of the water. And then she'd phone for help.

After that my story takes a split. One line ends up with me dead, buried in the soil of the land I refused to leave, despite my mother's plans. The other sends me to hospital. Imagine my consternation when I wake up there, head pounding, totally parched, and heavy white packs on both wrists.

I think I would scream. I know I would want to. I'm not one of those people who would send out a "cry for help." (How I hate that expression.) It would've been real, that suicide, if I'd done it.

And I suppose you'll want to know why I was even poised to do it. Whether I wrote a note. Whether I thought it would hurt anyone when they found out. If I didn't feel loved. If I felt life wasn't worth it. If it was because I'm gay.

Well, I didn't write a note. For one thing, what would it say? "Mum, I can't believe you've done this to me. Dad would never have done anything like this if it had been you who died."

For another, not everyone is capable of appreciating how well I write. The last thing I would do is leave my final words to be judged, picked apart, criticised after I'm gone by people who wouldn't know good writing if it fell from the sky, with or without colours.

And it wasn't because I'm gay. I have no problem with *that*, thank you very much. Even though I haven't told Mum yet.

So what did she do that was so horrid, you ask?

Here's what she did. She fell in love with a man, an architect, from Boston, Massachusetts—that's bad enough. He was here in the UK to dig up (not really; couldn't resist) some Welsh ancestors in—guess where? Caerphilly. So he's not only from Boston, but he's also Welsh. Worse still. And Mum has married him! Severe punishment indicated for this transgression.

Pale Green, Bright Yellow, Kelly Green, Lilac (Five)

Sorry. I'm sure this is getting tedious. Maybe I'll just leave some kind of blank space when I have to shut off the laptop and go scream into my pillow, instead of starting new entries every time. It's also, no doubt, getting tedious to see the entries coloured out. So I'll stop that, too. I think you get the point, anyway.

Just so we're clear, though, understand that even though *b* is sky blue and *r* is bright red, it's only coincidental that each of those main colours begins with the letter in question. G is not green, as it happens. It's fuchsia. I refer you again to the appendix.

So, back to the break that ended the last entry.

Trying again.

And she's making me move with her—with them—to Boston.

Entry Six

I'm trying not to hate her. Truly. I never used to. I mean, I was always closer to my father; it just seemed easier, somehow. He always seemed more approachable. I don't think it was just the shared synaesthesia, either. I wasn't able to put words to it when I was little, but looking back over my relationship with my parents now, what I see in my mind when I think about my mother is a kind of shield—transparent maybe, but solid—between her and me. And I don't think I constructed it. Or imagined it.

This distance between us, whatever it is, didn't bother me in any conscious way until Dad died. Then it was just the two of us, her and me, and this thing between us that neither of us had ever acknowledged to the other.

I'm probably making it sound bigger and more impenetrable than it is. My relationship with my mum is not terrible or anything. Or, it wasn't, until she dropped this bomb on me.

I'll need a way to refer to *him*. I guess I could use his name, but that feels like giving him so much more respect than he deserves. It's not just that he's half Welsh, either, though that's bad enough.

Do I need to explain that? Let's see. Wales. A country that fought England for far too long in a vain and misguided attempt to resist a superior form of government. We're talking about the twelfth century, here, but remember that England, unlike America, actually has a history and a very long memory.

Wales. Where separate little fiefdoms fought amongst each other at least as much as they fought against the Crown—fiefdoms led by so-called princes whose homes were practically stone huts compared to the castles and palaces of England and France. Wales, a country where a man could decide to leave his entire fortune (not that it would have amounted to much) to a bastard child instead of his legitimate son if he took a notion. A country where a wife who caught her husband in bed with a consort was within her rights to set the bed afire. While they were in it. All of this strikes me as rather . . . well, barbaric. And I'm not alone. But—deep sigh— we're all one now, supposedly. One United Kingdom.

I'll grant you that since King Edward I completed the conquest of Wales, things there have changed for the better, but their culture is still limited to singing and mining and fishing and charging money for tourists to see the sad ruins of Marcher Lord castles, which the local peasantry picked apart stone by stone after the English lords no longer needed to fortify the border.

But I think it's their attitude that bothers me the most. It seems to me that they don't take anything seriously enough. They treat everything as though it's just . . . I don't know, part of life. What I mean is, nothing seems to carry enough weight. Or maybe it's that the weight they give to serious things isn't heavier enough, in my estimation, than the weight they give to the less serious things. No doubt they would call it pragmatic. And in a way, I suppose it is. But let's just say that if my boyfriend Graeme and I decided to go to the town green at Abergavenny one night and have sex right there, they'd be more likely to rope off the area and sell tickets than to arrest us. It's not that they're money-grubbing. I don't think they deserve *that* criticism. It's just that they want to make the most of a situation in a way that doesn't always give it the weight it should have. And, all right, my example isn't a very good one; I chose it mostly for shock value. And it was an excuse to mention my boyfriend. But my point is, they just don't take things seriously enough.

So I'm reluctant to take my mother's new husband seriously. But I guess avoiding his name altogether is not going to work. He wants me to call him by his first name, but I can't bring myself to do that. I address him as Mr. Morgan. When I don't merely call him "him."

His name is Brian Morgan. BM. (Heh. I think that's how I'll refer to him.) And he has a daughter I've never met. Her name—I hope you're sitting down—is Persephone. I mean, really. *Persephone?* Not sure whether I'm more tempted to call her Percy, which is a favourite name for small dogs in England, or Phony. Evidently they do call her Percy, only with a different spelling: Persie. I think she's nine. Or maybe eleven. BM showed me her picture. Very proud, he was. Don't know why. She looks odd. Dark hair like his, below shoulder length, but even though it's a posed photograph, she's not smiling, and she's not quite looking at the camera. She almost looks like there's no one home, if you know what I mean. And I'll be unable to avoid her if (notice the subjunctive) I end up moving over there.

Mum met BM last January, only seven months ago. How's that for a whirlwind courtship? She was leaving one of her museum committee meetings on a cold and rainy afternoon, typical for London in January, the raw air making it feel colder than it actually was. Mum is nothing if not dignified, and hailing a cab is one of her least favourite things to do, so she has an account with London Black Cabs, and they give her priority when she calls them. The committee meeting was at the Tate Modern, not in the most accessible area of the city, and she had a car scheduled to pick her up. The taxi was late because of the weather and the afternoon traffic, so she was trying to stay out of the rain whilst she waited. There were two men waiting as well, men she didn't know.

A London Black Cab pulled up with a sign saying FITZROY-HUNT, our last name, displayed in the passenger rear-door window, and according to the story that Mum and BM (who was one of the two men) tell, she popped her brolly, said, "At last!" and headed towards it.

The other man dashed ahead of her and opened the door, and at first she thought he was being a true gentleman and opening it for her. But no, he threw a satchel into the backseat, got in, and shut the door behind him.

It's unlikely that the driver would ever have driven off; my family's account with the company is long-standing. Still, here was this cad of an interloper in the car, and Mum standing in the rain, staring in disbelief at the taxi from several feet away. The way she tells it, BM went flying past her, yanked the door open, and ordered the man out. A tug-of-war ensued on the door whilst the driver, turned around to face the back, yelled at the cad. Finally BM let go, ran around the car, opened the other passenger door, and took the satchel out. With the illicit passenger shouting at him, BM stood in front of the taxi, unfastened some of the satchel's pockets, and was starting to dump things onto the rainy pavement when the fellow gave up and got out. By now the driver was also out of the car, so the cad must have felt outnumbered. He collected his belongings and fled.

BM, dripping wet, held the door open gallantly (per Mum) as she climbed in. She offered to drop him off wherever he needed to go. And on the way to his hotel, they arranged to have dinner the following night.

The rest is history. I'll just give you the outline. He's a bit of a genealogy buff, and he'd indulged in a trip to Wales to research his lineage; his paternal grandparents had immigrated to the US when his father was five. He had included a few days in London before his return home, and he loves modern art, so he went to the Tate Modern on his first day in the city.

I didn't meet him on that trip. Mum told me about the incident with the taxi, and I knew she had met him for dinner, but I didn't know for a long time about the late-night phone calls and the letters and the e-mails and so on and so on. He came back to London once or twice over the next four months, and there was even one trip Mum took to Boston, and I did begin to worry. But I never believed it would come to this.

It was 1 June, I remember specifically, when the full extent of my mother's betrayal was made known to me. She sat me down, showed me photographs of Persie and of BM's house in Boston, which she assures me has a piano even better than ours, and informed me (she probably thought she was much gentler than that, but it could never have been gentle enough) that they would be married in two weeks, and that she and I would move there in late August.

I was supposed to go to the wedding. It wasn't a church affair, just a short ceremony at the British Humanist Association. But I locked myself in my room and refused to come out. Childish, perhaps, but necessary. Not only did the whole thing seem outrageously precipitous, and not only was she forsaking my father's last name for this man's, but also it meant forcing me to cut my own life completely off and relocate to a small, provincial city I don't know and don't want to know.

Oh, my God, we had so many conversations about this. Did I say conversations? Arguments. Battles, more like. I remember one in particular.

Mum seemed to think she could spin things. "I do understand that this seems like the end of the world to you. But it's not. It's the beginning of a new one."

"I have one word for you, Mother. Oxford."

"Oh, Simon, you don't have any worries there. You know that you're brilliant, your school career has been outstanding, and my father was at Magdalen College, so even though he's deceased you have a connection."

"What if I don't want to be at Magdalen?"

"That's fine. Your application will be reviewed by other colleges as well, and any one or any five of them might offer you a place." She shook her head. "Simon, you will have the world at your feet."

"All I want is London and Oxford. To hell with the rest of the world."

Her tone told me she was beginning to get annoyed. "Aren't you at all intrigued by the adventure this represents? The opportunity? America, Simon. Think of it."

"My life is here! My school, my friends . . ."

Mum's face took on an odd expression. "Simon, how many times have you told me you don't have any real friends? Certainly you're not close to anyone *I* know about."

I couldn't really argue that point. I'm not a friendly person, and although I don't really have enemies, I'm not exactly chummy with anyone, either. I once actually overheard some twit at school refer to me as a "nobby no-mates." Most of my socialising, such as it's been, has been with adults. My parents' friends. I lose patience with people my age; they seem so childish. But I came close—so close—to saying something to Mum about Graeme.

Instead, I said, "What about music? You know I've been studying with Dr. Ingerman for ten years! If you interrupt that now, I'll never know how far I could have gone."

"With piano? Simon, dear, you're very talented. But you know quite well you don't have what it takes to play professionally, to become a concert pianist. We'll find you an excellent teacher in Boston; don't worry about that. You should continue; you're very good. But it doesn't have to be here."

I didn't want to admit that she was right, or that I didn't even *want* to be a concert pianist, but neither did I want to give that point up so quickly. In trying to come up with a stronger argument,

I must have hesitated too long, and she jumped back into the university topic.

"You know, you could consider taking a gap year before starting at university, and spend it studying whatever you want in Boston or New York. Simon, don't underestimate what these opportunities could add to your scholastic résumé, wherever you end up studying."

Before I could come up with a way to find fault with that argument, Mum threw another stone at my defences. "You should also keep in mind that once you're in the US, you might even want to consider universities there. Harvard, Princeton, Yale, Brown—or you could consider schools in California. Your whole world will open up, Simon. And Oxford is still here."

"I told you! I don't want the whole world! I want only my parts of it! *My* parts, Mother! Not yours!" This seemed like the only argument I had: just my stubborn hold on the land of my birth, and that hard line, as wide as an ocean, between what she wanted and what I wouldn't let go of. I turned my back on her and headed upstairs towards my room.

Behind me, Mum said, "Don't forget to make sure your room is presentable. There's another showing this afternoon."

I slammed my door. Adding insult to injury, total strangers had begun tramping through the house, criticising and judging, any one of them potentially purchasing my home and yanking it out from under me, and for this treatment I had to keep making my room "presentable."

If everything I've told you isn't enough to convince you how terrible this move is, let me remind you: My boyfriend is here in London.

Graeme Godfrey. Gorgeous Graeme. That's what I call him, and to be equally alliterative, and equally admiring, he calls me Sexy Simon. Reddish fuchsia (him), blood red (me). The two together are a rich, heady combination, magnificently exciting when swirled together like marbled paper.

Or like the red in my bathwater.

In that second story line, I picture Graeme visiting me in hospital. He comes in whilst I'm asleep, and I wake up to see him in a chair beside my bed, his blond curls all I can see of his head as he buries his face in the sheets and weeps quietly. I reach out a hand heavy with bandages and stroke those curls, and he sits up quickly.

"Simon! Oh my God, how could you do this? How could you almost leave me like this?"

My head falls back onto the pillow. My voice weary with the weight of the world, I reply, "I have to leave you one way or another. I just wanted to choose the method myself."

He kisses the ends of my fingers and then stands so he can kiss my mouth.

And I vow that kiss will stay with me always, whatever "always" turns out to be. After I get home, every time I see him, he takes me greedily, like he's afraid every time together will be our last.

And even though that hospital scene didn't really happen, I'm keenly aware that every time I see him will be closer and closer to being our last.

Entry Seven

I've done everything I can think of to arrange a different reality, to stop this thing moving forwards. Mostly all I've been able to do is drag my feet, and I've done that as much as possible. For example, the school they've decided I'll attend in Boston—which Mum has tried to assure me has a reputation equal to that of Swithin for Oxford prep—sent a whole packet of material, from colourful, glossy brochures to lists of things like dress codes and class schedules. I looked at them long enough to see what they were and dropped them on the floor, where Mum saw them.

"Simon, have you decided on the electives you'd like to request for your first semester? It's rather a long list. Lots of interesting subjects."

"I'll get to it."

"Will we sit down together and go over it?"

"We will not. I said, I'll get to it."

Another procrastination I indulged in to make it clear to my mother that this move couldn't happen was to refuse to help pack. So at first I refused to participate in the decision tree that happened with every item she pointed to or picked up. It goes like this:

Is this something we should keep or not?

If we keep it, does it go into storage for us to consider later, or do we pack it for the move?

If we don't keep it, is it something we should throw away or give away?

If give away, to whom? Which person or organisation? When and how do we arrange it?

Obviously, her goal has been to pack as few things for the move as possible and then assess how important the stored stuff is, for a potential follow-up move. Pretty quickly she figured out that she could force me to cooperate by starting on *my* stuff. Like yesterday morning.

"That's fine, Simon. If you don't want to help, then I'll just make all the decisions myself. Now, what about this music collection, hmmm? Seems to me we don't need all these CDs. How many different versions do we really need of the *Goldberg Variations*? And surely not *all* of Mozart's piano sonatas need to come with us."

I know what you're thinking. *Bach? Mozart?* And here's my answer: Yes. I have some contemporary stuff, too; don't worry about that. KT Tunstall sees into my soul; the Indigo Girls prove they know what I'm going through with "Share the Moon"; and One Direction are great fun for a lark. But I love the classics, and whilst there are a few sonatas I think Mozart must have written in his sleep, I have at least one recording of most of the important ones. And having Daniel Barenboim's piano rendering of the *Goldbergs* as well as Trevor Pinnock's harpsichord is not the redundancy it might seem like to some.

My mother knows this. I really shouldn't have let her push my buttons like that, but my tolerance for irritants was never great, and this move, this project of packing, has shrunk it further. Lately I snap at everything and everyone. Sometimes it feels good. Mostly it doesn't.

Finally I told Mum, "Stop it. Go away."

BM, meanwhile, keeps swooping in from the States. I hate it when he's here even more than when he's not. It's August now, so they've been married for a couple of months, and he stays with her in her room. My father's room. My father's bed.

How can she *do* that?!?

I really do try not to think about it. Where was I? Oh, yes. Packing. And BM. He's here now for a few days, as it happens. And he came into my room not long after Mum left me alone with my music collection.

With a quick glance around he said, "I know this isn't any fun. I could help, if you'd like. Be glad to." And he stood there, waiting, a dorky look on his face that caused me to notice yet again how much too big his forehead is. The first time I saw him, I thought it was just that his hairline is receding, which it is; his dull brown hair is fading with age and pulling away from his face—a face that almost asks to be pulled away from, in my opinion. But it's also that his forehead is just too big. At least he's not doing a comb-over. That would be the limit; I'd sneak into my father's room at night and chop those hideous strings off.

I gave BM a look that said, *You must be mental.* What I said was, "That would not be a good idea, no." And I turned away so I could silence the scream that wanted to escape.

He went back to the packing job Mum was leading in the room next to mine, and I heard him say, "Em?" (I hate that he calls her that! Her name is Emma, and he should use it.) "Don't you think we should tread a little carefully with Simon? Tough love might not be the best approach."

The packing noises stopped, and I heard an exasperated sigh. "I know him; you don't. Coddle Simon at all, and he'll walk all over you. He'll lose respect for you."

Like I ever had any respect for BM.

I could almost hear him shrug. "Okay. If that's what you think is right. I just wish there were something that would get me at least a foothold on his good side."

"I am sorry, Brian. I'm really sorry it has to be like this. We're uprooting him completely, and he's just going to hate both of us until he doesn't hate us anymore. Can't be helped."

"Has he chosen his electives for St. Boniface?"

"I don't know. I've been after him about it."

"Well . . . has he said anything about the school?"

"Not to me, no." She didn't sound like she was enjoying this interrogation. The packing noises picked up again.

"It might help if he understood how good the school is. Have you explained that they're an IB school? That they have International Baccalaureate standing and their college prep is up to Oxford's standards? I know he expects to go there. Many St. Boniface students—"

"Brian, can we just get on with what we're doing? I promise you, I've sung the praises of his new school more than sufficiently. Simon has had every opportunity, and then some, to help himself. If he doesn't do what he needs to do, he'll have dug his own grave."

Little does she know. . . .

Whatever St. Boniface has to offer, Swithin is *famous* for its preparation. They send massive numbers of students to Oxford and Cambridge. I'll bet St. Bony can't make that claim. Gritting my teeth, breathing hard through my nose, I turned my attention back to my piles, and after an hour or so I'd made some progress, at least in terms of decisions. Hadn't actually packed anything yet. Mum and BM had moved downstairs.

I sensed rather than heard someone in my bedroom doorway, and when I turned I saw Graeme. (He's very good at finding me without my even knowing he's in the house. It helps, I suppose, that I gave him a copy of my key.) One hand was on the doorframe over his head, and he looked at me as though a truly intense gaze might keep me here. He stepped in and silently closed the door behind him.

I was in his arms so fast, and he was in mine, and we stood there like that, willing time to stop. It didn't, of course. I reached behind him and turned the lock.

We lay on my bed for a while, mostly kissing, touching, sighing. Before too long, though, his hand found its way to my waistband, then to my dick, and he teased and tugged and stroked until I came, really quietly, almost peacefully. He kissed me again, and I buried my face against his shoulder until I drifted off.

I'll never forget the first time he kissed me. It was at a birthday party last year for this girl at school. It was at her family's country house. One of the activities was a treasure hunt in a privet maze that had been on the property for generations. There were little favours hidden in the hedges, and whoever found the most would get some prize. What it was, I've forgotten; I got *my* prize.

I'd collected a few of those meaningless, colourful doodads and had found my way into a dead end. I circled back and somehow ran smack into another one. Or maybe it was even the same one again. Facing the direction I had come from, I stood still to listen, thinking maybe if I could hear someone else moving around, I could at least get to where they were, when around the near corner came Graeme. I'd admired him for months and months, from a distance, never dreaming he'd noticed me.

He stood there, looked around to see that it was a dead end, and I thought he'd turn to leave. But he didn't. He came towards me, watching my face. I was stunned and just stood there, waiting. When we were maybe a foot apart he stopped, put his hands on my shoulders, and leaned his face towards mine. It was a sweet kiss.

"I've wanted to do that for a while," he said.

"Would you like to do it again?"

The next kisses were not what I'd call sweet. Even today, my body tingles at the memory. And there have been oh, so many kisses since then.

This is what I'm losing. This is what's being torn away from me.

* * *

I woke up to the sound of Mum calling my name through the door. I saw that Graeme was gone, and my heart tumbled. Nearly tripping over packing paraphernalia, I went to the door and yanked it open.

"What?" My tone was so angry it surprised me.

Mum and I both have quick tempers, and she didn't back down any more than I would have. She repeated something she's said my whole life, something I've never understood and she has never explained. "I have asked you not to lock doors!"

We stared at each other. Glared, really. I flung the door open so it bounced against the wall and waited for her to walk away.

Facing the bed, looking through a red haze, I saw Tinker Bell there, front paws tucked under her chest, green eyes looking at me as though to say, *Life sucks, and then you die.*

No, that's not right. Cats don't really have that attitude. People do. I do. I sat on the edge of the bed where I could stroke her dense fur, mostly a bluish-grey with the occasional patch of white.

So if she wasn't saying the same thing I was thinking, what was her message? I sat quietly and listened.

You're leaving me.

I buried my nose in her neck and dropped tears onto her fur.

Entry Eight

Our next fight, Mum's and mine, was the very next day, and it was about Tinker Bell.

Before Mum had dropped the bombshell on me about marrying BM and packing us off to the colonies, and without saying anything to me of course, she had already made arrangements for Tink, which were to give her to one of Mum's friends for her little daughter, a few days before we leave. It's upsetting enough to have to give Tink up at all, but to learn that she'd go to a child—

who wouldn't understand Tink in particular or cats in general and would no doubt make Tink's life miserable—was adding insult to injury. It had been presented to me as a fait accompli because, as Mum had put it, "You don't want Tinker Bell to have to suffer through a terrifying quarantine period, which would be required for her to come with us to the US."

Of course I'd replied that neither Tink nor I wanted to go at all, and that discussion had ended in a shouting match that changed nothing.

For this latest fight, I was more prepared. After that heartbreaking accusation from Tink about how I was leaving her, I looked all over the Internet for information about the quarantine business, how long it was, what the conditions were, and what I'd found out is that all you need to bring a cat into the US is a health certificate from the cat's vet in the UK. The vet gives you a sort of animal passport that includes rabies vaccination verification. There is no quarantine period. The biggest hurdle is transportation.

"You lied to me!" I shouted at Mum, waving a printout of what I'd found as proof. "I'm not going anywhere without Tinker Bell!"

Mum didn't rise to the occasion the way I would have expected. She and BM were kneeling on the floor in Dad's study, packing books, and she was looking very tired and a little sad. All she said was, "I told you that for a reason, Simon. I knew it would be easier for you to leave her if you thought she had to go through a quarantine period and risk being destroyed."

I stood there, dumbfounded, printout dangling impotently in my hand, trying to wrap my brain around what she was saying. "But—that makes no sense . . . unless your real intent is to destroy me completely! Why would you try to make me leave her behind at all?" Mum and BM exchanged an odd look that went on too long. "Well? No answer? That settles it, then. If I'm going, so is Tink."

Mum got to her feet, slowly and awkwardly, and sat in Dad's reading chair. She took a deep breath whilst I waited for something I knew was going to be really horrid. Finally she said, "The reason we can't bring Tink with us is that Persie is allergic to cats."

Well, this put me right over the edge. "I didn't ask for this! I don't want to leave home at all! I don't want to live with him"—and I gestured at BM without looking at him—"or his daughter with the stupid name. And I am not—repeat, *not*—giving up my cat to do so!"

I stomped upstairs to my room in a righteous rage, ignoring the fact that Mum was following me. By the time she got upstairs, my door was shut and locked, and I was throwing things into a duffle bag. I don't like Aunt Phillippa very much, and I had no reason to think she's any more enthusiastic about me, but this had ripped it. Desperate times call for desperate measures.

"Simon? Simon, please, open the door. I need to talk to you about this. About Tink." I didn't respond to her in any way; as far as I was concerned there was nothing to say. "Please?"

Half a minute later I heard BM's calm voice. "Come on, Em. He's not going to talk with anyone right now. Wait until things have cooled down."

I almost shouted through the door, "Things will *never* cool down! I hate both of you, now and forever!" But then I realised that they had not only cooled down; they had frozen. Or, at least I had frozen. I was in a rage, but it was a cold rage.

I finished packing essentials for a few days and shoved the bag under my bed. I grabbed my mobile, unlocked my door, went downstairs to the hall cupboard, and dug Tink's carrying case out of the mess in there. I didn't take it out; I didn't want them to know what I was planning just yet. I knew where it was, and that's all I needed for the moment. Then, as quietly as possible, I headed out into the warm air of early August. I rang Aunt Phillippa. Bless her heart, she answered.

"This is Simon," I told her. "Um, we need to talk."

"All right." Her voice was friendly, if maybe a little wary. That was fine; I could work with that. She added, "What is it we need to talk about?"

"You know how Mum has married this Welsh American fellow? And you know she's planning to make me move with them to Boston?" I waited for acknowledgement and then unveiled my plan. "I can't go, Aunt Phillippa. All my friends"—all none of them—"my cat, my whole life—everything's here. I have to find a way to stay in London, and I think you're my only hope."

There was a second or two of heavy silence, and then, "Simon—"

I sensed negativity and tried to head it off with a plea for sympathy. "Aunt Phillippa, they expect me to give up my cat! Mum even lied to me and said Tink would have to go through quarantine. She wouldn't! That's not true! The only reason Tink can't go is because the guy's stupid daughter is allergic!" There was too much silence. So I added, "Please tell me you'll think about it? I can be ready any time."

"Simon, I'm so sorry. I'm allergic to cats, too. And as for having you live with me, well—my house is just too small."

I tried to breathe in; couldn't really do it. I tried to breathe out, and a half-cough, half-sob escaped me. Finally I managed to say, "What am I going to do?" My voice sounded like that of a little kid who couldn't find his way home. Or maybe a kid who couldn't go home because being there would kill him.

Aunt Phillippa mumbled something I didn't really hear, and then there was more silence, and I rang off. Phone back in my pocket, I started walking. I didn't know where I was going or why or how long I'd walk or whether I'd ever walk home again. I considered calling Graeme, but what could he do? I couldn't even give him my cat; he lives in a flat where no pets are allowed. I turned my phone off, thinking, *If Mum wonders where I am, well . . . let her wonder.*

Without really thinking about it, I headed for Hampstead Heath, following Platt's Lane to the entry point on West Heath Road. If I'd had any grandparents still living, I'd have tried that option, but they're all deceased. I began forming this plan where I really would kill myself, and this time I'd take Tink with me. A kind of suicide pact. Surely Tink would rather that than have to go live with a little girl who'd pull her tail and make her wear disgusting lace hats and aprons. But then it occurred to me that I was willing to live with Aunt Phillippa, unpleasant in so many ways though that would have been. So it might be that Tink would rather go live with the little girl than check out altogether. It wouldn't be fair of me to make that decision for her.

I think of the Heath as my park. It's so close to our house on Hermitage Lane that I've spent a lot of time there. It's massive, with fields and ponds and horse trails and woodland paths. I've always been drawn to the woodland paths, the less frequented by others the better.

I left Sandy Road, the horse/bicycle trail, as soon as possible and pointed myself towards my favourite tree, a weeping red beech. The branches cascade down from high above in a grand expanse like a great skirt, and I can lean on the trunk, standing or sitting on the ground, and no one going by can see me.

I sat in my usual spot, a soft concave between two thick roots, and leaned back against that solid, constant, trustworthy tree. Knees up, I laid my forearms across them and dropped my head on the backs of my poor, battered wrists, as they appeared in my imagination.

To keep the tears away, I allowed myself the painful pleasure of dwelling on the ultimate fate of Earth and everyone, everything on it. Because, you know, it won't last. It's doomed.

I skimmed the possible topics. There have been enough cataclysms through the millennia to satisfy even my imagination. One of my favourites is the Great Dying, which killed about 90 percent of life on Earth at the time—250 million years ago. But life recovered. I was more in the mood for something we couldn't recover from.

Everyone knows that the stability of Earth's magnetic field is decreasing, and that this field is our main defence against radiation from the sun. Satellites and even telescopes are already being affected. The ethereal beauty of the auroras borealis and australis increases as the magnetic field struggles to protect us. Once or twice in the distant past, the magnetic field has weakened in a way that caused the north and south poles to switch their locations. This is going on right now, and anything might happen—even to the unlikely but still possible point of radiation's killing off all life on the planet. Mind you, even if this happened, it would take a while.

There's no need for anyone alive today to see this phenomenon as a cue to hurry up with their bucket list. But it's doom, and it suited my mood.

In the shady gloom, I had to focus deliberately to see the three black ants on the dirt under my legs. I watched them for several seconds, or maybe several minutes, fascinated and appalled at the apparent randomness of their meanderings. It struck me that most people seem to meander rather aimlessly through their own lives, and if someone were looking down from above they'd probably be about as unimpressed with us as I was with the ants. And yet these ants keep going, like it matters. Like life matters. Like their lives matter.

Suddenly I heard a soft rustle that told me someone was invading my sacred space. A sharp glance up told me it was all right: It was Graeme. He sat beside me so that our shoulders touched.

"How did you find me here?"

He leaned his head back against the tree. "It seemed likely. This is your spot, where you come when you're upset. I rang and got voice mail." He turned his face towards me. "And here you are."

"And here I won't be much longer." We let that hang in the air, and then I added, "You haven't heard the latest." I could practically hear his teeth grinding, bracing for more bad news and angry for me about it already. "Mum lied to me." I waited, but still he was silent, so I told him there was no quarantine after all.

He said, "I can't wait to hear the rest. I'm sure there's more."

"That horrid girl, Persephone, is allergic."

In a quick, angry move, Graeme repositioned himself, facing me. *"What?!?"*

"I know."

"But . . . but that's . . . Oh, Simon!"

"I've just tried to get Aunt Phillippa to take me in. She wasn't enthusiastic, and also she's allergic, too. What's with that, anyway? Is it even a real thing?"

Graeme just looked at me, his beautiful face contorted into an expression between anger and pity. Softly, gently, he took one of my hands and leaned his face towards it, kissing first the skin on my wrist where bandages almost had been, and then the centre of my palm. I love when he does that.

"What we need," he said between kisses, "is one of those large cone snails."

I almost laughed. He meant a particular variety of snail that sometimes stings people at tropical seashores. There's no antivenom for its poison, and people who are stung usually die, sometimes within minutes. The shell is incredibly beautiful, and people are tempted to pick the snail up. It might not do anything right away, but eventually—gotcha! A harpoon-like tooth, capable of penetrating even a wetsuit if it's one of the larger snails, shoots deadly poison into you. There's pain, swelling, paralysis, respiratory distress, lots of nasty symptoms. If you're not taken someplace immediately where they can keep you on life support until the toxin is metabolised, you'll almost certainly die.

Graeme shares my fascination for things doom-oriented. Just one of the many things I love about him. I wrapped my tattered wrists around his neck, and he leaned back so he was lying on the ground, bringing my body onto his, and we kissed. For a long time.

Graeme walked me most of the way home. I stopped a few houses away, knowing Mum would be furious with me, not wanting to face that. I pulled out my mobile and turned it on; sure enough, there were five missed calls from her.

"Will I come in?" Graeme asked, perhaps thinking his presence would prevent a total explosion.

I shook my head. "No point in putting both of us through it. The sky will fall now, or it will fall later. May as well get it over with."

Graeme ran a hand tenderly down my arm and smiled sadly, and I headed towards the house. I made as much noise as reasonable unlocking and opening the door: Don't let anyone think I'm the least bit penitent.

"Simon?" Mum came running towards me. "Your Aunt Phillippa called. Where have you been?" Her tone and her facial expression ran the gamut from afraid to thankful to furious in the space of those few words.

"Out." I tried to get around her to the stairs and the haven of my bedroom. She wasn't cooperating.

"Do you know that I very nearly rang the police?"

"Of course I don't. I wasn't here." I managed to get upstairs, nearly at a run, and I was in the process of shutting my bedroom door when I felt pressure from the other side. She pushed the door open, glaring at me. I'm sure she would have shouted something at me if BM hadn't appeared and taken over.

He put his hands on her shoulders. "Em, let me talk to him." His voice was so calm, and the way he was touching her released something in her, and her face relaxed a little. In the nanosecond it took for her to turn away, a flash of recognition hit me and nearly made me choke: BM knows how to approach her, just like my father used to. Dad could calm her down, or calm me down, from almost anything. It's no wonder we're falling apart now that he's not with us anymore. He was the buffer. He was the bringer of peace.

Maybe Mum is willing to let BM step into that role. I am not.

I couldn't slam the door shut with him in the way, so I turned my back on him. I sat on my bed, browsing through my phone like I cared about what I might find there.

His voice still annoyingly calm, he asked, "Are there things you'd like to say to me, Simon?"

I turned to look at him. He was leaning against the doorframe, no doubt trying to look casual. I blinked stupidly for about three seconds. Was he really prodding me to lay into him? And if I did, what would the consequences be? Doing my best not to shout, because I wanted to sound eminently sane, I said, "Do you have *any* concept of what this is doing to me? Wrenching me away from everything in my life? And if that's not enough, it'll ruin my chances of getting into university where both my father and I want me to go, one of the best in the *world*, where I could get myself set up *for the rest of my life!*" I shouted that last bit. So much for sanity.

He blinked softly, rather like a cat when she's looking at you and wants to let you know it isn't a confrontational stare she's giving you. Silence.

"*Well?!?*" I slammed my phone onto the bed as punctuation.

His voice still calm and soft, he said, "I have a feeling there's more. Why don't you get it all out into the open?"

I stood, hands clenched at my sides. At first, words failed me, but not because I didn't know what to say. I didn't know where to *start*. I glared at him, willing my eyes to shoot fire.

"Fine. You and Mum have made me into the red-haired stepchild, literally and figuratively. You've ganged up together, and I'm odd man out. If you insist on being married, you could have waited long enough for me to finish one more year of school, and I'd be on my own, at university. Or if you couldn't wait to do unmentionable things together in my father's bed, you could move to London instead of ripping me out of my home during my almost-finished formative years. Your daughter's young enough to be flexible. There are all kinds of ways you could proceed without ripping my life to shreds. And my dear mother"—I wanted to spit at this point, but it would have been uncouth—"is proceeding with all these plans that destroy my life, and she lies to me to make it more convenient for herself."

I was breathing hard through my nose, all those things I'd been dying to say strewn about the floor.

He blinked again, that soft gesture. "Have you said all this to her? Those alternatives?"

"Oh, trust me, there's nothing left unmentioned."

"And what did she tell you were the reasons?"

"All she said was that we're doing it. There are no reasons. 'Because,' that's why."

"You're sure?" Something in his voice told me this was not a surprise to him, that he was merely verifying the information.

"Look, I don't know where you're going with this—"

"I think you deserve to understand what's behind our decisions. I know your mother's been reluctant to tell you, and she has her reasons, but I think you need to hear everything." He gestured towards the stairs. "Please. Let's go where we can talk together, all three of us."

He had my attention; that was certain. He seemed to think there were things I didn't know about this horror show, things I needed to know, things Mum had kept from me. That is, *more* things she'd kept from me. Wary though I was, curiosity got the better of me. I followed him downstairs to the sitting room and set-tled into my favourite chair, a big, overstuffed thing that we will no doubt leave behind. Legs tucked under me, huddled into this giant lap for comfort and protection, I waited whilst BM went to fetch Mum from the kitchen. I heard a teacup settle onto its saucer, and then a short, nearly whispered conversation.

"Em, it's time. We need to let him know the whole story."

"Brian—"

"Em." His calm voice took on—not an edge, exactly. It was a tone of finality.

"No, listen. I was going to tell him. That's why I followed him upstairs earlier."

"Then let's tell him now."

When Mum appeared, she looked almost meek. I couldn't make any sense out of it. They sat side by side on the couch, and BM took Mum's hand. It was an odd moment for this, but I took a good look at her for the first time in quite a while. She had more grey than I remembered, shot through her wavy auburn hair. It was pulled back rather severely at the moment, but at more re-laxed times it flowed about her shoulders. As it was now, it ex-posed and perhaps even exaggerated small wrinkles I hadn't noticed. I've always known she was older than my dad, but only by four years. She's forty-six now, and my guess is that BM is about the same age.

I watched, and waited, whilst they settled. He looked at her, like it was her job to tell me the "whole story," but she kept her eyes on their clasped hands. So he turned to me.

"You know that I'm divorced." I nodded. "What you don't know is why. It has to do with my daughter. Persie has Asperger syndrome, which is a form of autism. I encourage you to look it up so you can understand more about it."

He stopped, no doubt to see if I had any questions. What was going through my mind was that this explained the way Persie looked in the photo I had seen.

"My ex-wife had a very hard time dealing with it. A very hard time. She decided to leave me, and Persie, two years ago. Persie . . . well, she needs a lot of care. She is not what they call high-functioning, although a lot of people with AS manage to deal well with the rest of society. I can afford to provide her with the care she needs, but moving her anywhere would probably send her into a catatonic state. People with AS and related issues usually don't handle change well. So that explains why she and I can't move to London."

This was definitely news to me. But Mum must have known. I risked a glance at her, but she was still staring down at her hands, and what I could see of her face told me that something about what BM had said was upsetting for her, which puzzled me. I mean, sure, it's a sad thing to have your child be like that (whatever "that" means; I will look this thing up), but it's not *her* child.

I looked at BM, since he was the one with all the answers. "Why is this the first I'm hearing about this?"

BM glanced towards Mum. "Em, I think you should explain about Clive."

I couldn't help asking. "Who's Clive?"

It was obvious, even to me, that it took a huge effort, but Mum sat up straight. She looked at me and said, "My younger brother. You never knew him. You never knew *of* him, even. I wasn't planning to have any children, because I was afraid of having a child like him. A child with autism. It's more common in boys, and when I found out you were a boy, I was terrified. I didn't want you to be like him."

She took another half-minute or so to collect herself, and I used the time to try and wrap my mind around what she was telling me. She'd said he *was* her brother. "What happened to him?"

Her answer was more of a story, and she ploughed forwards with it as though a pause would make it impossible for her to continue.

"He was three years younger than I was. Because of his autism, he was a burden to my parents and an embarrassment to me. I didn't want to have friends over, and I loathed being seen in public with him. I never understood how to act around him, and it seemed like every day I'd do or say something to set him off. One day when I was thirteen, our parents went out together for maybe half an hour, leaving him in my care. Something upset him, as usual. He locked himself in his room, and I just left him in there, relieved not to have to deal with him. When my parents came home, my father had to break down the locked door. Clive was facedown on his bed, nose buried in his pillow. He'd stopped breathing, or he'd suffocated. He was dead." Her breath caught, and it was several seconds before she could finish. "I remember feeling incredibly relieved."

BM handed her a tissue, and she blew her nose. "I didn't tell your father about Clive before we married. It wasn't until I was pregnant with you and found out you were a boy that it all came out, because I was so afraid for you. And I was so very ashamed."

A really nasty thought occurred to me at this point. I ground my teeth to try and keep it from escaping, but it got out anyway. "So you married *him*," I tilted my head towards BM, "out of guilt?"

Suddenly she was all composure. "Since you have raised this question, I married Brian because I love him, because he loves me. I am no longer the confused girl who couldn't face her brother's condition. In fact, now I know that not only *can* I face this challenge, but I actually welcome it."

"You still get freaked out by locked doors. Do you really think being Persie's stepmum will make up for Clive? And even if it can, this purging pilgrimage can't wait a year? You're dragging me into this mess right now because . . . ?"

BM's voice surprised me. "That's quite a sharp tongue you have, Simon."

Quick as a flash, I said, "It is. And the worse my life gets, the sharper it will be. Get used to it, or let me stay where I belong."

For the first time since I'd met him, I saw a flash of anger on BM's face. And he was not the only one struck by what I'd said. It's true, I've always had a bit of an acerbic quality to my personality, but the last few things I'd said were over the top, even for me. It came from desperation. There was a headiness about it that made me feel a little dizzy.

Mum leaned forwards. "Simon, I'm sorry I waited so long to tell you about Clive and about Persie's situation. It's just that you were already so angry with me that I was trying to ration out how many things I told you at once. And not having told you about Persie, I tried to find a way to explain about Tink that would give me a little more time."

It would have been decidedly unwise to say anything that smacked of intolerance for dear Persie, but I decided to play a certain card one more time. "You haven't answered my question. Why now?"

BM interjected. "Your mother and I can't spend the next year travelling back and forth to visit with each other, for two reasons. First, it upsets Persie immensely when I'm not home on a regular schedule. But it's not only Persie who has trouble dealing with my absence. I don't have the luxury of taking a week or two away every now and then. Exceptions can be made for emergencies or planned vacations, of course, but not for constant interruptions just because my wife and I live in different countries. In fact, I've already lost two clients in the past several months because they felt I wasn't available enough. Second, until your mother takes up residence with me, Persie won't have a chance to become accustomed to her. She can't adjust to irregular comings and goings. So either we live together, your mother and I, or we see each other once or twice a year for short periods of time. I'm sure you can see that only one of these options is acceptable."

I crossed my arms over my chest and tried not to let my lower lip stick out in an obvious sulk. "So your business, and Persie's problems, and the fact that you can't live without each other for one year all add up to outweigh—oh, I don't know, the rest of my life." I turned towards Mum. "It's like you set me up to have a great opportunity and then snatched it away right in front of me, as soon as I was ready to take hold of it!"

"What are you talking about?"

I sat up straight suddenly, as though struck by lightning. "Oxford! Good God, Mother, how many times do I have to say it? You know that only the *best* marks, the *best* preparation, the *best* résumé will get me in! And it's much harder for students outside the UK!"

She sat back dramatically. "Are you *still* worried about that?"

Speechless, I made some kind of wild gesture with my arms. "Simon, how many times have we had this conversation? You know very well that all you need to do is to have a good year anywhere. It doesn't need to be at Swithin. St. Boniface is a very prestigious Anglican—"

"Episcopalian," BM interrupted.

"Episcopalian public school—"

"Private school, Em. Public school in the US means government school."

She let out an irritated breath. "A very prestigious International Baccalaureate school, right in Boston, a very cultural city with lots of serious music and literature and art going on. And New York City is not very far away. And you don't need to give up your citizenship, which means you can apply to Oxford as a British citizen. Besides, you might even be of *more* interest to them, having lived in the US."

I'd already taken these things into account. I just don't want to leave. It's as simple as that. True, I placed a lot of emphasis on Oxford, tried multiple times to play that card because of Swithin's reputation, but that's because it's something concrete. My feelings? Well, they might be figuratively concrete to me, but it appears they are not important to anyone else.

I had only one card left, other than Graeme; I expected he wouldn't mean anything to her. "What about Tink?"

Mum looked wary. "What about her?"

"Is Persie really allergic? Even though you didn't tell me about that syndrome, you could have told me about her allergy. But you didn't. So is that another lie?"

Mum closed her eyes, and BM answered.

"You haven't seen yet what it's like to live with someone who has Persie's condition. She doesn't understand a lot of the rules you and I live by. I'm afraid she would not react well to a cat, and the cat could attack her, and if that situation got bad we'd have to get rid of the cat anyway. This, after transporting the poor thing all the way to the US. Tink is attached to you; it's true. But more, she's attached to her environment. She'll have to leave this house;

that will be bad enough. Don't force her to endure international travel, probable torment by someone who doesn't know any better, and almost certain relocation yet again, to yet another home and another family. If we could even find one to take her. And anyway, when you go off to Oxford, you'd be leaving her alone in Boston. There *is* a quarantine from the US to Britain."

I ignored the comment about Oxford; it didn't fit into my sulk. What I heard was that Tink would be put to death if she dared put one tiny little scratch mark in the pink flesh of his handicapped daughter.

I felt decidedly trapped. I'd played every card I had by now, or any card that might have influenced where I spent next year. In my mind was an image of poor Tink, cornered in a strange house by one little girl or another, hunched into a prickly ball of teeth and claws, ears back and eyes wide with fear and fury. I identify with this image; this is me. Maybe that's what made me lash out with my last card, which wasn't a card but a handful of information I hoped would sting.

As though it were a blade, I flung this at them: "I hope you realise that I'm gay."

From my hunched position, teeth and claws still bared, I watched their faces. I couldn't quite identify anything specific. I expected shock, distaste, anger, confusion, something definite. Mostly, though, Mum just looked blank, and BM looked bland.

He spoke first. "So . . . ?" His tone was not challenging; it was his usual calm voice.

So?!? How very Welsh of him, not to take that announcement seriously. But I had to believe he was bluffing, that he was really horrified or at least worried about his image or his friends or his family or something. He just didn't want me to know I'd landed a hit. I decided to ignore him and looked at Mum. I could almost smell the wood burning inside her head, asking: *How should I respond to this?*

I watched as her expression moved slowly towards sadness. If she'd said something like, "You can't be serious," or "What utter nonsense," it would've led to a knock-down, drag-out battle that might have provided some chance of . . . I don't know, something to stop this train to hell moving forwards. But still she didn't say anything. So I sat up in the chair, strong and proud now, and dropped another bomb.

"I have a boyfriend."

"Oh, Simon!" The sadness was obvious now. Of course, to me, this said that I'd dealt her a terrible blow. Her precious boy, her only child, is a deviant, a pariah. If she'd been embarrassed by Clive, what would this do to her? I couldn't recall that she'd ever said anything negative about gay people, but neither had she said anything in support. So it had to have been a blow. I wanted it to be a blow. She stood and moved to stare out the window.

"You seem pretty unhappy about it." My tone was almost gloating.

She turned to face me. "Am I sorry to hear this? Of course I am. Your life will be much more difficult, I don't understand homosexuality at all, and instead of telling me at a time when we could have a genuine conversation, you have just thrown this news at me in the middle of the discussion about other things to muddy the waters and try and make me feel guilty—"

I rose out of my defensive ball in the chair to stand in front of her, wishing she weren't just a hair taller than I am. "Oh, Mum, I *really* don't need to do that. You should feel so bloody guilty already—"

"Enough!" BM's voice shocked us both into silence. I'd never heard him raise his voice, or seen him do anything to take control before today.

He stood near Mum and me, but sort of opposed to us. He looked at me. "Do you have any idea how lucky you are? How good you have it? No money worries, no health problems, a mind well into the genius category, and a future brighter than most people could reasonably expect. You have a mother who adores you and a stepfather who would like to get to know you—yes, gay or not, that makes no difference to me—and provide you with even more opportunities. I don't want to make light of your leaving your boyfriend, but you're smart enough to know you haven't yet met anyone you want to spend the rest of your life with. And despite all these advantages, what do you do? How do you react? If your charmed life means so little to you that you'd destroy it with hatred and verbal brutality, then let's find a way to turn it over to me so that I can give it to the little girl waiting at home for me."

He took a few audible breaths and turned to Mum. "Em, I know you're sensitive to what Simon's going through. And yet you let him push your buttons, and you push his, and you end up in an argument with him every time you talk. He's a young man, not a child, and he deserves to know the full truth of what's happening and why. No more secrets. No more half-truths."

Back to me again. "I will help you prepare for this move any way I can, and once you're in Boston I'll do everything I can to make sure you're as comfortable as possible. It will be up to you to make sure you're happy. No one expects you to make your mother happy, but you have it in your power to make her miserable. I hope you're better than that."

I'd been waiting for him to take a breath, and I pounced. "If I'm not a child, then I should be able to—"

"If you're not a child, you're old enough to understand that making others miserable will make you miserable as well. This is an extremely difficult move for you; I know that. And it's not your choice. Your success in life will depend on how good you are at finding opportunity when life changes unexpectedly. If you're smart enough and brave enough, you'll take advantage of these openings. Because if there's one thing we can be sure of in life, it's change."

No one said anything for about five seconds. BM broke the silence, his voice calm again but still assertive. "So. I think we might go out for dinner. It's rather late, and I doubt anyone feels like cooking. Any objection?"

Perhaps as a conciliatory gesture, Mum suggested one of my favourite places where she knew they'd give her a table despite the late notice. But it had been a long time since I enjoyed doing anything like going out to dinner, and I knew I wouldn't enjoy this little outing. Especially after having just been told off by BM, who seemed to have found a backbone suddenly. Inconveniently. I said something along the lines of "I'm not hungry." But BM, in his newfound voice, said, "Everyone's going for dinner. No discussion."

He took control during the dinner conversation, too. I, of course, was trying to say as little as possible, but BM seemed determined to get to know me, as he'd said during his castigation earlier.

"So, Simon, this synaesthesia condition. I understand that letters have colours, and that it's consistent for any given letter." He and Mum both looked at me, but I was not feeling conversational. So he asked, "Does it have a genetic component? Is it inheritable?"

I spoke quickly before Mum could say anything. "My father had it." I glued my eyes to his in a warning: *Do not go there.* I saw a flash of understanding.

"Do you find that it helps you in any way?"

We waited in silence whilst the waiter placed our main course dishes in front of us. Then I said, "It helps with spelling."

"Wouldn't there be too many different colours, though? I mean, for it to be really useful?"

"Not at all. Oxford, for example, is terra cotta overall. There's also dove grey, pale green, bright red, and dark brown, and if you took out the grey, the shade of terra cotta would be darker. If you don't have it, I'm not likely to be able to explain it to you."

"I see." He took a mouthful of food, and I was hoping he'd turn to Mum next, but he didn't. "So, on a lighter topic that I've been meaning to ask you about, do you have an interest in oceanic subjects? Boston has a historic relationship with the sea just as England does."

It was everything I could do not to say, *My, but we're trying very hard, aren't we?* Certain that he was expecting me to say something about sea battles or whales, I decided to see how much stomach he has for my doom-oriented interests. "I'm partial to the blue-ringed octopus."

"I don't think I've heard of that one. What's special about it?"

"It's a beautiful creature. Very small for an octopus. You wouldn't know how beautiful it is unless you annoy it. Then it turns the most gorgeous shades of neon blues and yellows. Its bite carries the most powerful neurotoxin in nature. It kills a human within min-utes. There is no known antivenom. The female carries her fer-tilised eggs in her arms until they hatch, and then she dies."

As though I'd said nothing out of the ordinary, I bent over my dinner and took a forkful of roast chicken in veal reduction deco-rated with bits of lardon.

After BM's outburst, calling me on the carpet and Mum at least to some piece of accusatory furniture, the pace of packing and other preparation increased. And now I'm limited to the music stored on my phone, and most of my personal stuff is wrapped and padded and boxed.

One thing I made sure found its way into my personal baggage was a small, black leather case, with two packets of single-edge razor blades. You never know.

Entry Nine

After BM left for the States that time, saying he'd return briefly to help with the move itself, two things happened. One was that he sent both Mum and me, via e-mail, links to resources where Amer-ican English and British English terminology is translated. "Please do your best to use American terminology around Persie," he wrote, "to help keep the peace. She can be rigid about things."

I nearly wrote back, "Here's one term I think translates well: Fuck off!"

The other thing was that Mum called me into the sitting room to have "the conversation." That is, the one about my being gay.

"Simon, I want you to know that I love you, and I will always love you. You are my son, my only child, and I wouldn't want you to be anything other than what you are. Being gay is just one of those things." She gave me a chance to say something, but I didn't take it.

"But there's no denying that gay people have a harder time of it, so forgive me if my initial reaction wasn't enthusiastic. And I do need you to know that this changes some things about the way I see you. That is, until I get used to it. I've always pictured your future with a wife and maybe children in it." She smiled. "To be truthful, I've imagined you becoming a venerable Oxford don, with a brilliant, beautiful wife who's distinguished in her field in some vague way I haven't clarified." She waited again, and again I didn't speak.

"You could still be that Oxford don. That might suit you very well. Maybe even with children. I just need to see a man at your side. I have a lot of images of your future that I've stored up over the years. Parents can't help doing this. And in all of them you have a wife. It will take me a while to sift through them and make this change."

"How very difficult for you." My voice dripped sarcasm, and on her face I saw it strike home.

She let out an irritated sigh. "What I'm trying to tell you is that this new knowledge—and remember, it is new to me, even if you've known it for a while—doesn't change how I feel about you. I'm merely asking for your patience as I learn how to integrate it. And yes, Simon, it will be difficult, and I will make mistakes and probably say stupid things without knowing they're stupid. This is fair warning that I don't want them to be stupid, that I accept you the way you present yourself to me. But I'll need some time."

I just stared at her.

"I daresay it took you some time, as you began to realise this about yourself, to get used to the idea. To be sure it was real, and that it's right for you. I'm not arguing about whether it's right for you, even if it's not what I would wish for you. But now it's my turn. I need some time." Another pause. "Do I know your boyfriend?"

"If you did I wouldn't tell you who it was."

"Why not?"

"I'd never out anyone. May I go now?"

She let out a breath that sent exasperation into the room. "Simon, I'm trying to stay on an even keel with you. I'm trying very hard not to get upset. But you make it very difficult."

I managed to keep my tone low, but it was still acidic. I have some toxin at my command. "So you're finding this difficult. Welcome to my world. You're forcing me to leave my entire life behind me, Mother. *My entire life.* The only part of my former life that's still going to be there is you, and it's you making me go through this horror. Maybe you can force me to do it, but you can't force me to pretend I accept it. And you'll never force me to forgive you." I watched as she struggled to keep her temper, to avoid pushing back, as though BM were watching to make sure she didn't let me drag her into yet another argument. "Now, do I have permission to leave?"

She closed her eyes for about two seconds. "As long as you understand what I've said."

I got up and went to my room, shut the door, and leaned against it. I wanted to ring Graeme and tear apart everything she'd just said. The problem was, I was having some trouble finding fault with it, as far as the gay question is concerned. What was awful was that she didn't seem to understand that I don't even care whether she accepts me as gay or not. As far as I'm concerned, tearing my life apart the way she's doing proves that she doesn't understand any part of me, and that she doesn't care about me despite her insistence that she does.

Most of the final preparations were a blur to me. One thing that got left to the end was procuring a wardrobe to comply with the dress code for St. Boniface, which is pretty much what you'd expect—not quite a uniform, but close to it: blues from navy to pale sky, red and maroon, white, and khaki, with the odd yellow and pink thrown in. At least, the girls are allowed pink. I'm not. I'm contemplating instigating a protest about this, but it wouldn't look good with my red hair, anyway.

I'm making an effort not to sulk. Really, I am. But a couple of realisations are making it harder than ever to accept what's happening. For one thing, I really do believe that it's Mum's guilt about Clive that's pushing her to go and take care of Persie, and for Mum, meeting her own needs obviously means more than what I need. It means so much more that she won't even let it wait one more year before she starts her penance.

The second thing makes the first one fall into place: She didn't want children. This might go a long way towards explaining that invisible shield I'd always sensed between us.

The day she'd told me about Clive, she'd said she hadn't planned to have children. And she never had any other than me. So I was an accident. And she didn't want me.

Entry Ten

We're leaving in a week. And I have only four days left with Tink.

I'm not sure you can understand how much I love my cat. Part of it is that my dad gave her to me, and part of it is that she's so wonderful, and we have an incredible relationship. You've probably heard the expression that goes, "Dogs think you're God. Cats know they are." But an attitude like this from a cat happens when the human isn't treating the cat like a cat. I guess you don't actually have to be stupid to anthropomorphise an animal, but it probably helps.

A cat is a cat and should not be treated like a human or have human characteristics projected onto it. We're supposed to be smarter than cats. If that's true, we should know better than to think the cat should learn how to be like us. On the contrary; the best relationship a human can have with a cat is one in which the human understands the kind of relationship the *cat* needs, and then provides it. A cat lives by rules it makes for itself, and the smarter human's job is to figure out how to influence that process so that the rules work for the human as well as for the cat; otherwise you could end up with a demanding, obstreperous cat. And it wouldn't be the cat's fault.

Twice I went to visit Margaret, the little girl Tink is going to. I gave her lessons in how to establish her place as Top Cat gently, so Tink will be peaceful and content and won't think she has to make rules for the humans as well as for herself. I wanted to make sure Margaret's house is ready for Tink, and that Margaret and her parents know how to take care of her. I've made it abundantly clear that the less change they subject her to, the more quickly she'll adjust, so she needs all the same possessions she's had here. I've told them where her scratching posts and her carpeted perch need to go. I've made sure they know where the litter box belongs and what brand of litter to use. I've told them where her dishes need to be placed in the kitchen and what kinds of food to buy. I've made doubly sure they understand that she is never, ever, *ever,* under any circumstances to go outside unless they use her harness and leash. I even gave Margaret a lesson, though I had to do it without the cat, about how to trim her claws—how she should do it when Tink is sleepy, or at least very relaxed; how Margaret must be calm and gentle but still firm; and how she must always give Tink treats immediately afterwards.

At least it seemed like Margaret took this all very seriously. She's only ten, but she's smart and seems to really want a cat. I've told her she's getting the best possible cat, one who already understands her place in life and is delighted with it. And I've told her it's her responsibility to make sure this doesn't change. It's Margaret's job to make sure Tink never knows how lucky she is.

But all the packing and moving around of things at home, in Tink's environment, has put a huge amount of stress on her. She began hiding a lot, under things, in boxes, burrowed into piles of clothes or blankets. And yesterday, she stopped eating. This told me it was time.

So this morning I rang Margaret's mum and asked if I could bring Tink to them this afternoon, instead of waiting three more days. I barely got through the conversation without bursting into tears, and as soon as I rang off the deluge began. I threw myself onto my bed and sobbed. My heart was being ripped out of my chest.

I sat with Tink for half an hour before we left, mourning this horrible, horrible loss. No more soft bundle of love to hold on my shoulder. No more rubbing of her face against the side of my neck. No more of that sweet, singing purr in my ear. I don't know how I'm going to stand this.

I cleaned out her litter box in the bathroom whilst Mum packed her bowls and the food we'd already bought. When I came out with Tink's clean litter box, Mum was on the couch, crying. It surprised me, but I was glad. I want her to hurt.

Tink was hiding under my bed. I brought her carrying case in, shut the door, and coaxed her out with chicken-flavoured treats and cooing sounds that kept being interrupted by sobs. Finally she came to me. Such a betrayal.

I can't even write about what it felt like to leave Tink at Margaret's. Driving back without her, my arms already aching—aching!—to hold my cat again, I tried to console myself with the knowledge that Mum could have done much worse for Tink's new family. But—she's not my cat any longer. I won't be able to have a cat at all, at least until I'm on my own. Not with Persie around, itching to pull tails and yank ears and generally mistreat an animal.

I will miss Tink *so much*. And I don't want her to miss me at all.

At home, I glared at Mum through my tears. As I turned to head towards my room I told her, "I hate you."

There's no way to describe what it felt like to part with Graeme. There were kisses and hugs and tears and screaming about what's happening and promises we don't know how we'll keep. We talked about how we'll both see the same sun, the same moon and stars, how we'll text and write and try to arrange visits. None of it helped.

Part II

Exile

Part II

Exile

Boston, Day One, Saturday, 25 August

We're here. And I wish there were something good to report.

Actually, the house itself is pretty nice. It's a large townhouse on Marlborough Street, with more bedrooms and (though I hate to admit it) more bathrooms—and nicer ones—than we had in our detached house on Hermitage Lane, which was pretty nice itself. BM never exactly bragged about how much money he has, or makes, unless you count that comment about how he can afford to give Persie all the care she needs, but a house like this in London would have cost many millions of pounds.

BM wanted to give us the grand tour right away, mumbling something about how it would be easier for Persie this way, so he could go to her sooner and stay with her until dinner, despite the fact that Mum and I were both nearly falling over with exhaustion. It was mid-afternoon Boston time, but of course that's much later London time, and we'd been working ourselves to the bone to get ready. Yes, that included me; I've decided that my only realistic option is to go along with things until I can make the changes I want (read: Get back to England).

Mum convinced BM that we needed to collapse someplace comfortable and have some refreshments before trying to take everything in. I was just glad that the place was air-conditioned; the wave of moist heat that hit me getting into the car at Logan Airport was like nothing I remember experiencing at home. So much for the Northeast US having cool weather. I gather it sometimes snows quite a bit here in winter, but you'd never know it in August.

As we passed through the various rooms on our way to the

kitchen, I did take note of some things, and I have to say that whoever decorated the place has good taste. Hand-knotted Pakistani
rugs everywhere, which I recognised because I helped Mum shop
for a few replacement rugs at home last year. The muted pastel
wall colours don't interfere with the furniture upholstery, and
there are beautifully restored ornate ceilings in the formal rooms.
BM turned conspicuously to me as we passed the music room,
where there's a baby grand Steinway along with shelves and shelves
of CDs.

In the kitchen, which is large and very modern, BM had us sit at
the table for six at the far end of the room, in front of a large window that overlooks a small bricked patio at the back of the house.
He served us himself, though it was all laid out—no doubt by
someone else—and Mum and I could have served ourselves:
chilled San Pellegrino with lime in stemmed wine glasses, pâté,
cheese, carrot sticks, light crackers, and olives.

Mum and I were both pretty quiet, though not for all the same
reasons. She was hot, exhausted, and overwhelmed; I was hot, exhausted, and bitter. As I said, I'm going along, for now, but I don't
have to like it.

BM took us upstairs next. The master suite is here, running
front to back of the house and taking up rather a lot of space. With
its own sitting room and the sliding glass doors in the back onto its
own large balcony with a weatherproof table and two chairs, it's really
its own flat; all it lacks is a kitchen. Someone had already brought
Mum's baggage up.

"Oh, thank God! Brian, I'm going to have a bath immediately
and then maybe a nap."

"You don't want to see Simon's room first?"

She hesitated, like she'd already started drawing her bathwater.
"You're right, of course." But I could tell she'd much rather not.

Persie's rooms—bedroom, bath, and playroom, BM told us—are
on this floor, too, I guess where BM can keep an eye on her. He
pointed towards the closed door that leads to them but didn't approach it. His voice low, he told us, "Persie is in there now with
Anna Tourneau, her live-in tutor."

I couldn't resist. "Her tutor *lives* here? Isn't that a little pre-Victorian?"

"During the week, she stays here. As I mentioned before, it takes a lot to care for Persie. Anna has her own apartment elsewhere, and usually she has weekends off. She's here this weekend to help Persie adjust to your arrival."

From behind the door I could hear what must have been Persie having some kind of tantrum that Anna was apparently unable to control. She was screaming "Nevermore!" rather like Poe's raven. Shrieking it, actually. Over and over. Mum turned to BM, her face white and strained. "Is that my fault because of insisting we wait for the tour? Oh, Brian, I'm so sorry!"

BM didn't quite say it was or it wasn't. "She knows I'm home, and the rule—her rule—is that I go to her immediately and spend some time with her. We've upset the rule. I'll be able to calm her down soon."

My eyes flew to BM's face. He'd just told me, essentially, that Persie is a cat, and he's let her decide for herself what all the rules are. So she's a misbehaving cat, a cat that's been given too free a hand. Suddenly I was more interested in Persie than before. But I must say I didn't especially want to meet her right then.

The stairway to the top floor is behind a locked door, which BM unlocked with a key before handing it to me.

"Your room is on the third floor. I don't want Persie wandering up there, so please keep this door locked. If there's an emergency, there's a fire escape at the back of the house."

I wondered how Mum would take it that I'd just been told that I *must* lock a door. Not looking at her, but intending this comment for her, I asked, "Is Persie's door locked?"

It was an odd question, but BM didn't miss a beat. "Never. Just this one. The house cleaners and Anna are the only others who have keys to the third floor."

As I took the small silver key, I said, "And you."

"Pardon?"

"You have your own key as well, yes?"

"Oh. Yes, I do. But I don't recall the last time I used it."

"Why does Anna need a key?"

"Her room is up there, directly over Persie's bedroom. She has her own bathroom, so you won't cross paths very often. There is a third room, a guest room, and if anyone used it they'd share your hall bathroom. But we don't have overnight visitors. It upsets Persie. I send anyone who comes from out of town to a hotel, usually the Taj or the Four Seasons."

"And will I get other keys to the house?"

"Yes, of course. I'll give you and your mother keys to the external doors later."

"I don't really need you to come up with me. Let Mum have her bath. Maybe I'll do the same. And you can go be with Persie." I wasn't really being kind, here, or considerate. Persie was just a good excuse; I didn't *want* him coming up with me.

Mum gave me a half-smile like she hoped this would help things work out better, and BM stared at me like he was going through a cost-benefit analysis: *How much do I lose if I let Simon have his way, and what do I gain if I insist?* Finally he said, "Your room is at the top of the stairs in the back, immediately to your left. To the right is Anna's room. I'll be with Persie for a while, so you probably won't be able to reach me. There's an intercom near the dumbwaiter upstairs, to the left of the door that goes to the roof garden. It connects to the kitchen, so if no one answers it's because no one is in the kitchen."

Without another word, I walked through the door, and as I pulled it shut I heard BM add, "I hope you like your room. I find it delightful."

Initially my impression of the top floor was that it's kind of gloomy. The landing at the top of the stairs faces the back of the house, and directly ahead is the only source of light: the window in the door to a roof garden that must extend over the master suite and part of Persie's space. Both bedroom doors, Anna's and mine, were closed. I couldn't hear Persie's screams from here, though probably from inside Anna's room I could have.

Alone in the room I'm to call mine whilst I'm here, I stood and looked around, seeing nothing, really. I felt light-headed and almost like I could have fainted, if I were the fainting type. My throat and chest felt tight, constricted, almost painful. I reached out to steady myself against the tallboy to the right of the door, closed my eyes, and willed myself to be calm.

When my breathing settled, I opened my eyes and moved slowly from place to place, first trying out the chair at the desk along the left wall, where there was already a colour printer and a laptop computer, user ID and password written on a piece of paper beside it. Then I tried the overstuffed reading chair in the far left corner, floor lamp and small table beside it. Sitting there, facing the bay window in the back wall of the room, which has a window seat, I could see the roof garden. I had to admit it's a big, luxurious room, and with the locked door, and with Anna mostly spending time with Persie, I could almost have had a cat up here. But I won't be here long enough.

There are light blue papered walls, and a thick navy and cream Chinese rug on the cream carpeting. But the best feature is the skylight. I'll be able to lie on the bed and gaze up at the sky whilst Graeme is doing the same thing.

Graeme!

A wave of tears washed over my eyes, fight them though I tried. I held my breath to keep from sobbing, and then I picked up one of the pillows on the bed and screamed into it a few times. That helped take the edge off this empty, gaping loneliness. I hugged the pillow and heard my own voice say, "Oh, Tinker Bell!" and then I couldn't keep the tears back any longer. I fell sideways onto the bed.

After my cry, my abdomen hurt; the sobs had been that wrenching. I sat up, massaging my middle, and noticed that my baggage was already here. But I wasn't quite ready to start unpacking, so I wandered out onto the roof. It's a large, open space with raked gravel underfoot, two separate round metal tables with three chairs each, and several potted evergreens. With that dumbwaiter, I could have whatever meals I wanted to eat alone up here. There's nothing to shield from the rain, though, and as I said it gets cold enough to snow here, so there are limits. The view isn't much; the building isn't tall enough to see over some of its bigger neighbours. But it'll be like having my own private patio, unless Anna uses it, too. I'll have to see about discouraging that.

Back inside, I passed by my door and headed down the hall that leads to the front of the house. On my right I noticed the door to the bathroom, standing open, and ahead was the guest bedroom BM had mentioned. Vaguely curious, I decided to see whether he had given me the better of these two rooms.

The front bedroom is huge—a little larger than mine—but instead of the refreshing blue, this one is in heavy, deep maroons and browns. There's a skylight here, too, and the room needs it. And there's a bay window overlooking the street. It's a quiet street, but I expect my room will be quieter than this one. Plus I like the light feel of the blue. I considered leaving BM with the impression that I thought he had given me the lesser room, but I don't want him to call my bluff; I'd rather have the blue one.

Rather than a bath, which Mum was probably having right now, I decided I did need a shower. But I had to unpack enough to find my robe, slippers, and a change of clothes first, and rather than just unearth a few things, I decided to get the unpacking over with.

It felt so odd, placing familiar clothes and personal things into drawers that smelled like they belong to someone else. They weren't bad smells. Actually, the drawers had been scented with something rather nice. But they weren't mine. This is only a hotel room. This stay is temporary.

There's a love seat at the end of the queen-size bed, upholstered in a flocked fabric that matches the walls. With my phone in hand, I curled into one end of it. Just as I was about to text Graeme, he texted me.

Hey SS.
GG! I want to come home.
Then come!
If only.
Is it bad?
Could be worse. Big room, roof garden just for me.
Sounds nice. What's next 4 u there?
Walk tomorrow, sights. Monday a test at St Bony to see which classes I take.
Bony! LOL! Met sis yet?

No. Locked away in her rooms with tutor Anna.
I miss you so much.
I miss YOU so much. Wait for me?
Always and forever.
XXXXXXXOOOOOOOOOOOOOOOOOOOOOO

I don't know whether I felt better or worse after this exchange, but I decided not to dwell on it. I headed for the bathroom, which turned out to be rather impressive. It's a huge room, for starters, with a glass-walled, marble shower big enough for Graeme and me together, a separate claw-foot tub, a vanity table and chair, an armoire, and, of course, a skylight, which is good because there are no windows. I played with a few of the switches, and a faint whirring startled me until I realised it was the skylight opening up above a screen protecting the room from bugs or whatever. I left it open, started the water, stripped, and indulged in a long, hot shower.

I'd rinsed my shampooed hair and was just soaping my chest when suddenly Graeme was with me. He opened the glass door to the shower, naked and incredibly beautiful, already erect. Before I could say a word, I was pinned against the marble tiles, his tongue deep inside my mouth, his hands everywhere at once. Then he was on his knees, my dick in that sweet mouth, and he worked me until I came. He stood and kissed me, sharing everything.

I was asleep on the bed, dressed in only my underwear, when I heard a knock and then, "Simon?" It was Mum. My body jerked. "Are you awake, dear? We're about to have supper. It has to be now because of Persie's schedule. We can't upset it again."

"Hang on." I stumbled to the door and opened it. "I'm not hungry."

"Sweetie, you've been asleep. You can't tell yet whether you're hungry. I'll wait whilst you throw something on." She stepped into the room. "Oh, this *is* a lovely room, isn't it?"

"Mum, cut it out. Go downstairs. I'm not dressing with you standing there."

She looked at me as though she wasn't quite sure about trusting me. "All right, but come down as soon as you're dressed. We're waiting for you in the dining room."

"How did you even get up here?"

"Brian's key, of course."

For a nanosecond, I considered demanding that they send my supper up in the dumbwaiter so I could be alone in the roof garden, but I decided to fight that battle another time. Besides it was hot and humid outside.

It took me some time to decide what to wear, and I was moving slowly, like a sleepwalker, or someone on barbiturates or drunk. It did register, though, that I was hungry after all.

By the time I got into the dining room, everyone was already eating. BM was at one end of the rectangular table, and Persie, from her chair on BM's right, glared in my general direction. "Dinner is on time. You're late. Late. Late. Late. Late. Late. Late . . ." With a fork in her right fist, she began pounding the handle down on the table with each repetition.

BM stood and pulled her chair out from the table, and she bent forwards so she could keep pounding. When she couldn't reach the table without standing, she screamed one final, "LATE!" and was suddenly very still. By now, the woman who must be Anna and who had been seated on the other side of Persie, was beside BM, helping him reposition her chair so Persie could reach her plate again. All seemed quiet, and then Persie uttered one more, nearly silent, "Late." And she went back to her meal as though nothing had happened.

Mum was at the other end of the table from BM, and I walked around to the chair beside her, across from Anna, who smiled at me and nodded. No one made a move to do anything by way of introduction. I glanced at Mum, confused.

"It's all right, Simon. Go ahead and help yourself to dinner from the sideboard and sit down."

Her voice was a little odd. I put this all together and interpreted it as letting me know Persie didn't approve of introductions, and that according to some rule of her making I'll be somehow incorporated into the group informally. Again, what occurred to me is that she is a cat who needs an authority adjustment. That's not something I'll be taking on. Not now, certainly, and probably not ever. As I took my place at table I watched Persie go through her mealtime routines, organising the food on her plate, eating a bit of one thing, then a bit of something else. Eventually it dawned on me that what she was doing was eating each item in order, all around her plate, and around again, calculating how much she needed to eat of each food so that she'd finish everything in the final sweep.

There was some conversation, though Persie was quiet for the moment. BM told Mum and me that he has someone named Ned Salazar who does food shopping and prepares meals. During the week, and sometimes on weekends, he stays to cook dinner, but tonight he'd left a prepared cold meal for us, which is what was laid out on the sideboard.

One thing I do like about meals with BM is that he always has wine, and I always get some. Mum likes wine well enough, but she's no oenophile. Dad was, and he taught me some things. I want to learn more. At one point before we'd left home, BM—no doubt trying to tempt me—had said he has a wine cellar. Now that I'm here, I plan to get to know it. In fact, I'll take advantage of everything I can whilst I'm here, and the wine cellar is on the list. Tonight, with the cold sliced chicken and the avocado potato salad with asparagus, we had a sauvignon blanc from New Zealand that reminded me of grapefruit.

Anna is somewhere under thirty years old, not unattractive but no showstopper—a little heavy, with dark-blond hair in a ponytail. I didn't get much of a sense of her, because most of her attention was on Persie. BM watched Persie a lot as well. I wondered how his time with her had gone, and how much trouble he'd had calming her down, assuring her that her life isn't turning completely upside down. You see, *he* loves *his* child.

BM said that tomorrow, Sunday, he'll take Mum and me on a walk around the neighbourhood. Somehow he thinks the Public

Garden is going to be my new Hampstead Heath. He has no idea. Then we're going into Cambridge to see Harvard. Pointless.

When Anna and Persie left, I said "Good night" to them. Anna returned the greeting; Persie did not.

BM told me, "She doesn't understand the need for social niceties. Don't take offense that she didn't return your 'good night.' "

Living with her is going to be *so* much fun.

So I'm alone in my room now, feeling decidedly displaced but not like I'm in hell altogether. Or, if it's hell, at least it's well-appointed. And, of course, this is pre-St. Boniface; the school could turn out to be dreadful.

I've looked up Boston on Google Maps and researched some Internet sites. It's tiny. Provincial. No matter how much money BM has, or how much fine wine he pours for me, it can't make up for this poor excuse for a city. There's just nothing here.

Boston, Day Two, Sunday, 26 August

This morning, Boston time, there was another text exchange with Gorgeous Graeme. You know, we used to find so much to talk about when we were in the same place. Texting doesn't hold a candle to a real conversation, and of course there's no physical touch, either. So this latest exchange didn't cover much ground—pretty much the same as the one the day before, with the only difference being that we agreed I'd ring him tonight as soon as I have an opportunity, even if it's in the middle of his night. I had thought texting would be a good way to connect real-time, but real-time doesn't make up for what texting lacks. I'm beginning to lean towards e-mails, which will at least allow me to pour my heart out. Maybe I'll send him bits from this journal.

It was cooler today, almost chilly out on the bricked patio where we breakfasted. Persie wasn't there, and Mum told me she has breakfast in her rooms. That's a relief, not having to take every meal under the tyrant thumb of that little girl.

BM prepared everything for us. Evidently breakfast is some big thing for him. It was a typical American meal with too much food, but I was really hungry again. I wanted to turn my nose up at the pancakes, which were like a thick, crude crêpe (I did decline something called maple syrup and opted instead for fruit preserves on mine), and the bacon, and the fresh fruit, but I decided not complimenting BM with every bite was enough of a statement; no need to starve myself. Mum was gushing over everything, veneration to veneration, so maybe he didn't even notice my silence. Too bad.

At least Mum had taught him how to make tea properly. I wonder whether he had drunk nasty tea before they met, or if he's a reformed coffee drinker, forcing himself to convert so he can impress Mum. England has gone largely over to coffee and teabags, but I refuse; and my tea must be loose-leaf and brewed correctly, according to its variety and when it's served. I want Assam for breakfast, Darjeeling or Earl Grey for afternoon tea, and a pale green Formosa oolong if I have tea at night.

As I had predicted, and in fact as I had seen on Google Maps, Boston Common and the Public Garden were unimpressive and tiny. Honestly, BM has been in Hampstead Heath, and in the Regent's Park; he ought to know better than to expect a good reaction out of me to the little postage stamps he calls parks here.

BM pointed to two live swans floating on a pond. "Romeo and Juliet," he said. "They take them to the Franklin Park Zoo for the winter, because the water here freezes."

"Really? Romeo and Juliet?" I said, scornful. "Didn't anyone explain that those two teenagers committed suicide because they weren't allowed to be together?"

No one responded. I wasn't sure whether I was being ignored or what.

Later, we were standing on the bridge over the water in the Public Garden, watching the silly swan boats paddle tourists about, and BM asked, "Would you like a ride?"

Before Mum could say anything, I replied, "No, thanks."

Mum glared at me, and BM said, "I'm sorry you're not enjoying the Garden, Simon. I realise it must seem rather small to you. Perhaps we'll take a trip out to the Arnold Arboretum in the fall, when the leaves turn colour. It's almost three hundred acres." He looked at me, but I just stared straight ahead and lifted one shoulder. That should have said it all.

BM's car service picked us up on Charles Street, and BM explained that he'd made a reservation for Mum and me to have lunch at an outdoor café on Newbury Street whilst he goes home to lunch with Persie. I glanced at Mum, and it seemed she already knew about this plan.

So we were sitting under an umbrella at some restaurant, I don't remember which one. All I remember is being hot and unhappy.

"How do you like your room, Simon?"

"My room? Really? You're starting there?"

"What do you mean?"

"It's the old elephant-in-the-room syndrome. Persie is the elephant, in case that needs pointing out."

She toyed with her salad for a minute. Then, "She will take some getting used to. I think it will be less stressful once we've learned the rules to follow, because she's less likely to get upset when they're observed."

"From what I've seen so far, there must be a book full of them."

"Yes." She took a sip of wine. "So, do you like your room?"

"It's fine. Large, nicely furnished."

"The bathroom is lovely." So she'd peeked around up there.

I decided to throw her a crumb. "I like the skylights."

"And after the weather cools down, the roof garden looks like a wonderful place to read."

So far we'd spent only a few sentences on Persie, who represented the most disruptive aspect of this living situation, barring the move itself, and Mum wanted small talk about the house's features? I took the elephant by the tusks.

"Why wasn't I introduced to Persie last night? Or to Anna, for that matter?"

More wine for Mum. "You missed Brian's explanation. He's been preparing her for our arrival for some time, so Persie knew she'd see us, and she even knew where we'd sit at table. You chose the right chair, by the way."

"Oh, good."

She ignored my sarcastic tone. "Some people with Asperger syndrome—I'll just refer to it as AS, the way Brian does—handle social interaction better than others. Persie finds it more difficult than many AS sufferers, evidently. If Brian had introduced anyone at dinner—I wasn't introduced either, just so you know—not only would it have been a break in Persie's dinner routine, but also she would have been forced to interact with you socially. Brian says she remains much less agitated if the people she's expecting just show up, and she isn't required to interact with them until she feels ready."

"She certainly interacted with me."

Mum actually chuckled. "She told you that you were late, yes, but it was not exactly an interaction. You never spoke to her, and that was the right thing to do."

"So we're to learn her rules and follow them?"

Mum's smile was almost wry. "It would seem so." She sighed. "Actually, I expected this. One thing I remember about living with Clive is the routines, the insistence on no change. AS isn't the same form of autism that he had, but Persie's condition is severe enough that the two types evidently have this in common."

"I wasn't introduced to Anna, either."

"There's that routine again. Persie allows conversation, but it must follow certain parameters. An introduction is its own routine."

"Persie *allows*—?"

"I know, I know, Simon. It seems extreme. But Persie's condition *is* extreme. And it helps explain why Brian's first wife—whose name was Miranda, by the way—had such a hard time dealing with it. Brian hasn't told me much about her, but I gather she had her own brand of inflexibility going on. Perhaps she had a touch of AS, herself. I don't know."

I sat back and studied Mum's face. "How much of this did you understand before you agreed to live with it?"

Mum watched a few people stroll past, and I was thinking she hadn't heard me when she said, "I knew as much as Brian could explain. *Understanding*, though, is going to take a while. If you recall, I did visit him here once, but I stayed at the Taj. I didn't meet Persie. But Brian talked about her a lot. He gave me as clear a sense as he could of what it would be like to live with her."

"And how do you think you'll do?"

She looked directly at me. "With time, better and better. And in case you're wondering, it's unlikely Persie will ever be able to be independent."

"So you'll be saddled with her as long as you're with him?"

"Don't say 'saddled,' Simon. But, yes, unless something changes, she'll be around, always."

It occurred to me that I don't know my mother very well. This sacrifice, this penance, or this generosity—however you look at it—does not jibe with my picture of her.

BM was in the car that picked us up and whisked us off to Cambridge. On the way, he said, "I'm trying not to overwhelm the two of you by showing you too much in one day. Boston may not be London, but there's a lot of history here, and lots of things to do. At home, I've got some guidebooks for you." Mum smiled at him. I stared out the window, carefully not saying that Boston barely knows what history is.

Harvard Yard was so much smaller than even I had thought it would be. I had expected this supposedly prestigious school's centrepiece to look like more than it does—just an odd assortment of buildings that people here seem to think are old and charming, around a bit of greensward that's more bare earth than grass, crisscrossed with walkways the students obviously ignore. I realise there are other buildings outside the "yard" that are part of the university, but—really, it's *nothing* like Oxford, where there are thirty-eight colleges all over the city with their own "yards" to brag about. To be sure, many of them are quite small, but still. If this were Harvard *College*, I might be more lenient. But it calls itself a university. And

Cambridge—the one in Massachusetts, I mean—is . . . well, tiny. They make a big fuss over Harvard Square, but really most of the fuss should be about the horrible traffic.

Back in Boston, BM had the car drop us all off at St. Bony, which is farther down Marlborough Street from his house, in the opposite direction from the park. The front of the main building is unassuming and fits right in with the area, row houses along the tree-lined street. The street entrance opens to a hallway with a tiled floor, large black-and-white squares, and that hideous fluorescent lighting that makes everyone look sick. School won't start until later this week, and there was a guard at a desk who told us we couldn't go any farther without a school ID or an escort.

After the walk down Marlborough Street to the house, Mum said she was exhausted and needed to rest a little. I mumbled something along the same lines and went upstairs to be with Graeme.

He answered on the first ring.

"Hey, Sexy Simon."

My throat started to close with emotion, but I managed, "Hey, Gorgeous Graeme."

There was silence as we listened to each other breathe for a few seconds. Then he said, "How were the sights? Did you see St. Bony? Anything worth a few minutes of complaining?"

I chuckled. "I'm not that bad, am I?"

"Perennially. It's one of your charms."

I love this guy. "Puny parks, puny Harvard Yard, puny Cambridge. I'd say puny school, but all we did was walk in the front entrance."

"Which was—let me guess—puny."

"How did you know?"

"So, what will the test tomorrow be like?"

This wasn't what I wanted to talk about, so I made short work of it. Basically, I'll spend most of the day in a room with a monitor and some number of other students, and take some kind of test in several different subjects, so they'll know what my course load will be.

Then I asked, "You all ready for your upper sixth?" Graeme, of course, is also extremely intelligent and aiming for Oxford as well.

He sighed. "No way I can be ready for that. You're supposed to be helping me."

With an effort I kept my voice from breaking. "We'll still be at New College together."

"We'll sing in the chapel."

"We'll lounge in the back garden when it's sunny and quiz each other for exams."

"We'll have the best table in the dining room. Everyone will want to sit with us, and we'll select only the people we like."

My teeth ground together. "A year, Graeme. A whole, fucking year."

"I know."

More silence, maybe thirty seconds. Then there was a knock at my door. I covered the phone and nearly shouted, *"What?"*

BM's voice said, "Dinner is always at six thirty, Simon. Please don't be late tonight."

I glanced at my watch: a quarter past. "Be there shortly." To Graeme I said, "I'm not to be late to dinner tonight, which Persie insists is served promptly at half six. I wasn't in my seat on time last night, and I thought she was going to have a cow, shouting, 'Late!' at me. Honestly, the way they let that girl dictate terms around here . . ."

"I guess you'd better go down."

We agreed I'd ring him again on Wednesday night. Then I needed a few minutes to collect myself. Blow my nose. Throw some water on my face.

Ned was here tonight—a bonus, as far as I'm concerned, as I'm sure he's gay. And he's attractive. Maybe twenty-five or so? He's black. I do hope I'm not expected to say African American all the time; it's too long. How do I know his family aren't from Jamaica, or whether he was born in Kenya? His voice is rich and incredibly deep. And he understands cuisine, which is huge in my book, especially since I don't want to be lumped in with that antiquated idea that there's no good food in England. Anyway, he's tall and slender and has the most gorgeous eyes.

He gave a brief description of each dish as he served it, and he knows what he's doing. Tonight's main course was the tenderest pork medallions in a red wine sauce, served with an Oregon pinot noir I would have loved to take to bed with me.

Of course I got no introduction to him, either. I'm sure I caught his eye a few times by the end of the soup course, though.

BM is so ignorant about most things English. For example, he keeps referring to what would have been my final UK school year before Oxford as my senior year. Over dinner he sang the praises of St. Bony.

"So you know, I've informed the administration at St. Boniface that you intend on going to Oxford. They said they'd make sure your classes reflect that. And, believe me, they know what Oxford requires. Their baccalaureate programme is excellent. Something tells me you haven't spent a lot of time looking into what the school has to offer, but many St. Boniface graduates have gone on to universities such as Oxford and Cambridge. You can be as prepared as you want to be." Then he added, "And more challenged than you might expect."

Mum said, "That's good news, isn't it, Simon?"

"The best." I kept my tone even and low; no enthusiasm, no rebellion. And, if BM was listening carefully, no credibility.

I wasn't expecting to be called on the carpet by little Miss Prissy Persie tonight, but it seemed I could do no right. She hadn't spoken at all, and I was trying to speak as seldom as possible, per my usual practice for months now, but for some reason I used the term "join the dots." Evidently in the US they say "connect the dots." It wasn't in any of those resources Brian had pointed me towards, wasn't amongst the host of Britishisms I'm expected not to utter. As soon as the phrase was out of my mouth, Persie's head snapped up, her attention on the calculations necessary to even out portions of the various food groups on her plate forsaken in favour of shouting at me.

"*Connect* the dots!" she shrieked. "Connect! Connect the dots! Connect! Connect!"

It went on like that for a while, and it took both BM and Anna to calm her down. At one point Anna suggested taking her upstairs, but BM, irritated, said that Anna knows that just makes things worse. It wasn't clear to me how this could be true; she'd be shrieking in her own rooms, which would certainly have been better for most of us.

No one spoke for a good five minutes after Persie quieted down, and then BM turned towards me and, in a low voice, explained, "Figures of speech, metaphors, anything represented in the abstract, can be extremely challenging for her. The expression you used is one of the few she's mastered. But she understands it in the American usage, and hearing a different version of it was profoundly disturbing."

"So, can she participate in a conversation at all?"

"Of course I can."

I jumped. I think Mum did, too. I said, "All right. Why is it important to divide up your food portions so precisely?"

"So I can finish them all together."

"I get that, but why is that important?"

"Because they're all on the same plate." A plate she never looked up from.

I decided not to pursue that further. But I wanted to know what else she focuses on. "What did you do today?"

"I woke up. I put on my slippers. I took three drinks of water. I went into the bathroom. I sat on the toilet. . . ."

"I'm sorry, Persie," BM said as he leaned towards her and gently laid a hand on her arm. "I think that's probably more than Simon wants to know. Why don't you tell him about your new book? You read that today, didn't you?"

"Yes. *Analysis of Tonal Music: A Schenkerian Approach.* By Allen Cadwallader and David Gagné. September 3, 2010. An introduction to the fundamental principles of Schenkerian technique. Oxford University Press, USA. Four hundred and thirty-two pages. I read one hundred and sixty-seven pages today. It focuses more on the music and less on reduction itself than Allen Forte and Steven E. Gilbert's *Introduction to Schenkerian Analysis: Form and Content in Tonal Music.* I don't know yet whether I like it more or less, because I do like reduction. But I also like music." She stopped and turned her head towards BM as if she wanted to know if she should say more.

BM leaned over and kissed the side of her forehead. "That's my girl." I didn't see any indication whether the kiss or the implied praise meant anything to her.

Schenkerian analysis? And she's how old? *Eleven? Twelve?* Ye gods. I have only a vague idea what it's about, and this girl is reading graduate school texts on it. And, it would seem, understanding them.

I did my best to bring my jaw back into position from where it had fallen and asked her, "Are you a music savant?"

"I don't know what that is."

"Like *Rain Man?* The Dustin Hoffman film where he plays the mathematic savant?"

She shook her head, then harder, then harder still. BM leaned over yet again. "It's all right, Persie. I'll explain. You don't need to." She calmed down immediately. To me he said, "Persie doesn't watch movies. She's tried, but they upset her. Fiction is rather a foreign concept."

"So is she a savant?"

"That's not an easy question to answer. Certainly she has astounding comprehension of music. But from what I've seen, she doesn't mix her experience of music with her analytic abilities. I mean, she either listens and is transported, or she applies only intellect and analyses."

"Done," Persie announced, and suddenly Ned was there to take her plate. And as though she meant "done" to apply to the discussion of Schenker, we all fell silent again. I caught Ned's eye, lifted an eyebrow and dropped it again, and he winked at me.

As Ned was serving the pudding (slap my wrist! I mean dessert), key lime pie with whipped cream on a chocolate crust, Mum and BM chatted about something, and Anna was focused on

Persie. Ned set my plate down and whispered, "It really is easiest if we all follow the rules."

Sotto voce, I said, "Where is that book, anyway?" I turned my head to look into his eyes.

His hand landed oh, so briefly on my shoulder. "Don't worry; you'll get it." And he moved on.

If there's anything I'm going to like about living here, it's going to be all about the kitchen: Ned, good food, and wine. Things could be worse.

Later, I had just gone upstairs and was puttering around my room, working out the best placement for things that belonged back home in my room in London, when BM knocked on my door. Whether I wanted to hear it or not, he was here to tell me more about Persie's behaviour at dinner. He went on for a few minutes about how in the worst cases, people with AS don't always understand how other people want to be treated, that they might not know how to have a conversation that doesn't relate directly to them, that they might have trouble understanding what it means to be polite, or considerate. He added that Persie's case is rather extreme.

I guess I must have looked interested, because he didn't stop there.

"The extreme degree of her condition means that there's very little understanding of, and almost no empathy for, other people. On the other hand, she doesn't expect empathy *from* anyone, either. Also, many people with AS and other forms of autism don't want to be touched. Persie doesn't mind some people touching her. I can, and so can Anna, as long as it's a firm, definite touch and not just a light one. But she seldom makes eye contact."

"She doesn't expect empathy? She sure expects to be obeyed."

"I understand that it seems like that. Not all people with AS are as removed from others as she is. Many people with AS work through their issues and manage to lead fairly normal lives. Persie will not."

"How can you be sure? She seems extremely intelligent."

He gave me a wan smile that somehow seemed patronising. "You'll have to trust me."

After he left, I pictured Persie, heard her voice in my head explaining about Schenkerian analysis, her voice a fairly flat monotone. And then I remembered how puzzled she'd looked, even panicked, when I'd asked her about *Rain Man*. And then there was the kerfuffle of the connecting dots.

Maybe he was right. And it wasn't my problem, anyway.

Boston, Day Three, Monday, 27 August

The material from St. Bony, in talking about what today would be like, neglected to indicate whether I was to follow the dress code. School isn't in session yet, but I erred on the side of caution and donned a pair of khaki slacks and a light blue Oxford (of course) shirt. I was too nervous for breakfast, though of course Mum made me eat as much as I could. A few spoonfuls of a muesli were all I could manage; the tiny bits of dried mango in it made me suspect Ned had put it together. I wished I could have enjoyed it more, but all these tests were hanging over me today.

There was an insulated satchel on the counter and a piece of paper in front of it that said, "Good luck, Simon—in case you need any."

"Who's this from?" I asked Mum. It wasn't from her; it wasn't her handwriting, and it's unlikely she'd have left it because she'd be walking me down to the school so she could talk with the headmistress, whom she hadn't met yet. Evidently BM had pulled quite a few strings to get me into St. Bony, and Mum wanted to thank Dr. Healy in person.

"Ned left that for you. Remember that the school material recommended you bring lunch today; the canteen isn't open yet, and there won't be a lot of time for you to come here or look elsewhere for lunch." She smiled. "I think you'll be pleased with what he's prepared. And here. Keys to all outside doors except for Brian's office, in case you need to let yourself in after your exams."

"Thanks. Let's get going." I just wanted to get this day started. I test well, but I'm often nervous before a test begins. Once I'm into it, I'm fine.

I didn't say much on the walk down Marlborough Street. It felt awkward and also comforting to have Mum walk with me, like going back and forth between being a child and . . . well, being a child. She didn't go to the test room with me, though; we were met at the front entrance by an academic-looking man, maybe forty and decidedly following the dress code, who introduced himself as Dr. Metcalf. What he teaches, or what he does here, I didn't quite catch. He ushered me away, telling Mum he'd have someone collect her to see Dr. Healy.

We walked down several hallways until I was thoroughly turned around and ended up in a classroom with huge windows overlooking a small close with green grass, some benches, and a few ornamental trees. No people in sight. I was pleased, actually; if I have to gaze at something whilst I'm thinking, I like to have a pleasant but non-distracting view. There were several other students in the room, also from outside the US. I didn't make any effort to remember their names; I'll get to know them if I need to.

Dr. Metcalf, half sitting on the desk at the front of the room, explained the rules for the exams and said that the results would have some bearing on our schedules, which we'd be e-mailed by end of day tomorrow. Orientation for seniors, he said, is on Wednesday, and classes for everyone begin on Thursday.

Most of the exams were predictable, on subjects like maths, biology, history, English, a few others. I'm sure I did quite well on all of them but one. History. It's a subject I've always excelled at, and it's one that Oxford will expect me to be good at. A great memory and my synaesthesia help me remember how to spell everything from place names like Afon Tryweryn to emperors like Zhu Yuanzhang, but history is a strong suit for me.

Which is why I couldn't understand why I was struggling a little with this test. Or, rather, there was an obvious reason. It was that so many questions pertained to points of US history, some of them so esoteric that I didn't quite know what was being asked or how to answer. The only questions I'm convinced I did well on were those about the history of Europe, India, and Russia, and a couple about the Chinese dynasties.

Back at the house, I used my newly acquired front door key to let myself in. In my room I found a surprise. There was a package on my desk, and a note, which I read first.

> *Simon—*
> *I thought you might like something along the lines of what your classmates will have, so here's an iPhone. Charges will go to my account, but I'm not checking up on the calls. I realize you're likely to call England. Hope you like the blue bumper.*
> *If you don't want the iPhone at all, that's fine—just let me know. And if you suspect I'm trying to win you over with gifts, well . . . it can't hurt to try!* ☺

I showered and changed, and then I played with the iPhone, located the phone number, and texted GG to say the exam ordeal was over and I did fine, and got *X*s and *O*s back. I hadn't decided whether to keep the thing, so I didn't change any of the default settings.

Downstairs I heard voices, Mum's and Ned's, and laughter, coming from the kitchen. It appeared Ned was having her help him prepare dinner, apparently salmon, and they were getting along like old chums. They hadn't seen me yet, so I watched from the door, and it came to me that Mum used to cook a lot before Dad died. She was very good, too; taught me a lot of what I know about cuisine, as a matter of fact. I'd kind of forgotten that.

Finally Ned looked up. "Simon! How goes it? I'm sure you wowed them. But did you wow yourself?"

I shrugged and tried to subdue a temptation to grin.

"Your mom made you a treat. A reward for your hard day." He

held out a small, pristine, white plate with several tiny balls arranged on it. Tea butter balls. They're made from butter (of course), flour, butter, confectioners' sugar, butter, vanilla (we always used Tahitian, but I don't know what's in this kitchen), finely chopped walnuts, and—did I mention butter? While they're still barely warm from the oven, you shake them up with more confectioners' sugar to coat the outsides. I think they're my favourite biscuit. I looked up at Mum as I took the plate and the napkin Ned handed me.

Mum smiled but didn't take any active credit. She said, "We're having barbied salmon with scallion horseradish mayonnaise. I'm making that, and the raspberry fool for the pudding. Um, dessert. Ned's making a surprise soup. He says it's one of Persie's favourites, but he won't tell me what it is."

"Now, Emma, we say 'grilled' here, not 'barbied.' Miss Persie will have you hog-tied if she hears you. Hey, Simon, Brian tells me you're quite the wine aficionado. Wanna help me pick something out from the cellar for tonight?"

Now, *that* I would love to do. And I felt an unwilling rush of something like pleasure at the thought of BM's noticing this about me and even sharing it in a good way with Ned. I tried to curb my enthusiasm. "Sure. When?"

He turned to Mum. "You've got this covered, right?"

She laughed, something I haven't heard her do lately. Hands waving dramatically in the air, she put on a pseudo French accent and said, "But of course!"

I set down the biscuits and followed Ned towards the back of the kitchen, where the door to the wine cellar is. The stairs lead back under the kitchen and into an area that far exceeded my expectations: several tall, glass-fronted, temperature- and moisture-controlled storage units, each partially full of bottles.

"Miranda—Brian's ex—was responsible for keeping these full of wine. When I got here there wasn't a lot left, so I've been working to restock. Brian seemed to have lost interest." Ned turned to watch my face. "He'd lost interest in a lot of things. And then he met your mother."

That was a place I'd rather not go. "You call him Brian?"

"Oh, sure. We're all friends here."

"Um, where does he get his money? In England, at least, an architect would have to be quite the success to have a place like this."

He grinned. "Well, his clients do like him. He gets lots of referrals. But this house was in his family, and I expect he got money from them, too. There's no mortgage, I don't think, though the property taxes are probably hefty. Now, on to the wine."

He moved from case to case: lighter whites, meaty whites, light reds, heavy reds, rosés, each case divided into countries and regions of origin. There was also a case for sparkling wines, and one for brandies, cognacs, ports, after-dinner wines. Very impressive.

Returning to stand near the lighter whites case, Ned crossed his arms casually and leaned against a post that supported the floor above. "So, what would you like for tonight?"

You. It almost slipped out. "You've led me to this case. Is this the category you'd recommend?"

His smile was cryptic. "Maybe I led you to the one most people would choose. Doesn't mean it's the best choice. Sometimes it pays to take a risk. Let me ask you this: If the salmon were given a heavier treatment"—he waved a hand in the air—"something less summery, what would you drink?"

"Probably a pinot noir, maybe a white burgundy. Depends."

"So, for a lighter treatment, would you go red at all?"

"Maybe a rosé?"

He made a slight face. "Not bad in concept, but would it hold up to the horseradish?"

As soon as he said horseradish, I headed for the sparkling wine case, looked for a pink foil over a large cork, opened the door, and pulled out a bottle at random. It was a rosé prosecco.

Ned laughed and clapped his hands. "I love it!" He bowed obsequiously and imitated a pretentious waiter by saying, "Excellent choice, sir."

I moved over to the sweet wines. I was looking for a sauterne my father used to love, but I didn't see it. There were sauternes here, but nothing I recognised.

Ned said, "Another excellent idea—fabulous with fool. Do you want a recommendation?"

"Please."

He moved to stand beside me, and in the cool cellar the warmth of his body was almost like a wave, or a gentle pulse. In a trance, I watched him, not the bottles. He pulled one out and handed it to me. "This one, I think." He didn't move away. "You know, I think it's great that we're celebrating tonight. And I think we're celebrating not just your day, but also your mom's coming out of her shell." He closed the case and stepped back.

"Shell."

He laughed and headed towards the stairs. "Don't tell me I gave you too much credit. I know teenagers mostly don't even know their parents are people, let alone sympathise with their difficulties, but—yes, shell. She's seemed so wound up, so tight, since she got here. But not this afternoon. Did she teach you to love wine?"

"No. My father."

"Well, you could learn a few things about cooking from her. She's no slouch." He took the stairs two at a time. I followed, watching him from behind, watching his behind, and once again thought that things could be worse.

Back in the kitchen, I picked up the plate of tea balls. "Thanks, Mum. Haven't had these in a while." The relatively friendly comment was more for Ned, so maybe he'd give me back a little credit, but Mum beamed like I'd given her an unsolicited hug. To Ned, I said, "Any reason I can't take these into the music room?"

He feigned a scolding tone. "If Miss Persie finds one tiny smudge of dusty sugar on that piano, you'll hear about it for the rest of your life. Here." He handed me a glass of San Pell, two-thirds full, with a submerged lime wedge. "Don't spill one drop!"   '

There was a table with coasters in the music room, so I set my water and plate down, ate two biscuits, wiped sugar from my fingers, and perused the CD collection. It was massive. Everything from Tantric Buddhist monks to Tippett. There was also an area devoted to less erudite recordings. It seems BM—and perhaps Miranda?—enjoyed the popular music of the 1980s. Plus The Beatles, of course. Too soon, I'd finished the plate of biscuits. If it hadn't been for the dinner Ned and Mum had planned, I'd have gone looking for more. I turned away from the CD rack I'd been browsing—and nearly dropped the plate.

Persie had come in, very quietly, and she was sitting on the piano bench, facing me with her side towards the keyboard. I did my best to hide my fright. "No Anna?"

"She has today off. It's not the right schedule." Probably compensation for the tantrums she had to deal with all weekend. "Daddy's grilling fish. Ned is cooking." She didn't look at me.

"My mum is cooking, too."

No response. All right, I would avoid referring to anyone who hasn't been here long enough to become the norm. That would include me, of course, so I asked something about her.

"Did you do any Schenkerian reductions today?" She hummed three notes. "What's that?"

"Beethoven, *Cello Sonata, Opus 69 in A minor,* second movement. Scherzo, allegro molto."

I know only so much about Schenker's method. A whole movement down to three notes? "Why that movement?"

"It's fun."

"Why Beethoven?"

"I wanted to start with something easy." Her tone was flat; there was no bragging in it. No expectation of praise or admiration.

I nodded like I understood. "Are you sure those are the right notes?"

"I have perfect pitch." And she played the three notes on the keyboard at her side.

So there was no question in her mind that I would ever challenge her reduction—that is, whether those three notes accurately represent the sonata movement by Schenkerian rules—just the actual tones she had hummed. I might have met my match for arrogance.

Then she added, "I might try Berg next, though. The Beethoven was too easy."

Nope. She has me beat for arrogance. I can't even *listen* to Alban Berg's music. "Let me know how that goes."

She looked at me, briefly, without expression, and then away. Remembering what BM had said about her lack of expectations regarding empathy and politeness, I decided to give it a test, hoping she wouldn't go into one of her tantrums.

"I took placement exams for my school today." Still no response. No *How did that go?* I plunged ahead. "Most of it was pretty easy, of course. Though I'm not sure about the history section. It's . . . well, it's rather upsetting, actually. I mean, I'm very good at history. But I'm worried about this test, because it was mostly about US history. The proctor said it's to see how much I know, coming from England." I paused and got nothing. "Do you know who shot Abraham Lincoln?"

"John Wilkes Booth."

So she was listening, anyway. I didn't let on that I hadn't known. "I did really well on the English section, of course. I had to use the words *irenic, nugatory, neologism, sartorial,* and *ersatz* in as few sentences as possible." I was about to describe how I'd done it, but she got up and wandered over to an end table. She picked up a glass object that looked like a bird of some kind, and sat on the chair beside the table. I had to reposition myself to be able to see her. She didn't say anything, though, and she showed no signs of exploding. She was looking at the glass bird so intently it was almost like she was meditating on it. But I wanted to talk more about my day, and GG wasn't here. I didn't want to talk to Mum or BM, and Ned was busy. So I just kept talking to the un-protesting, unresponsive Persie.

"Then they had fifty uncommon words, some of which were misspelled, and I had to correct those. *Iliopsoas* gave me pause, but when I considered that the *p* might be silent, I knew it was Greek and I should leave it alone. And I almost missed an incorrect one, but then I realised it must be Greek too, so I added an *r* and got it right."

Persie was still intent on her bauble. I didn't know whether it was her silence or my knowing that she didn't care at all what had happened to me today, but I ended up telling her something I would probably not have told anyone else. Even GG.

"That Greek word was *arrhostia*. I thought I was correct in leaving it alone. But the proctor, Dr. Metcalf, came by and said that I'd made one mistake in the whole list, and that if I found it he'd give me credit. I was shocked that I'd missed something, actually. Shouldn't have been, maybe, because I hadn't seen some of those words before. I hadn't ever seen *arrhostia*. For a minute I suspected Dr. Metcalf of playing a trick on me."

No response to that. So I tried another test. "*A* is pale yellow. *R* is bright red, so it's bright red twice after I made the correction."

Something about what I said caught Persie's attention. She watched my face as I went on. "*H* is cream; *o* is terra cotta; *s* is blood red; *t* is bright blue; *i* is bright yellow; and the final *a* at the end is another pale yellow. So the overall effect is creamy yellow, with a brownish-purple swirl. That swirl is almost brown if you take out that second *r*."

"Because of less red with the blue, and the brown tone of the terra cotta." She looked away again.

"Exactly." These are rules. Rules for letters, to be sure, but I'll bet the concept appeals to her.

"What colour is *p*?"

"Black."

"What colour is *e*?"

I knew where she was going. "Your name is black, lilac, bright red, blood red, bright yellow, lilac."

She laughed. Actually laughed. And clapped her hands a few times. "It's like a painting by Clyfford Still!" Before I could ask *Who's Clyfford Still*, she was up, out of the room, and pounding up the stairs. I wasn't sure whether I should follow her or not; could she get herself into some kind of trouble? But—BM left her alone sometimes, and it wasn't like she was an imbecile or something. I took the stairs two at once, just the same.

The door to her rooms was open, but I didn't feel I could just wander in. I peeked in, though, and it looked really lovely. Lots of pastels, all used to very good effect. I called out, "Hello?"

"Here it is. Here it is. Here it is." She repeated this phrase several times and then trotted out and sat at one end of a love seat in the upstairs foyer, her hands flying over the keyboard of a laptop. "Here it is. Here it is."

"May I sit at this end?" I knew I had to ask for permission.

"Yes. Here it is. Here it is. Here it is." And finally, triumphant, she turned the laptop so I could see the screen. And she was absolutely right. There was a painting, *Untitled, 1974*. It must be oil, must be huge. It's abstract, and the effect is the same as if Still had painted the entire canvas black and then added jagged areas of a purple colour with swirls of creams and pale yellows and reds in it, and finished it off by adding small but equally jagged areas of bright red, bluish white, and just a dab of sunshine yellow.

I looked up at Persie, and she was grinning from ear to ear. I had to smile, too; couldn't help it. "Yes," I told her, even though the purple was more purple than lilac. "This is you."

"Simon," she said with finality, not like she wanted to address me, more like it was just a word. "What colour is *m?*"

"Brick red."

"What colour is *n?*"

"Coral."

Evidently she remembered the other letters that make up my name, because she was back at her laptop again. "Here it is. Here it is." When she turned the screen again I was dumbfounded.

The painting is called *1947-R-No. 1*, and the Web page said it's just over five feet square, a little taller than wide. Blood red overall, large irregular edgy shapes in terra cotta, a squiggle of yellow, and a small starburst of orangey-coral. There are also areas of edgy black and a squiggle of white, but they don't upset the total effect. I was staring at it in a kind of trance when I heard BM's voice from downstairs.

"Persie? Simon?"

"Here!" Persie's reply made me think it was one of their routines: He calls; she answers immediately and with just that word.

"Simon?"

I looked at Persie, who was looking at me. I called out, "Here!"

There was a moment of silence, almost like BM didn't know what to say next. Then I heard, "Dinner. Now."

Persie jumped, slammed her laptop. "Oh no. Oh no. Oh no." This went on as she ran back into her rooms with the laptop, back out, and down the stairs. "Oh no. Oh no."

I was halfway down, going more slowly than she went, before I saw on my watch that it was two minutes past dinnertime. I guess Persie doesn't allow even herself a grace period.

Mum, BM, and Persie were seated in the dining room, deep white soup bowls with pyramid piles of tiny, pea shapes of carrot at each place setting. I took my assigned chair. While Ned went around and ladled bright green chilled soup over everyone's carrots, BM looked at Persie, then at me.

"You weren't in Persie's rooms, were you?"

"No. The love seat on the landing."

"I can't wait to learn what on earth captured her attention so profoundly as to make her late for dinner."

"Late," Persie said between spoonfuls of soup, but she was talking to herself, not shouting. "Late. Late. Late."

BM leaned towards her. "It's all right, Persie. Don't worry."

I said, "This soup is amazing." The colours were striking, but the flavours were so well blended I couldn't quite tell what they were, other than fresh peas making the soup so bright green swirling around the little orange "peas."

"So," BM said, "what was so fascinating?"

I looked at Persie, but she didn't seem to want to explain. So I did. "I described my synaesthesia to her, and she ran upstairs for her laptop. We sat on the love seat, and she showed me Web pages with images of paintings by Clyfford Still. She seemed to think they represented something similar to how I see words."

"And did they?"

I nodded. "She found one for her name right away. Then she found one for mine."

BM put his spoon down and stared at me. "She did what?"

How would I know what he wanted? "What part didn't you get?"

"She found a painting for *your* name?"

"Yes."

"Did you ask her to?"

"No."

Now he was staring at Persie, who had about finished her soup. "Persie, you looked for Simon's name?"

"Blood red, bright yellow, brick red, terra cotta, coral. *1947-R-No. 1.*"

BM sat back like he'd forgotten his own name. Mum asked, "Brian, what is it?"

"She looked for Simon's name. She never takes that step, focusing on the other person. At least never so quickly, or without being asked." Back to Persie: "What colour is your name, Persie?"

"Black, lilac, bright red, blood red, bright yellow, lilac. *Untitled, 1974.*"

He stared at me again, more like he didn't know what else to do than for any other reason.

Mum said, "Why Clyfford Still?"

Persie answered as though she'd been asked who he was. She wouldn't know that there weren't very many contemporary artists Mum would not know about. "A leader in Abstract Expressionism. Contemporary with Rothko and Pollock. Born 1904, died 1980. Two daughters, one named Sandra Still Campbell, the driving force behind the Clyfford Still Museum in Denver, Colorado. I want to go there."

It was no surprise to anyone that Persie would have the information about Still's life at her command, and would deliver it in an unmodulated tone. But that last sentence, in the same monotone, floored BM yet again. Watching his face, I was convinced he was trying desperately hard not to reveal an astonishment bordering on shock. Keeping his voice calm must have been an effort. "You want to visit the museum in Denver, Persie?"

"Yes."

"Even though it's in Denver?"

"Yes."

"Even though it's abstract art?" She looked up at her father; I couldn't tell whether she was confused about the question itself or

about why he would ask it. He said, "It's fine, Persie. I'm asking
because you prefer art that's more literally representative."

"*Untitled, 1974.*" And she polished off the last of her soup.
"Done."

I suggested, "Maybe the fact that these works have titles that
don't try to represent the art itself helps?"

BM sounded puzzled. "Perhaps."

After dinner, Persie asked me for a list of colours. "Your letter
colours," she called it. I told her I'd make up a chart tonight and
leave it for her on the love seat outside her rooms. She nodded and
said she was going to read upstairs. Mum helped Ned clean up despite his protests, and BM went out to the patio to clean the bar-
bie. Grill. For want of anything else to do, I wandered out to take a
look at said grill. BM saw me and nodded. "How'd your exams go,
Simon?"

"Fine, I think. History was a bit chauvinistic."

"How so?"

"It was mostly US history. I asked about it, and they said it was
because I'm not from the US and they wanted to know the extent
of my knowledge. Something like that."

He grinned. "And did you know the answers?"

I gave him an abridged version of an essay that had been required for one of the questions. If he was impressed, I couldn't
tell.

"That was a fascinating wine selection tonight, that prosecco. I
would never have gone there, but it worked very well."

There was that reluctant beam of pleasure again, both from this
praise and also because I decided to believe it was Ned, not Mum,
who'd told him it had been my idea.

I wandered for a bit around the patio. It's not very big, but from
another angle I could see the entire grill. It looked formidable,
dials and controls and different levels. Before I could stop myself,
I blurted out, "Thanks for the iPhone."

"You're welcome. Glad you like it." And he turned back to his
chore. I half expected him to say more about it, which I didn't

want him to do. But he didn't. Did he know he'd make more points with me by keeping quiet?

Back in the kitchen, I saw Mum had left, and Ned was still working. The dishwasher was churning away. I pulled a chair out from the table and sat, trying to think of something to talk with him about. My opening was weak. "Where's Mum?"

He was finishing up the last of the hand-wash items. "Gone to the other room to read, or watch TV, or something. I shooed her out. She's done more than her share for today."

I got up and reached for a drying towel. "I haven't." He grinned at me as I took things out of the drying rack. I didn't know where anything went, so I set dried items on the forest green granite of the island, which Ned had already cleaned.

"When do you eat dinner?" I asked.

"Oh, don't worry about me. It varies. Depends on the meal and the degree of fussing between courses. Sometimes I eat first, sometimes after, and tonight I ate pretty much while you all did. It takes me less time than you. No conversation."

"Why don't you eat with us?"

He laughed. "This is my job, Simon. And I get paid to eat while I work; pretty good deal."

I set a dried grill fork on the island. "But we're all friends here. That's what you said."

He dumped the last of the dishwater and ran the disposal. "It would be pretty awkward, always jumping up from the table for one thing and another. Besides, like I said, this is my job." Towelling his hands off, leaning a hip against the sink, he said, "What on earth did you do to Miss Persie tonight?"

"What do you mean?"

"Well"—he slapped the towel on a counter and picked up a glass I hadn't noticed, which appeared to contain sauterne—"first of all, she's never late for dinner. Or anything else, for that matter. That was the first clue." He took a sip. "Would you like a little more of this?"

"Sure."

"Help yourself. Glasses are there"—and he pointed—"and the

wine is in the stone cooler over there. Next, she's upstairs with you. She barely knows you. This just doesn't happen. It takes her a long time to get to know someone well enough to be alone with them."

"She came into the music room. I was already there, and she came in behind me, silently, and just sat down. Scared the willies out of me."

He laughed. "That's Persie. Doesn't see the need to announce herself. Still, it's surprising, since you were the only one in there. So you were talking about colours?"

"When I see a letter, it has a colour. The same colour every time. It's called synaesthesia. My father had it like I do, only the colours were different. My Aunt Phillippa once said that when she listens to the third movement of the sixth *Brandenburg*, she sees green lines and pink bubbles."

Ned had to set his glass down, he was laughing that hard. "Oh, that's amazing! Wouldn't that be great? Let's see, what about something like "Somewhere Over the Rainbow"? That's got colours already. Might be too much of a muchness."

I considered telling Ned about my conquest in vocabulary during the test today, but before I could begin, BM's voice behind us startled me.

"Simon, how did Persie go from—wherever she started, to Denver?"

BM had sneaked in and sat in the chair I'd vacated. I was irritated that he'd horned in on my conversation with Ned, but I couldn't ignore him.

"I was talking about the spelling portion of the exams today, and I mentioned my synaesthesia. She got it immediately."

"She . . . she doesn't have it, though."

I shook my head. "Don't think so. What I mean is, she understood it. Translated it into something important to her. She's deep into this artist."

"So it would seem. But how did you get her to show you the images?"

"It was her idea. I'd never heard of Clyfford Still."

He looked at me a minute, assessing. "She trusts you, somehow."

"She's a cat."

"What?"

They were both staring at me like I was bonkers. But I knew I was right. "Cats live by rules they make based on their environment and experiences. If you can tell what a cat's rules are, you can fit into the picture it has of its world, or at least you can convince it to give you a chance. Respect the rules, ask when you don't know what they are, and it works. Once you're in, you might be able to influence a few changes."

Ned wanted to know, "How do you ask a cat what the rules are?"

"You just assume there's a rule for everything, and you tread carefully. If the cat starts to react badly, back off and see if you can figure out what would fit into its world better. Just wait and observe."

"Well, I'll be." BM shook his head. "Simon, if you find yourself casting about for a career choice, you could consider working with autistic individuals. You'd be fantastic." He chuckled. "That must be why she asked you about *your* name. You did something to fit into her world picture, so you became part of it." He pointed at me. "And I'm putting you on official notice. If and when we go to that museum in Denver, you are coming with us."

Actually, I wouldn't mind seeing the museum. I really liked the images I saw of Still's works. But going with BM and Persie would not be my first choice. I told myself this trip was beyond unlikely, so I didn't have to reply. Instead I drained the end of my sauterne. I held the glass out. "Will I wash this, Ned?"

"Nah. Give it here."

"I'm going upstairs, then. See you tomorrow." And I headed out before BM could interrogate me any more about his daughter's metamorphosis.

Upstairs, after making up my colour chart for Persie, I curled into the reading chair with the course catalogue from St. Bony. About time to decide on a course from the arts and humanities category. Going through the options, my eye fell on one that surprised and intrigued me. Beginning Schenkerian Analysis. Perfect.

Boston, Day Four, Tuesday, 28 August

After being awakened by the cleaning crew, who evidently start on the top floor and work their way down, I spent most of the day scoping out the house and watching for an e-mail from St. Bony to tell me what classes I have. One thing I was looking for was BM's office, and eventually I figured out where it is. There's a door off to the side of the front entrance with a small nameplate: BRIAN MORGAN, AIA. Must be some architectural credential. There was a buzzer to the side, which led me to believe that the door would be locked. I didn't know whether BM was in his inner sanctum. Back in the house, I located the office's interior access door behind the front stairs, very inconspicuous. It was closed.

Finally, around half three, that e-mail arrived. And I hit the ceiling.

Carrying the printout I stormed about the house, looking for someone who might be able to fix things, until I located Mum on a chaise longue out on the brick patio, reading. Ned looked at me oddly as I stormed through the kitchen. I didn't dare say anything to him.

I slapped the paper down on the table beside Mum, next to a glass of something I didn't recognise. She marked her place in her book with a finger and looked up at me. "Something upset you, Simon?"

"This is unacceptable." I pointed to the paper.

"Why don't you summarise for me?"

I crossed my arms. "There are at least two things on the schedule they've given me that can't stand," I opened. "For one thing, they've given me a history class that's intended for their *junior* year, not senior. It's History of the Americas. Second, they've sent a list of arts and humanities classes that I'm to choose from, and the one I want the most isn't on it."

"What is it you want to take?"

"Schenkerian Analysis."

"I see." Her voice sounded rather tongue-in-cheek. "Do they say why it's not on the list?"

"It says these are the elective classes in which there are still openings."

"Well, I feel I must point out that if you had made your selection early in the summer—"

"Yes, Mother, I realise that. But the problem is happening now. We need to do something."

She looked at me for a few seconds. "I think what *we* need to do is that *you* need to select something from the list of classes with openings."

My teeth ground together, and I nearly bit a hole in the side of my tongue. "Are you telling me you won't do anything? You won't help me?"

"Simon, I don't know what you expect me to do."

"You could talk to your husband. He's the one with strings at the school, yes?"

She sat up and swung her legs so her feet were on the bricks. Her voice was quiet, but there was finality in it. "Brian pulled an enormous number of strings to get you into this school. If you have no idea how much weight he threw around, it's because no one told you. That's not your fault. So I'm telling you now: There are no more strings. You've put yourself in this position, Simon. Don't expect someone else to get you out of it."

I stood there like a stunned fish, mouth opening and closing.

"I think the best thing you can do now is to assess the electives on that list and choose the one most geared towards Oxford's admission requirements. Would you like me to help you?"

Through gritted teeth I said, "No, thank you." I stormed back through the kitchen and up to my room. I don't swear often, but when it's called for, for example at times like this one, I do: I felt so fucking helpless! I had been forced to uproot my life, make this poor exchange—London for Boston, Swithin for St. Boniface—and now I can't even get into the classes that will get me home again!

I threw the paper on my desk and nearly fell into the chair. If anything would catch Oxford's attention, it's Schenkerian Analysis. It's unusual and very advanced. It requires the student to be intelligent, independent, analytical, and musical all at once. It was nearly yelling at me, *This is the perfect course*. And I can't take it.

I was just contemplating picking up my pillow and screaming into it when I heard an unfamiliar sound. Someone was calling my name. But who was it, and where were they? Then I realised it was coming from the intercom beside the dumbwaiter. It wasn't Mum. Maybe it was BM, and he'd decided to help me. I dashed into the hall and pressed the Speak button. "Yes?"

"Simon, it's Ned. Do you have a few minutes for me?"

I had no idea what he meant. "I have all the time in the world." I knew my voice sounded angry, but I couldn't help it.

"May I come up? I'm sending gifts."

There were strange noises coming from the dumbwaiter. When it got to my level I saw that Ned had sent up a tray with tea butter biscuits, a pitcher of that stuff Mum had been drinking, and a wet sponge. I took the tray out to the roof garden and headed down to open the door to my level for Ned.

He used the sponge to wipe down the chairs and the table and then settled in like it was his own house. I sat also, not sure what he wanted, and not inclined to ask.

"You're planning on Oxford, I gather. That's ambitious." I shrugged, not sure where he was going, or how he even knew this. He smiled at me and, as though he'd read my thoughts, he said, "It's the perennial servant-master relationship. We hear everything that goes on in the house. In this case, I believe you need to talk about this impasse, and I think you're comfortable talking to me. Am I wrong? Say the word, and I'll take my dollies and tea set and go home."

I couldn't help smiling back. "I doubt anyone here thinks of you as a servant."

"Good thing. I'd disabuse them in rather unpleasant ways. Listen, Simon, am I right that you feel let down by the school and by your mother?"

"That about sums it up."

"May I see the list?"

Another shrug, and I fetched it. Ned had poured our glasses full of something pale-tea-coloured with lemon slices and ice cubes. And it dawned on me that it was iced tea. I saw it occasionally in London, but really it's for tourists. I'd never had it. I handed him the list.

"Thanks. Try the iced tea." And he started reading. Feeling obstinate, I took a biscuit instead. Without looking up, Ned said, "Your mom says that's your favourite cookie."

Tricked. He'd tricked me into accepting a biscuit from Mum by telling me to go for the iced tea. I nearly spit it out, but it was too good. Plus, he'd silently reminded me I wasn't supposed to use the word "biscuit" when Persie would want that particular baked confection to be called a "cookie." I set that imperative aside.

I waited a full two minutes before I took a sip of the tea. Unfortunately, I liked it.

"This class on twentieth-century literature looks interesting. Did you know Thomas Mann was gay?" he asked without looking at me.

"Yes. Why do you mention it?"

He gave me an arch look. "As I said, we hear everything. And I'm gay, so don't try to hide anything from me." He set the list down. "What major are you aiming for at Oxford?"

I considered pursuing the question of who had been talking in Ned's hearing about my sexual orientation, but I wasn't sure I cared. "We don't have 'majors' in the UK. I'm considering Oxford's Psychology, Philosophy, and Linguistics course of study."

"What languages have you studied? Other than English, of course."

"Italian. Latin. A little German."

He shook his head. "Too predictable. And too easy, for you." He picked up the list and pointed. "If I wanted to impress a place like Oxford, I'd go for this. Beginning Chinese."

I blinked. This idea hadn't occurred to me. "Why that?"

"Why? Well, for one thing, because all the world is facing east now and will be for a while to come. And even if that weren't true, learning a language that doesn't look or sound anything like the one in which you've already proven yourself is a massive undertaking. It's almost got an 'Abandon All Hope' banner over it. In fact, it sort of does, except that it adds, 'unless you're really, really smart.' " He handed me the list. "You, Simon Fitzroy-Hunt, are really smart. And if you don't do something that stands out, you might be seen as having done only what you need to do. You won't be seen as having stretched yourself." He shrugged. "It doesn't have to be Chinese. But it needs to be something that will catch their attention in a good way."

"Schenkerian Analysis would have done that."

"Maybe, maybe. You know Oxford better than I do. But consider this: If the course is full now, it might be offered again next semester. Get your name in now."

"It's a two-semester course."

"Better yet! Someone's bound to drop out, either during first semester or between semesters. Are you good enough at it to start behind the other students and keep up? Maybe you could get Persie to help you get a head start." He popped a biscuit into his mouth. "Just a thought."

"Persie is *twelve*."

"Eleven, actually. What's your point?" I didn't speak, so he said, "She knows this stuff better than you do. Admit it." He grinned at me, expecting an answer this time.

I had to fight the smile that wanted to spread across my face. I sipped more tea to hide it. "Well, she's been working at it."

"And you haven't. So she's ahead of you. But she doesn't judge. She doesn't gloat. There isn't a drop of arrogance in her blood. Unlike *some* people." He lifted his glass. "I will say she'd be a very difficult taskmaster. No sympathy. She might not be patient enough with you."

"I'm not stupid, you know. I know you're baiting me."

"Sometimes we have to be pushed into doing what we want to do. No man is an island, and we need each other. Right now, you need someone to push you. That might be Persie. It might be me. Or it might be the Beginning Chinese teacher."

"What makes you think I need pushing?"

"You're stuck."

"Stuck?"

He set his glass on the tray. "Look, Simon, I know you didn't want to come here. And I understand why not. But you're here. Take advantage of what you can, and use it to put yourself back on the course you would have chosen. And believe me, there's lots here to take advantage of." He stood. "Call me on the intercom when you're ready to send the tray down." And he headed for the door.

I called a challenge after him. "You're really too smart for this job. Do you need some pushing?"

His hand on the doorknob, he turned and said, "I've finished my master's degree in food chemistry. Just taking a break to earn some money and figure out where I want to go next." And he was gone.

Sitting there, watching the light change on the buildings as the sun got lower in the sky, I tried to regain my sulk, but it wouldn't cooperate. Finally I picked up the list again. If there was one thing Ned had said that I should listen to, it was that Oxford will expect me to stand out. Even with the connection through my dead grandfather, there's the question of which fellow I'll be assigned. I'm not saying Oxford would have any unacceptable fellows, but a good match can make all the difference.

Other than Chinese, was there something else I might want to bargain for? Flipping through the course list my eye fell on African Studies, Doing Business in India, Ancient Rome, Environmental Systems and Societies, Information Technology in a Global Society, Public Speaking, and The City: A Living Palimpsest.

Palimpsest. Not a word typically used for anything alive. Scraping off an old manuscript to reuse it doesn't sync up with city life for me. I shook myself and went over the list again.

It's no good! I want that Schenker course.

Think, Simon. You're smart. Think. Who else might be able to help?

I picked up my new iPhone and rang up the main number on St. Bony's Web site. When they answered, I said, "This is Simon Fitzroy-Hunt. I'm enrolled for the first time this year, as a senior, and I have a question about my electives. Is there someone I can speak with?"

"Certainly. Your assigned counsellor . . . hold on, please . . . is Dr. Metcalf. He's in his office at the moment. I'll connect you."

Perfect. He already knew me a little. I hadn't given any thought to what I would say; bad planning. So when he got on the line I plunged in. "I have my schedule, and there are a couple of things. . . . Well, first, why is it that I'm registered for the junior year History of the Americas?"

"I have your placement exam in front of me. You show a solid understanding of connections around the globe over time, but if I were to graph your depth of knowledge on a map, the coverage of the Americas in general and the US in particular isn't enough to support your application to schools here in the US. Before you protest," he added quickly, "I realise that you have your sights set on Oxford, and I know of no reason to worry. However, it's always a good idea to have a few backup schools, and it's also possible you'll change your mind about where you want to go."

"I'll be submitting my application very soon. I'm not going to change my mind."

"Then consider it insurance for your backup plan."

"I don't need—"

"Simon, this is knowledge that will stand you in good stead, whatever your future."

"Is there no one else I can talk to about this?"

"Certainly. You can speak to anyone all the way up to Dr. Healy if you like. It won't change anything, however." He paused whilst I ground my teeth some more. "Was there another question?"

"Yes. There is. I had expected to take Schenkerian Analysis, but it's fully subscribed. What do I need to do to get a place in that class?"

"Ah, yes. Not a course we offer frequently. It's currently over-subscribed with a waiting list. We can put you on that, but I must warn you that you'll be around number four or five."

"Can I get into it for second semester if someone drops out?"

"It's not an easy course to drop into. And it would depend on how many names are still on the waiting list."

"And is there anything I can do to move up higher on that list?"

"I don't know of anything, other than waiting your turn."

"Financial generosity would not be rewarded?"

He laughed. He actually laughed. "Good try, but the reward for generosity would not be in the form of a waiting-list advancement. It would be in the knowledge that you're supporting a worthy institution."

I was trying to be calm, but I was also getting desperate. Talk about a backup plan . . . "Then, Beginning Chinese?"

There was a brief silence. "It looks like as of a few minutes ago, that class is full, too." It was everything I could do not to scream. "Tell me a little about yourself, Simon. What plans do you have for your future?"

I could feel my jaw working as I tried to hold my temper in check. "I'm planning on the Psychology, Philosophy, and Linguistics course." I wanted to know if he knew what I meant by that.

He didn't miss a beat. "That course of study has a very broad scope. Would it be fair to say, then, that you're not the kind of person who has one or two very focused academic passions? That your interests are more diverse?"

That was easy. "I'm interested in many different things. And I'm good at most of them." I couldn't resist. "Like history."

"Good. Then you could consider the City course."

"The Living Palimpsest one? What on earth for?"

He chuckled. "If you think that's an easy course, you're very much mistaken. Students have to find their own way around the city, and you're not allowed to use any kind of chauffeured service, private or taxis. You'll look at every aspect of Boston, figure out why these aspects developed as they did, and translate that into a conceptual model transferable to any world city. Your final exam will include a written paper and a thirty-minute presentation to a large group of staff and students." I was quiet for long enough that he asked, "Do you know the meaning of *palimpsest?*"

I almost snorted. "Of course."

"Picture how a city—London is a wonderful example—is built, rebuilt, reorganised, destroyed or partially destroyed, rebuilt—on and on. Each time a city changes, there are driving forces behind those changes. If you know what these forces are and understand how they drive the development of cities, all kinds of academic doors will open for you. And here's a suggestion. If you take that course, it would allow you to kill a few birds with one stone."

"Oh?"

"It's a two-semester course, and it meets the IB requirement for the Individuals and Societies class. If we add one extra assignment in the course specifically for you about Boston's influence over US history for, say, one hundred years after the American Revolution, we could remove the History of the Americas requirement. And because it includes the city's cultural development, it could fulfil the arts and humanities requirement as well. What do you think?"

I was trying not to get sucked in, even if this was sounding more interesting. "Two semesters . . ."

"You couldn't do it justice in one. Are you comfortable with public speaking?"

"I delivered presentations to large groups at Swithin."

"I have to say, Simon, you seem like an ideal candidate for this course. And I would not say that to very many students. I think you have what it takes. And there's yet a *third* bonus." His voice took on weight. "Students who do well in this course receive a special commendation from the headmistress that's noticed by university deans of admissions."

"Why don't more students take it, then?"

"It's a very challenging course. Time-consuming. And many students prefer to focus on one or possibly two disciplines rather than spend a lot of energy on this expansive curriculum."

"How many of last year's graduates are at Oxford now?"

"Two. And one of them took this course. The other is a mathematician."

I had expected him to say "none." St. Bony is not a large school; I think there will be just over two hundred students as of this autumn, across four grade levels. "What if I take the first semester and want to drop the second part?"

"There's no penalty grade-wise, but there would be a note on your record. You'd need to include an explanation. And you might be required to pick up two second-semester courses. As I said, this one is very demanding."

"How many openings are there for it now?"

"Let me check . . . It looks like there are two openings."

God. What should I do? "What were the other courses with openings, again?"

We went down the list, but nothing stood out. "So, Simon, shall I sign you up for The City?"

Oxford will take notice. It will make an impression.

"Are you concerned it would be too much for you?"

If I had reservations, they had more to do with Boston, which I've disparaged so many times to so many people. I didn't want to be put into the position of having to eat my hat. But I also didn't want to pass up an opportunity to get noticed at Oxford. "No."

"Then . . . what would you like to do?"

"I'll take it."

"Excellent. Hang on. . . . Okay, I've just entered you. I'll need to make some adjustments to your schedule, move a class or two around, to accommodate the City course. I'll send you an amended version of your schedule this evening, so watch your e-mail. And tomorrow we'll go over your CAS IB course. As you know, the International Baccalaureate programme requires three core classes, and Creativity, Action, Service is one of them."

"Yes, I know about the course." I didn't admit that I'd forgotten about it.

"Then you know that we assign each student a unique project. After your orientation tomorrow, have the front office give me a call. We'll talk about it then."

Christ, what next? "Do I have to come prepared with ideas?"

"No, actually, we've got your project pretty well defined; just a couple more details to iron out."

"And you can't give me the basics about it now?"

"Best to speak in person, I think. See you tomorrow, Simon."

I rang off, but I wasn't happy with this turn of events. Sure, the City course sounded interesting, and it would stand out on my résumé, but so would the Schenker course. I know I love music; I don't look forward favourably on the idea of traipsing all over Boston. Crap. And now there's a "unique" project?

I considered texting GG, but there was too much to say. So I rang him.

He didn't answer.

Boston, Day Five, Wednesday, 29 August

Wait, just wait until you hear what my CAS project is. I'm nearly apoplectic.

Orientation was about what you'd expect; they gave us our badges, then dragged us through the buildings on Marlborough Street and out for short tours—or at least drive-bys in buses—of locations they use for sport activities.

Back at the school, around half three, the receptionist—a perky girl in a ponytail and a green polka-dot blouse—sent me to Dr. Metcalf's office. We exchanged a couple of comments about the orientation, but I didn't want to waste time. I asked about the CAS project.

He told me, "The first thing you'll need to do is brush up on rules and preparation for the annual Scripps spelling championship, which takes place at the end of May."

"Not to compete, I presume."

"No. You're well past the grade level and age for contestants. As I'm sure you know, you flew through the spelling portion of the placement exam. I was very impressed that out of fifty words, you missed only one, and when I told you there was an error it took you no time to identify and correct it." He sat back in his chair. "Your file indicates that you have synaesthesia. Specifically, letters have colours for you. Do you feel that has affected your ability in the area of spelling?"

"Definitely. I know what colour a word should be, not just what its letters are."

"So I assume you hadn't seen *arrhostia* before. Yet you found it quickly."

"Once I knew there was an error, I knew it had to be one of the words I hadn't seen before. I decided that with only one *r, arrhostia* didn't make sense."

"Why not?"

"It didn't seem to fit any category. You know, medical, legal, linguistic, geographic, that sort of thing. So I played with changing letters, and finally it made sense that it was Greek. So adding the *r* made sense."

"Have you studied etymology, Simon?"

"Not extensively. But I've studied Italian, Latin, and German, so if something has a Latin or a Germanic root, I recognise that. I've been exposed to enough Greek to be a little familiar with what its roots look like. Shall I go on?"

"No, you've made your point. And it's where I was hoping you'd go. I think you'll enjoy this project." He opened a folder on the desk. "There's an eleven-year-old boy named Toby Lloyd at the Academy of New England, a private IB school. Young Toby has won spelling bee after spelling bee, and he's nearly qualified for the national level. One more victory at a bee in March, and he's on his way." He shook his head thoughtfully. "The spelling abilities of these kids are unbelievable. I watch the televised competition every year, and I wouldn't be able to spell very many of the words they're given."

He closed the file again and handed it to me. "Toby needs a coach. We want that coach to be you."

Shock. Utter shock. I didn't even open the folder. "What?"

"You'll meet him tomorrow afternoon at his home in Brookline. The address is in the folder. He'll be expecting you as soon as you can get there after lunch. His school has allowed him to devote Thursday afternoons to this work, so you should plan to stay with him at least until four. You won't need to have study materials; he'll have lots of that sort of thing. By the way, he's thrilled that you're English. He can't wait to meet you."

How can I *stop* this? "What other projects are there?"

"If this one turns out to be problematic, we could reassess. However, the justification would need to be solid. Do you have some concern in particular?"

"I—I don't get on well with children." The truth is, I don't get on well with *anyone.*

"Toby is extremely bright; you'll get along fine."

"What if we *don't* get along, though?"

"As I said, if the reasons are strong enough, we'll revisit."

"How am I marked on this? What if he doesn't win?" My voice was starting to sound squeaky with panic.

"You and I will meet each week about your career here, and this project is one of the things we'll discuss. I'll monitor your progress, I'll speak with Toby and his parents a few times, and I'll write a report about your overall success at working with Toby. Your final assessment won't be based on the outcome of the competition. It will be based on your interaction with him, on the effort you put into it, and on our discussions. He doesn't have to like you, or you, him. But you need to find a way to help him prepare."

I was struggling to come up with some other angle. I really, *really* did not want this project, but without that CAS credit, Oxford won't consider me.

There are so very many things I'm being forced to do that I don't want to do, but this? This was the icing on the cake. The final straw. Whatever metaphor you like. I'd reached critical mass.

"Simon, I know that moving to Boston was not something you wanted to do, and I completely understand that. But the best choices you can make now must be rooted in reality. You are here, and we're very well prepared to support your goal. But you have to work with us. At this point, rebelling against your current situation will work against your future one. My job is to help you. So, given that, and keeping in mind the current reality, is there anything I can do to help you help yourself?"

My eyes stung. I *refused* to cry! I lifted my chin to keep tears from falling. I knew that if I spoke, my voice would crack and I'd lose my battle. I grabbed the folder, turned my back on my supposed counsellor, and left.

I couldn't get out of there fast enough. A couple of students I'd met during orientation stood like obstacles between me and the exit, and I nodded at them as best I could without slowing my frantic pace.

The near jog between the school and BM's house was a blur. If a dog had jumped out and bitten me along the way, I don't think it would have registered.

Everyone keeps telling me to work with what I've got, to look for opportunities in the changes. What they don't get is that *everything else* was taken away from me. So everything I wanted is gone, and they keep handing me things I don't want and saying, "Here. Work with this." And there's not a fucking thing I can do about it!

Every time I think, *All right, this could be worse*, it gets worse. First the house isn't bad, but then there's Persie to deal with. So I managed to get to a place where Persie is at least interesting, and St. Boniface tries to make me take remedial history. The IB programme requirements point me towards art, and there's a course I actually *want* to take, but no, I can't have that one. So they push me into a demanding, year-long course that most students know better than to sign up for. And now? Now they want me to cater to some *child* who can't learn to spell by himself! And through it all, they keep telling me not to fight it, not to rebel, not to complain.

FUCK THAT SHIT!

At the house I got upstairs as fast as possible. Unlocking the door to my staircase, I was shaking so badly that I dropped my keys at least three times.

My bedroom door has a lock, and I used it. Screaming into my pillow, I didn't hear Mum's knocking until it turned into pounding. "Simon! Simon, what's wrong? What's happened?"

"Go away! Stay away from me! This is all your fault!"

"I'm not going anywhere. I'm going to stay right here until you open the door."

There was no way I could go on screaming as though I were alone. I got up and threw the door open.

"You've taken everything else, and now I can't even have any fucking privacy! Get the hell away from me!" I've rarely sworn in front of my mother, and never *at* her.

She stepped into the room and tried to embrace me. I stepped away. "Get out, damn you! Get out and leave me alone!" We stared at each other for two, three seconds maybe, and gradually she turned and left, an odd expression on her face that I couldn't read. And I didn't care.

I went back to pounding on my bed, but there didn't seem to be any tears. Maybe I'd used them all up by now. Sliding down to the floor, back against the mattress, I longed for Graeme. I was supposed to ring him today. *Maybe I should ring him now. Maybe I should text him. Maybe it would be cathartic to write a long, heartfelt e-mail.*

Maybe I should just face the truth. There is no Graeme.

This hit me smack in the middle of my chest, hard enough to take my breath away.

The Graeme who loves me, the Graeme whose kisses make me wild, doesn't exist.

The real Graeme, the one I love but who barely knows I'm alive, isn't even gay. That day in the maze? The treasure hunt where he ended up in the same dead end with me? That happened. What didn't happen was his kissing me. Or even looking like the idea had ever crossed his mind. There have been no exchanges about being at New College together, or about singing in the chapel or lounging in the garden or creating a dining routine everyone wants to join. I've wanted him for over a year, dreamed about him, dreamed of him loving me. None of it was real.

As the self-delusion about Graeme wormed its way into my psyche, it made me vulnerable to another secret I'd tried to hide from myself: I don't believe Oxford will want me.

It was my dad's idea, Oxford. It was his belief in me that made it seem possible. And ever since he died, I've been trying to prop up his idea—with less and less conviction. And if I'm honest with myself, I have to admit this was part of the reason I'd picked up the razor blade at home.

The other part had been the same damned reason I was in despair again now. Graeme. I'd known he had a girlfriend, but he'd been talkative enough about it that I felt sure he hadn't had sex with her, because he'd never mentioned anything like that, which meant there was still hope. But then, just before Mum informed me about this move, his talk had changed. And I knew it had happened, and I knew he had liked it.

Looking back, mentally seeing that blade in my hands, I don't know why I didn't go through with it. What had stopped me? What had seemed like it was worth going on for? Whatever the reason, not using that blade meant I'd had to find some way to go on living, at least for a time, at least until I could decide what to do. I couldn't change the move, but I'd managed to reconstruct my love affair. It had been imaginary all along; why couldn't it continue that way?

Now, with both these things hitting me again on top of the critical mass reached today, I realised that these two delusions together—Oxford and Graeme—were nothing more than a hollow shell merely pretending to be a solid, unstoppable mass. And I was the cowardly lion, pretending to be fearless. I was huddled into a soggy ball and crying out, "Who pulled my tail?" when it was me, hanging onto it out of terror.

There were sobs now, painful and deep, and when they faded I sat there on the floor, considering my options. I could refuse to do any of the things that are being thrown at me, and lose any remote chance at Oxford or any other decent school. I could toe the line for the rest of this fucking year, absorb all those awful things that keep flying at me like rotten meat thrown by a bloodthirsty crowd, and get out of this fucking city and back home, even if I have to disappoint my father and go to some other school.

Or I could let the bloodthirsty crowd win. I could die.

The next thing I registered was that I was in that huge, beautiful bathroom, staring at the claw-foot tub. It would be a lovely place to die, actually. I took off my St. Boniface clothes, folded them neatly, and stacked them on the floor, leaving only my undershorts on. Experimentally, I lay in the empty tub for a few minutes and decided that yes, it would work. I got up, opened the skylight, and from a drawer in the antique oak armoire I fetched my panic kit: that black leather case with the single-edge razor blades.

They looked clean, objective, without judgement or intent or emotion. They were just blades. I selected one and held it so the light caught on it, and I felt a peaceful calm come to me.

Everything was in slow motion now. First, I locked the door. Next, I placed the vanity chair under the doorknob in the event Mum came looking for me again. Next, I set the plug into the tub drain. Next, I turned only the hot water on. I watched the water fill the tub. *Water:* Navy. Pale yellow. Bright blue. Lilac. Bright red. A few times, I tested the water temperature, adding cold water as needed.

Water off, I stared up at the skylight and, through it, sent a final farewell to Graeme. Aloud, I said, "I loved you. I loved you so much. If only you knew."

I set the blade in the soap dish and stepped into the tub.

Reclining there, I let my arms float in the clear water, water that wasn't just clear but was also a swirl of bluish purple with a dash of yellow. I was about to add so much red to it. It would be truly beautiful. Persie would be fascinated. And that's all she would be. Persie is like the razor blade. No judgement, no attachment.

In my mind, Persie picked up the blade that was actually in my right hand now. She didn't look at my face. This wasn't about me, for her. Aloof, emotionally removed, she leaned over her task, and with the corner of the blade she pricked the skin on my left forearm, just to see what would happen, and pulled the blade away. A thin stream of red swirled into the water and gradually disappeared. Again, blade to skin, she made the cut a little longer. No deeper yet, but longer. More swirls, more gradual fading away, rather like my life would do soon. If there was pain, it didn't touch me.

A little deeper now, and the swirls were richer. I watched them dissipate, but there was enough that the clear water was changing. Suddenly it wasn't blue or purple or yellow or even red. Suddenly it was an ugly shade of greenish brown. I raced through the letters; what was brown? *C,* and *d.* Different shades, but both browns. What was green? *F, q,* and *v. Q* for *queer,* maybe? But together these letters made no sense. They were twisting in my brain into ugliness. They turned into brown snakes with hideous green markings, and they curled around my legs, my waist, and up my chest.

Suddenly I was standing in the tub, screaming, but without making any sound. Silent screams. Silent snakes. With my hands, I brushed frantically at my ribs, pushing the snakes down, pushing them off my legs, until I could get out of the tub. I stood on the marble tiled floor, dripping green-brown water that slowly faded to the palest pink.

My legs wouldn't support me, and I lowered myself to the floor. On all fours, I felt my lungs heave as though something had pulled me underwater and I'd barely escaped. The panic waned, and from my left arm a squiggly wet stream of watery blood made its way to the floor. I watched it without caring in the least what it was or what it meant.

Fully on the floor now, I lay on my side, curled into an embryonic ball. There were no tears. There was no pain. All that existed were the hard, cold floor and my own heartbeat. And then I heard it. My father's voice.

"What's green and brown, Simon, is the word *stop*."

His colours were different to mine. I don't know what all his colours were. All I could do was believe the voice.

The knocking on the door went on for a while before I noticed it. Then I heard, "Simon? It's Ned. Can I come in?"

I pointed my brain in that direction, struggling to understand. My eyes opened, but still I couldn't see very well. It was late enough that there was not much light coming from overhead. From inside my embryonic cocoon I managed, "What?"

"Are you all right? Can I come in?"

"Wait." At least I knew he must wait; nothing would happen quickly. I unfolded my arms first, checked to be sure my left arm was no longer bleeding, then straightened my legs as much as I could, and finally I sat up. "Wait," I said again, just in case.

There was blood on the floor.

Standing slowly, I located first a light switch and then a sponge, which I wet in the pale pink water of the tub. I swiped at the floor.

"Simon?"

"Wait." My brain started to kick in, and I realised this wasn't enough. So I added, "I'm just getting out of the bathtub, all right?"

There would be a stain between the floor tiles. No getting around that. I rinsed the sponge as well as I could and drained the tub, swiping with the sponge at the pink ring the water left behind. The blade, which I had dropped, lodged in the drain, and I picked it up carefully, wrapped it in a wad of toilet paper, and set it in the wastebasket.

At the sink I rinsed my arm. The cut wasn't very big. It would heal.

"Simon?" His tone had become more insistent.

"Wait! I said wait!" I was irritated now. Again, no privacy. I looked around the room to be sure it was as unrevealing as possible. Wrapping a towel around my waist, holding it with my left hand, my inner arm pressed against me to hide the wound, I moved the chair as quietly as I could and then unlocked and opened the door. "What is it?"

"You didn't come down for dinner." He half grinned. "Persie will have your head. Anyway, I've brought your dinner up for you, along with mine. Why don't you get dressed, and then come out to the roof. We can eat together."

"I'm not hungry."

"Come out anyway. I'll be waiting." He turned and left.

Feeling stunned and empty, moving slowly, I located a box of bandages and applied one in case the bleeding started again. In my room I peeled off my damp underwear, put on a dry pair, and wrapped myself in my bathrobe. Ordinarily, this robe gives me pleasure. It's a rich gold silk with dark blue silk edging sewn around the cuffs and along the shawl collar. But tonight, it was just a robe. Stepping into slippers, I made my sluggish way out to the roof.

Ned had the table set, complete with placemats, cloth napkins, and sterling silver. There was a half-bottle of wine in a marble stone cooler and two glasses. On the plates were Cornish game hens, something that looked like haricots, and something white and red.

"Gorgeous robe. It's almost dark enough for the light. Do you need it?"

"There's a light out here?"

"Sure."

I sat. "No. No light."

He poured some wine into the glasses. I didn't look at the label. I didn't care. Then he picked up his glass, holding it in my general direction. "Prosit," he said, practically forcing me to lift mine. Once I had it in my hand, I took a sip. It was chilled, but it felt warm and buttery. "One of the Mersault selections. There wasn't a lot in half bottles. But I like this one."

It was an effort to set my glass down carefully, I felt that weak. And then it was too much effort to pick up my utensils. So I just sat. So did Ned.

"I know something happened today that upset you very much. I hope you'll tell me what it was."

My head wouldn't raise, but I did my best to look at him. I didn't want to talk about it. And I did want to talk about it. I didn't say anything.

"Is it about school?"

Was it? Yes, but so much more. I have no boyfriend. I have no cat. I have no parents. I have no home. I have no friends. I have no chance. I have no hope. How much of that could I say? To anyone?

"It's everything," I managed finally. "There's nothing left. Nothing of me left. It's all someone else's life now."

"Someone else? Like, who?"

My life has felt like a sham for so long. So I cast the blame in the most obvious direction. "My mother. It's her life. It's all about her. Everything that was me is gone. And they keep dumping more and more and more"—my head lifted now, and my voice got louder— "and more crap on my head. More shit I have to do that I don't want to do. More shit I have to deal with. It's like—it's almost like someone's cast an evil spell over me. And everyone keeps telling me to accept it, to work with it, or I can't go home. I feel like fucking Dorothy. And the witch who cried, 'Surrender, Dorothy' has had her way."

"So you want to go back to Kansas?"

I glared at him. "This is not funny!"

"Sorry. Couldn't help myself. So, getting back to London would make everything all right?"

I took a very, very shaky breath. Would it? Oxford or no Oxford, would I rather be in England? *Yes. Absolutely, yes.* "Every shred of me is back in England. I could be myself there. I can say 'biscuit' there. I feel out of it here, out of everything. I want my cat back. I want to be able to visit my father's grave. I want a chance to build my life where I started it, where my roots go back further into history than people here can begin to imagine, where I feel like I belong. They ripped me away from it, and they're trying to make me believe that I can't have it back unless I do all this shit they're telling me to do."

His face had an odd look on it. Almost angry. And as I realised that his own African roots were as old and as deep as mine, knowing that his ancestors had been yanked much more cruelly out of their soil than I had been, I shrank back into my chair. A challenge in his voice, he said, "What shit would that be?"

But he didn't have the right to challenge me. My problems were no less real than they had been five minutes before, and he wasn't the one who had arrived on these shores in the stinking, crowded cargo hold of a small ship. I stood so suddenly that the chair went over backwards. "All of it! Boston, this house, Brian, Persie, the fucking school, a course load that could kill me when I'm feeling good—and I'm feeling like shit—and now this latest thing—"

Turning away from the table I walked quickly to the far end of the roof, to the waist-high brick wall. I leaned my hands on the granite that tops the brick and looked over. It might or might not be fatal to fall from here. Everything would depend on the position I'd be in when I landed. Plus I'd have to be sure to clear the fire escape that's back here.

Ned was beside me, and almost under my breath I said, "I know I sound like a whingy little kid. But it just goes on and on, one thing after another."

His voice was calm again, soothing. "And what's this latest thing?"

"It doesn't matter." I turned and slithered down until I was sitting on the gravel. The sharp stones would have hurt if they hadn't felt good. "It doesn't matter."

Ned lowered himself to sit beside me. His voice gentle, he said, "Let's think about time. Let's imagine eight or nine months. Picture how large that amount of time looks against seventy or eighty years. Just see that in your mind for a minute."

He waited, then, "Now let's take those proportions, and instead of time, fit them into a landscape. Those eight or nine months, they're brambles, and maybe some nettles and poison ivy. Nasty stuff. But you have a long stick and a scythe. Getting through this part might not be fun, but once you're clear of it, on the other side—even from here you can see it—lovely, open, green pasture, a sweet little village, and in the distance a beautiful, lively city."

Emerald City? But no, that wasn't Dorothy's real home. Ned was painting an English landscape. "I know what you're doing."

"Good. And do you know what *you're* doing?"

"What do you mean?"

"Do you know what you're going to do next?" I shook my head. "No? I do. You're going to come with me back to the table and enjoy that scrumptious meal I put together for us." He stood and held a hand out. "One step at a time, Simon. You'll get through the brambles." I took the hand, and he pulled me to my feet and into his arms for a quick, firm hug.

Ned brought an oil lantern to the table and lit it. We didn't talk whilst we ate. Outdoors, it didn't matter that the game hens, the beans, and the tiny red potatoes had gone cold. It was more like a picnic this way. The wine was cool, and that was perfect. The only sounds that registered for me were the tiny clinks of sterling silver on china, which—when I hear them outdoors—always seem to be the very sound of luxury.

As Ned poured the last of the wine, he said, "Dessert, which is a divine almond torta served with vanilla bean ice cream and the richest fudge sauce you have ever tasted, is in the kitchen. And before you can have any, you have to tell me what today's load of shit was all about."

I took a sip of wine and set the glass down carefully. "I have to help an eleven-year-old boy named Toby Lloyd—Christ, another Welshman, *and* another eleven-year-old—prepare for some national spelling bee."

Ned sat up straight. "The Scripps National? Wow. That's a huge, *huge* deal, Simon. So, you're his coach?"

"Yes."

"And how is this appropriate for you?"

"There's this course IB students have to take, almost like a community service sort of thing. But mine is *special*." My tone of voice reflected how special I thought it was. "I can spell anything. Well, anything I've seen once, and most words I haven't. I have a really good memory, and of course there are the colours. The synaesthesia."

"Mmmm-*hmm*. How is your synaesthesia going to help young Mr. Lloyd, do you think?"

He was right. "I don't know."

"Because if I remember rightly, the words those kids have to spell would challenge even you. They aren't words most people ever see, really. The kids have to know etymology, derivations—that sort of thing. So I doubt the colours would help you, and I certainly don't see how they're going to help Toby."

"They won't. That's not something I can teach him."

"So it looks like you'll need to figure out what *will* help him. And I guess you can't really begin to do that until you meet him. When does that happen?"

"I'm supposed to go to his house tomorrow afternoon. Brookline, wherever that is. Two o'clock, for a couple of hours. Every week."

"Are you taking a cab, or do you want to try your hand at the T? I can help you figure out how to get there."

"What's the T?"

"It's the subway. Only not all of it's underground. *T* stands for transit, I guess."

I hadn't thought about that option. "A taxi, I suppose. But you're talking like it's really going to happen."

"Isn't it?" That question hung in the air for maybe a minute. When I didn't agree or disagree, he asked, "If you were in London, and your school there gave you this project, would you take it on more willingly?"

"Maybe."

"So, here, it's just a case of all this shit getting to you. You might actually enjoy it, you know. I get that you're wading through a lot of crap that's been thrown at you. I really do. So figure out which bits aren't really shit, focus on those, and hack your way through the rest of it."

I toyed with my glass, sulking, not looking at him.

"Life's not fair, Simon. I'm sure you've heard that before. Now you're living it."

"It's my mother's fault." I tried that again, though it was rather halfhearted by now. Maybe she hadn't lost Oxford for me, or Graeme, but she'd made me lose home, and Tink.

"I'm not arguing. But it kind of doesn't matter. Laying blame isn't terribly useful. What's useful is figuring out how to get out of the mess you're in. And for you, time will be a big factor. Once you wrap your inestimable brain around that, you'll make the rest fall into place. If you never forgive your mother, that's up to you. But when we find ourselves standing in shit, we need to wade through it to get out. You'll get out, I promise."

"I told her I have a boyfriend." I don't know what possessed me to say this; maybe it was so I wouldn't blab that I'd almost taken another path out of that shit just a little while ago.

Something in my voice tipped him off that there was some question about it. He asked, "And . . . do you?"

I shook my head. "He's straight. But I love him. I've wanted him to be my boyfriend. I almost convinced myself he was."

"Ah, Simon, if I had a dollar for every straight guy I've fallen for, I think I'd have . . . I'd have maybe two dollars." He laughed at the look on my face. "They're fun to fantasise about, but they're like knife grass. Wander in there, and you'll come out bleeding from a thousand cuts that don't go very deep but that sting like hell." He shook his head like he was remembering something. "Well, I ain't tellin' yo mama. You want her to think you gave up even more than you did, that's fine by me."

"Speaking of my 'mama,' how did it end up being you who came up to find me?"

"I gather there were—shall we say, words—between you and your mom earlier. When you didn't show up for dinner there was a lot of discussion about whether she should come upstairs, or Brian should, and it started to get a little heated. Persie . . . didn't react well to your absence, or to the discussion. And even though Anna's here tonight, Brian didn't feel he could leave Persie without things getting worse, and he was sure you'd react badly again, yourself, if your mom did. So I offered to come up, and your mom offered to finish serving dinner."

"I see. So now I'm as bad as Persie?"

"I didn't say Persie was bad."

"But I'm as obstreperous as she is. You might as well have said that."

He gave me a wry smile. "It's true that there are two offspring requiring special handling in the house, if that's what you mean." He chuckled. "I think she missed you, actually."

I couldn't begin to understand the weird jolt this gave me, so I ignored it. "Special handling won't help."

"It might, if they knew what the rules were. Do you know what the rules are?"

"My only rule was, 'Don't make me leave home.' They ignored that one. I told them they were ignoring it at their peril, but they ignored that, too. And here I am."

"And if someone puts a cat into a new home, does it or does it not establish a new set of rules to fit the new situation?"

"Yes." My voice sounded sulky. "But I'm not a cat!"

"Aren't you? If you were a dog, you'd be happy wherever you were as long as you were with your people. Cats bond to their people because the people are part of their world, so losing their people is upsetting, but it's really their place, their home, they're attached to. Am I right?"

This was true, and BM had said something very like this to me once. But somehow this made Ned more like BM than the other way around, and that made me angry. "I'm still not a cat. I don't have to be a cat *or* a dog."

"Maybe not, but you might let cats instruct you a little. You might want to think about what your new rules should be. That would help you, and it would help others treat you the way you want to be treated."

"The way I wanted to be treated was ignored! I was yanked out of my home—"

"Yes, you were. And that sucks. That sucks big-time. You're mad at everyone involved, and I don't blame you. But as you said a minute ago, here you are. Now what?"

I crossed my arms on my chest and stared at him. "I'll tell you 'now what.' Now I get all this shit dumped on me, shit I didn't ask for and don't want." Even as I heard myself say this, I was tired of hearing it. I just wasn't ready to give up the mantra.

"Seems to me people around you are looking for the rules. They're trying to make sure the things you have to do are things that pertain to you in some way. Take this spelling coaching thing. What do you know about this kid? Anything?"

I got up, went into my room, grabbed the folder, and practically threw it at him before I sat again. He skimmed through the information, raising his eyebrows a couple of times. Once, he looked up at me intently and then back at the material. "Did you look up Longwood Towers?"

"No."

"It's pretty ritzy, for condominiums. And did you happen to see this photo of Toby?" He handed me a page.

"What's a condominium?"

"Condo? You don't have those in England?" Based on the description he gave me, it's similar to something we call a commonhold, or a share of freehold.

I looked at the page, and my first impression seemed unlikely, so I held it closer to the light to be sure I'd seen it right. I had. I wouldn't have guessed there was that much clothing a boy could buy that was pink. The way he'd combed his dark hair made his face look like a girl's, and the pose he'd struck added to the effeminate effect.

Ned said, "Seems to me Toby ain't just gay, honey. Seems to me he's royalty."

Royalty? And then I got it: a queen. "So they gave him to me because I'm gay?"

"Do they know you're gay?"

Good question. "BM . . . I mean, Brian could have told them."

After Ned stopped laughing, he said, "He wouldn't have done that." He chuckled and wiped his eyes. " 'BM.' That's priceless."

I did my best to stifle a smile, and then I remembered the college entrance requirement called the extended essay, which I'd begun last year at Swithin and will have to complete this year. It's a four-thousand-word research paper on a topic the student chooses. I chose to compare several major world cultures' views on homosexuality. Dr. Metcalf probably knows this, even though I'm not due to hand the first draft in for a few weeks. Of course, it didn't even matter whether he saw a connection to me in that area or not. It's the spelling that's the connection to Toby, not our sexual orientation.

I think.

Ned said, "They, um, cast this particular 'spell' on you because of your capabilities. You can handle it, can't you?"

I almost groaned at the pun. "Of course I can."

"So handle it." He leaned forwards. "Simon, I don't think doing your best to get back home is giving in to the people who ignored you. I think it shows them you meant what you said. You were serious. And it proves that nothing they've done has changed your mind." He sat back and grinned. "You could take a lesson from Miss Dorothy. She did whatever it took."

I took a moment to put it all together. The IB course load is heavy, and the classes won't be easy, but the City course takes two of the requirements off. Of course, the City will take time, but I don't doubt I can do it. And this thing with Toby . . . I picked up the photo again. Dr. Metcalf had said Toby was thrilled that I'm English. That might mean he'll be easier to get along with.

"It's mostly that you don't want to be here, isn't it." Not a question this time. "Good. We've got that settled. And you know what you need to do to make sure you're not here any longer than you have to be. Now, how about you put on something a little *less* comfortable, and we'll mosey on down to the kitchen and have some dessert. Sound like a plan?"

I don't understand why, but Ned makes me smile. And I think he knows this. I think this is why he's the one who came upstairs.

BM and Mum were sitting across the kitchen table from each other, deep in some intense conversation, and I couldn't help assuming that it had to do with me in one way or another. I sat on one of the stools at the island in the middle of the room, but Ned walked to the table. "Simon and I dined alfresco tonight. I'm about to feed him some of my famous almond torta. Would either of you care for seconds?"

Mum's eyes had been on me since I came into the room. Without answering Ned she got up and came to stand across the island from me. "Are you all right, Simon? I was very worried about you."

My talk with Ned had pulled me out of the ditch I was in, but now I was angry again, and I still needed someone to blame. Mum was an easy—and not an altogether inappropriate—target. "I had some unpleasant news at school. Just one more thing I hate, one more thing I very much don't want to do, one more thing I have no choice about. One more thing"—and I almost glanced at Ned here—"I have to overcome before I can go home again. So it's same-old, same-old." Adding even more edge to my tone, I added, "Nothing you need to concern yourself with."

Worried? Perhaps she was. But now she was also cheesed off. She was trying to control her temper, and it looked like she was about to lose the fight. BM came behind her and put a gentle hand on her shoulder. She shrugged it off. "Simon, I don't know what else to do. Are you going to be mad at me for the rest of your life?"

"The rest of yours, probably. I intend to outlive you." And I realised almost with a shock that I do intend just this. I'll do whatever it takes.

BM gave me a look that would have cut glass, but he said nothing. Still gentle, he touched Mum's shoulder again and coaxed her out of the room.

On my way upstairs later, after devouring the torta that was every bit as delicious as Ned had promised, as I stopped to unlock the door to the top floor I heard voices from the master suite. I couldn't help it; I listened.

What came through first was Mum, crying. If Ned had told me an hour ago that this sound wouldn't give me a feeling of unholy glee, I'd have laughed in his face. But now . . . I couldn't say it made me sad, exactly. But it did make me feel sorry for her.

I had to listen hard to make out what she was saying.

"I should never have done this. It was a mistake. It was too much to ask of him. And—Brian, I feel as though I've traded Simon's happiness for mine. Just because what he said was cruel doesn't make it wrong."

There was nothing but sobbing for a few seconds, and then Brian said, "This decision, this move, is for the rest of your life, Em. I'm not saying it was easy on Simon. It's not. But he's a lot tougher than he lets on. And this is just one year out of his life compared to the rest of yours."

"If I've ruined his life, that would ruin the rest of *my* life, Brian!"

If only she knew how close I came this afternoon. If only *I* knew.

"I understand that, and I don't make light of it. But remember that he's still a teenager, and life's events seem to loom very large for him at this age. But what he said just now tells me he'll fight. As long as he's angry, he'll work hard to prove us wrong, to show us we can't ruin his life." There was a pause in which I pictured him holding her. "He and Ned seem to have established a friendship. I trust Ned to let me know if he's worried."

Mum's voice was low, almost like she was talking to herself. "Sometimes I think I should go back. Pack Simon up, and just go back."

It was several seconds before BM said, "And if you did, would that put everything back to where it was? Would he go back to being merely arrogant and standoffish instead of hateful and venomous?"

My back stiffened. But—he wasn't wrong.

A short laugh escaped through Mum's tears. "I don't know." And then, "There really is no going back, is there?"

"I'm not saying he's going to stop being angry at you—at us—anytime soon. Maybe not ever. But once he gets involved with his classes, makes a couple of friends, he'll have a lot more in his life than he has right now. He'll have something else to focus on besides his anger at us. It should at least get easier."

"And if it doesn't? Simon does not make friends easily."

"We'll cross that bridge if we come to it."

I had allowed myself a glimmer of hope when Mum mentioned going home, but in my heart of hearts I know this is not going to happen. And I also know BM is right; we can't go back, not the way we were. I'll go back alone.

Upstairs, I set my alarm; tomorrow is school. Then I lie on the bed for a bit before undressing, eyes on the skylight, wondering whether Graeme had any idea how I felt. If he even registered that I was alive on the planet, let alone missing from school, from home.

Somehow, Ned's understanding of my problems—and his giving me his permission not to forgive Mum—makes it easier for me to be mad at her without feeling desperate about it. The anger, the hatred or whatever, feels less heavy. It's easier to carry now, so I feel like I might be able to move forwards. Emphasis on "might."

And, I remind myself, I will still apply at Oxford. If they don't want me, they're going to have to tell me that.

Boston, Day Six, Thursday, 30 August

I had set my alarm for very early, because I hadn't felt like doing any research last night on the spelling bee thingy. So I'd given myself half an hour this morning to gain a little familiarity; I didn't want to show up at Toby's with no knowledge at all. I tried to put an odd mix of depression and excitement behind me as I waited for my PC to wake up.

Eligibility, competition rules—all the expected stuff was on their Web site. Nothing surprising, other than the size of the prizes: thirty thousand dollars; a US savings bond; a complete reference library. And then I found links to the word lists. *Rhipidate. Bisbigliando. Heiau. Cholecystitis. Lymphopoiesis. Chamaephyte.* It was easy enough for me to look at them and see that the way they're spelled made sense, but if I were standing on a stage, hundreds of people plus television cameras trained on me, and someone spoke the word *axolotl* . . . If I hadn't studied that particular word, and I couldn't *see* the *x* or the *tl*, would it help enough to be told that it derives from Nahuatl, and that it's a Mexican salamander? I don't know. But Toby will have to do it. And I will have to help him get to where he can.

I was puzzling over how the hell I'll be able to coach a kid who can probably already spell several times better than I can when I heard my old mobile's tone for an incoming text.

Graeme!

Right. I knew better than to expect anything from him even before I admitted he isn't there for me. Isn't texting me. Isn't in love with me. So—who would text me on any phone?

The text was from Margaret, the girl who has Tink now. It said, *Pics! Check yr e-mail.*

My fingers flew over the keys to log onto my e-mail account, and—yes! Pictures and pictures. Oh, sweet Margaret!

There was Tink in her perch, basking in the sun, and the perch seemed to be right where I had told them to place it. There was Tink the huntress with a feathered toy in her mouth, green and white feathers against her soft white and blue-grey fur, eyes bright with excitement. Tink sitting on the floor, her sweet face turned up and intent, the look in her big, round eyes telling me she was expecting something really delicious, immediately. Tink in her harness, on the patio, pawing at iris leaves. Tink on a lovely blue rug, on her back in her signature pose, front and rear paws gently curled, her adorable face at a relaxed angle, her eyes almost closed. Tink nestled on Margaret's shoulder, both girl and cat smiling. I could almost hear the purr.

Oh, Tink! I was laughing and crying at once, delighted that Tink seemed so happy and devastated that it wasn't my shoulder she was settled on. Much as I truly don't want her to miss me, it hurts that she doesn't seem to. And it hurts that I miss her so much.

I went through the images once more before I shut the PC down and went in for a shower, knowing that their being here for me to see again tonight will help me get through the day. I decided to send Margaret a thank-you reply later; couldn't take the time now.

The strangest thing happened in the shower. Maybe I'd just grown so accustomed to imagining Graeme with me that he'd become real somehow, but there he was in the shower with me. And it was all right. It wasn't the Graeme of reality; it was the Graeme who's there only for me, to be whatever I need him to be, to do . . . whatever I need him to do. And after he did what I needed him to, I stood there, water hammering the back of my neck as I stared at the drain, calm for the moment, almost happy for the moment, whilst around the edges of my mind there was a voice trying to get in. It was saying things like, *This isn't healthy. Imaginary lovers are not good for you; they make you want what you can't have. They make you expect perfection you can never get from anyone real. You'll be alone all your life.*

"I don't care." The sound of my voice startled me. I turned off the water and focused hard on that "one step at a time" Ned had advised me to take. To keep that inner voice at bay, to keep my mind too busy to hear it, I forced myself to notice every detail of reaching for the towel, drying my hair and back and chest and legs and feet, shaving carefully and noticing every *tick* the blade made on every whisker it encountered.

In my room, I aimed the same mental focus at each tiny step involved in dressing, right down to socks and shoes, and then each tiny step of putting my school bag together. I moved towards my closed door, but before I could reach the knob someone stepped in my way, put his hands on my face and his mouth on mine. I dropped the bag and gave in to the imaginary but oh, so real embrace of Graeme's arms. When finally I opened the door and walked into the hallway, I was smiling, sure in the knowledge that he, too, would be right there when I got back from school.

Mum, obviously exhausted whilst forcing herself to appear cheerful, was putting my breakfast together. She smiled as well as she could when she saw me. "Good morning, Simon. Sit wherever you like—table, island, wherever."

I set my school bag down inside the entrance to the kitchen and moved towards the island, and I stood watching as she set a place for me, with a bowl of corn flakes and sliced bananas beside a pitcher of milk and a bowl of sugar. She gave me another smile that I knew she intended to look cheerful and then started to turn away, no doubt to pour me some juice or fetch the tea, but I touched her arm to stop her. When she turned her face towards me again, there was so much sorrow behind that forced smile that it hurt even me. She must have seen this, because she wrapped her arms around me, and mine went around her, and we embraced for several seconds. Perhaps it was what I'd heard last night, knowing how sorry she is for what she's done, knowing that she understands how I see it, that softened something in me. But only so much.

As I pulled away, I told her, "Don't worry about me, Mum. Brian's right, and I'm not a child any longer." With a start, I realised that might be the first time I'd referred to him in her hearing as anything other than Mr. Morgan. She swiped at her eyes as she moved towards the counter where my tea was waiting.

St. Bony started things off at a run. Most classes are on Mondays, Wednesdays, and Fridays, leaving students time on Tuesdays and Thursdays to focus on the various required papers and presentations, as well as our CAS projects. But perhaps it was because we hadn't officially started that work yet that this first Thursday we had Wednesday classes. Except for those of us taking The City, because that course has a one-hour eight o'clock session on Thursdays. Evidently The City trumps most other classes, so whilst several of my peers were in the first "Wednesday" German class, I went to my first City meeting.

In that first class, we found out what the time commitment for The City will be. Dr. Metcalf had warned me, I suppose. Every week, we'll spend the entire day on Tuesday—unless the teacher calls a meeting, which will happen sometimes—independently taking whatever action we need to: travelling around the city, researching, meeting with classmates for the occasional team assignment, putting our interim papers together in a way that will lead up to the final report and presentation in May.

Our very first assignment was in teams, which I hate. There's only one other boy in the class; perhaps this broad curriculum appeals more to girls. And evidently I was the last person to sign up, so there are nine students, and Dr. Osgood made three teams of us. But starting that team project won't be the first thing we do. Next Tuesday we'll do a Freedom Trail tour in the morning and a walking tour of Beacon Hill in the afternoon, as Dr. Osgood put it, "to get your feet under you, as it were."

We had a short huddle in teams for the first assignment. I was put with Olivia Steele, a dark-haired, prim-looking girl in a pale yellow shirt with a Peter Pan collar, and red-haired Madeleine Westfield—in a pink blouse despite that hair—who is as talkative and invasive as Olivia is reserved. We're to call her Maddy, she informed us.

Each team was assigned a general topic. We got education (or, more specifically, institutions of higher learning), and the other two got arts and medicine. Dr. Osgood told us that whilst we're to do this first segment in teams, we'll all be working on the other two topics individually, and then other topics of our own choosing.

Before I left the classroom at the end of the hour, I decided to ask Dr. Osgood about getting to Toby's house the same way I'll have to get around Boston, which means no taxi.

"I'm so glad you asked!" she said. She pawed through things on a rather disorderly bookshelf and came up with a pile of maps. "This has the subway and bus routes, and also the train routes to the suburbs, though you won't need that for the class. Where are you going?"

"Longwood Towers in Brookline. It's for my CAS."

"Nice!" She opened a map and pointed as she spoke. "Turn right up Marlborough to Mass Ave and then turn left. Stay on the left side of the street. You'll walk for a few minutes before you come to the T stop for Hynes Auditorium. Follow signs to outbound trains, and wait on the platform for a D train. You'll go three stops—Kenmore, Fenway, and get out at Longwood. Cross the street and walk up this way, and this," she jabbed with a finger, "is Longwood Towers. Oh, do you have a mass transit pass?"

"Not yet."

"Here"—and she dug in a different pile of stuff. "I'm going to hand these out next week, but you can have yours now."

It was a colourful, stiff plastic card with a cartoonish man hanging out of a train window. "CharlieCard?" I asked, reading the heading, noting the absence of a space—a modern gimmick that I find irritating.

"Charlie on the MTA?" she said, as though I would recognise the phrase. I shook my head. "Tell you what. Between now and Tuesday, you look that up, and at our next meeting you can tell the class what it is. Locals, and maybe some others, will know, but they won't expect you to know, and there will be others who don't." She grinned broadly at me, like this was some special treat. "Now, off you go! Don't want to be late to your next class."

I had Biology HL (Higher Level) II, then Language and Literature HL, and then IB Math SL (Standard Level) before lunch, which I took in the canteen. Despite Ned's cookery, most likely I won't bring lunches, I decided; the café isn't bad.

I'm not going to write in my journal everything that happens in all these classes; I'll be busy enough doing the work for them.

After lunch, I debated. Should I take a taxi this first time to Toby's, or should I just dive into mass transit? I used the tube at home, though Mum never descended into it. And London's underground system is far more complex than Boston's. Which will no doubt be puny. It was a little drizzly today, but as a Londoner I wasn't fazed. I pulled out my folding brolly, settled my bag on my shoulder, and headed towards Massachusetts Avenue. Might as well get started clearing away some brambles.

Puny, yes. Almost laughable, compared to London's underground. But serviceable. I had no trouble finding Longwood Towers, though I did have a few minutes of trepidation, of hating that I have to do this, of wanting to leave Queen Toby to his own devices. But the doors opened inevitably at the Longwood stop, and I stepped out.

I pulled out my iPhone and sent a text to the number in Toby's file for his mobile to let him know I was approaching the building. It was the first contact we'd had. Within nanoseconds I saw, *Fabulous! I'll be in the lobby.*

There were three towers, and in the couple of minutes it took me to locate the one named Alden, the sun came out and made everything steamy. The grounds are immaculate and beautifully landscaped, curved walkways leading the way to each tower. I told the doorman Toby Lloyd was meeting me inside, and he let me in but watched me. As I entered the lobby, I had to blink several times to adjust to the cool dimness. When my vision cleared, I saw lots of dark wood in a massive room, floors that appeared to be large cork squares, a beam-and-plaster ceiling high overhead. There was low-key but extremely contemporary furniture placed on islands of equally contemporary area rugs, a softly-lit reception area, and a very excited boy dressed in lime green and white, practically bouncing across the floor towards me.

"Simon! You're here! Oh, this will be so fabulous!"

I did my best to smile. "How do you do," I said, falling back on formality by default. This made Toby laugh delightedly.

"Oh, you're so English! I love England. We were there last year for a few weeks. London was fabulous! Why would you ever leave it?" The child speaks in exclamation points.

"Sometimes we don't choose what happens to us."

I followed him around a corner to a bank of lifts. "We call these elevators," he said as though I'd pronounced "lifts" aloud. "Will you go back, do you think?"

"As soon as ever I'm able." The massive doors slid shut, and Toby pressed the number seven. But he didn't stop talking.

"We're not quite at the top, but we have great views! You can see the John Hancock building and the Prudential Center from our living room. How soon do you think you'll be able?"

"Able?" I'd lost track of where his ramblings were going.

"Able to go back."

"Ah. That. If all goes as planned, I'll be at university next year in England." Somewhere.

"Really? I want to go to Cambridge. Or maybe Yale. Mommy wants me to go to Princeton. So I guess I'll apply there, too. Doesn't hurt to have a backup, you know?"

"I expect you're right." Ye gods; my own father didn't mention Oxford until I was maybe thirteen. And this kid already has a number of schools in mind?

The lift doors opened almost silently, and Toby bounced out into a carpeted hallway with occasional furniture placed demurely here and there, as though waiting for someone to settle and watch the wallpaper or admire the art on the walls.

He opened the door to his apartment and walked into a short hallway. "That's my room," he said, pointing to the right, "and that's Mommy's office." He pointed to the left. Out of politeness, I didn't look into either of them. Past Toby ahead of me I could see a room full of light and a huge bay window that did, indeed, have an amazing view of the city. Toby jumped and landed amid beige and gold pillows on a love seat built into the window.

"See? Isn't this magnificent?"

"Really lovely," I said, hoping that was enthusiastic enough.

Behind me I heard a woman's soft Irish brogue say, "Welcome, Simon. I'm Colleen."

I turned, surprised; Toby's mother's name is Abby, or so the file said. But then I saw this woman was quite young, perhaps early twenties. "How do you do," I offered.

She gestured towards the kitchen. "I'm the Jill-of-all-trades here, during the day. I've made some biscuits and lemonade for you to keep your energy up. Let me know if you need anything." She was lovely: black hair in a pixie-like cut and that clear, pale Irish skin. Startling blue eyes. If I didn't believe Toby to be gay, I'd have expected him to be head-over-heels about her.

Behind her and around the corner of a supporting column I could see the bar that separates the kitchen from the dining area and sitting room, a platter of biscuits and lemonade in a pitcher waiting there. Toby bounced over. "Cookie?"

"I've just had lunch. Perhaps in a little while."

"Cookie. From the Dutch *koekje*, k-o-e-k-j-e, diminutive of *koek*, or cake, from the Middle Dutch *koeke*, k-o-e-k-e."

"Of course." What was I going to do with this child? How could I help someone who'd taken the trouble to learn the etymology of a word he won't even be asked to spell competitively? "Where will we work, then?"

He clapped his hands. "I love it! Only English people say that."

"Say . . . what?"

"You said, 'Where *will* we work, then?' Using 'will' there instead of 'shall' or 'should,' and finishing the question with 'then' is *so* English!"

I looked over at Colleen, wondering if he subjected her to this scrutiny. She lifted an eyebrow, smiled, and turned towards the kitchen. I would guess he does.

"And the answer?" I prodded.

"My room. Come on!" More bouncing, and I was thinking he could live in a flat—condo—only if it were built as well as this one; otherwise the downstairs neighbours would be complaining constantly. I followed Toby, hoping he'd calm down soon; I needed to get along well with this child, and so far I wasn't even sure how I'd manage an afternoon with him.

His room was a bit of a gender-bender. The canopied bed, which by default for canopied beds in girls' rooms everywhere really should have been covered with white or pink or yellow, was denim blue, and what should have been a ruffle around the canopy edge was more of a flat panel. The bureau and desk were a clean design, possibly cherrywood; but instead of model airplanes or plastic dinosaurs scattered about, I saw sweet little trinket boxes made of wood or stone—including a vivid green malachite specimen—some with carving or mother-of-pearl inlay. I was afraid to ask what was in them; the answer would have taken the rest of the afternoon and no doubt would have required much faked enthusiasm.

On the desk was a bright pink pencil cup with several colourful pens and pencils, including one with a troll head, its bright yellow hair combed up into a sculpted swirl. The bookcases above and beside the desk were filled with books, and on the desk surface I saw reference materials for the spelling bee and a huge dictionary.

The hardwood floor was mostly covered by a dark blue Chinese oriental rug, but on top of this beside the bed was a circle throw rug, in a sculpted floral pattern of rose and cream.

The overall feeling I got was that this "boy" is, as Ned had guessed, royalty. It was as though someone had laid the room's design foundations for what would be appropriate for a boy, and someone else had added touches suitable to a girl to mitigate the masculinity. Surely, his parents know. . . .

"I read fifty dictionary pages a day," he informed me, a smile on his androgynous face. "That's *almost* good enough. Some kids read sixty or seventy. And some have read two dictionaries, cover to cover. I have to get up to at least sixty-five."

I set my bag down and got a good grip on the dictionary. Toby hadn't said how he wanted to proceed, but I reckoned I might as well dig in. There was an upholstered chair, blue with a soft rose-coloured throw, and I sat there, opened the book towards the back, and dropped my finger. *"Schadenfreude."*

Toby stood before me as though on stage already. "Language of origin, please?"

"German." I didn't need to look at the book to know this.

"Is it from *Schaden*, harm or damage, and *Freude*, joy?"

"Yes." I knew this, too. I was surprised he did, though.

"Definition, please."

I consulted the dictionary for this one; this book is the bee's official version, and what I say should match what Toby will hear in the competition. "Delight in another's misfortune."

"Are there alternate pronunciations?"

Not that I knew of, but I looked to be sure. And I saw that whilst I had given the word its genuine German pronunciation, there was another that was more anglicised. I said that as best I could, knowing I was massacring the wonderful Germanic sounds.

"Spelling, please?" I looked up from the book, and Toby giggled. "Just kidding! Can I have it in a sentence, please?"

"The girl's schadenfreude at hearing her main competitor misspell *arrhostia* gave her pangs of guilt." I knew he was asking every question he was allowed by the bee's rules, though I was sure he knew the word.

"Schadenfreude." He used the fingers of his right hand to scribble on his left palm. "Schadenfreude. *S-c-h-a-d-e-n-f-r-e-u-d-e.* Schadenfreude."

"Ding!" I gave the sound indicating an error, and his jaw dropped. "Just kidding!"

More delighted laugher. "I knew that! Another word. Something really unusual."

It went on like this for nearly an hour. I did my best to trip him up, and once—with the word *Ugaritic*—I did stump him. He put an *e* before the *u* and turned the *a* into an *e*. He demanded to see the word.

He stared at the page for perhaps twenty seconds. "I was going to tell you your pronunciation was wrong," he said, "but this kind of thing happens a lot, where the phonetics make a letter sound like something else, and you just have to know the word or the derivation so well that you can get it right anyway. Stuti Mishra lost to Snigdha Nandipati because she didn't know that there should be an umlaut over the *a* in *schwärmerei*. That makes the *a* sound like an *e* when it's said aloud, and that's how Stuti spelled it." He handed me back the book and picked up a notebook. "I keep lists of everything I miss."

"Toby, what would be most helpful for you?"

"Actually, this is great. On my own, I can't fake myself out with pronunciation the way you just did."

"My accent isn't getting in the way?"

He smiled, shook his head. "Nope. Time for cookies and lemonade?"

"Tell me the derivation of lemon first."

"I . . . I can't do that." He looked almost ashamed.

I smiled at him. "I can't, either. I doubt they'll ask you that one." I opened to lemon in the dictionary. "From Middle English *limon*, through Old French, Italian *limone*, from Arabic and originally from Persian." I closed the book. "Now we know."

"It might come in handy for some word that has the same root. Thanks!" He made another entry in his "mistakes" notebook and then bounced out of the room.

Colleen must have put the pitcher of lemonade in the fridge; the ice cubes floating in it had barely melted when she brought it to the dining table. Just as I was sitting in a chair, a movement under a table on the far side of the living room caught my eye.

A cat! A beautiful, sleek, all-black cat. But what was wrong with its ears?

"Who's that?" I asked Toby, nodding towards the animal.

"Shangri-La. We call her La La. Isn't she pretty? She's my mom's cat."

La La sat several feet away as if to allow me to admire her, her huge, round, amber eyes trained on me. The ears were folded forwards entirely, very nearly giving the appearance that she hadn't any. "What happened to her ears?"

Toby laughed. "You should know!"

"Why is that?"

"She's a Scottish fold! Her father is a British shorthair, and her mother is a folded fold. The original fold was a white British shorthair named Susie who lived on a farm in Scotland." He went on at length about how it took geneticists decades to figure out how to breed for the cartilage weakness in the ears without cartilage weaknesses elsewhere, which would result in deformed kittens. It seems the doctor who finally solved the puzzle had been from just outside Boston.

La La stretched, walked nearly to the table, and sat, watching me. Almost to myself, I said, "I love cats."

"You can pet her if you want."

"I'll let her get used to me first." In fact, I had to remind myself not to stare at her, which she would have interpreted as confrontational. I allowed my eyelids to lower just a bit, and she did the same. Excellent. Now I just needed to wait for her to make the next move. I turned my attention to the lemonade.

More to make conversation than anything else, trapped as I was at this table with this child, I asked about his parents, where they work, that sort of thing. His father does something in finance for Blue Cross Blue Shield, and his mother is a junior partner at some law firm specialising in environmental law. I took this in and filed it away, not knowing whether I'd ever need to know it; I might not ever even meet these people.

Toby babbled on for a bit about his past conquests at spelling bees, relating some of the words others missed, detailing a couple of close calls he had when he was given a word he didn't know.

"I gather that the strategy is to know as many words as possible, then," I asked, "rather than merely having enough background to try to figure out how to spell them when you're standing there?"

Toby nodded, swallowed some biscuit, and said, "You still ask all the questions you can, just to be really, really, really sure, because there's no going back. I mean, you can start the spell again, but you can't change any of the letters you've already given. So taking your time helps you be sure it really is the word you think it is. 'Cause, I mean, you have to know so many, you know? The similar words start to blur together."

"And so my calling out words to you is the best way for me to help you?"

"Yup. Some coaches do other stuff, like test you on etymology. You could do that, if you want. Like, tips for when the word comes from Latin, which means the middle vowels are usually *i*, there is no *k*, that sort of thing."

"And Aztec words often end in *tl*."

"Right! So that stuff is good. But the practices . . . That's the best. Especially when the pronunciation can cause problems. Like *schwärmerei*. You just have to know the word. The more words I miss with you, the more I'll learn."

He was telling me my task was simply locating words that are as unusual as possible, and words that sound the least like they're spelled. "That seems almost too easy. For me, that is."

"It's time-consuming, though. You'll help me, right?"

It was on the tip of my tongue to say that I had no choice, but I caught those words before they could escape. "Of course."

"All the way through to the contest?"

"The end of May, correct?"

"Coaches get to come and watch. It's near Washington, D.C. You'll come, won't you?" I hesitated just a little too long; no one had mentioned this to me. Toby's face fell, and he reached for another biscuit. "It's okay. You don't have to."

"I might. I just didn't know it was an option."

"You like me, right? I like you."

Eleven, is he? Seemed more like five, emotionally. I leaned on my cultural roots to avoid a declaration. "Now, Toby, you know I'm English, yes? You know how reserved we English are. I don't know of any reason I wouldn't—"

"Because if you do, I'll tell you a secret. A really important secret."

This wasn't part of the deal. "I can't promise to tell you one back."

He blinked. "I hadn't thought of that. Okay, you don't have to. Can I tell you?"

How would I stop him? "If you like."

"You won't tell anyone?"

This gave me pause, even though he'd already called it a secret. "Does anyone else know?"

He looked around, furtive, even a little scared. "Nobody."

This might not be such a good idea. "Are you sure you should tell me?"

"I have to tell someone! I'll explode!" His hoarse whisper had a note of desperation in it.

"Why not your parents?" He made a face I couldn't quite interpret, let alone describe, but he didn't say anything. "All right, then. We can't have you exploding."

He leaned forwards, looked around again, opened his mouth, and evidently decided he was still too exposed. Out of his chair, he leaned towards my ear, cupped his hand, and whispered, "I'm a girl."

This revelation caused some lightbulb to go on in my head. On some level, it made perfect sense. But is he biologically a girl dressed like a boy, or a biological boy with a girl trapped inside?

On another level, it made no sense to me at all. This was not something I'd encountered before—heard about, sure, but not had to deal with. My brain fired in a few different directions at once, and finally I decided the only reasonable course of action for me to take was to accept the information at face value.

He'd scampered back to his chair and was bent over a biscuit, watching me intently. Keeping my voice low, I asked, "So, your parents don't know? You're sure?"

Sotto voce, he said, "I'm sure. They think I'm a boy."

That was one answer, then. Biologically, he's male. "Why haven't you told them? It seems very important."

"I don't know what they'd do. They might get rid of me, or something."

The weight of this crashed into my brain. Even if the fear were unfounded, it would be earth-shattering to live with the possibility—with the very *idea*—that one's parents might actually discard one, toss one out with the garbage. "Why tell *me?*"

"I just felt like you'd understand."

In the spirit of acceptance, wanting to avoid admitting that I didn't understand at all and hoping he wouldn't toss *me* out, I said, "Well, I will tell you a secret—maybe a semi-secret—about me. I'm gay."

"Ha! I knew it."

"You did?"

"Not really. But I could tell there was something special about you."

I felt a soft weight land on one of my feet, and when I looked down Shangri-La was on her back, front paws curled against her chest, hindquarters squarely on the toe of my shoe. Enjoying the cat's approval, I glanced back at Toby and asked a question that might or might not help me grasp this thing. "Do you like girls or boys?"

"Oh, boys! I'm not gay."

"I see. Straight boys, then?" I had to stop a sardonic chuckle; maybe he'll do better than I had.

"Of course. You've got nothing to worry about. I like you, but not that way."

Well, that was a relief, even if it hadn't occurred to me. "Your parents don't guess, with all the pink going on in your bedroom?"

He toyed with a crumb beside his plate. "My mom might have guessed. I'm not sure."

"She might just think you're gay."

He nodded. "But I'm not gay. I know all about being gay."

"Do you, now?"

"So many kids at school call me gay. Always have. Well, for a long time, anyway. I wanted to make sure I knew what it meant, so I researched it. But I haven't told them what I *am*."

I nodded, and thinking to provide a little comfort, I said, "I got called names, too, mostly because of my hair. Some kids used to call me Ginger."

"That's not so bad."

"Oh, but it is. In England, it's a mean thing to say. It's intended to be derogatory."

"Not as bad as gay, though."

"No? What's wrong with being gay?"

"Well . . . I mean . . . you know."

"No, I don't, actually. I don't think there's anything wrong with being gay."

"Not if you really are gay. And there's nothing wrong with having red hair, either."

To my surprise, I laughed. "You've got me there. Will we go practise some more?"

I didn't know what to do with this confession. Really, there's nothing I *could* do. And this isn't my problem.

As I was about to leave, Shangri-La trotted over to me, bouncing on her little black feet, and threw herself on the floor, belly up, her head at a sweet angle. Fur colour and ears aside, she looked so much like Tink I felt tears well up in my eyes. I leaned over, let her sniff my fingers, and scratched under her chin. She tilted her head up so I couldn't see her eyes and let me go on for a while as I scratched from ear to ear and back again.

Toby asked, "D'you wanna pick her up?"

I shook my head. "She hasn't given me permission to do that yet."

"How do you know?"

"She's staying on her back, which doesn't give me access to pick her up. If she rubs against my legs and then stands still, I might pick her up. Maybe next time."

He glanced around—I was sure—to see if Colleen was nearby. "You're not creeped out?"

"You mean, about the girl thing?" He nodded. I lied, "Not at all."

"So you'll come back?"

"I'll be here next week, same time. Good to meet you, Toby."

"Maybe next time, I'll tell you my real name. My girl name."

"I look forward to it." What else could I say?

The trolley car was more crowded on the way back. The time went by quickly, though; my mind was back on Toby and his—her predicament. Transgender issues confuse me. I have no thoughts or feelings about being anything other than male. But I've heard about men trapped in women's bodies and vice versa. I believe them, I guess; I just don't understand them. And I wonder what Parents Lloyd would make of it.

I was still preoccupied with the topic over dinner, and still keenly aware that whatever I thought about it, it was not my secret to share, so when Mum—no doubt encouraged by our hug over breakfast—asked about my first school day, I didn't go on at length. Of course, I hadn't exactly been a chatterbox about anything lately. Plus, it occurred to me rather suddenly that I hadn't told anyone but Ned about Toby or my coaching job. As this thought was bouncing around in my brain, Mum must have said something else to me, and I didn't take it in or respond. But I did notice the silence.

I looked around the table; all eyes but Persie's were on me. "Sorry. Just a little preoccupied with something." I did my best to provide a little more information about my day without going into details. Then Mum asked if I'll be going on the apple-picking outing the last Saturday of September. Evidently families are invited. There was some back and forth about it—I hadn't even noticed it on the schedule—and finally I did my best to pacify her with "Probably."

Brian asked, "What steps will your City team take to complete your first assignment, do you think?"

"We haven't discussed it yet. I suppose we'll select a few schools, visit them, research the history and the current focus, that sort of thing. Why? Any suggestions?"

"I'll be interested in where Harvard falls in your analysis."

I let my hand fall onto the table beside my plate, fork pointing towards him. "I'm not applying there, you know." Even if Oxford won't have me, I wasn't impressed with Harvard.

"I ask, because I went to Harvard."

"Oh. Well, I'll let you know, if you like."

I did my best to fall out of the conversation again after this, though I accidentally set Persie off. Preoccupied as I was, when Mum asked me what time I'd gotten to bed last night, no doubt because I looked tired, I said "half eleven."

Persie's head jerked up. "That's not a time. What is it?"

I glanced at Brian and knew I was in trouble. "It's eleven thirty."

"It's not!" she shrieked. "It's five-point-five! Five-point-five! Five-point-five!"

Oh, boy. Here we go again. It took Brian and Anna a few minutes to quiet her down. At one point I mouthed "Sorry" to Brian, silently. He didn't look forgiving.

I had rather a lot of homework already, and I hadn't gotten

enough of it done between getting back from Toby's and dinner-time. But when Ned set a piece of fruit pie in front of me, he whispered, "Cat got your tongue?"

There was an intense look on his face, which I took to mean he'd be available later if I wanted to talk. And he must have noticed that I hadn't mentioned Toby.

So after I finished most of my homework, I wandered down to the kitchen, glad to see he was still here, marinating something to get a head start on tomorrow's dinner. I grabbed a bowl, scooped some chocolate ice cream for myself, and sat at the island.

"You'll wash that yourself, young man." He grinned at me. "How did it go?"

"The coaching, you mean?" He put a hand on his hip as though to say, *Duh*, and I told him, "Weird." I took a spoonful of ice cream. "This is one thing you Yanks do better," I said around the silky melting lump in my mouth, pointing towards the bowl with my spoon.

"Knock it off, kid. What was weird?" He leaned on the island across from me.

"What do you know about people who are transgender?"

"I've known one or two. Why? Something you want to tell me?"

"Not about me. But our queen isn't a queen. Or, she really is a queen. At least, that's what he said. What she said."

"This is Toby we're talking about?"

I nodded and dug into my ice cream bowl. "Next time I go there, I'll learn his girl's name, or so he promised."

Something about my tone must have clued Ned in to the fact that I wasn't entirely on board with this phenomenon. He didn't say anything until I looked up from my bowl. "What did your mother say when you told her you're gay?"

"Don't recall, exactly. Why?"

"Did she say, 'Don't be ridiculous' or, 'Where did you get that idea?' or, 'That makes no sense to me'?"

"No."

"Do you think she could know what you feel inside yourself? Do you think anyone should be able to tell you that what you feel is wrong because it doesn't make sense to them?"

"No. I get it, all right?"

"Good." He picked up a towel and started drying pans. "I know that there are boys who really like girl things, and they dress like girls at least some of the time, but they still want to be thought of as boys. What did Toby say, exactly?"

"His very words were, 'I'm a girl.' "

"There you go."

I shook my head, confused. "How can he just ignore what he's got for equipment?"

"Well . . ." Ned tapped a finger on the counter, thinking. "If your mother, and all your friends, all your teachers, if everyone you know insisted on calling you Susan and treating you as though you were a girl, I'll bet that whenever someone did that, your dick wouldn't be the first thing you thought of. And I'll bet if you were forced to wear girls' clothes and use the little girls' room, it would just be so utterly, completely wrong that it would have less to do with your body and more to do with your internal identity. With how you think of yourself, and how horribly out of sync that is with how you have to present yourself to the world."

"I suppose so."

"How out is he?"

"Not at all. Evidently I'm the first to know. His parents don't know; his friends don't know."

"And he told you because . . ."

"Because he likes me, because he could tell there was something 'special' about me."

Ned grinned, and then his face grew serious. "This is huge, Simon, a huge thing he's trusting you with. How do you feel about that?"

"The trust? I don't know. It feels like a lot of responsibility. I mean, I can't tell anyone. He made me promise. I shouldn't be telling you, but I felt like you could help me understand."

"He'll tell others when he's ready."

"So, is he really a gay boy who's at the extreme far end of the spectrum? So far that he becomes a she?"

"I don't think it works like that, actually. Does he like girls or boys?"

"Straight boys."

He laughed. "You found out rather a lot, eh? But—the spectrum picture doesn't seem to fit. I couldn't really say why; it just feels wrong."

"Should I refer to Toby as 'he' or 'she'?"

"You'll have to ask."

"This is so confusing."

"You got that right. People are not simple creatures, Simon." He watched me finish my ice cream. "You haven't told your mom about this coaching job yet, I take it."

"No."

"And that's because . . . ?"

"Hasn't been a good time. If you'll recall, I was rather out of sorts last night. Today was school, and she was out when I got home. And it's a good thing I didn't say any more than I did at dinner, or I'd have been hauled on the carpet for speaking English English. Any other probing questions you'd care to ask?" He just looked at me until I dropped my eyes. "Sorry."

"So, change of subject here, are you gonna like this City thing? I heard you talk about it over dinner."

I shrugged. "It'll be fine."

"What's the deadline to submit your Oxford application? Or have you already done that?" Our eyes connected for a little too long. "Simon?"

I got off my stool, carried the bowl and spoon to the sink, and leaned my back against the counter. "The application deadline is 15 October. Interviews are in December, and offers go out in the middle of January."

"Have you already taken the SAT?"

"In the UK and for students here in IB schools like St. Bony"— Ned chuckled obligingly—"A levels and high marks alone are enough. No SAT necessary. But even if I get an offer, my marks have to be high through the end of the year."

"*If?* I thought you were certain." He was grinning at me like he was stating the obvious. And again, I stalled, and he lost the grin. "Simon, you're not having second thoughts, are you?"

I chewed my tongue for a few seconds. "More like doubts."

"Why?" He looked honestly confused, and it did help a little to see that.

I shook my head. I didn't want to admit the extent—or the longevity—of my doubts. "It's just . . . there are so many things out of place. Nothing is happening the way it was supposed to."

"Well, this much I know: You're still you. And, Simon, what you are is someone who can get into any school he wants to, provided he *wants* to. So don't procrastinate on that application."

I lifted a shoulder, dropped it. "I have more homework."

He gave me a wry grin. "Homework, and on the first day." He stepped over and gave me a quick hug. "Get up there, then." I looked at the bowl in the sink, the one I was told I'd have to wash. "Will you *go?*" And he pushed my shoulder.

As I sat at my PC to do a little online research for the biology assignment, I realised I'd been so preoccupied with Toby's situation that I'd almost forgotten about Tink's photos, and I hadn't gotten a thank-you off to Margaret. She was certainly asleep, now, so I wrote that I'd had an insane first day of school, and that the pics of Tink had made the whole day so much brighter. I told her she can't possibly send too many.

The research for biology was to see what might inspire me to do a paper, because I need to turn in a general outline for a project tomorrow. But thinking of cats brought La La to mind—La La with her genetic cartilage weakness that puzzled geneticists for so long. I decided that would be a great project. We don't have to come up with any new findings, just something unusual to research and report on. My title will be, "The Genetic Mutations of Scottish Fold Felines." It's almost a tribute to Tink, who is a British shorthair, after all, like the original fold. And even I think it's a little cool that the solution arose so close to Boston.

Getting ready for bed, my mind turned again towards Toby's predicament. For it must be a real predicament to be a girl trapped in a boy's body. I hate to admit it, but Ned had been right to call me on the carpet.

To see if I could get a sense of what Toby feels like, I tried to picture myself in a girl's body, but I couldn't get there; my thoughts slipped away as though I'd tried to catch a fish with my hands in oily water, and my body shivered—almost convulsed—involuntarily.

So I'll just accept what Toby has told me and not try to puzzle it out. And, really, this is not my problem. I can't allow this distraction too far into my mind or it could jeopardise my own priorities. To push this profoundly uncomfortable feeling away, I'll make sure that before I go to sleep, Graeme reminds me quite thoroughly who I am.

Boston, Thursday, 6 September

This idea of writing something every day is just not going to work. I have to spend way too much time on schoolwork if I'm going to apply to Oxford (which I've decided I will do, though I'll also apply to a few other places). But I don't want to lose this thread, so I'll recap a little.

Saturday I told Mum and Brian over breakfast about my coaching assignment. I played it down as much as possible and made it sound like the task would be beyond simple for me so they wouldn't be tempted to interrogate me about it later. Mum was interested in the family, but of course I didn't have much information to give her. Instead, I described the home and, getting a certain unholy pleasure from it, the cat.

Classes are pretty much what I'd expected. My biology project was approved, so that will be kind of fun, and it will let me dive into cats—always a good thing.

My weekly consultation with Dr. Metcalf is Fridays at two, and last Friday he pretty much won me over, in terms of how our relationship will work. He said nothing that reminded me of how I'd run from his office the last time I was there; he simply asked how it had gone with Toby, and he approved of my approach.

I didn't tell him Toby is a she. It didn't seem like something he needed to know—at least, not at this point. Though when I left his office, I did feel as though I could talk to him about it in the future if things got . . . I don't know, awkward, or difficult, something like that.

I almost forgot to look up the significance of the cartoon man on the CharlieCard, which would have been bad because Dr. Osgood did *not* forget, and I acquitted myself well enough, explaining to the class on Tuesday that it refers to a satirical song about a political issue in the mid-twentieth century. The song says the fares were raised whilst this fellow was riding the subway, and he didn't have the money to pay the extra when he tried to get off. Now "he rides forever 'neath the streets of Boston." He'll never be able to return home.

As I took my seat again, some nasty voice in my brain told me I would be the man who never returned to England. I didn't have time to dwell on that, because first Dr. Osgood used that story as a demonstration about what drives the development of a city, and then she herded us all out for our Freedom Trail tour.

I managed to avoid getting stuck walking with any one person for too long. I took photos with my iPhone of places that might be relevant to future assignments. Maddy kept trying to insert herself into my shots. "The redhead shooting the redhead!" as she put it. Irritating girl.

I liked the walking tour of Beacon Hill. Louisburg Square seemed very genteel and civilised, almost Parisian, and I decided that if I had to live in Boston, that's where it would be. But that isn't about to happen.

Thursday, back at Toby's, I had done some preparation. I knew, for example, that only one Massachusetts speller had ever won the competition, and that was way back in 1939. And I had scads of words, though I hadn't had time to make note of the etymology of them, knowing his dictionary would provide that.

"Chionablepsia," I threw at him. He got it. "Capharnaum." He got that. "Projicient." Another one down. But he put two *l*s into *phalarope* and put an *a* instead of an *o* in the middle of *sciophyte*, which really was not a mistake he should have made, so it was a very good one for me to have chosen. We went over it thoroughly until he understood the reasons for the spelling, inside and out.

"Excellent!" he said. "This is fabulous! You found some great words." I had thought I'd found rather a lot of great words, but he knew so many of them that I realised I'd have to put even more effort into it.

During our break (iced tea this time), he chatted on about things that had happened at school until Colleen disappeared. Then Toby leaned towards me and whispered, "Kay." He sat back and grinned at me.

At first I thought he was shortening "okay," but I couldn't imagine what he was referring to. Then it came to me. "That's your name, is it?"

He nodded. "In Welsh, it means 'rejoiced in.' Actually, it might be given to a girl *or* a boy. My last name is Welsh, you know."

"Yes." My tone indicated ambiguity at worst, I hoped.

He squealed with delight. "Oh, you sound so British, the way you say that!"

"English," I corrected. "I sounded English." Which prompted him to ask me lots of questions about what Great Britain comprises, how it differs from the United Kingdom, the British Isles, the British Islands, and Ireland, all of which cost me a good deal of effort to avoid sounding disparaging of the non-English parts, especially Wales and all things Welsh.

Finally I suggested we resume our work. As we left the table I asked, "How many dictionary pages have you been reading per day?"

"Ooh, good question to ask me. Keep the standard high. Sixty-five!"

"And do you think you'll be ready for the regional competition in March?"

"I have to be. And then I have to get at least to the semifinals."

"The semifinals? Not the *finals?* Don't you want to *win?*"

He closed his bedroom door quietly, and as I took my chair he said, "I do want to win. Of course. But the semifinal event is the first time there are cameras on us, on stage. What I really, truly want is to be able to be me, the real me, for all the world. I'll show you."

He disappeared behind me, poked in the clothes cupboard where I couldn't see him, and when he came into view again he was transformed. His dark hair was brushed up into a fluffier shape, and he was wearing a white blouse with soft ruffles for a collar and a pale rose-coloured skirt. His face beamed. And I was in the presence of Miss Kay Lloyd.

"You have been dying to show this to someone, haven't you, Kay?"

He practically threw himself at me, and as I stood to make the embrace less awkward I felt his body shaking. He was crying, though I couldn't tell whether it was from joy or pain.

He backed away, wiping at his eyes. "Thank you," he managed through little gasps, "for calling me that." He held his head up. "This is who I am. Only *you* know the truth."

"This might seem obvious, but—do you want to be referred to as he or she?"

We locked eyes whilst he considered this carefully. Then he said, "It would mean you'd be talking to someone *about* me, wouldn't it? You wouldn't use those pronouns talking *to* me."

I nodded, not quite sure I wanted to tell him I was committing all this to a written journal, and that that was the main reason for my question. "I guess that's right."

"Then I guess it has to be 'he.'" He sat hard onto the desk chair. "But I *am* a she. And now that I've told someone, I don't know how I'll be able to go back to being a boy again!"

"Why don't you just be a boy except when we're alone, like you've been doing?"

"Because I want to *be* who I *am!*" He looked like he was about to cry again, for a very different reason this time. "But I guess I don't have a choice."

From the other room came the sound of a man's voice, and I saw Kay shrink noticeably. Head down, Toby looked at me from under his eyebrows. "That's Father."

"You call him Father?" He nodded. I had to ask: "Are you afraid of him?"

"He . . . he can't see me like this." He jumped up to transform himself back into an apparent boy, or as close to it as Toby ever got. Then we went back to our work, but it was obvious his attention wasn't on the words.

"It's a quarter to four," I said. "Shall we call it a day?" He didn't say anything, just looked at the floor, so I started putting my things together. I almost didn't recognise Toby; his behaviour was so subdued. "Till next Thursday, then."

"Can you leave without me going out of the room with you?"

This seemed odd, rather like skulking out, but I could tell there was something going on I didn't understand. "Sure." I stood and moved towards the door, where I turned back. He was looking frantically around the room, possibly for any clues that would reveal his true nature. "Are you all right?"

"Yes . . . yes. But . . . You know, I do have to go out with you. I have to introduce you."

He walked around me, his body tight with tension, shrunken into itself. I followed close behind him, feeling almost protective, watching like a sniper for danger. What I saw was the man who must be Mr. Lloyd, standing in the kitchen. He moved suddenly as though surprised. And his motion was away from Colleen.

His voice was a little too loud, his tone a little too cheerful. "Toby. Is this your spelling tutor?"

Toby mumbled my name as I held my right hand out. Mr. Lloyd took it and said, "Speak up, Toby. Don't mumble."

Behind him, Colleen busied herself with something, and Toby said, "Simon Fitzroy-Hunt," more loudly.

To me, Mr. Lloyd said, "You're an expert, I gather?"

"In my own way, yes."

He seemed not to know what to make of that. "Are you a past champion or something?"

"No. Never competed." I wanted to leave it there, make him puzzle over me. But he might protest to St. Bony. If I were to fail at this project, I didn't want it to be the doing of this man. So I added, "I have an aptitude for spelling and a knack for productive study. St. Boniface felt I would be able to help Toby, and I think I will."

"What's your strategy?"

A voice inside my head said, *Whom does he think he's dealing with?* Another one sent a silent thank-you to Dr. Metcalf, who had already made me articulate my approach.

Aloud, I told him, "Toby is very good at studying the words and their origins; he doesn't need any help there. But no amount of dictionary study or etymology will help him spell *schwärmerei* correctly if he doesn't know that it's pronounced as though the *a*-umlaut were an *e*. So my strategy"—I had to force myself not to lean sarcastically on the word—"is to seek out words that don't sound like they're spelled and give Toby only the spoken word to work from. He must be as comfortable as possible with being put on the spot with a word he hasn't studied."

Mr. Lloyd laughed. "They weren't kidding about you," he said.

"Really?" I tried not to sound especially interested. "What did 'they' say?"

"That you were smart and skilled and—they didn't put it quite like this, but I'll say, a little full of yourself."

I raised my chin just slightly and allowed one side of my mouth to curl upwards. My tone cryptic, giving away neither agreement nor quarrel, I said, "Indeed." I turned to Toby. "See you next Thursday. Say good-bye to La La for me." And to Mr. Lloyd, I lied: "A pleasure to meet you, sir."

Boston, Sunday, 9 September

Oxford's deadline for application is the fifteenth of October, and I really don't want to be seen as waiting until the eleventh hour. So this weekend I've made short work of my homework so I could dedicate myself to completing the application. I had already started it, of course, some time ago, but I got sidetracked with the move to Boston and with my lack of confidence rising to the surface the way it did. But I'm back on track, now. And although on the forms I did mention my grandfather's being at Magdalen, I'm submitting an open application rather than focusing on one college. I'm almost afraid of New College, after all my fantasies of being there with GG, but if that's the only one that offers me a position, I'll take it.

After putting the finishing touches on the application package, I did take a little break this afternoon to realign my brain cells before digging into the schoolwork that waited for me. Mozart does that better than anything else, so whilst Brian (yes, I've decided to have mercy on him and use his actual name) and Mum were out walking Persie—a prescribed route that doesn't vary, evidently a large circle around several neighbourhood blocks—I dug out my book of Mozart's piano sonatas and played through a few of my favourites. Time got away from me, and I was in the middle of the first movement of No. 17, K. 576, which is fairly boisterous (at least for Mozart), when everyone came home. I didn't hear them, so when Persie appeared silently at my side I jumped about a foot off the bench. It took me several seconds to realise she had her laptop with her.

"More Clyfford Still art?" I asked her, my heart still pounding a little. From the corner of my eye, I could see Mum and Brian standing in the entrance to the music room, watching.

Persie stood on my right and looked down at the piano bench, and I took this to mean she wanted to sit there, so I scooted over to the left, wondering how soon I could get back upstairs.

She opened the laptop, which was displaying something on YouTube, and she clicked Play. It was that scene from the film *Deliverance* with the "Dueling Banjos" number, even though it's a banjo and a guitar. I'd heard the piece before—who hasn't?—but I hadn't seen the film, and I didn't know the banjo player was supposed to have a condition that appears to be something between deformity and autism. He won't speak to the guitar player, who's visiting the area with some other men, but his face lights up as he plays.

As I wondered how Persie had stumbled upon this clip, knowing she doesn't like films, wondering if she thinks the scene on

YouTube is real, she let the video play all the way through. Then she shut the laptop and set it on a table. Right hand on the keyboard, she picked out the opening theme and waited. She was waiting for me, I realised, so I echoed the notes an octave down. She repeated the theme, and so did I, and then she launched into the tune. I don't know it as well as she evidently does, but I could follow the harmonic progression, which is pretty simple. So I improvised chords in the lower register to follow her melody, in a lively rhythm that kept everything moving. Her fingers flew over the keyboard almost as fast as the banjo player had fingered his notes. Finally she began a kind of musical coda that told me she was closing in on the end, and we raced together to the final cadence.

In my peripheral vision, I saw Mum start to applaud, but Brian caught her hands before she could make a sound. Persie turned her face towards me, grinning from ear to ear. I couldn't help smiling back. She stood, still smiling, picked up her laptop, and walked past Mum and Brian without acknowledging their presence.

Mum turned to watch as Persie headed towards the stairs, and then she turned back to me. "Oh, Simon! That was marvellous!" As I stood, she came over and hugged me briefly. I felt almost like Persie; didn't really want to say anything. And then I noticed Brian, who stood where he'd been. He was rubbing the heel of his hand on his eyes, wiping away tears.

To Mum I said, "Thanks. Um, guess I'll go back to my homework."

Brian caught my arm gently as I came near him. "Thank you," he said.

"My pleasure." It was the polite thing to say, but as I said it, I realised it was true.

Back upstairs, it wasn't easy to focus on homework. When I'd headed downstairs to play Mozart I had been avoiding coming up with a topic for my Theory of Knowledge project (TOK), a requirement for the IB curriculum. TOK is about the nature and limitations of knowledge, determining the meaning and validity of critical thinking, or so the course description says. With "Dueling

Banjos" still playing in my head, it occurred to me that I should be able to work out a topic inspired by Persie. Applying the course concepts to the way she acquires and exhibits knowledge, and the limitations she faces, could be just the thing to make my project unique. I made a note to ask her about how she perceives that video. How she even found it.

By the time I went down to dinner I had a pretty good basic outline of what I want my project to look like. I was ready for the Monday afternoon class. Thanks to Persie. Though that duelling tune refused to leave my head for the whole next day.

Boston, Tuesday, 11 September

It's Tuesday night, and we've had our first full City day on our own as teams. And I think this particular day will haunt me for a long time.

With our assignment being institutions of higher learning, Olivia, Maddy, and I decided to visit the registrar offices at Harvard and at Boston University, or BU. It was a warm day, and I was annoyed that we'd be required to wear school-sanctioned clothes, which meant I was in a long-sleeved shirt and had to wear a tie. I mutinied a little and left my blazer at home.

Harvard was about what you'd expect, and we collected printed material and spoke for a little while with some administrator about the school's history and its influence on Cambridge and Boston. Then there was the obligatory walk around Harvard Yard, which was a little more interesting in present company, but not much. Then on to BU, which was also about what you'd expect, except that an hour after we left the registrar, my life changed.

It had become apparent to me as this hot day progressed that Maddy had set her cap at me, as the saying goes. She exhibited all the signs, and she's not a shy girl. Even Olivia noticed, and I caught a look on her face more than once that basically said, "Oh, I can't believe this." I'd had about enough of Maddy "accidentally" bumping into me on the T, but as we left the BU registrar she was up for more and suggested going back to school to pull together what we'd learned. I lobbied hard to find someplace air-conditioned nearby instead where we could order something to drink whilst we talked, and Olivia (bless her) agreed with me.

After our consultation, I begged off when they got up to head back into town. "I might go back up the street to the fine arts building. Maybe check out the Stone Gallery."

This was too specific; it gave Maddy an opening. "Ooh, I love art! I'll come with you."

Think fast, Simon. "Um, I hope you won't mind, but I really prefer looking at art alone. I'll see you at school tomorrow." I gave her my sweetest smile.

Now, having said what I'd said, I had to go look at art, which I love doing, but I was feeling tired and a little grumpy from the heat and from my efforts to avoid Maddy's attentions all day. But I reasoned that art would take my mind off all that, so I loosened my tie until the knot hung a couple of inches low, rolled up my shirt-sleeves, hefted my school bag, and walked down Comm Ave, as they call it here.

I wasn't taking anything in, really, just wandering vaguely from one piece to another, letting the cool air and the slightly echoing sounds from other people wash over me, until I noticed him. He was standing near a piece of ambiguous sculpture made of various materials, but he wasn't looking at it. He was looking at me. And when I looked at him, he didn't turn away.

Dark hair, slightly long, gentle waves around his face, a long, Roman nose, and dark, intense eyes. A latter-day Romeo. He made no move, and I was unsure what to do. Should I walk towards him? Ignore him? Pretend I didn't see him? No, too late for that. So I gave him as cryptic a smile as I could and turned back to the art on the wall near me. I moved to the next work and stared at it without taking it in, insisting to myself, *I will not look around. I will not look around. I will not . . .*

"I know the girl who painted this one."

Steady, Simon. Be calm. Wait two beats, and then turn your head slowly. "Do you?"

"She was in the art history class I took here over the summer."

I looked back at the painting. "What's your medium?"

"Sculpture."

Still not looking at him, I asked, "Was that your piece, where you were standing just now?"

"Yes. Do you like it?"

I turned to face him again, tilting my head and smiling just slightly. He had perhaps two inches on me, height-wise. Two well-built inches. "That's a brazen question."

He shrugged, a smooth motion that allowed me to imagine the slide of muscles under his skin. Speaking of sculpture . . .

He said, "I can be brazen when the need arises."

"What need do you have now?"

"For you to like my art."

He was flirting with me. I was sure of it. As I turned so I could see the piece better, I know his eyes stayed on my face. I studied the piece for a few seconds, and then walked away from him towards it, around it, stopped a few times, and around again. I looked for the title. *"Discord."*

"Well?" he prodded.

"It makes me feel off-balance."

"Perfect."

"What was your inspiration?"

He turned his head to look at nothing in particular, collecting his thoughts perhaps, and I noticed a small, stylised X tattooed on the right side of his neck. He looked back at me. "Ever hear of Straight Edge?"

"Is that a music group, or something?"

His scornful expression made it appear he thought I'd said something stupid. No doubt having identified my accent, he told me, "It's only a cultural revolution, that's all. It's in England too, y'know."

If he was flirting, he was failing with me. And if he thought he could out-smug me, he was about to learn a thing or two. I gave a tiny snort, decided to ignore the certain hyperbole of "revolution," and said, "There are rather a lot of things going on in England, as it happens. Why should Straight Edge mean anything to me?"

"Maybe you should look it up."

"Maybe you should stop talking to strangers. You don't do it very well." I turned my back on him and moved off, but before I got all the way to the next painting on the wall he was in front of me.

"Sorry. And you're right; I don't talk to strangers very well. Can I treat you to a soda or something? Make it up to you?"

I looked him up and down, taking in the jeans, the roughed-up, olive-green trainers on his feet, the scuffed maroon messenger bag, the black T-shirt with STRAIGHT EDGE scrawled across it in grey letters so faded I had to look hard to make out what it said. I looked back at his face again, thinking I'd turn down this odd offer. But my eyes caught on his, and I heard my voice say, "And you'll tell me about this Straight Edge thing in civil tones?"

He grinned. "Promise. Look." He turned around long enough for me to read the back of the shirt: LIVE TRUE. LIVE FREE. LIVE BETTER. "Let's get outta here."

We went from the cool gallery to the hot pavement. "How about the Oven?" he asked.

Thinking we'd just stepped into one, I shook my head. "Don't know that, either."

"Amalfi Oven? In the GSU?" More head shaking on my part. "How long have you been here? I'm a freshman, and I know the Oven already."

"I'm not a student here. What's the GSU?"

He paused for just a second, taking in this information about me. "George Sherman Union. Food, cultural events, a kind of student hub. So you just happened to stop in at the Stone?"

"I was . . . I was in the area. Sorry if that sounds lame. Doing research for some coursework."

"So where *do* you go to school?"

"St. Boniface, Marlborough Street. Senior year," I specified, not wanting him to think of me as a child.

"You some kind of brainiac?"

Okay, I thought, going anywhere with this guy was a bad idea, no matter how gorgeous he was, no matter what effect his smile had on me. "Yes. Look, maybe I should just head back." He stopped in his tracks, gave me a vaguely amused look, and laughed. And I got irritated again. Intending it to be a parting shot, I said, "Good luck with your off-balance sculpture."

"No, wait. I wasn't laughing at you. It's just that you surprised me." He shook his head, chuckled. " 'Yes.' A brainiac. Simple as that." He held out his right hand. "Michael Vitale."

Michael: brick red, bright yellow, pale brown, cream, pale yellow, lilac, bright orange.

Vitale: Kelly green, bright yellow, bright blue, pale yellow, bright orange, lilac.

Both names had so many similar colours in them; it was a good thing they started with different letters. The total effect of his name struck me as Mediterranean. Italian, of course. Warm, bright but not overwhelming, alive.

I gave him my hand. "Simon Fitzroy-Hunt."

Another grin. They were growing on me for sure. "Your name is as English as your accent. Mine's Italian."

"Sì, è evidente."

And again he stopped. "You speak Italian?"

"Solo una piccola."

"I don't know what that means. But my *nonna* would. I mean, my grandmother."

"So, this Amalfi place sounds Italian." I took a step, and we were back in motion again.

"After a fashion. Italian inspired, at least. So, what do you expect St. Boniface to do for you, anyway?"

"Get me into Oxford University."

He whistled. "And then?"

"Not sure. I expect I'll figure that out whilst I'm there."

"What are you doing in Boston? I know they have good prep schools in England."

I gave him a thumbnail sketch of my life for the past few months, told him a little about my City course and why I was in this neighbourhood today, and by the time we were at a table with our drinks and two slices of sausage pizza for Michael, I told him I was ready for an explanation of his shirt, of Straight Edge.

He knitted his eyebrows and glanced down at his plate. "If I were really good about it, I'd be vegan. No cheese, and for sure no sausage."

"So there's a dietary component?"

He lifted a shoulder and dropped it, took a few swallows of his drink, waved his hand in a circle. "Maybe a little. You were closer with the music group idea. Straight Edge is a lifestyle. We take a vow to live right. No alcohol. No drugs. No sex until marriage. Lots of music, though." He dug in his bag and pulled out an iPhone and some earbuds, selected something, and handed the buds across the table. Before I lifted them to my ears the raucous sounds hit me like a wave. I tried to focus, but the words "no sex until marriage" were ringing too loudly in my brain.

Now, I hardly expected to end up in the sack with this guy—at least, not immediately, if at all. I've never even kissed anyone real. Even so, his gorgeous face and attempts at flirting had drawn me in and allowed me to hope that I hadn't misread his initial approach. But I must have been wrong. I mean, if he was so focused on this pristine way of life, "marriage" for him would necessarily involve a woman.

I handed the earbuds back. "Quite a sound," I said, deliberately vague.

He selected something else and gave me the earbuds again. This time the music was harmonious, much easier to listen to, but still my mind was on other things. Like, *I am so not falling for another guy who doesn't want me. A "straight" edge guy, at that. No way.*

By the time I gave him back his earbuds he had pretty much finished his pizza. "So, seriously," he said, "you should look it up. You'll be able to get a much better sense than I can give you in a few minutes. A friend of mine got me into it last year. It's changed my life."

"Oh?" I wasn't sure I wanted to know. I was working towards an exit line but didn't say anything quickly enough.

"Truly. Live true, live free, live better. I used to be different."

"Got into lots of trouble, or something?"

He shook his head. "I, uh . . . I was fighting something, really hard, and losing. I was afraid I was . . . I'm not ashamed to say it now. I thought I might be gay."

A lift of my chin, narrowed eyes, tongue-in-cheek: I wanted to leave no doubt about my self-confidence. I slid out of my chair, picked up my bag, and shot my exit line at him. "I'm gay. And I'm not ashamed of *that*, either."

I didn't look back to see whether he watched me leave.

Michael's face kept sliding into my mind's eye as I tried to focus on homework after dinner. *He thought he might be gay.* Which almost certainly means he is. And now he's—what? Straight Edge? Which isn't the same thing as straight, though maybe he's deluded himself into thinking it is. I decided against looking this thing up; it would only serve to keep my attention on him.

But if he really is gay, that means I'd been right about his approach. He *had* been flirting with me. Whether he would ever admit it was a different matter.

Vitale. Vital. Italian, from *vita*, life.

It was tempting to go downstairs, see if Ned was still here, and talk with him about it. But that would be no better—and maybe even worse—than looking up Straight Edge, in terms of keeping Michael on my mind.

Note to self: *Forget it, Simon. The only thing worse than falling for a straight guy is falling for a gay guy who won't admit the truth about himself.* Live true, indeed. Ha.

Boston, Wednesday, 12 September

This afternoon, classes over, on my way out of the school entrance I was trying to shake Maddy, who was ostensibly interested in my approach for our latest City assignment, but who was really asking questions she didn't need to ask, about things that didn't matter, so she could talk to me. I wasn't paying attention to where I was going and nearly walked into someone who stepped in front of me.

Michael Vitale.

Maddy was still talking, not noticing or maybe not caring that I'd frozen in place.

"Hey, Simon." His smile had something intimate in it.

I recovered as quickly as possible and said, "Michael." I hoped my tone was as even and unrevealing as I intended it to be. For a nanosecond, I considered continuing my conversation with Maddy as though it were the most natural thing in the world that Michael was standing there, and as though hello was the be-all and end-all of what we might say to each other. But I couldn't move, and I couldn't drop my gaze from his face.

"Simon?" Maddy finally realised she didn't have my full attention.

I yanked my gaze away from Michael long enough to tell her, "See you tomorrow, Maddy."

Michael said, "Walk with me."

"I beg your pardon?" *Who does he think he is? My boss? My commanding officer?*

"Please? I'll carry your books."

Ignoring his teasing tone, I glared at him. He might be gorgeous, but he was also clueless. "You're going from bad to worse. What do you want?"

"I . . . Simon, look. I'm just trying to make a connection."

"Why?"

"I feel there's something between us. I'd like to know what it is. Wouldn't you?"

"You remember I'm gay, right?"

He grinned. "I remember. And you remember I almost was, right?"

"That might be clear to *you*." What I was thinking was that avoiding sex is hardly the same thing as changing how you feel about it.

"Let's go someplace where we can talk about that. Newbury Street?"

He looked like he thought he had hooked a fish, or could at least see it approaching the bait. Maybe I wanted to be caught. "Can we sit outside?"

Maybe ten minutes later we were at a café table close enough to the street to watch the pedestrians file past, at adjacent sides of a square table so we weren't facing each other directly. He ordered a Coke and chips, and I got an iced tea, with a silent nod to Ned. And now that we were here, he seemed reluctant to begin. So I opened.

"I hope you realise I don't buy this 'almost gay' idea."

"You don't know the power of Straight Edge."

"I'd bet on biology any day. And is this why you're stalking me, by the way? You want to convert me?" I glanced sideways at him, away from the parade of people.

"Okay, look. I'm not stalking you. And I'm not out to convert anybody. That isn't what Straight Edge is about. It's just that you seemed . . . I don't know, different. Yesterday, in the gallery."

"I am different. I'm English, and I'm gay." I turned my gaze back to the parade.

"And you're incredibly smart. You must be, to be at that school."

My tone sarcastic, I said, "So, put all that together and you come up with someone you can't get out of your mind?"

He was quiet long enough to make me look at him. "Maybe not for the reason you think."

I wasn't sure what I wanted to do about this tension. If he'd admitted to being gay, I would have liked it a lot. I turned fully towards him. "Back at the school, you said you sensed something between us. Would you like to know what I think that is?"

"Sure."

"You're attracted to me. And I'm attracted to you. There are probably a lot of reasons for this, and one of them is that we're both gay." If that didn't send him packing, nothing would.

"Just because I find you interesting doesn't mean I'm attracted to you sexually."

"How, then? In what way are you attracted to me?" And why *didn't* that send him packing? Did *he* want to be caught?

"There's something edgy, something cool about you. And you're smart. Really smart. I was always one of those kids who wouldn't admit they're smarter than they act. You know the type? Boys, mostly. If we have a brain, we hide it. And talent in art is like the plague. Not cool. Me, I barely got into BU. But I know I have the brain power and the talent to stay, and maybe enough to go on after that." He pointed the straw from his drink in my direction. "You? You're the whole deal. I can't speak to talent, but on top of everything else, you like art."

"And you think I'll—what? Open doors into your true inner self?"

He grinned. " 'Live True.' No, I'm the only one who can open my doors. But, see, if there's anything we can make a friendship out of, I'd like to do that. Because I gotta get away from my home crowd. I'm from Boston, y'see. And some kids who see me like I used to be are still around me, at BU. Skipping classes, getting drunk, that kind of scene. I'm over that. They're not. And college is a great place to reinvent yourself. So I'm looking for new friends." He waved the straw around as he spoke. "And you're not the only one. I've been watching people, talking to people I don't know. Girls can take it the wrong way, so I'm limiting myself to guys for now. And you're new to Boston, so I figure maybe we can help each other."

My mind had caught on how he's limiting himself to boys, and the helping each other bit nearly threw me. "What makes you think you can help me?"

"This course you're doing. The City one. I was thinking that part of what makes a city a city is the people, and in Boston most people have come from someplace else. Like Italy. My *nonna* lives in the North End. That's mostly Italian, in case you don't know. Won't move out. You can speak Italian to her—just a few words would give her a thrill—and she'll tell you anything you want to know. In English."

This gave me pause. It would be an interesting angle.

"And then there's Straight Edge. X. Like 'this tattoo, which I know you've noticed. You said part of what you need to show is how culture connects cities, right? Well, X is all over the world. Like I told you, it's in England. So right there you've got Italian immigration and how it affected Boston's development, and I can give you the goods on X as it is here, and both those influences apply to cities everywhere." He shrugged. "So, yeah, I have something to offer. Something I'll bet the other brainiacs in your class won't be able to match."

I was speechless. He was right; there were doors he could open for me. I might even want to make Italian immigration or Straight Edge—X—the focus of my final presentation, kind of like a thesis. It seemed unlikely there was a connection between the two, but I could choose one or the other. X would be more unusual, and the fact that it's contemporary would help get me noticed at Oxford.

And in return, I must offer him friendship. Didn't seem like a fair trade, really. That aside, though, I searched his face for a few seconds. What kind of toll would this take on me, to spend time with this artistic Roman god and not be able to touch him?

Finally I said, "There must be more to this arrangement for you."

"All right, look, there's something else I want to get out of this, too. I have a course where I've been given an assignment, comparing art in Italy and England. And I just don't get English art. Maybe you can help me with that."

"I must say, you've given this a lot of thought."

"We were told to 'think outside the box' for an approach." He chuckled. "You're outside the box, all right."

Trite expression. "So, why the coy camouflage? Why start this conversation by trying to pretend you had a less pragmatic motive?"

"Dunno. I guess . . . I guess I'm not used to being up front about anything academic. And, like I told you already, I don't talk to strangers easily."

This still seemed rather thin. And I wasn't so sure he found it difficult to talk to strangers. Which made it all the more likely that his real reasons for talking to me were ones he wasn't admitting to himself. This should have sent *me* packing. It didn't. Holding my straw between first and second fingers, I bounced it on the table. "How would this work, then?"

He leaned forwards, his face intense. "I'll give you a quick intro to X. Play you some of the music, show you some of the stuff on-line, maybe introduce you to a couple of guys I know who are in it. And you and I go to the Museum of Fine Arts; we focus on Italian and English art. By that time, I'll have told my *nonna* I have a friend who speaks Italian—"

"Only a little Italian. Please understand that."

"Fine. And she'll probably invite us to dinner, and she's a great cook, and you can pick her brain. Make friends, you know. And then you can use her as a resource. She loves to talk about Italy and what it was like to leave, and what she thinks about Boston."

I tried to force my brain to focus on what he was offering towards my academic success, but his face was so gorgeous, intense eyes trained on me, mouth partially open and tempting me to wonder what he'd do if I leaned forwards and kissed it. I turned deliberately back towards the street just as a tall, obviously gay man walked by, a Siamese cat in a red harness perched on his shoulder. I watched his retreating figure and then turned to Michael.

"It won't bother you that I'm gay?"

"Will it bother you that I'm not?"

"Maybe." Yes. Or, it will bother me that he thinks he's not.

He laughed. "I like your honesty. And as long as we're honest with each other, I think this will work. What are you doing tomorrow afternoon?"

"I'm not at uni yet, y'know. Thursday is a school day." I decided not to go into my spelling coach job with him.

"Okay, well, the museum is open until nine forty-five. How about we go there after school lets out for you?"

My voice teasing, I said, "So you get your art before I get my Italian?"

"How's this, then. We go to the museum, spend a couple of hours, then you can come back to my dorm and meet the guy in the room next to mine. He's not Italian, but he's X. We could start there. Go out to dinner together. We'll tell you everything. Plan?"

"I'll be free by four. Should we meet at the museum after that?"

"Plan."

As we were about to head different ways, Michael asked for my phone number. "I'll call you tomorrow to confirm, and you'll get my number that way." He laughed when I had to fish out my iPhone to look up the number.

"I just got it," I told him by way of explanation as I began to go through the icons.

"And you don't have it memorised yet? You, the brainiac?" I looked up at him, and he winked.

"*I'll* ring *you*," I said. "What's your number?"

And just like that, I had the Roman god's contact information stored in my phone—the Roman god who might as well be a stone statue, cold to my touch.

Boston, Saturday, 15 September

Thank the gods I have Graeme—my fantasy version of Graeme— to keep me warm. As it were. Otherwise I think I'd go berserk thinking about Michael all the time.

I was not especially attentive to Toby Thursday afternoon. First, I was late, because I'd stopped at the house to drop off my books so I wouldn't be lugging those around all evening, and I also wanted to change my St. Bony shirt to something more intentional.

On a single sheet of paper I had a list of words I'd looked up for Toby, but it wasn't long enough, and I had a hard time using his dictionary to find words at random of sufficient obscurity to stump him. I was going to have to put in more effort; that was sure. I was so distracted that at one point, when he finally missed a word, I said, "No, there's more yellow. You missed the second *i*." Which of course made him quiz me about what that meant until I had to tell him about my synaesthesia.

"Wow! If I had that, I'd win for sure! Would they even have let you compete? I mean, when you were younger? Or would that be considered cheating?"

"I'm sure I don't know." I hoped my dismissive tone would discourage more questions, but no; it seemed he wanted to know the colour of every single letter. Finally I pointed out that he was wasting time better spent on practice, and he buckled down again.

During our break, with Colleen puttering about in the kitchen and Toby rambling on about how much he loves the film *Close Encounters of the Third Kind* and speculating about the coloured lights that flash when the alien ship is sending out tones and whether the aliens had synaesthesia, my mind wandered away again towards Michael and what it would be like spending the evening with him. I tried to refocus by reminding myself that he was not to be touched, but that just ended up making me feel sad and vulnerable.

Toby was explaining how *Close Encounters* is all about being open to other creatures we can learn to understand when La La surprised me by jumping onto my lap. Automatically, my fingers began to rub behind her ears, and suddenly my eyes stung with tears. I squinted hard to keep them away.

Toby, unfortunately, noticed. "Simon! Are you all right? What's wrong?"

My voice would break, I knew, if I spoke right away, so I shook my head and coughed, which sent La La back to the floor. I managed, "I'll tell you another time."

There was no putting him off forever, though. During the rest of our practice, he deliberately misspelled some words, I think to try and make me feel better. Finally I had to tell him that I'd had to leave my cat behind in England. He jumped up and threw his arms around my shoulders as best he could. I didn't get out of my chair to make it any easier. As he sat down again, he wiped tears from his own eyes.

No Mr. Lloyd appeared to darken the rest of Toby's afternoon.

When I was downstairs in the entrance lobby, alone at last, I pulled out my phone, brought up the entry for Michael's number, and sat there staring at it until the screen dimmed. I touched the phone to brighten it again. This went on for some number of times I lost track of until I finally just hit the Call icon. He answered on the second ring.

"Michael, Simon here. Ready for your art lesson?"

"Primo. I can be at the entrance on Museum Road in twenty. You?"

"Same. See you." And I rang off before anything in my voice could give away that I was shaking a little.

I sat where I was for another couple of minutes, trying to talk myself out of this funk. *Get it together, Simon. What is wrong with you? You're acting like a child. Grow a pair. Find your backbone.*

I spotted him immediately, leaning against the side of the building, casual, at ease, and oh, so handsome. He wore a white cotton shirt tucked loosely into blue jeans, sleeves rolled up to reveal well-formed forearms in that olive tone of his heritage that contrasts beautifully with white. A couple of girls passed by him ahead of me, and they both turned to look at him. But he was watching me.

Inside, he led us right to the museum's permanent European collection. He had some specific works in mind that he wanted to examine, some paintings and some sculpture. I think I impressed him by drawing his attention to other types of art: silver work, furniture, textiles—other works in which he might detect the patterns that were distinctly English or Italian.

It was intoxicating, standing close to him for minutes at a time, examining a work of art, inhaling the scent of him: wool, warmed by the sun. No cologne, no added fragrance. I stumbled on the technique of asking him a leading question and then basking in his nearness as he formulated an analysis. I listened to his responses only enough to tell that he knows a heck of a lot more about art than I do, and to come up with another question so we wouldn't have to move on and, inevitably, apart any sooner than necessary.

It came to an end at last, though later than Michael had planned. "We'll have to hoof it or we won't have much time to talk with Chas."

A taxi was just dropping a passenger off, and I hailed it. Michael said, "Whoa, there, that's pricey."

I smiled at him and held the door. "My treat." And I sat as close to him in the backseat as could possibly be deemed reasonable, not quite but almost touching. He didn't move away.

"Aberdeen Street," he said to the driver. I tried to pay attention to how we got there from the museum, but the distraction of Michael's leg or shoulder occasionally touching mine was too much for me.

Aberdeen turned out to be a short block of underwhelming buildings. We got out of the taxi with a row of cars between us and the building. I paid for the ride and was putting my wallet away when my eye fell on a sticker on the bumper of a parked car. Michael was greeting someone, undoubtedly another college student, who had just come out of the nearest doorway and had unlocked this same car, his remote causing a short *beep* of the horn. But my attention was on that bumper sticker. It read, LOST YOUR CAT? CHECK MY TIRE TREADS.

"Simon," Michael was saying to me, "this is Dick. He lives on the first floor."

Dick, a large fellow, lots of bulk to him and rather unattractive, was holding his hand out. I didn't take it. Instead, looking right at him, I said, "Dick, is it? How appropriate."

Dick lowered his hand and scowled at me. "What's your problem?"

"Not my problem. Yours." I pointed to the bumper sticker. "Did you put this on here?"

"What if I did?"

Michael, unsure what was going on, moved to where he could see the sticker. He looked at it, looked at me, looked at Dick.

Dick repeated, "What's your problem, dude? You some kind of cat lover?"

"Well, *your* attitude towards cats is hanging on your proverbial sleeve. You realise," I said to him in a voice that suggested sarcastic confusion, "that cats can't read, right?"

"So?"

"So your problem must be with people who like cats. So your problem is with me." I lifted a foot and dragged the sole of my shoe across the nasty thing. "*This* is a prehistoric attitude to project towards people you haven't even met. You don't know me, but you want me to be angry with you." I shook my head. "Primitive. Michael, are we going inside?" I turned my back on "Dick" and headed towards the doorway.

No doubt more to avoid additional conflict than to do my bidding, Michael practically jumped towards the door. "See you later," he called to Dick.

"And that faggy limey had better not be here when I get back!"

Michael pulled the door open and held it, aiming a hoarse whisper at me as I passed. "What did you do that for?"

I halted in the doorway. "The question should be, 'What did *he* do that for?' He's a Neanderthal, Michael." I moved forwards, and he followed. "Though that's an insult to Neanderthals."

"Okay, but they're dangerous! I just hope he doesn't see you again later."

I decided against pursuing this discussion further.

The foyer was what you might expect: ancient, grimy floor tiles that might have started life as cream or maybe even white; dirt caked into corners and wherever the floor and a wall met; badly maintained wooden panelling on the walls below a chair rail, white marble with black veins above—badly in need of resurfacing. I followed him up two flights of stairs made of some unidentifiable stone, each step depressed in the centre from the wear of countless feet treading up and down and up and down. He shared three tiny rooms with a fellow who was seated at a desk on the left side of the room we entered from the hall. Without standing, this fellow turned towards me and held his hand out. I decided against annoying another of Michael's acquaintances and shook hands.

"Brad Tollman," he said. I gave him my name, and he turned back to his desk. There was another desk and a small couch in this windowless room. There were doors to two other rooms, both bedrooms with windows.

Michael turned to the right and gestured to a door. "Make yourself at home," he said to me. "I'll go roust Chas, and we can head out."

Michael's bedroom. I was alone in Michael's bedroom. I would have expected to notice the bed first, but the posters on the wall were so intense they practically assaulted me. Straight Edge imagery, bands with trap sets and electric guitars and keyboards, one image of some shirtless guy holding his tattooed shoulder so close to the camera that the rest of him was blurred. Xs all over the place. The only poster I could tolerate looking at for more than a few seconds was over the head of his bed: Van Gogh's *Starry Night*, outlandishly out of place.

The bedcover was a hideous red corduroy, worn in places where someone—Michael, presumably—had sat on it countless times. It was a twin bed; no room for anything bigger in here. But what was interesting was that the bedspread fit it, and it wasn't new, which made me wonder if it had been on Michael's twin bed at his parents' home. I'd always slept in a queen-size bed, or at least since I was twelve or so. Maybe thirteen. And I'd always had a room plenty large enough to accommodate it. The quality of the bedspread—or the lack thereof—and the size gave me the impression that Michael's family were not well-off, financially. Looking around the room I noticed a similar lack of quality, though the furniture itself was possibly provided by the school. The lamps, one on the bed table and one on the bureau, were small and cheaply made. I had just begun to examine the personal items on the bed table when I heard Michael return, someone in tow.

"Chas Dakin," said the fellow, holding his hand out to me. I shook it and gave him my name, trying not to stare at the two barbell piercings through his right eyebrow or the grey X-inspired T-shirt he wore untucked over a charcoal pair of those hideous not-quite-shorts, not-quite-trousers with the crotch that hangs about halfway down the thigh. Was there no place on this guy I could rest my eyes without wanting to turn away?

Behind me Michael dug into a bureau drawer. I turned in time to see him pull out something olive drab, no doubt another T-shirt. Greedily I took in his bare torso as he removed the white shirt, disappointed that he was rejecting it but enjoying the outline of his abdominal muscles, dropping my eyes down to follow the slanted lines of muscle that disappeared into his jeans. Why had he worn the white shirt to the museum, and why change it now?

Dressed again, he said to me, "You like?"

It was, of course, another X-related thing. A few playing cards were printed in black across his middle. Above them in brick red was, I'M STRAIGHT EDGE. Below them was, DEAL WITH IT. Why would I like it? "Do I get in trouble if I tell you how much I preferred the white shirt?"

He laughed without replying. "Shall we head out?"

As Chas turned I noticed a massive tattoo, a gothic-style X on the side of his calf, bright red outlined in thick black ink. I looked away.

We sat at a round table in a forgettable Chinese restaurant. With an effort, I pushed aside my frustrated feelings about Michael and focused my mind on the task at hand, which was to determine if there was enough to this X stuff for me to use it in my coursework, either centrally or peripherally. I learned that the movement had begun within punk, but became a protest against the self-indulgence and hedonism punk is known for. The name Straight Edge came from a song by a group called Minor Threat, and the X symbol was born when a Straight Edge band arrived to play at a club. It seems the band members were underage, and to allow them to stay but prevent them being served alcohol, the club management had put a large black *X* on their hands to alert club staff. Evidently this all goes back to 1980.

Chas, who said he grew up in Colorado, rambled on about how cool it was to be clean, to be able to say no to offers of drugs now that he was in X. He talked about how he'd been into drugs in high school until he'd ended up in hospital. After that, starting the summer before his senior year, he had dedicated himself to X. He'd been to the Sound and Fury Festival in Los Angeles over the summer, and he raved about bands with names like Rotting Out, Minus, Harms Way, and Take Offense.

The nasty bumper sticker still on my mind, I asked Michael, "Is cat-hater Dick in X?"

He shook his head. "No, he's just an asshole. And it's not 'in' X. It's just X."

Whatever. I asked Chas, "So what can you tell me about why these bands would deliberately give themselves names with dark or negative connotations, like Take Offense? What is the relationship between being clean, as you put it, and wilfully offending people?"

Chas laughed, but without humour. "If you were X, you'd know what it's like. There's even an X T-shirt that says, 'Straight Edge means I have no friends.' Being X puts you into a minority group, and we get a lot of grief from people who don't get it. So our response is, you know, 'In your face, fuckers!' " He grinned as though he'd love to have someone to say that to right this minute.

I glanced at Michael. How would he take it if I told this guy what it really means to have people hate you for no good reason, a reason you didn't choose? What if I told Chas he didn't have a clue? Or if I suggested he tell people he's gay, or maybe that he's really a girl, and see how many friends he had?

I opted for a less confrontational way to make my point, even though I knew it might be a conversation-stopper. Instead of asking if anyone had ever been killed by being tied to a fence and then beaten and tortured to death because they were X, I said, "I know what you mean, in a way. You see, I'm gay. There are people who wouldn't want to be my friend because of that."

I watched Chas's face. This was a kind of challenge for him. He was not gay; I had no doubt. So would *he* refuse to be *my* friend?

His grin drooped a little, and it was obvious to me he was struggling to maintain it as though I'd said nothing that disturbed him. I decided to take advantage. "How does X feel about gay people?"

Chas shrugged, which gave him a chance to change his facial expression and let go of the fake grin. "Sort of depends. I mean, X is kind of a tough crowd."

Fighting to keep sarcasm out of my voice, forcing myself not to tell him what kind of guts it takes to be openly gay, I said, "Then being devotees of bands like Rotting Out or Harms Way must validate you. Tell me, who knows about these bands, other than Xers?"

Chas blinked. "Well . . . I dunno. I mean, we play our music real loud. . . ."

"So you gang together at festivals like—what was it? Oh yes, Sound and Fury, which I'm guessing would be attended by Xers. It sounds like, really, you're tough for each other. Who else knows you're tough? Because I have to tell you, I'd never heard of you before the other day." The parallel between this exchange and my telling Dick that it wasn't cats he was offending almost made me laugh; I struggled to keep a "straight" face.

Chas glanced at Michael. I didn't dare do that; I'd probably just sealed my fate with him, spending the entire evening alienating everyone he introduced me to. Something in me was rebelling against the "movement" that I'd yet to hear anything good about other than avoiding drugs. In particular it bothered me that X gave Michael permission to lie to himself about who he is and call that "living true." And I was beginning to realise that the kind of thesis X would fit into would be more along the lines of groupthink psychology than the social culture of cities. X obviously has nothing to do with cities.

With Chas dumbstruck and Michael with his nose practically on his plate rather than look at anyone, I decided to refocus the conversation. "What does X here, do you think, have in common with X in another country? Is X in Boston more different or more similar to, say, X in London?"

Chas perked up a little. "Oh, X is X! It's worldwide, and . . . well, of course there will be some differences. But that's just because the members are, y'know, English or German rather than American. But the promise is the same."

"Right. No drugs, no booze, no sex. Is there any kind of leader?"

He went on for a while about some prominent Xers who mostly seemed to be associated with bands, and he made a strong point about how even though some people think Xers are like gangs, the vast majority are nonviolent. He said there's a group called Boston Hardcore that's a Straight Edge group, and that they are more likely to be seen as troublemakers than the regular X group here. But it sounded as though the phenomenon is essentially autonomous from group to group, city to city, from what Chas could tell me.

Then he started quoting lyrics from some of his favourite songs, all of them dark, depressed and depressing, fatalistic. From different songs he quoted phrases like, "Youth is a wound time won't mend." "The rusty gates of Eden lock to never let me in." "We'll hold those barren bodies bereft of any soul."

"About the sex, though," he offered, "not all Xers swear off sex. We swear off promiscuity. And you have to decide for yourself whether it's possible to have sex before marriage without being promiscuous."

"And how about you? Have you sworn off sex until marriage?"

I could tell he was avoiding looking at Michael; not sure how I knew, but I did. Had Michael confessed to Chas his struggles with sexuality?

Chas grinned almost shyly. "Well, not exactly, no. I mean, you know."

"Earlier when I asked you about homosexuality, I didn't get a good sense of the X attitude towards it. Anything else you can say about that?"

He sounded a little more sure of himself this time. "Like I said, we swear off promiscuity. And lots of us swear off premarital sex. So if you don't have sex until you're married, you can't ever have it with guys."

"Of course you can."

Both Michael and Chas said, "What?"

I looked at Michael. "Come on. We're sitting here in the first state in the US that supported marriage equality. And it's not the only state anymore." I looked back at Chas, who had started babbling something, but I interrupted him. "And from what you just said, should I infer that gays would be unwelcome in X under any circumstances, or only if they refuse to be chaste? Or are they welcome if they lie about it? Are they welcome if they marry some poor, unsuspecting woman?"

Chas sat up straight. His tone giving the impression he was

dealing me some kind of lethal blow, he said, "Have you considered that maybe if you became X you could leave that part of you behind?"

"Have you considered that maybe there's no earthly reason someone would want to be something other than gay, if that's who they are?" He was still staring at me, trying to take this in, when I added, "Would you be willing to leave a part of yourself behind? Your leg, perhaps? A hip? Your penis?"

Chas looked at Michael. "Did you know he was just going to find fault with us? Did you know he was just one of them?"

Michael opened his mouth, but nothing came out.

I said, " 'One of them'? You mean the people who don't like you? *I* didn't know I was 'one of them.' So no, Michael didn't know. I don't know that I'm 'one of them,' now, either. But I can tell you I've heard almost nothing tonight I find appealing about X. You've even named your bands with terms designed to turn people away, so it stands to reason that you have detractors. In fact, it would seem you go out of your way to make sure you do." I smiled to try and soften my approach. "But that's not why I'm here, you know. I'm not here to like or dislike X. I'm here to learn about it. And I think I know all I need to."

I looked at Michael, who was still staring down at his empty plate. A sadness hit me; my sarcasm and antagonism had alienated him. The most I could hope for out of this meeting was that maybe he'd rethink what X is and is not, rethink what's true and what isn't. No more art lessons. No Italian dinners made by his *nonna* in the North End. Maybe it was for the best.

I dropped a couple of twenties on the table. Quietly, directly to Michael, I said, "I'll get a taxi home. Thanks for trying."

Chas watched me leave the table. Michael didn't look up.

On the ride home I watched sightlessly as the nighttime streets of Boston moved past my window. I repeated *Maybe it was for the best* to myself several times, eventually dropping the "maybe." By the time the taxi arrived at the house I was feeling resigned but also a little sulky, and all I wanted was to get upstairs and do as much damage control as I could, in terms of homework, so that I wouldn't earn demerits in *all* my Friday classes.

I turned the front door lock as quietly as possible and scoped out where people might be so I could avoid them. I was in luck; the only people I could detect were Mum and Brian, evidently in the kitchen, talking. I headed for the carpeted stairs and would have tiptoed up them, but two things happened. First, I heard a loud thud as something struck a wooden surface upstairs. Second, I heard Brian say, "Em, I just don't think this is going to work. I'd love for you to help with the interviews, but as for taking care of her yourself . . . It's a specialised skill. You're not trained."

Taking care of whom? And could the answer be anyone other than Persie?

Mum's voice sounded . . . offended, maybe? "You don't trust me."

"It has nothing to do with trust. And, Em, it has nothing to do with Clive."

"So that's your problem? You think that because of how I treated him, I can't treat Persie well, either?"

"There, see, that just proves my point. No matter how well she's treated, no matter how much she's *loved*, what she needs even more is someone who *understands* her. Who's been trained to work with people with autism. That's not you, Em. I'm sorry, but that's not you."

I wasn't sure why, but I didn't want them fighting. It wasn't just that I didn't want to witness it, though that was true as well. I didn't want them fighting. I opened and closed the front door loudly as though just making my entrance to the house, and I headed for the kitchen.

They both turned to look at me, and even if I hadn't overheard anything I'd have known something was wrong. So I said, "What is it? What's happened?"

Mum stood and carried a teacup and saucer to the sink. "Anna has given notice."

I nearly gasped; I knew what this would mean to Persie. "How soon?"

Brian said, "She tried to give two weeks' notice."

"And evidently I've ruined that," Mum said, her tone angry and sarcastic.

I decided against opening that door. "Why is she leaving?"

"She's found a clinic position," Brian said. "She wants more of a personal life, and regular office hours will make that possible. I can't say that I blame her. But she's the best tutor Persie's ever had."

I added, "And even small changes are giant ones in this house."

"Exactly."

There was an elephant in the room, an amorphous blob of lilac and blue and pale yellow and black, keeping to the shadows. But where had it come from?

Leaning her back against the counter, arms crossed over her chest, Mum said, "Evidently I destroyed all hope of a gentle preparation, because Persie overheard me talking with Anna about tutoring Persie myself. So she found out suddenly, and now she's furious and won't talk to anyone. Anna will probably need to leave right away."

"So that thump I heard a minute ago . . . that was Persie throwing something?"

Brian's face, already strained, took on an alarmed expression, and he got up and nearly ran out of the room.

Mum told me, "She threw a glass figurine at me. She missed, but it was a beautiful thing she loved, and it's in shards." She sounded near tears.

I turned and went into the music room. The day Persie had told me about Clyfford Still, she'd been toying with a glass bird. It was gone. Upstairs, Persie was now screaming.

I was torn as to whether to try and console Mum or try to help Persie. I didn't know what I could do in the kitchen, but maybe I could do something for the cat in pain upstairs. I raced past Persie's screams and up to the top floor, turned on my computer, and searched for Still's paintings. I wanted one in blood red, bright blue, bright yellow, and orange, the colours in the name, Still, and also in the word *still*, meaning calm. And I wanted one in sky blue, bright red, lilac, pale yellow, bright blue, and cream. *Breathe.* This one was harder to find, but there was one that was pretty close. I captured the images on separate screens with their words in capital letters beneath them and sent them to the colour printer, standing impatiently over the thing, willing it to work faster, hoping fervently that Persie had memorised the letter colour chart she'd asked for.

Printouts in hand, I thundered down one flight and saw Anna standing tentatively just inside the door to Persie's room, as though trying to come up with an action that would quiet the girl. I went in, past her and a grey-faced Brian, without saying anything; it would take too long to explain. I walked past as though I were Persie, only my goal in mind, and stopped in the middle of her playroom.

Persie sat on the floor, objects around her that had obviously been yanked from their proper places and thrown indiscriminately. She saw me and froze. I knew that not asking her permission to come in would not be good, but I couldn't risk rejection. Knowing also that to a cat, a long look usually means confrontation, I glanced only briefly at her before placing the first sheet of paper on the floor. I set it far enough away from her that she couldn't reach it easily and shred it, but she could see it and read the word *STILL*. Then I watched her face. She looked at the paper, her gaze moving from the art to the letters and back several times, and then her eyes flicked to mine and away.

Beside *STILL* I placed *BREATHE*. She stared at this one a long time. Finally, in her usual unmodulated tone, she said, "It's not right." It was not criticism; it was fact. She got up, went to her own laptop, and pretty soon I heard, "Here it is. Here it is." She brought the computer towards me and held it for me to see.

She'd found it, the perfect *BREATHE* Still.

"Yes," I said. "Will you do that?"

"I am breathing. I'm always breathing."

I closed my eyes, took a long, deep breath, and let it out slowly. Lazily I opened my eyes on her and saw her close her eyes before following my example. Before opening her eyes again she took four of these long, deep breaths. Then she set the laptop back where it had been.

To Anna she said, "I don't want you anymore. Go away." To me she said, "I'm going to bed now." And she turned away, presumably to do just that.

I looked at Anna, wondering how she'd take this, but she was turned towards the door, where Mum now stood just outside the room. Her voice tense, anger barely controlled, Anna said, "This was not the way to handle things."

Mum, her voice nearly breaking, said, "I'm sorry. I've said that several times already."

Anna mumbled, "Excuse me," and headed towards the top-floor stairs.

Holding her composure somehow, Mum turned towards the rooms she shared with Brian, went in, and very quietly shut the door.

Brian asked, "What do you think? Should we put things back where they were before she threw them?"

"Do you know precisely where they all go?"

He shook his head, and together we left Persie's rooms. Shutting the door behind us, he said, "I suppose Anna will need to do that while Persie's not in her rooms at some point tomorrow."

"Persie might put them back herself. She won't like that they're out of place."

Before I got as far as the top-floor staircase, still intent on doing at least *some* homework tonight, Brian asked, "How did you know, Simon? How did you know to do that?"

"I didn't know. I felt it." If this came as a surprise to him, it was an even bigger one for me. I don't just "feel" anything. My brain is always engaged. Yet somehow I had *felt* what I needed to do for Persie. The only thing I can figure is that cats get under my defences. Or maybe I'm really a cat, myself, as Ned had suggested. It would account for a lot.

Boston, Friday, 21 September

I didn't see Michael all week. Didn't expect to. Except, well . . . I did see him in my mind's eye every night trying to fall asleep. Graeme helped some, but even after his attentions, Michael would show up just as I was about to drift off. I'd see him concentrating on an art object at the museum, or changing his shirt, or not looking at me as I left the Chinese restaurant. The images, and the feelings, bounced around from longing to lust to loneliness.

I put Michael aside as best I could that week, focusing hard on my schoolwork and trying not to get involved as a steady stream of applicants for Anna's job ebbed and flowed. I even avoided Ned, because talking with him tended to make me vulnerable to all things that are important, and I didn't have time for anything other than the single-minded pursuit of excellent marks and making good impressions on my teachers. It was difficult, I found, to talk with Dr. Metcalf about Toby and not bring his transgender state into the mix. But I had to.

One fun thing that happened is that I went for a haircut. Ordinarily, this is just a basic thing—a nice cut from a good stylist. I had asked Ned for a recommendation, and I ended up going to a salon on Newbury Street. I had a man named Daniel, obviously gay, wacky sense of humour. He suggested we let the front area grow a little so it could be formed into a section that wouldn't quite curl over my forehead—my hair is straight as a board—but that could, with the aid of a tiny bit of product, be shaped into a fringe to cover just a small portion of one side of my forehead. He showed me what he meant with a lock of a hairpiece. At first it didn't look like me. But then another customer walked by on his way to a chair, a gorgeous man with a head of golden curls not unlike Graeme's. He stopped in his tracks, staring at me in the mirror. I looked at his reflection, and the look in his eyes convinced me.

"Let's do that," I said to Daniel.

So now I have a new style, or at least a new style in the making.

* * *

When I arrived at the Lloyds' flat yesterday, it was Colleen who let me in. She looked very sober, and my first thought was that something had happened to La La. But then I saw the cat in a sunny spot on the rug, legs curled under her. Even she looked tense, though.

"Is something wrong?" I asked Colleen.

"I think Toby should tell you, if he wants to. He's in his room."

If he wants to? Well, there was no point standing here interrogating Colleen, so I followed the sounds of Gloria Gaynor that emanated from behind Toby's door. "I will survive!" she was wailing to the world, to the man who had hurt her.

I knocked but heard no answer. Louder knocking; still no response. I opened the door, and was nearly assaulted by the music. Toby was facedown on his bed, and over Gloria I could just hear his sobs. I closed the door and waited for several seconds to see if he knew I was there, taking in the conspicuous absence of anything pink or girlie. The little rug, the throw, even the yellow-haired troll was missing. I located the volume control on the stereo set and turned it down. Toby sat up suddenly, eyes wild with an odd combination of fear and fury.

He made an attempt to speak which I translated as, "It's you."

"What's happened?" I was afraid I already knew.

This question, or perhaps the difficulty of answering it, brought on a new fit of weeping. I sat on the side of the bed and waited until Toby could sit quietly beside me, a box of tissues at his elbow. "He found out."

"He?"

"My father."

Ah. It was as I had feared. "How?"

Between hiccoughs Toby explained that yesterday he'd been dressed as Kay, singing along to something by Taylor Swift, when his father had arrived home unexpectedly. He had opened the door to tell Toby to turn the volume down and had caught full sight of his "daughter." When Toby had gotten home from school today, his room had been purged of femininity.

Something like this had been bound to happen, one of life's inevitabilities. Still, I couldn't help thinking that cracking the metaphorical door to show me who she really was had made Kay more vulnerable and had exposed her sooner than would have happened otherwise.

"How do things stand now?"

His voice practically squeaking, Toby gestured to take in the room with a sweep of his arm. "Look at it! It's decimated! I'm destroyed! Even my music. He's killed all the girls!"

Gloria began her song for maybe the third time since I'd arrived; evidently Toby had it on repeat. "Where'd you get Gloria, then?"

He blew his nose. "It's an old iPod I'd thrown into a drawer."

"What's the etymology of *draconian?*"

"Simon, I don't care! My life is ruined. Can't you see that?"

"I was merely trying to sympathise in a way that might calm you down. Bad idea; sorry." We sat there for a few minutes whilst Toby played with damp tissues, his breath catching from time to time. Then I asked, "How do you know you're Kay?"

"What?"

"Without the pink, or the skirts, or the music even. Are you still Kay, or was she all trappings and no substance?"

He was on his feet, facing me, glaring at me. "How dare you? I'm Kay! I'm Kay Lloyd!"

"So your father didn't take that away from you."

"Of course not!" He breathed in and out a few times through his nose, somewhat juicily.

"And do you still want to get on that stage and present yourself as you really are?"

"How can you even ask that?!"

"Then I would advise that you keep your head down, let him think he's won. Otherwise you could lose his support for this competition."

"It's not fair."

"No. It isn't. Nor was it fair when my mother took me away from everything and everyone I'd known, made me give up my cat, and forced me to move to a place I have no intention of staying. My sole focus right now is on what will get me back home."

"And getting there will take you out of your mother's control. You'll be on your own. I won't."

"True, not right away." This was a crucial difference; he was correct. "So are you having second thoughts?"

"No. I just have to find a way to make him understand."

"Probably not the best way to keep your head down."

"I suppose not."

"Did he tell your mother?"

He sat on the bed again. "No. And he made me promise not to." "Why?"

"I . . . I don't know."

"How did he get rid of all this stuff without her knowing?"

"He made Colleen do it today."

"So, does Colleen know?"

"Well, she had to deal with the girls' clothing, so probably."

"Aren't you afraid he'll come home early again and find the iPod?"

Toby jumped up and switched off the music. "I just had to hear that."

"Does he come home early very often?"

"No. Well, sometimes."

"Because he did one day when I was here, and I haven't been here very many times."

"Well . . . he never used to."

Thinking back to the day I'd met him, I remembered how hastily he'd drawn away from Colleen. It was a distinct possibility that he'd started coming home early when he began to—well, spend time with her. A slow burn of anger started inside me at the injustice of an adulterous man ripping his child's identity away in the name of—of what? "When he saw you, what did he say?"

Toby's voice was sulky. "He called it nonsense. He said it was twisted. 'This is the last straw,' he said. 'No more of this girl stuff.' He called it a phase and said it was time I got over it." Toby's voice rose. "It's not a phase! It's not!"

"I believe you. I don't pretend to understand it, but I believe you." Suddenly, it occurred to me to ask, "You know you're not alone, right?"

"What do you mean?"

"There are lots of people who are not the same sex inside as they are on the outside. Lots of boys who are really girls, and vice versa."

"Are you sure? Where are they?"

My heart twisted. This poor kid, thinking he was unique in this trap, and yet being brave enough to go as far as he had before he'd hit this brick wall . . . "Look up the term *transgender*. I'll bet transgender kids communicate over the Internet, and I'll also bet quite a few of them are in Boston. Do you want to do that now?" Some things, I felt, were more important than spelling practice.

He practically flew to his computer and was opening link after link faster than I could follow him. Watching over his shoulder, I was astounded at the number of hits. There was the Boston Area Transgender Support group, whose Web site said they supported people teenage and older. There was the Boston Alliance of GLBT Youth. There was TransAction, sponsored by Gay and Lesbian Adolescent Social Services. There was Massachusetts Transgender Legal Advocates, a group of lawyers dedicated to protecting the rights of transgender people. The list went on.

And suddenly the screen stopped changing. Toby stood and threw his arms around me. He sobbed and sobbed, and held me tighter and tighter. How long, I wondered, had he been in pain like this, not understanding how this could have happened to him, how this could be true in a world where—for all he knew—no one else was like him, terrified of being himself, terrified of what would happen to him if he allowed—if *she* allowed herself to be open, to relax for even one second? And now—now to see that this is a real thing, a phenomenon that's as true and as real for other people as it is for her?

I have a damned good imagination. And I could barely imagine what this must be like. When I realised I was gay, it's true that I had felt alone at first, and I had believed I needed to hide the truth. But I was sure in the knowledge that there were lots of others like me, that someday I would be able to come out, and that when I did there would be a community of people like me, and other people who accepted me even if they weren't gay. Mind you, I know gay people have to put up with a lot of shit, but so far I've encountered precious little of it. And it was never like this, like it is for Kay, for me. Never.

I led Kay over to the bed and reached for the box of tissues. When she was able to speak, she said, "Thank you. I didn't know. I thought—" and she went into a fresh bout of weeping. "I thought it was just me. I thought I was just weird."

I laughed. "You might be weird, Kay Lloyd, but if so, it's not because of this."

Taking a ragged breath, she said, "Now I just need to figure out how to get to them."

"Them?"

"My people." She got off the bed and stood in front of me again. "I have to meet them. I *have* to, do you understand?" Her voice was intense, strained, desperate.

"I do. So figure out which organisations are working with people your age, and contact them."

She nodded, but despite the conviction of a moment ago, she looked anxious. "What if he finds out about this, too?"

I didn't suppose it would help much that her father hadn't forbidden her to contact anyone about it. Then I remembered that she had said her mother suspected something. "Listen, what do you think your mother would do if she found out?"

"I told you. I promised I wouldn't tell."

"Hypothetically. What do you think she would say?"

"I—I don't know. But it might make them fight."

"So you think she'd be more accepting than your father?"

"I think so. But I don't want them to fight any more than they already are."

More than they already are . . . I shook myself mentally. This is not my problem! "Well, maybe it's enough for now that you know there are others like you out there."

"But I told you, I have to meet them!"

"Life's full of compromises, Toby. Kay. Full of choices that conflict. Either you keep your head down between now and the semifinals, or you risk not getting there at all. Of course, you know, if you don't make it past the March bee—"

"That's not an option!"

"Fine. I was just going to say you'd have less left to lose in that case. But, as I said, if you want to be yourself on that stage, you need to get there, first. So, do you feel up to some practice? I have some really tough words for you today."

We worked for a little while, though Kay wasn't up to her best performance. No biscuit break today. At one point there was a thump against the door, and Kay said, "That's La La. Can you let her in?"

I opened the door, and La La trotted across the room and scooted under the bed. Kay and I went back to practising, and soon La La came out and rubbed against my leg. I picked her up, and she settled onto my lap like she was born for it. I could go on reading words to Kay like this, but with La La on my lap, that dictionary was unmanageable. I was about to put La La down, but Kay stopped me.

"It's okay. I'll spell the words and then look them up myself to make sure I have the etymology right. That's almost as good. You hold her. I know you miss Tinker Bell." Then she added, "I just noticed your hair's different. I like it."

This week Dr. Metcalf asked me about my college admissions progress. He was rather irritated to learn I hadn't seriously considered any place other than Oxford.

"Simon, since you don't seem to have anywhere in particular in mind, I'm going to suggest a few schools, and I want you to apply to them. No one—and I mean, no one with any sense—applies only to one school." He started digging through some files as he asked, "Are you enjoying working with Toby?"

"Reasonably," I said, hoping he wouldn't ask me to explain that;

with yesterday's development still on my mind, I wasn't sure what I might reveal.

"What are his chances, do you think?"

"Not knowing very much about the competition, I couldn't say."

"I'm going to send you a link to videos of the competition this past May, the semifinals and finals. I think you're on the right track with the training approach, but I want to make sure you're working hard enough to help him. Watch your e-mail."

And he did send it, and I watched it, and he was right. I did have to work harder. And this was fine, because I was trying to keep my mind from focusing on Michael.

Plus now I guess I'll have to complete some more applications. Dr. Metcalf handed me information about several, and I think I'll do just a few. Maybe Princeton, and Yale, and Stanford. I'm deliberately avoiding Harvard, of course. I think Princeton would be my first choice of these. They have an early-admission process, which I really want to do so I know something as soon as possible. This means I can't apply early admission to the other two; so be it.

This afternoon, shouldering my bag on my way out of the building after school, I heard my name called by a now familiar voice. And when I turned, I saw it was, indeed, Michael. My heart racing, I waited for him to approach me. It had been a full week since our museum visit, since I'd caused a scene with Dick the dick, since I'd walked out on Michael and Chas.

He grinned a lopsided grin at me.

"What do you want?" I hadn't intended to be antagonistic; it was almost as though I couldn't help myself.

But my response didn't seem to dampen his mood. "Well . . . what *I* want isn't the question. I thought *you* wanted to meet my *nonna* and ask her questions about emigrating from Italy. *And* get a really great Italian meal at the same time. She's very excited about meeting you." He looked harder at me. "New do. Looks good."

It took me a second to realise he meant my hair. I stepped out of the way of other pedestrians and dropped my bag to the ground. "So . . . you're not angry with me?"

He shrugged. "You were a bit of a prick last week; that's for sure. I was a little pissed, yeah. I don't think you gave Chas a very good chance to explain X."

"I gave him every chance. But not only is it not going to be something I can use for my class work, but also nothing he said helped me understand what's good about it, other than keeping kids off of drugs and booze."

"That's a lot!"

"Sure, sorry, I didn't mean that's small beer. As it were. But as I've already told you, I'm gay, and not only do I not intend to try and do anything about that, I don't think there's any reason I should want to. I'm pretty sure he and X both disagree with me."

"And that makes X bad?"

"Michael, anything, anyone who tries to force you to be something you're not is bad. But that's not the only reason—" I searched the sky for words. "Here's the thing, Michael. When Chas said that Xers have no friends and he wants to shout, 'In your face, fuckers,' I get that. Because I also get 'We're here; we're queer; get used to it.' Both of these make good battle cries at a pep rally for the indoctrinated. For the members. These battle cries don't do so well when your audience is anyone outside the group, unless you actually *want* to make enemies. I don't know if all Xers are looking to make enemies, but it sure sounds like a lot of them are. And besides that, Chas wants me to allow him his battle cry, but he won't let me have mine."

From the look on his face, either Michael didn't see what I meant, or he disagreed with me. I tried again. "It sounded to me as though the only thing that connects one X group to another—outside of the behaviour modification—is the music. X would seem to have nothing to do with the growth of a city's social structure, and little or nothing about it connects one city to another. So it doesn't help my project, but, okay, that's not a judgement. What bothers me is that mostly X seems to be about cheesing off everyone who isn't in the club. And Chas proved it by telling me I should turn my back on my true self. It's just another kind of fundamentalism. 'Belong to our club, do what we say, or fuck off.' "

"Y'know, you don't exactly bring out the best in people."

"What's that supposed to mean?"

"You walk around with this chip on your shoulder. It doesn't take much to set you off, and when you're set off, you let everyone know it. Maybe Chas was just reacting to that."

"Chas thinks he's persecuted because he's X. Tell him to google Matthew Shepard." I picked up my satchel. "I hope your *nonna* hasn't gone to a lot of trouble. Please apologise to her. *She's* done nothing to 'set me off.' " I turned my back on him and started to walk away.

"See, now, this is what I mean." He caught up with me and walked alongside.

"I don't see. The *chip* is on *Chas's* shoulder. It's shaped like an *X*. And anyone who disagrees with him is just plain wrong."

He sighed. "All right, so be pissed at Chas if you want. But don't disappoint my *nonna*."

It took several more paces for me to get off my high horse. "Fine. When's dinner?"

"Saturday? Is that all right?"

I hadn't mentioned anything about this to Mum or Brian or Ned, but I didn't expect any pushback. Saturday, though . . . Date night. Interesting.

"I'm sure it will be. I'll ring you if there's any problem. Where should we meet?"

"Where do you live?"

I hesitated for just a moment as a combination of *Do I want him to know where I live* and *Do I want him to know how different our financial situations are* flashed through my brain. Then another voice prompted, *What difference does it make? You don't think this is going anyplace, do you?* And then it occurred to me that if Ned were around and had a chance to meet Michael, he might be able to give me his impression: Is Michael straight, or just Straight Edge? This would be worth breaking my intention not to talk to Ned about Michael.

"If you walk another few blocks, you'll see."

"You live here? On Marlborough Street?"

"Yes."

"Holy shit."

"No, I think that location is at least half a mile away."

It wasn't that funny, but he laughed anyway. "I guess I should have known. It fits."

I decided not to pursue that; didn't want to get "set off" again. "It's not actually my house, you know. It's my stepfather's. Will you text me your grandmother's address?"

"It's kind of hard to find Nonna's if you don't know the North End. I'll stop by your place."

I debated whether to point out that I could take a taxi and probably find anything, but I just said, "What time?"

"Five thirty? That way we can have some antipasto and talk for a bit. I've asked her to make manicotti; it's her signature dish."

"I'll text you in the morning if there's any problem. Or you can walk me home now and go in with me, and we can be sure right away." This would be tantamount to "meeting the parents." Would he do it?

There was just a slight hesitation, and then, "Okay. Sure."

If he was impressed by Brian's house, he gave no indication. I walked him through to the kitchen, where I expected Ned would be, and he was. I introduced them, told Ned that Michael was helping me gather resource material for a school project, and left them alone whilst I went to talk to Mum, who was on the patio.

It took me two seconds to secure permission for my Italian dinner, though I noticed that Mum seemed rather down. "Everything okay?" I asked, not really sure I wanted to know.

She sighed. "I think Brian's just about decided on Anna's replacement."

"Is this a bad thing?"

"It's just that I've spent a lot of time with Persie this week, and I think we're getting on very well. I suppose I was holding out hope that I'd at least have more time with her, even if Brian doesn't think I could manage the job itself."

"Well . . . Even if you're not in the job officially, can't you still spend time with her?"

"It won't be the same."

Well, of course not, but . . . "Mum, I don't mean to be imperti-nent, really, but are you trying to make up for Clive?"

"Brian accused me of that, too."

"Hey, I wasn't accusing."

"Do you really think I hadn't considered it? And as a matter of fact, it's watching you with her that's inspired me. You don't even seem to be trying, and yet you've made a lot of headway with her. She trusts you. I've watched how that has happened, and I under-stand at least some of it. As you put it once, I'm going to be 'sad-dled' with her for the rest of my life. So why not be as involved as possible? It would be better for everyone."

Carefully not allowing myself to get set off, I said, "Okay, but you could be involved with her in ways other than tutoring her. Anna was a whole lot more than a tutor, but it was only Persie and Brian in the house then. What's this new person's role?"

"That's the problem. Brian and I disagree over the best candi-date. He wants a woman who would be another Anna. I voted for someone who wouldn't live here and would be here on weekdays only. My candidate would also be available for temporary overnight stays. If Brian and I were to go away for a week, for example, we could arrange for her to stay in the house. Brian thinks that would be too much irregularity for Persie."

"I don't." I didn't know where that came from, but there it was. I agreed with Mum that Persie didn't need quite as much protec-tion as Brian believed.

"You . . . you agree with me?" Her astonishment seemed gen-uine.

"In principle. I haven't met these candidates, and of course Brian knows Persie better than we do. But, yes, I think Persie could handle it. Though, of course, if it doesn't work out for some reason, that's more change for Persie, because you'd have to find another Anna after all."

Mum nodded. "Yes, but I can't help thinking that if we don't expose Persie to a manageable level of challenge, she won't grow. She won't learn to function at a higher level. Even autistic individ-uals can often learn to interact. Look at Temple Grandin."

"So you've explored this difference? Between AS and other forms of autism, I mean?"

"While you've been at school, I've had several consultations with experts who specialise in supporting people with AS. I don't put myself forwards as an expert by any means, but yes, I understand the difference. And I think Persie can grow."

Wow. Like, wow. And I never use "like" like that. "Where is she now?"

"As of twenty minutes ago, she was in her rooms reading a book that's a visual history of paleontology. She was telling me about a bacterium that still exists today that appeared 3.8 billion years ago, the earliest known form of life on Earth."

I didn't quite know what else to say about this situation, and I had to get back to the kitchen. "Um, anyway, I need to let Michael know we're on. He's in the kitchen."

"Aren't you bringing him out? I want to meet him."

"He's just a friend, Mum."

"I can't meet your friends?" It didn't escape my notice that she gave no indication of surprise that I would even *have* a friend.

The last thing I want is for Mum or anyone else to fixate on Michael as a romantic figure in my life. I don't need anyone encouraging me to think that way. But there didn't seem any way out of this introduction. "Fine; I'll get him."

"Never mind; I'll come in with you."

I trusted Ned not to say anything awkward, even though he must know that I find Michael attractive. He didn't disappoint. Mum asked Michael a few questions about his studies, and then about his art. She actually said she'd love to see some of his work, that she and Brian are very fond of contemporary art. He responded enthusiastically whilst I groaned inwardly; I do not want this guy integrated into what passes for family in my life.

After Michael left, promising to return at half five tomorrow, I went back into the kitchen, hoping to find Ned alone. He wasn't, but Mum didn't hang around for very long before going back outside.

Ned raised an eyebrow. "You were planning to keep Romeo a secret for—how long, exactly?"

Funny how we'd both landed on the same metaphorical name. "Yeah, about that . . ." I rummaged around for something sweet, found a fresh batch of brownies that I know Mum made, and settled myself on a stool at the island. "He's not gay, you know."

"Oh, honey, tell me another one."

"I'm just telling you what he told me." So Ned agreed with me; Michael is fooling only himself. I took a bite of brownie, examining the other half; you can *see* the richness in Mum's brownies. "He almost was, you see. But then he found Straight Edge."

Ned was silent so long that I lifted my gaze from the brownie to look at him, and his expression told me he did not like what he'd just heard. Finally, he said, "Those groups have caused problems in a lot of places."

I knew what Chas had said, but I wondered if Ned had anything specific to relate. "Boston one of them?"

"I don't recall."

"What kind of problems?"

"I gather their, um, music get-togethers can get quite rowdy. Very loud, very animated. And every once in a while you hear about some group of them starting fights. From what I've heard, they don't take kindly to suggestions that they consider how their activities affect other people."

"Mmmm," I agreed, swallowing the second half of my brownie. "I gather they revel in their lack of friends. Proud of it, even. But I think the beating-up part might be done by just a few hardliners."

"And is Romeo trying to get you to join their ranks?"

My snort nearly brought up brownie crumbs. "Wouldn't matter if he were; they're so not my style. I met one of Michael's X cohorts last week. X is how they refer to it, at least sometimes. Between the guy's appearance and his attitude, I'll be staying pretty far away from that crowd."

"But not far away from Michael."

"You know, that's what's odd. I keep trying to stay away from him, and he keeps following me around. Waits for me outside school. That sort of thing."

Ned laughed, delighted. "Well, you are irresistible, Simon." Before I had time to enjoy that, he turned serious. "You could get cut bad on this one, sweetie. Even if he's not really straight."

We locked eyes for a few seconds. I asked, "What did you think of him?"

"Gorgeous is as gorgeous does, my dear. How does he treat you?"

"He doesn't 'treat' me at all. We don't have that kind of relationship."

"Mmmm-*hmm*. How many piercings does he have?"

I blinked, surprised that I hadn't wondered this myself. "I don't know of any. But then, all I've seen of him is his face, his neck, his . . . Well, all right, I've seen his chest. But I didn't see any metal."

"I saw the tattoo. Didn't realise what it meant."

"The *X* on his neck."

"Yup. See any more of those?"

"No other ink I've seen, no. Um, you haven't told me what you think."

Ned turned towards the sink, picked up a knife, and went to work chopping something. Affecting an accent that isn't the Ned I know, he said, "It won't do me no good to tell you what I think. You're gonna do what you're gonna do, and you're gonna get hurt doin' it. Tha's all there is to it."

This irritated me. I'd been counting on him for support. Support for what, exactly, I couldn't have said, but still. . . . "Mum seemed to like him." I tried hard not to sound sulky; not sure I succeeded.

"She asked about his art. Don't take that for liking him."

"Well, for your information, I have no intention of putting myself in harm's way here. It doesn't matter whether you or Mum or anyone else approves of him as a boyfriend for me, because that's not where this is headed."

Ned stood very still for a few seconds. Then he set down the knife, walked over to me, and wrapped his arms as far around me as he could. "You do what you need to do, kid. I'll be here when you need me."

He went back to chopping, and I grabbed another brownie and

headed upstairs. When I fired up my laptop and checked for e-mail, I saw Margaret had sent more photos of Tink.

Sweet Margaret. Sweeter Tink.

I'm up. It's half two in the friggin' morning.

These are not my problems! Toby/Kay, Mr. Lloyd. Persie, Brian, Mum. Why are they keeping me up? Initially I had trouble dozing off because I was fixating on Michael. But that led to my conversation with Ned, and then to my conversation with Mum about Persie, and somehow I ended up having an imaginary conversation with Mr. Lloyd in which I gave him what-for. Of course, I always win these imaginary conversations.

The next thing I knew, I was having one with Brian. I told him he had a blind spot when it came to his daughter. I told him he was keeping her in a bubble without knowing whether she really needed to stay in there, or if she just needed it as a safe harbour. I told him he loved his place in her life more than he loved her. Of course, that's when he exploded and I couldn't reason with him any longer, so I'm not sure I could be said to have won that one. But Mum's approach is making more and more sense to me. Why wouldn't Brian want his daughter to grow?

Just to get away from that situation, I went back to Michael, but everything about him is so vague. Why is he stalking me? Because, really, he is. *Am* I irresistible? No one has ever seemed to think so before. But Ned does. And maybe Michael does.

I'll have dinner with his *nonna*. I'll see whether there's enough material there to be useful to my project. I'm so torn, though! If there is, I might be seeing more of Michael. And if there isn't . . . I'll almost certainly be seeing more of Michael, anyway. And the more of him I see, the less of a good idea it seems, unless he'd be willing to be true to himself instead of to X.

Seeing more of Michael, and taking that literally and physically, has . . . um . . . brought up something else. Think I'll go join Graeme in bed now.

Boston, Saturday, 22 September

After breakfast, which Mum and I had alone because Brian has
been having breakfast with Persie in her rooms since Anna left,
Mum asked me if I would stand guard near the bottom of the stairs
whilst she and Brian discussed the question of whom to hire.
They'd be in the kitchen, the farthest room from Persie's.

Mum said, "We just don't want her to have to hear all the ins
and outs of the situation."

"Why don't you go into the den instead? You could shut the
door."

"She's upstairs, reading, and if she comes out I want you to be
able to let us know immediately."

I reckoned it was a crap shoot either way. "Has anyone asked
her what *she* wants?"

"Interesting you would ask that. I wanted to. Brian said no. He
said that once she expresses a preference, the decision would be
out of our hands."

"Well, that's probably true. So the solution would be not to suggest a candidate you couldn't live with."

"I know, I know. It's—he's so afraid for her."

Everything I've heard from Mum about the next stage of Persie's care has sounded better to me than Brian's position. I looked
at Mum with a new sense of respect and said, "Let me go and
fetch some work, and I'll set up in the music room where I can see
the stairs."

When I got downstairs with my laptop and a few books, Mum
and Brian were at the kitchen table. The kitchen is on the other
side of the living room from the music room, and at first their
voices were low, so I was able to concentrate on homework. Then
I heard Mum's voice, raised, say, "That's not fair! You can't keep
holding that over my head! Persie is *not* Clive. She's not autistic;
she has AS."

Brian shushed her, and they were quiet again for a bit, but gradually the volume rose enough for me to tell that the conflict Mum

had described to me yesterday was still alive and well. I kept glancing up the stairs towards Persie's door, which remained shut.

I renewed my attempts to concentrate on my homework, but I could no longer quite ignore the discussion in the kitchen, which was definitely louder now than when it had started. At one point Mum asked a question that sounded particularly challenging.

"Brian, where do you see her ten years from now?"

"Here." His answer was very quick, spoken possibly without thought at all.

"Do you see her as ever being able to live apart from us?"

"I don't see how."

"It's likely that she'll outlive both of us."

"I've provided for that. She has a generous trust fund, and I've appointed people to manage her care for the rest of her life."

"Do you think that when she's, maybe, twenty-five or thirty, she might rebel and want a little more autonomy?"

At last, something he didn't have a quick answer for. "It seems unlikely."

"Or she could begin to feel like that after we're gone. And that could happen suddenly—a plane crash, something like that. She'd be on her own abruptly. She'd have been insulated all her life, completely, and there would be no safe way for her to find out how well she might manage without complete and total support."

Mum waited, perhaps to see if he'd take it from there, and I looked up to watch, not able merely to listen any longer. After a pause all he said was, "What's your point?"

"If you open the door for her *now*, just a little, to give her more latitude, she might be able to grow. And if she can't, if that turns out to be something she just can't manage, she still has a safe place to retreat to."

"I don't want her to *have* to retreat. That's *my* point."

Mum stood and paced the floor, clenching her hands and no doubt trying to come up with another angle to get him to understand the importance of what she was saying to him.

I tried to reconcile this Brian with the Brian I'd thought he was: someone who was open to new things; someone who would meet a woman in a foreign country, woo her, marry her, carry her home, with every expectation that it would work. Someone who even knew how to talk about my cat in a way I couldn't argue with. It didn't make any sense. And that's when I couldn't just sit there and listen any longer.

Abandoning my post, I headed into the kitchen and stopped at the far end of the island, facing the table. Brian looked at me, evidently surprised I would just step into this conversation—this confrontation—so boldly.

"You might remember," I said to him, "that I once told you that Persie is a cat. What I meant by that was that she makes the rules, and they're more or less sacred. What I didn't tell you was that she's a cat who needs an authority adjustment."

As I spoke, Mum headed towards the music room, no doubt to take up my guard post. Brian sat back and crossed his arms on his chest.

"That's ridiculous, Simon. You—"

I talked over him. "If you take a cat out of its environment, it freaks. But then it adjusts. And it makes new rules, based on its new environment. And when that happens, its caretakers have a chance to influence what rules it makes. Anna's leaving has changed Persie's environment, and she's busy now making new rules. This is your chance to introduce change, because she'll see it as part of the change that's already happening. And it might be the best opening you'll ever have to give her a chance. To give her a chance to grow. And if it doesn't work, then, yes, there's one more change. It will involve another new person, but it would just be the same old routine."

"Simon, we can't have just anyone in here."

"That's what you're for, to make sure that doesn't happen. And from what I gather, you haven't asked her yet which candidate *she* likes. But that aside, there's no reason you can't find the right person. You have the luxury of time, with Mum here to bridge the gap." Would he say anything to *me* about Clive?

He didn't say anything right away, so I took another risk. "And, given that you work, and presuming you don't chase Mum away, presuming that she stays longer than the next tutor, isn't she providing the best kind of bridge—a consistent one?"

He stared at me for several seconds and then leaned forwards, elbows on the table, rubbing his forehead with his fingers. I waited; he who speaks first, now, loses. And, finally, he spoke.

"I can't stand to see her suffer." His voice was tight, as though holding emotion in check.

With an effort, I kept my tone soft. "No doubt I haven't seen the worst she can get, but I've seen enough to know what it might be like. Even so, would you rather see her stagnate? Would you rather see her dry up and fade?"

He looked at me, but I had the sense he wasn't seeing *me*. And suddenly what *I* saw was Persie in the Clyfford Still Museum in Denver. "Should she be robbed of any chance to explore her creativity?"

He stood quickly and went to the patio door, facing outside. His back to me, he leaned both hands on the doorway. And I lobbed one more volley at him.

"Is it her pain or yours that frightens you more?"

He spun around. "That's enough!" His whisper was hoarse and forceful, but even in his fury he was mindful of his daughter upstairs, not wanting her to hear this strife.

It was on the tip of my tongue to say, "Is it? Is it enough?" But instead I left the room, knowing that anything else I might say would be pointless at best. So, yes, it was enough. Maybe more than enough.

Mum was standing in the doorway to the music room. As I got closer, she reached out and ran a hand down my arm. "Thank you. Thank you for trying, and for supporting me."

Supporting her had not been my objective, but I decided against pointing that out. "I hope it all works out," was the inane response that came out instead.

She nodded. "Give him some time. He's a good man, Simon. He really wants to do what's best for her."

And once again, it hit me how what was best for me had been ignored. Nearly knocked me over. "Of course." I collected my things. "Think I'll go out for a while."

"Anyplace special?"

"No." Afraid of saying something that would cause a fight and benefit no one, I left her standing there, dropped off my school-work upstairs, and headed out the front door.

I had no idea where I was going. All I knew was that I needed to try and get away from my own thoughts, my own emotions. I walked hard and fast, down Marlborough Street a few blocks, and then turned south where I saw more people; I wasn't looking to in-teract with anyone, but I felt I needed the distraction a crowd of strangers can provide.

As it happens, I'd turned onto Dartmouth Street, and after I crossed the green island at Commonwealth it wasn't long before I was at Copley Square, where the stone Trinity Church, from the 1870s, is dwarfed by that glass Tower of Babel called the John Hancock building. Turning slowly away from this juxtaposition, my attention went next across Dartmouth to the Boston Public Li-brary, a place I'd been meaning to visit. So I did.

Boston became a completely different city to me that afternoon. The library's initial statement alone—with the main entrance flanked by huge sculptures of human female forms representing Art and Science—impressed me beyond any expectations I'd had. The fact that it was the first public library in the world was what had made me want to see it, and I'd heard it was full of art, but I wasn't prepared for what I saw. Inside, it was apparent that this li-brary is at least as much a museum, and form and function become one in no better way than here.

Lions guard the massive marble grand staircase, which is so large it dwarfs people as surely as the Hancock dwarfs Trinity. The stone is rich with colour and patterns, and where walls follow up-wards around the staircase there are huge murals; it took me some time to get up the stairs for gazing at the art.

The place is chock-full of sculpture as well as painted art. I stopped before *The Child and the Swan* sculpture and wondered if Michael had seen it. I wanted to take it home.

There's a café that's also a map room. A café in a library . . .
unique, surely. There's a courtyard, in Italian Renaissance style,
that feels almost like a cathedral cloister, with any ecclesiastical
misapprehension dispersed by the delightful, pagan-inspired *Bac-
chante and Infant Faun* sculpture in the middle of the fountain.

I could go on for days, but one thing I knew was that if Michael
had not yet seen this place, we would explore it together. With
that in mind, I denied myself further investigation other than to
see the main reading room. It goes on for days under a ceiling
vaulted so high I couldn't guess at the distance from the marble
floor to the huge arches overhead. I walked slowly down the centre, with long wooden tables on either side lit by green shaded
lamps, enjoying the hush of books being opened and shut, pages
being turned, the low, almost whispered sound of the occasional
quiet conversation. And then, in a whisper that carried, I heard my
name.

At first I didn't react; who here, I reasoned, would know me,
and how many people must there be in Boston named Simon? But
it was repeated with more urgency, and when I looked in that direction I saw it was Toby. He wasn't alone.

Grinning from ear to ear, no doubt struggling to contain his bois-
terous spirit in this place of reverent hush, he introduced me to a
Dean Furley, who appeared to be a few years older than I am.
Toby pulled me immediately down into a chair beside him, and
Dean resumed his seat across the table.

"Simon, this is so fabulous! Guess who Dean is?"

I shook my head. "I'm terrified to try. Please tell me."

Toby smiled broadly at Dean and back at me. "I met him in a
transgender chat room. He's going to help me. Dean was born a
girl. Diane. Can you believe it?" To Dean he said, "Simon is the
spelling coach I told you about." Back to me: "Simon, I hope it's
okay that I told Dean you're gay."

I glanced at Dean again, and he smiled. It was apparent that
he'd had hormone treatments; the muscle definition was remark-
able, and he obviously shaved that dark beard frequently.

"I don't think it's a problem that you told him," I said to Toby, "but it's a better policy not to out someone else."

"I'm sorry." Before I could think what else to say, Toby shoved a periodical towards me, open to an article by Norman Spack, MD, titled "Transgenderism." He didn't give me a chance to read, launching right into what it was that had captured his attention in particular.

"The thing is, Simon, that I have to do what Dean did. His parents let him get hormone treatments before he hit puberty as a girl. If you wait, that's a huge mistake! Without the treatments, your body develops fully the wrong way, and even if you do sex-change surgery, it's really hard for a man's face to look feminine. The only reason to wait is if you're not really, really sure. And you know I'm really, really sure, right? So this is what I need to do!" He stabbed the journal with his finger as though the force of that alone would make this therapy happen for him.

I picked up the journal, scanned for Spack's credentials, and nearly gasped; he's right here, at Boston Children's Hospital. I set the paper down again.

"So, what are you going to do?" By which I meant not so much what did he want to do as what was he going to be able to do, given his home situation.

"I guess I'm gonna have to come out to my folks. I have to tell them. Because I have to get these treatments. Dean's going to help."

Dean is, is he? Dean probably looked about how the Parents Lloyd were expecting Toby to look in several years.

I asked Dean, "What are you going to be able to do for Toby?"

He shook his head. "I'm going to help *Kay*. If her parents react badly, and if they won't let her see me again, I'll find someone else who can help. Maybe a woman next time, M to F." I understood this to mean male to female.

Dean went on as if reciting promotional material. "We have lots of educational material, including information about what's in store for people who are forced to mature against their sexual identities. I can give the Lloyds references to specialists, to counselling if they're open, or just to medical people. I know people who can put them in touch with parents who've seen their children safely into new identities. And if necessary, there are parents willing to talk about what happened when they didn't support their transgender child, and how they wish they had." It hung in the air why they might have wished this, and I presumed that suicide was involved.

Then Dean lobbed another information bomb. "Did you know that the brain structure of transgender individuals is that of their desired gender, not of their apparent one?"

I blinked at him, stupidly. "I did not." If that's true for everyone who's transgender, I have to say it's rather compelling. To Kay, I said, "When are you going to do this? Tell your parents, I mean?"

"Tonight." Her face was set into an expression that was hopeful, determined, and terrified all at once.

"And I'll be available," Dean told me, "to hear how it went and help figure out the next steps."

I couldn't imagine that it would go well. "What if Kay's parents prevent her from contacting you afterwards?"

"I'll find her at school if necessary. Don't worry. I won't leave her on her own."

Well, I *was* worried; I'd seen how afraid Kay is of her father, even when she's not expecting him to explode. Just introducing me to him had taken courage. This wasn't my business. Even so, I couldn't avoid asking this question. "Kay, has your father ever struck you?"

"When I was younger. Spankings, sometimes. That's all."

"And are you afraid he's going to?"

"I—not exactly."

Hardly a rousing vote of confidence. "Why were you so reluctant to introduce me to him?"

Kay's voice rose a little. "It's because he's so mean about letting me be who I am." Dean hushed her, and she relaxed a little. "My mom's the one who let me decorate my room. She fought with Father about it. They had another fight when she found out he'd made Colleen take it all away again."

"Does he strike your mother?"

"No. He doesn't hit people, Simon. Why do you think that?"

"I don't. I'm just trying to understand where your fear is coming from." I looked at Dean. "And I should think Dean would want to know whether there's any danger in this outpouring you're planning."

Dean said, "We've talked about that. I didn't overlook it."

I had another question for him. "Are you straight?"

"Yes. I like girls."

"Girls like Kay?"

I had expected this to take Dean by surprise, but it didn't. "I have a girlfriend. And Kay is far too young for me."

"And how does Kay feel about you? She's straight, too, you know."

Kay interrupted. "Simon, really, you don't have to worry."

Dean smiled at me. "I like that you're so protective of her."

I ignored that and said, "I'm assuming that there are trans men who like men, and trans women who like women."

That annoyed him. "Of course there are. We're all just people, you know."

I nodded at him and looked at Kay. "All right, then. I guess I'll find out next Thursday how things went, eh?"

"You don't want me to call you tonight?"

"I'll be out tonight."

"On a date?"

"Sort of." No point in trying to explain. "You can e-mail me, if you'd like. How's that?"

"It's a plan!"

I stood, and Kay stood, and impulsively I embraced her. "Good luck, Kay. I hope it goes really well."

She smiled bravely and nodded. I shook Dean's hand and left the reading room, reminding myself yet again that this was not my problem, not my worry, not my concern.

But I was worried.

*　*　*

Back at the house, Brian called to me from the music room as I closed the front door. "Simon, is that you?"

I stood in the doorway and saw he was in an upholstered wing chair, listening to Chopin's nocturnes. It looked like that was all he was doing; there was no sign of reading material or a computer, nothing to distract him.

"Come in, please."

Without going too far into the room—not knowing what to expect—I kept as much distance between us as was reasonable without being impolite.

"Your mother's gone to the Museum of Fine Arts," he opened.

I think he would have continued, but I was too shocked and had to interrupt. "On a Saturday? She never goes to museums on weekends."

"I think she needed the escape. And while she's been gone, I've decided that she—and you—are right about asking Persie about the candidates."

Wow. I was right about something? And he admitted it? "Thanks. For telling me. I, um, need to go get ready to go out."

"Ah, yes, your date."

"It's not a date. He's just a friend."

"Sorry. Really. I don't mean to presume. But—I thought you were meeting his family."

"I'm meeting *with* his grandmother to hear her experiences in immigrating to the US from Italy. She might be able to provide material I can use for a school project. The dinner is just a fun way to do that."

"I see. Well, enjoy yourself."

As I climbed the stairs, my brain bounced back and forth. *Brian took me seriously and is going to do what Mum and I recommended* alternated with *I'm sure she'll choose the non-Anna option, and then what if it turns out Brian was right?* I do not want that monkey on my back. If something goes wrong with this approach for Persie, will Brian blame me? I guess I could take that, but will he blame Mum? Do I care? And will I blame myself?

Ye gods, but I wish none of this had ever happened. I wish to hell we could have stayed where we were, where the only creature other than myself that I had to concern myself with was Tink. Now, not only is there Persie, and Mum's situation—having given up everything, including me, really, to start this new life—but also there's Toby/Kay and the horror of that situation. And there's Michael, beautiful, gay Michael, attracted to me, lying to himself about why, headed for some kind of brick wall for sure.

I don't like having to worry about all these other people. I don't like it at all.

And now I had to get freshened up to go and meet Michael's *nonna*. He hasn't said a lot, but his tone of voice when he's talked about her, the things he's said—all of it speaks to a tenderness that I think goes very deep. I'm kind of afraid to meet her. Does she know anything about who Michael really is? Will she guess about me? And what would that mean to her?

To distract myself, I located the North End on my mass transit map. There did not seem to be any good way to get there. I wondered if Michael would spring for a taxi.

I was laying out the clothes I'd wear when my mobile rang. It was Michael, cancelling. His grandmother had had a stroke.

"I called her to see if she needed me to bring anything. I didn't get an answer. When I got there—Simon, it was horrible! She was collapsed on the floor. Barely breathing. Dad and Naomi—my sister—met me at the emergency room. I'm outside now; they didn't want me to use my cell phone inside."

"I'm so sorry, Michael. Is she conscious?"

"No. And there's no telling how long it might be"—his voice caught, and he paused for a few seconds—"before we know if she'll even wake up. And she might not be able to talk, or move." He sounded on the verge of tears.

"I don't know what to say. Is there anything I can do?"

"No. I just wanted you to know so you wouldn't wonder where I was."

"Please let me know how things look for her, when you know more. I won't try to call you in case you're inside the hospital."

We rang off, and I put my clothes away. Out on the roof garden,

I leaned on that granite-topped brick wall, stared sightlessly at nearby buildings, and considered this development. Obviously, it was horrible for everyone in the family, but beyond that I couldn't help seeing it as one more in the series of things that never quite work out between Michael and me. It was as if the universe is agreeing with me that he is not for me, telling me to move forwards with my own issues and not get distracted by his trials and tribulations.

It was fairly warm this afternoon, so after I let Brian know I wouldn't be going out after all and why, I went back to my room, collected everything I'd need to do some schoolwork, and took it out onto the roof.

I was in my seat at the dinner table three minutes early; evidently that doesn't bother Miss Persie, even though she doesn't make an appearance until exactly half six. And perhaps I should have gone out someplace, even if it couldn't be the North End, because I goofed twice, referring to arugula as roquette and saying "amongst" instead of "among" at some point. The "roquette" annoyed her, but she didn't have a total tantrum over it, perhaps because it's really just the French word instead of the Italian word for that green. All she did was bring her fist down hard on the table with her fork pointing to the ceiling. But "amongst" put her over some edge, and she screamed, "Among! Among! Among!" There was no Anna any longer, and no replacement yet, so Brian was on his own. He spoke soothingly, to no avail. Mum started to get involved, but she didn't seem to know what to do, either.

Maybe it was just that the whole day had seemed like some kind of cock-up, but suddenly I'd had enough of Persie's tyranny. I stood, landed my hands hard on either side of my plate, and glared at her. She stopped shouting, gave me a nasty pout, waited for me to sit, and declared, "Among!" one more time as though getting the last word. But she settled down to her dinner again. As long as she shut up . . .

Brian and Mum looked at me like they didn't quite know what had just happened, but no one said anything—probably terrified of disturbing the quiet.

Around nine o'clock I felt a little peckish and headed down to the kitchen to see what I could scrounge. Brian and Mum were in the music room, dancing to band music from the 1940s. My breathing grew odd. It was almost like watching her with my father; they used to dance to this music. My appetite gone, I decided to sneak back upstairs without being seen; maybe I'd come down later and try again.

I started up the stairs but got no farther than the top of the first flight. Persie was on the love seat there, evidently waiting for me.

"Simon." It was more of a statement than a greeting, but from Persie that was normal.

"Persie," I responded, my tone just as flat. I kept moving towards the stairs to the top floor, hoping I was wrong about why she was there. But she spoke again.

"Help."

That got my attention. "What?"

"Help."

"You need my help? Is that what you're saying?"

"Yes."

This was not what I wanted, at the end of a difficult day topped off with what I'd just witnessed downstairs. But for Persie to ask for help . . . This seemed highly unusual. I stood where I was and waited.

"I want a real tutor this time. A tutor only."

"You mean, not someone who lives here? Not like Anna?" She nodded. So Brian had asked her. "Did you tell your father that?"

"Yes."

"Then why do you need my help?"

"He told me to think about it. He said don't decide quickly. But I told him I don't need to think anymore. I know."

"And he said . . . ?" Ye gods, but this was like pulling teeth.

"He said please take some time and think."

"What's wrong with that?"

"I think he wants the other choice."

The idea of Persie's considering what someone else thought

about anything was inconsistent with what Brian had told me. "What makes you say that?"

"He didn't ask me why I want the other kind."

Several seconds went by whilst my brain scrambled to understand what I was hearing. "Is this the first time you knew what your father was thinking when he didn't say it directly?"

Her turn to take several seconds. And then, "I don't know."

Not much help. I tried a different tack. "So can you tell *me* why you want only the tutor?"

"I don't like being watched all the time. I want to decide what I want to do more of the time. I want to learn about things Anna doesn't know about."

I nodded; made sense to me. "What kinds of things that Anna doesn't know about?"

"Art."

Art. As simple as that. Not terribly surprising, perhaps. "Anna doesn't know about art?"

"Anna knows about art therapy. I don't need art therapy."

"So you want a tutor who knows about art?"

"I want a tutor who knows how to find art. I want to go see art."

"Like the Clyfford Still Museum," I said, and she nodded. "What about other museums, here in Boston?"

"Yes."

"My mother knows about art."

"Yes."

Mum had said she'd spent time with Persie. Part of that time must have involved art. Who could have guessed? "So what do you think I can do to help?"

"Tell him. Tell him I want art. Tell him I want to go see art. Tell him you'll come with me."

"Mum can go with you."

"Yes. I want you, too."

Christ! What I don't need right now is more of someone else's need. "Why can't *you* tell him you want art?"

"I did. I told him about the Clyfford Still Museum."

"That one time? That was all?"

"Yes."

"Tell him again, Persie. That once was a big surprise to him, and it's not likely he's thinking of it in terms of what you need right now, right here. Tell him again, and tell him about going to museums here. Just the fact that you bring it up again will mean a lot. Tell him—tell him you want to start with the public library. That's right around the corner, practically. Look it up online, and tell him specific things there that you want to go and see. That will help you."

"And you'll come?"

Think fast, Simon. "Yes, I'll go with you to the library. Now I need to go upstairs."

"All right."

As I started to turn away from her another thought came to me. "How do you feel about having breakfast downstairs, not just doing it in your rooms all the time?"

Her eyes flicked towards mine briefly; then, "I need to think about that."

I nodded. "If you decide you want to, tell your father. And the more carefully you say it, the more likely it is he'll say yes."

"Carefully?"

"Yes. Don't just say, 'I want breakfast downstairs.' Instead, say, 'Is it all right if I start having breakfast downstairs with everyone else?' If you make it a question, it sounds like you care about his opinion."

"What if he says no?"

"Well, I don't know why he would, but you wouldn't be any worse off than if you had just *told* him what you wanted and he said no. He's more likely to agree if you *ask*."

"Because I asked for his opinion."

"I tell you what, Persie. If you ask for his opinion, he'll be so startled and so amazed that he'll be likely to agree just because you asked. Trust me."

"I'll try it. Should I do it now?"

"I don't see why not. I think he's in a good mood." And it would interrupt the dancing.

"How can you tell?"

Patience. Think what it would be like not to have a clue about this sort of thing. "When I saw him, he was dancing with my mother, and they were both smiling and relaxed. And they were in the music room, not in a room with a door closed, so they weren't trying to be private about it. Does that help?"

"I don't know. But I'll try."

"Great. And now, good night." And rather than turn immediately away, I kept looking at her, willing her to say the same to me.

She started to turn towards her rooms, perhaps to look up the public library online, and I felt a keen disappointment. I had thought maybe I'd actually taught her something she could use. Rather like handing someone fishing tackle rather than just tossing them a trout. I almost sighed. But then she turned just her head towards me. "Good night."

If nothing else, I decided, I had gotten her to respond to a social greeting tonight.

I sat in the reading chair in my room with only the reading lamp on for maybe an hour, thinking over everything that had happened today, trying to sort out how I felt about all of it. Or any of it. There was the discussion with Brian about Persie, and then the fact that he actually listened to me—even if he really prefers the live-in tutor, as Persie suspects. Then there was the library, the beauty, the art, and Toby/Kay. . . . God! I need to remember to look for an e-mail from her. Then there was Michael's *nonna* practically dead on the floor. Then there was the picture of my mother dancing with someone who was not my father. And then Persie, acting almost like a person. That is, responding to life in a way I had been told she couldn't do.

A baby elephant can be kept in place by a rope around its ankle, tied to a stake stabbed deep in the ground. The baby isn't strong enough to pull the stake up. As the elephant grows, for some period of time it's still too weak to yank the stake up, but over time this is no longer true. But as long as that elephant has a rope around its ankle, it thinks it can't go anywhere, and only a sudden fright or something equally motivating would make the elephant forget the limitation of that rope and break free.

Maybe Persie is as much an elephant as a cat. And maybe the fright, or the motivation, of having to replace Anna has made her realise she's stronger than she thought. This is going to make fantastic material for my Theory of Knowledge course!

My mind went next to what it would be like to wake up in hospital, not having done anything to yourself to get there as I nearly did, and not to be able to move or speak. Unimaginable. I wondered how Signora Vitale was doing, and how Michael was reacting to it.

Michael. What did I want, anyway? Was Ned right that I was going to get hurt? And was it already too late to stop it? He's gay; I'm sure of it. But who am I to try and force him to look in that mirror? More responsibility for someone else; that's what it would be. But what about *my* feelings?

I decided I was going to have to pry this thing open. Which is to say, force Michael's hand in terms of what he does or doesn't feel for me. Because gay or not, he's attracted to me. And I want him to admit that and then say what he's willing to do about it, even if that's nothing. Then I can decide what I need to do.

I heaved a sigh and stood, giving up on the idea of coming to any conclusions on how to go about forcing Michael's anything.

At my desk, computer fired up, I checked for e-mails, and there was one from Kay. The subject was *Promise you won't be mad*. Inside, she confessed that she'd chickened out of saying anything tonight, because her parents were fighting about something and she didn't want to make things worse. I replied that she probably made the right decision (how would I know?). Even though I don't want this confession to interfere with her competition, I'm keenly aware that the longer she waits, the closer to puberty she'll get.

There was another e-mail, from Margaret, full of Tink pics. There was even a short video clip of Tink chasing a remote-controlled mouse around the kitchen floor. I would have thought this would make me cry, but instead I was laughing. Actually laughing.

I can't remember the last time that happened.

Later, I snuck downstairs to the kitchen, put some things together, added the remains of a bottle of pinot noir, threw a wet sponge and a hurricane lantern into the mix, and sent the whole thing upstairs on the dumbwaiter. On my own private rooftop deck, with Graeme in the chair across from me, I watched the moon make its way across the night sky. It was a little chilly, but I enjoyed it thoroughly.

I was nursing the last half-glass of wine when my phone rang. Michael.

"Simon, I'm sorry about the way tonight turned out."

"How's your *nonna?*"

"She's a little better. She woke up maybe an hour ago, which was a huge relief. The left side of her face is saggy, and she can't move that arm or that leg. She can't talk yet, but she can make sounds, so if she can just get a little more access to that side of her face, she'll talk again. Or she might learn to be understood with only half her mouth. The only trouble is that until one of those things happens, we won't know whether she'll be able to find words, even if she could form them."

"Wow. And that could take some time."

"The good news is she recognised us. All of us. And she seemed to understand what was going on when we told her."

"If you get a chance, please tell her I'm sorry I didn't get to meet her."

"Ah. Yes, well, about that. Would you still like to?"

"She's in hospital, Michael. And she can't talk."

"But I had an idea, and she nodded when she heard it. I know where she keeps a couple of shoe boxes full of letters that she received from family and friends back in Italy after she and my grandfather moved here. Now, I know you won't understand everything, but . . . they're in Italian, Simon. You could read them to her. Or, some of them, anyway. She would love that, so much! And you'd be able to get a little of the immigration picture."

What this looked like was yet more responsibility, at a time when I was beginning to have to ration any time not spent on studies. I tried to pawn it off. "Michael, I'm sure someone else in your family can read Italian to her."

"Not really, no. And when I heard you speak, your accent sounded really good. My dad can say a few things, but he can't read it and make it sound like Italian. And, besides, there might be some personal stuff in there that would be easier to hear read by a stranger."

I tried to think about what was in it for me. I came up empty, and I was silent too long.

"Okay, I wasn't going to say this, because she's not your grand-mother. But her doctor said it might be a really good thing for her, in terms of regaining mental capacity. What do you say, Simon? Will you do it? Just an hour or so tomorrow."

His voice was so full of hope; he sounded so young. And again the tenderness he must feel for her came through powerfully. "Will you be there?"

"Wouldn't miss it! So you'll do it?"

"All right, for maybe an hour. But I might not be able to do a convincing job, you know. I won't understand everything, and I might massacre the meaning too much."

"How about three o'clock?" He gave me her hospital and room number. Then he asked, "So did you get any dinner?" I described the alfresco scene before me rather than the earlier dinner, and he said, "There, you see? *Alfresco;* Italian. And it sounded like it. Wish I were there, too."

Ah. So did I. Sort of. I think. And then I had an idea of my own. "Well, if tomorrow's as nice as today, we could come back here after the hospital. Antipasto, *forse?* Perhaps? We could pick up something on the way." I stopped; I didn't trust my voice not to give away that this was a plan. A plan to get him alone long enough to test him. To test myself.

"Sounds good." His voice gave nothing away; if he gave even half a thought to what it might mean to be alone on a rooftop with me and some wine, I couldn't tell. And that was fine. "So I'll see you at three tomorrow."

"*Si. Fino a domani.* Until tomorrow. *Buonanotte*, Michael."
"I know that one! *Buonanotte*, Simon."
Buonanotte.

Boston, Sunday, 23 September

This morning, knowing my afternoon would be busy, I got an early start so I could get some homework out of the way, with special attention to documenting some ideas inspired by Persie for my TOK course. I also needed to work on the applications to some other schools Dr. Metcalf is pestering me about, though I didn't quite finish today.

Speaking of Persie, I half expected to see her at breakfast, but it was just Mum and Brian, and Brian had only tea, no food. So I guessed he had eaten with Persie in her rooms.

After I let Mum know Michael would be joining me for antipasto on my roof deck this afternoon, Brian asked me a question in a very pointed tone of voice.

"Did you happen to speak with Persie last night?"

Based on the way he asked, he already knew the answer. I had nothing to hide. "She was waiting for me on the landing."

"What did she want?"

"She asked for help figuring out how to tell you what she was thinking."

"She knows how to talk to me." There was definitely something accusatory there.

Deep breath; don't lose your temper, Simon. "But she has a hard time figuring out what your mood is. I got the impression she wanted to make sure you were in a good mood before she spoke to you."

"What did you tell her?"

"Gave her a few cues to look for, told her I thought your mood was pretty good at the moment."

"And do you know what she wanted to tell me?"

"Yes." Why was he turning this into an issue? What was wrong with what Persie had told me she wanted? I had been sure he'd be glad to hear all of it. I had even told Persie to trust me.

"Is that all you're going to say?"

"Look, she waylaid me on the landing, said she wanted more freedom, said she might like to take breakfast downstairs with everyone else, said she wanted to visit museums and to see more art, and that she wanted Mum and me to go with her. She also said it looked like you'd made up your mind about a tutor before asking her what she wanted."

"None of that sounds like Persie."

"So, what, am I lying through my teeth, then?"

"That's enough, young man."

"You keep telling me that. And this time, I'm quite sure it isn't." I set my fork down and glared at him, ignoring the tension coming from Mum in waves. "You know, I would have thought you'd be genuinely thrilled to have her express an interest in art—*and* in being part of the normal household routine, and even more delighted to have her approach you on her own to tell you that. Because it was *her* idea, not mine."

"Both of you, quiet. She'll hear you." Mum's voice was a hoarse whisper.

Brian lowered his voice. "It seems likely that someone has tried to influence her. I offered her the opportunity to meet both candidates, and immediately she said she wanted the one who wouldn't live here. She had already made up her mind."

"Well, you can't blame me for that. I never said a word to her until she approached me."

"And she had her mind even more made up after she spoke with you."

Suddenly it hit me what the problem was. "You thought she'd prefer the live-in tutor, didn't you?"

"You seem to think you know her better than I do."

Okay, that's another part of the problem. But—where did it come from? Careful, Simon. "What I know is that she wants to expand her

world badly enough to ask for my help on how to tell you that."
There were worlds between the words in that statement, beginning with the fact that she hadn't known how to talk to her own father about something very important to her.

"And what you don't know is what will happen when she fails."

"*When* she fails?" Mum's voice nearly squeaked. "You're not
giving her half a chance!"

I felt like Kay; the parental units are fighting, and I'm caught in
the churn.

Brian said, "Excuse me," and left the table.

Mum stared after him, looking as though she were considering
following him.

I said, "It was just a smoke screen, then, asking for her opinion.
Do you suppose he's jealous? Is he mad that she asked you and me
to show her art, and not him?"

"I don't know." She stood. "But I'm going to find out. This
can't go on."

Finally, alone. Breakfast in peace. And later, I avoided everyone
at lunchtime, sending a few things up on the dumbwaiter late in
the morning, leaving a note that said I had lots of homework.
Which was true enough.

Michael was already in the hospital room when I got there,
which was a relief; I'd been prepared to hang out in the hall and
wait, otherwise.

The dear lady was slightly propped up on the bed, tubes and
wires attached in various places. Her face was badly disfigured by
the sag on the left, but her eyes were bright and attentive. Michael
introduced me as though there were nothing wrong with her. Not
only did this impress me, but also it set the stage for my interaction
with her. She actually held out her right hand for me to shake, and
instead of shaking it, I kissed it, which caused her to make an odd
sound that I interpreted as laughter. So did Michael, to judge by
the smile on his face.

It seemed cruel to try and engage in small talk with her, so in
halting Italian I apologised for my unacceptable version of the lan-

guage and told her in English that I would do my best to read anything she cared to give me. She looked at Michael, who had a canvas shopping bag printed with big red and blue flowers—without a
doubt one of his grandmother's. He pulled out a shoe box that had
once held a pair of dark-red high-heeled shoes. Italian shoes.

"I made sure these were in date order this morning," he said.
"Nonna, do you want to start at the beginning?"

She made some gesture with her right hand, which Michael interpreted as asking him to sort through them; maybe she had a
favourite. He stopped when she grunted and handed the envelope
to me. I accepted it reverently, careful not to damage the envelope
or what it contained. I read the addressee information aloud, but
the return address was not legible. I'm not good with dates and
numbers, so I read the date in English. It was 20 September 1954.

Carissima sorella, it opened. *Dearest sister.* I made my way through it
as best I could, which I think wasn't too bad, recounting the sadness
the abandoned sister felt when Michael's grandmother and her husband, Victor Vitale (whom the sister evidently held in fairly low
esteem), left everyone and everything—*tutti e tutto*—behind, abandoning tradition and everyone who loved her for the hope of material gain in the US. There was mention of many children,
evidently nieces and nephews, as though sister Bianca were doing
her best to assail her sister Sofia (Nonna) with guilt that would
bring her home. At some points whilst I read, Signora Vitale would
roll her head and wave her right hand, which Michael interpreted
for me as an editorial on her sister's naked attempts to manipulate.
Signora Vitale even seemed to chuckle once or twice.

The next letter was from a school friend who supported the
move and who complained about her own husband, Rocco, for his
old-fashioned ideas about gender roles.

Most of the letters were newsy, full of family doings and mis-
doings, but occasionally they were more intimate, sometimes evidently in response to something Signora Vitale had written. It was
a little like reading some of St. Paul's Epistles and trying to con-
struct what letters or conversations he might have been responding to.

Around quarter past four, Signora Vitale's face began to sag more noticeably, and she wasn't responding to what I read with chuckles or groans or grunts any longer. Michael made leaving noises, and I kissed the signora's hand again and told her it had been a great honour to be allowed to read her letters to her.

Before we could exit she grabbed Michael's arm with her right hand. The right side of her face seemed to be trying to smile. She pulled on his arm a little, then released him and pointed at me, and then held her right hand up, staring at it as though willing it to do something. Finally she managed to fold her middle finger over the first, as though crossing them for luck. But then she pointed the entwined digits at Michael, at me, at Michael again, and smiled as best she could.

I couldn't see Michael's face as he bent over to kiss her good-bye. "No, Nonna. We're just friends. See you tomorrow."

So the signora knew the truth about Michael. Had she perceived this on her own? Had he confided in her when he was looking for an escape from himself? Neither of us spoke as we walked through the halls. Michael seemed embarrassed, which made me worried and annoyed that his grandmother had stolen my thunder before my lightning was ready.

Outside on the street, holding tight to the flowered shopping bag, Michael gazed about rather than look at me. He said, "Listen, can we not do this antipasto thing today?"

Yup; lightning fizzled. My best move at this point would be to seem not to care. "Of course. You taking the T back?" I knew there was a station not far away.

He shrugged and looked vacantly around him. "Yeah. Guess so."

"I'm going to locate a taxi. See you." And I turned back towards the hospital entrance, where the occasional taxi would no doubt drop off a passenger. I didn't turn around or look back, so I don't know how long he stood there. But before I reached the entrance I decided to take the T myself. I didn't want to get back to Marlborough Street as fast as a taxi would take me. Truth be told, I didn't really want to go back there at all. But I had so much homework to do. So I waited just long enough to be sure that Michael would already be on a train and that I wouldn't see him on the platform.

Dinner was a fairly silent affair. Everyone seemed to be angry with Brian, including Persie, who wouldn't speak. I took this to mean Brian must have denied one or more of her requests. She shook her head violently several times in answer to questions he asked her, which seemed to indicate that she wasn't responding. He didn't even try to ask me anything, and he and Mum acted like people who didn't know each other and didn't want to. I left as soon as possible to get back to my homework—a welcome escape.

I was at my desk, deep into work on my biology project about Scottish fold cats, when I heard someone coming up the stairs. It was Mum.

She sat in the reading chair. "I thought you might like to know what Brian has decided."

"Brian decided," I echoed. "Not Persie."

"Correct. He's planning to contact Maxine Leary tomorrow and offer her the job as Persie's tutor. Maxine will have the same schedule Anna did, with weekends off unless other arrangements are made. She'll live in Anna's room, so you'll have a neighbour again."

I'd never seen much of Anna, so I wasn't alarmed at the idea of Maxine's being up here. "You know, he's so afraid of Persie's reaction to—well, to anything she's not happy with. And yet he goes this route instead of doing it her way. What does he expect will happen? I mean, even I can see that Persie is likely to make Maxine's life miserable."

"I know. And I pointed that out to him."

"Has he said anything about Persie's request to go and look at art?"

She let a few beats go by. "He doesn't like the idea. Says Persie doesn't handle uncontrolled environments like that very well."

"Really. So . . . *is* he jealous, do you think?"

She exhaled loudly. "That wasn't a question I felt I could ask."

"Well, thanks for the update. When do you think she'll start?"

"Brian thinks it will be right away. She could be here as soon as Wednesday."

I nodded. "Thanks for telling me. I need to get back to my homework now."

But she didn't seem to want to leave. Maybe she just didn't want to go downstairs where Brian was. "How is your schoolwork going, Simon? What are you working on there?"

Trying to control my impatience, I explained as briefly as possible about the genetic aspects of folded ears in cats. She looked as though she'd like to say something, but didn't know how I might take it; this was cats, after all, and the ear fold began in a British shorthair like Tink. I considered showing her Margaret's photos, but decided against it; it would take too long, and I had no intention of forgiving my mother for tearing me away from Tink.

"Sounds fascinating," was all she said about the ear fold. And then, "I also wanted to ask about getting you a piano teacher. It would be a shame to let that drop. What do you think?"

I shook my head. "I don't have the focus for that right now. Between the coursework, and coaching Toby, and just being in a totally unfamiliar place—"

"How is that going? Coaching Toby?"

"Mostly we practise. I create word lists; I read a word; he spells it."

"Where do you meet with him?"

I'm sure I've told her all this before. "At his house. Condominium. Longwood Towers; it's very nice."

"Are you taking taxis, then?"

"No. The subway."

She sat up straight. "Simon, I don't want you doing that."

Little does she know I have to take mass transit everywhere I go for the City course. "Mum, I use it at home all the time. This system is nothing compared to that. And it's only a few stops, to a very nice area." It looked like she was about to protest, so I added, "Look, I really need to work now. There's stuff I have to hand in tomorrow." I stood and moved towards the door.

Mum sat in the chair for a few seconds, looking at me as though she weren't sure who I was. Then she got up, came to me, and laid her hand gently on the side of my face. She left without another word.

Boston, Sunday, 30 September

Maxine did, in fact, arrive on Wednesday, sometime after I left for school. And the shit hit the fan.

The first thing Persie demanded of Maxine was that they go to a museum to see art. Maxine sensibly said she'd check with Brian, and Persie—knowing he'd already said she couldn't go—threw the first of many tantrums for the week. Again, I was put in mind of the elephant with the rope around its ankle. Because although Persie had sometimes thrown fits around Anna, she had always submitted in the end without a physical struggle. But she fought Maxine, sometimes even slapping her. She was a bigger elephant now, and perhaps it was this denial of Brian's that had motivated her to challenge the rope. But he must have known it would be a mistake to offer Persie a choice and then snatch it away from her again. "Which lollipop do you want, my child, the yellow or the green? The green, you say? Here's the yellow one." And he had never intended to give her the green one in any case.

Friday when I got home in the afternoon, the screams hit me as soon as I opened the front door. I dropped my book bag just inside the music room and headed to the kitchen, where Ned was working on dinner.

"World War—what number are we up to, now?" I asked him.

He made a face. "Sit. Talk to me. Haven't chatted in days. What went on here over the weekend?"

I sat at the island, and magically a glass of San Pellegrino and a bowl of salted cashews appeared before me. "Thanks. Um, let's see. I think I'll have to summarise." I crunched a few cashews.

"Mum and Brian interviewed a number of candidates and got to a short list of two. One of them would be like Anna, live-in, and the other would be here only weekdays, with weekend care an occasional option. Brian preferred the live-in version, but Mum and I thought Persie could handle a little more latitude. We also thought Persie should be consulted. The three of us had a bit of a heated discussion Saturday morning, and Brian decided to offer Persie the chance to meet both candidates. Evidently, when he posed this idea to her, she pounced on the weekday option without meeting either of them. Which seems to have made Brian angry."

"But that's not who he hired."

I shook my head. Ned opened his mouth to speak again, but I waved at him. "I'm getting to that. I think he really expected her to choose another Anna. Personally, I don't think he gives Persie nearly enough credit for being able to handle things. And get this: Persie laid in wait for me after dinner Saturday to ask for my help—literally. She used that word." I gave Ned a quick rundown of what Persie had said.

"Wait. So, Miss Persie asked you how to talk to her father? And she wants an art escort?"

"Mmmm. Mum knows a lot about art, but Persie wanted me to go as well. I told her I'd do just one visit to start; I don't really have time to do a lot of museuming. So Persie told Brian that, and I think she also told him she might like to have breakfast downstairs."

Ned pulled a stool to the island and stared at me. "Simon, this is huge! Was he thrilled?"

"Far from it. He was *so* not thrilled he accused me of trying to influence Persie. Which I had by no means done. Well, maybe just about breakfast. And he decided that he would hire Maxine, ignoring Mum's opinion as well as Persie's request, which . . . Well, I'll stop short of criticising him, but you can imagine. He's said Persie's not to go museuming, and I haven't seen her downstairs for breakfast. Come to that, other than dinners I haven't seen much of her at all this week. Though I've heard rather a lot of her."

Ned scowled and stared over my shoulder at nothing. "This isn't like him."

"Maybe not in some ways. But he's always struck me as some-one who believes he's figured everything out."

Ned shook his head. "He can be moved by reason."

"I think he's jealous."

That got Ned's eyes back on me. "Of whom?"

"Persie didn't ask *Brian* to take her museuming."

"She knows he works."

"Right. And she's always so aware of everyone else's con-straints."

"You got me there."

"I'm at school all day, and I have massive amounts of homework at night. But she asked me. And this particular conflict began after I told him that she doesn't know how to ask him for what she wants. So she asked me for help. *Me.* Plus, Mum's been spending a lot of time with her, lots more than Brian could. Or, she had been, before Maxine."

"I hear you." More scowling. "Well, I'll be surprised if Maxine stays longer than the weekend. She's bruised and battered and traumatised. She said something to me today that sounded like she thought Brian had misrepresented Persie's mental state. I as-sured her that Persie has never been like this, but that probably just made her more convinced that she should leave. I don't know. . . ." He stood and went back to dinner preparation.

Just then we heard a thud from upstairs loud enough to startle us.

"Simon, you're so good with her. Do you think you could calm her down just a little? For our sake as well as for hers?"

Not my problem. Not my problem. "I doubt it."

"Try? Please?"

"You sound like my mother." Don't know why I said that, but there it was. I heaved a melodramatic sigh, went to collect my book bag, and headed up to the landing. Halfway up, I heard an-other loud thud and a near-scream from Maxine. I dashed to the door and opened it.

The room was a shambles, and Maxine was white as a ghost, her frizzy blond hair making the effect almost comical. Beside her on the floor was a three-ring binder, which I gathered Persie had thrown at Maxine without quite hitting her. The binder had popped open, and some papers were still on the rings, whilst others had been thrown loose. I bent over and picked up a loose one. It was *BREATHE* with the Still painting, the one Persie had found. I picked up a few other pages, each of which had a painting printed on it, each with a different word. I saw *PATIENCE* and *LONELY.* And I saw *BETRAYED.*

B is sky blue, and the word *BETRAYED* also has periwinkle and two lilacs in it. Only the *d* is brown. But this painting had so much brown in it. She had skewed the colour importance to choose the painting she wanted, evidently one that suited her mood.

Art therapy. She'd said she didn't need it, but this said otherwise.

I looked at Persie, who had sat down on a wooden chair, her arms crossed over her chest and her face in the deepest pout I think I've ever seen on anyone. At least she was quiet.

I pulled another chair away from the wall, planted it across from her, and sat down.

"No," she said, her voice loud and sulky. "It doesn't go there."

I gestured with my arm, taking in the entire mess. "A lot of things are not where they belong. I'm choosing to move this one." I did my best to look calm and unruffled, even though I knew I had just challenged her.

I watched her face for several seconds—though, of course, she wouldn't look at me—and then I said, "Persie, you don't want Maxine to be here, do you." Not a question.

"No. I told him."

"Do you mean you told your father you didn't want Maxine, or that you didn't want a live-in tutor?"

"No live-in tutor."

"And he hired a live-in tutor. But here's the thing, Persie. That's not Maxine's fault. So you're unhappy with your father's decision, but you're taking it out on Maxine."

She didn't say anything, just continued to pout.

"I'm not taking anything out on *you.*"

That got her attention. "Why would you do that?"

"Because when my mother forced me to move here with her, I

had to give up my friends; I had to give up my piano teacher; I even had to give up my cat. That was *horrible*, Persie. I love my cat very much. And do you know *why* I had to give up my cat?"

She shook her head.

"It was because of you."

If Persie had been a more typical child, this would have been a horrid thing to say to her. But if Brian was even half right about how AS affected her, it shouldn't cause guilt in Persie.

"Your father was afraid you and the cat wouldn't get along. So I had to lose my cat, my sweet, loving cat, whom I adore, a cat my father gave me before he *died*, Persie"—I had to clear my throat before going on—"because of you. I could have hated you for that. I could have hated you so much, and I could have treated you so badly. But would it have gotten me my cat back?"

She stared at the wall, silent, but here was another he-who-speaks-first-loses moment. I wasn't sure how it would play out with someone like Persie, and maybe this whole thing was point-less. Maybe it wouldn't matter at all to her that I'd wanted to hate her, or that I'd had to give up my beloved cat. So I waited. I heard Maxine shift her position behind me. I heard a car horn maybe a block away. I heard a timer go off in the kitchen.

Finally, "No."

"No. Correct. It would not. And it would have been a very, very mean thing to do to you, because it wasn't your fault." I couldn't tell whether that had sunk in or not, but I kept going. "And you're being very, very mean to Maxine. And it's not her fault you didn't get your way."

I got up and found *BETRAYED*, looked around for a pen, and found one on the floor next to a table. I crossed out *BETRAYED* and wrote *DETERMINED*. I handed it to Persie, who stared at it maybe ten seconds before taking it.

"This is a better word. Not only is the word colour better for this painting, but also it's a better way to get what you want. Maybe you feel betrayed, but that won't get you what you want any more than my being mean to you would get me my cat back. So be determined. Figure out what you need to do to get what you want, and be determined in how you go about getting it. Not mean. Not sulky. Determined. I know you can figure out how to do that."

"I can't! I don't know how!"

"So let's work it out. Maybe you start with what you want the most, or what would be easiest to get." I waited, and then realised she was waiting for a question. "What would you choose first? Where would you start?"

"Museums."

No hesitation at all. I turned to Maxine. "How much do you know about art?"

"Not as much as I'd like to."

Back to Persie. "So you need to convince your father that Mum and Maxine can both go with you. Have you ever heard of water torture?"

"Dripping until you go crazy."

"If your father has already said you can't go see art, you might try something like water torture." I hesitated, remembering that she wasn't comfortable with metaphor. "If you ask very sweetly, and smile—you do know how to smile, yes?" She just stared at the floor, so I moved on. "Maybe at dinner on Monday, you smile at him and ask very sweetly if my mother and Maxine could take you the next day. Don't treat it as though it's once and for all; treat it like you're asking only for Tuesday. If he says no, you just sigh sadly. No sulking, no pouting. Because all he's said is that you can't go on *Tuesday*. Tuesday at dinner, you do the same thing. Smile, and ask sweetly for Wednesday."

She was listening, I could tell; her pout was less pronounced. "Why start Monday?"

"If you ask tonight about tomorrow, he'll say no just because the museums are more crowded on Saturdays, and he would know that would make it harder for you. They're closed on Mondays. If you ask tonight about Tuesday, the best you'll probably get is 'We'll see,' because it's three days away. You want a firm yes. So start Monday. Do you think you can do that?"

"Of course."

"You say of course, but I'm not convinced that applies to smiling. Can you smile right now and show me?"

She pursed her lips, but at least that got rid of the pout. I waited, and then I smiled at her. She twisted her mouth in what she probably thought was a smile, but I gave her credit for it.

"That's good." I stood again. "And now, you need to help Maxine pick up all this stuff and put it back where it belongs. She won't know all the places yet, but you do, so you need to be patient. I'll see you at dinner." I set my own chair back where I'd found it to set an example.

As I passed Maxine on my way to the door, I barely heard her whisper, "Thank you."

I shut the door behind me and was immediately wrapped in Ned's arms. "That was magnificent," he said into my ear.

My trek up to the top floor was slow and plodding. With every step it hit me again what I'd just said to Persie. It was so very much like what everyone had been saying to me. *Figure out what's a bramble, hack it away, and focus on the good things. Keep moving forwards. Success depends on how you work through change. Be determined, not sulky.* Every step was another of these maxims, another nail driven into the coffin where my own sulk lay, where my own nasty, vindictive responses waited for good opportunities to jump out and slash at someone. All right, so my three-ring binders were aimed at the people who had fucked everything up for me rather than at a proxy like Maxine, but heaving things at these people would still not get me what I want. Only I can get me what I want.

Michael had said something like that to me once, that first day he'd shown up at St. Bony. He'd told me he was the only one who could open the doors to his true inner self.

Michael. I haven't heard from Michael since I turned away from him on Sunday, leaving him standing there holding that ridiculous bag. It was entirely possible I would never hear from him again. And I am not, I mean *not* going to contact him. If having his *nonna* see us as a couple disturbed him so much that he won't ring me again, what point would there be in my ringing him? This whole relationship was set up to fail, anyway.

I stood at the top of the stairs, coming to all these conclusions, when another one hit me. Michael is a bramble.

It was a chilly, overcast day, but I dropped my school bag and went out onto the roof. At the wall, the one I had contemplated jumping over, I stood there, leaning on the granite, until I was shivering. Then I stood there some more.

All these problems I don't want anything to do with! I have enough of my own, thank you very much. And how far will I get with them if I take the advice I'd just given Persie? What problem do I want to solve first—the most important, or the easiest to fix?

The most important, of course, is getting home and into Oxford. And to do that, I have to do just what I've been doing: nose to the grindstone and keep batting away other people's problems as best I can. And no Michael.

I sighed, and for some reason my mind went next to Kay. At least there'd been no drama with her this week. She'd been all business Thursday, partly I think because she was a little ashamed of chickening out about telling her parents she wants the hormone treatments. Can't say I blame her; that is going to be one awful scene.

Finally I decided I'd had enough shivering; it was beginning to feel like I was prolonging discomfort so I could feel mistreated, when I was doing it to myself.

Inside, before I hit the books, I called Mass General and was told that Sofia Vitale was still there and in good condition. They wouldn't tell me whether she could speak.

By breakfast Saturday morning, I'd already spent two hours on homework; I hadn't touched my extended essay—the one that compares different cultures' attitudes towards homosexuality—in months, and Dr. Metcalf wanted me to e-mail him my work to date over the weekend. I'd collected some really good research material that I intended to start working into the paper right after breakfast.

But as I poured myself some tea, Mum asked, "All ready for the seniors' apple-picking event today, Simon?"

"What apple-picking event?"

She leaned back in her chair and tilted her head at me. "Nashoba Valley Winery. They have orchards, and a restaurant—quite the outing. You've forgotten? You did agree to go. It's a family event, and Brian and I want to meet some of your classmates."

Not what I'd planned for my day, no. "What time?"

"We're to meet at the school at ten. They have buses picking us all up."

"Until when?"

"They'll have us back by three. We'll have lunch at the vineyard, courtesy of the school. It will be fun!"

It will decidedly *not* be fun. "I don't think I'll be able to go. I have an assignment I have to finish today."

"You've been working very hard, Simon. A little time off won't hurt you. And you can finish this evening, and tomorrow."

"I have to turn it in tomorrow. It's important, Mother. My extended essay. It's part of my Oxford entrance requirement."

"You've been working on that for a year."

"I have worked on it on and off over the past several months. I haven't touched it in a long time, and Dr. Metcalf expects a certain level of completion by tomorrow."

"Sunday?"

"Yes, Sunday. Tell you what. If you don't believe me, *you* can go apple picking, and if he's there, you can ask him."

"Well, I hope he is there; I want a chance to speak with him anyway. But you need to go, Simon."

"Why?" So much for not sulking.

She sighed, an exasperated exhale. "Oxford won't be looking only at your marks. They'll want to see what the staff at St. Boniface think of you as a person. If you spend all your time on academics, you will not appear well-rounded, which makes you a less desirable candidate."

"They are never going to know—or care—whether I go apple picking."

"St. Boniface will. And you know very well Oxford will want to know what they say about you. As a person."

I wanted to scream. I've been trying so hard to do what I need to do to get through these fucking brambles. It's already taking everything I've got.

"Five hours, Mum? Really? Do you know how much work I could get done in five hours?"

Brian chimed in. "Em, here's an idea. What if we three drive out ourselves in time to have lunch and be sociable, grab a few apples, and leave? We know where they're going. And we could get Simon back here well before three."

Wow. Brian, being nice to me? Ned must have told him what I did for Maxine. Good thing he doesn't yet know about Persie's up-coming water-torture routine.

Mum wasn't on board with this plan, though. "But that wouldn't give us much of a chance to talk with people."

"How much time do we really need?"

"We won't know until we meet them. And we'd be the only ones not staying the whole time."

"Maybe not. And I can't help thinking letting Simon finish his assignment is more important." Before she could protest again, he turned to me. "What about it, Simon? If we leave here at, say, eleven, and get back by two, would that be better?"

What would be better would be not going at all, but that seemed like a losing battle. So I accepted the compromise graciously. "Yes. Thanks. That works much better." I stood. "I'll just take a tray up-stairs now and get back to work. I'll be downstairs a few minutes before eleven." I gathered some food and left, noting the dark look Mum was giving Brian. Too bad; let her. Three hours wasted was better than five, and I'd take it.

The trip out to the Nashoba Valley wasn't bad, actually. Pretty countryside, lots of maple trees turning intense shades of yellow and orange. I was finally able to see what people meant when they rave about New England in the fall.

I managed to nab space with Olivia and her family for lunch, barely avoiding Maddy. I did notice Mum talking to Dr. Metcalf, and I hope she asked him about that assignment that's due tomorrow.

They released us into the orchard after lunch, and Mum wouldn't hear of leaving until I'd tried my hand at agriculture. Most of the trees near the parking lot were picked out already, of course, but

Mum made me pose a couple of times, holding an apple I had in fact not just picked, so she could snap a pic. Then I headed into the trees, thinking I'd just grab a few apples and that would do it. Mum didn't follow me, but guess who did.

I had just about enough fruit to give Ned something to work with and was backing away from a tree to see if it had any more low-hanging fruit to offer when I bumped right into Maddy.

"Jesus!" I hissed, startled.

"No. Maddy!" She laughed, and it took me a second to realise she'd pronounced her name in a way that she intended to be a loose allusion to Mary, as in mother of Jesus.

I pointed towards her meagre cache of apples. "Looks like you haven't picked very much."

"I was hoping someone taller could help me." Her smile said it all; I was someone taller.

"I think they have ladders you can use." Not very gracious, but I didn't want to waste time, and didn't want to spend any more of it alone with her.

As if I hadn't spoken, she pointed towards a nearby tree. "That one has lots of great-looking apples, just a little too high for me."

I gritted my teeth, set my bag down, and held my hand out for her bag. As quickly as possible, I harvested several bright red specimens, which brought her bag to nearly full. Handing the bag back to her, when I tried to pull my hand away it didn't come; she had clamped hers onto it and was stepping nearer to me. With my other hand I pushed on hers until I could free both of mine. The time had come.

"Maddy, look. You're a great girl, but you're not my type. And I mean *really* not my type, if you know what I mean." I thought this would be obvious. But it wasn't; not to her.

"What's your type, Simon? Give me a chance?"

Wow. Not wasting time on subtlety. I took a deep breath; I hadn't had to say this phrase to anyone at school yet, but . . . yes, the time had come. "I'm gay."

She scowled a little as though trying to take this in. "Maybe I could change that."

I laughed. I couldn't help it. And she looked hurt. "Maddy, the most seductive siren in the world couldn't change it. It's not a choice. It's a fact of life. My life. It would be cruel to both of us for me to pretend otherwise." I almost added, "I'm sorry," but I was afraid that would be misinterpreted.

She nodded, and in sad, quiet tones she said, "Don't worry. I won't tell anyone."

At which point I nearly said, "It's not a secret. It's who I am." But the truth was I also didn't want her blabbing it all over the place, either. I was still puzzling over what I might say to tread a middle ground between "I'm proud of who I am" and "It's no one's business who I am" when she held her right hand out.

"Friends?" she asked.

What else could I do? We shook hands. She smiled broadly at me, shades of sadness on the rest of her face, and walked away with her bag of apples. At least that problem was now off my plate. I threw a few more apples into my own bag and headed back to the main area.

We were back on the road by half one. And when the car pulled up to the house, who should be waiting there, sitting on the front steps and busy on his mobile, but young Mr. Vitale. And he had that flowered bag with him.

There was the obligatory small talk as we all bunched up near the steps, and Mum invited him in.

"Mum, I need a minute with Michael." I watched Mum and Brian disappear and turned to Michael. He smiled, and it was a huge effort for me to think *Bramble*. "Why are you here?"

He blinked at me, a puzzled look on his face. "That's not very friendly."

"Why can't you phone or text like a normal person?"

He thrust a hip out and planted a hand on it. "Why all the hostility?"

"Look, you're the one who keeps insisting there's nothing between us. We're 'only friends,' right? Showing up here like this flies right in the face of that. I've told Brian and Mum the same thing you told your grandmother, but showing up like this will make them doubt that. And anyway, I don't have time for a social call. Making sure it's a good time to drop by is why you reach out in advance. And this is not a good time."

"Okay, okay. You've made your point. I just thought you might like to read some more Italian. Nonna really loved it last week."

"That doesn't explain why you just show up. Could've saved yourself a trip. Because as it happens, I have a major amount of homework I have to finish this afternoon."

"Can't wait until tomorrow?"

"It's *due* tomorrow. And then there's more due for Monday. My school is a little more demanding than yours." All right, that was cutting, even mean. But it's also probably true. Still, the look on his face made me add, "Sorry. It's just that I've got a lot to do, and I've already had to waste three hours on something stupid I didn't want to do." He shrugged and looked down the street at nothing. So I asked, "How long were you waiting here?"

"Half an hour, maybe."

Which made me wonder how long he would have waited. I did a quick calculation: Would I have time to read to his grandmother and still get everything done for school by tomorrow night?

I would not. "Look, Michael, I'm really sorry. With this chunk that just got cut out of my day, I simply don't have time. I'm really sorry." I stopped before I repeated myself again.

He looked at me with an expression that said he wasn't quite ready to forgive me. "They're moving her to Spaulding Rehab Monday."

"Is that very far away?"

He shook his head. "It's actually about the same distance from her house as Mass General, just in a slightly different direction."

"So you'll still be able to visit her, then. That's good." He looked down at his feet, shuffled them, and I said, "I really have to get inside now and work. Ring me? Let me know how your grandmother is doing?"

"Sure. Bye." And he and that flowered bag turned and walked away. Something in me wanted to call out, to tell him that of course I could read to his *nonna*, that I wanted to try again for a rooftop repast. Something else in me said, "Don't be a fool."

* * *

I got the draft of my project off to Dr. Metcalf by one a.m. this morning. With so little sleep, I was late getting downstairs for Sunday breakfast, though that shouldn't matter the way "late" mattered for dinner. However, when I got to the kitchen, Mum and Brian were sitting across from each other, and beside Brian was Persie. I stopped dead in my tracks, and Persie looked up at me, which must have cost her. I was sure she was about to yell "Late" at me, but she smiled. It was a deliberate, forced smile, but it was a smile. I suppose she was practising for when she began her water torture, scheduled for tomorrow's dinner. Also, she hasn't had time to establish rules about breakfast yet, so I hadn't broken any of them. I decided against saying anything to indicate surprise at her presence, though I did smile back.

I took the chair across from Persie. It wasn't my usual kitchen seat, but I knew Persie wouldn't have had time to lay down the law on that, either. Then I saw that the cook in Mum had evidently been inspired by my apples, and as soon as I saw the dish I said, "I'll have some apple crumble, please."

Persie's head snapped towards me. "Apple crisp!" she shouted. "Crisp! Crisp! Crisp!"

Brian opened his mouth to say something, but before anything else could happen I stood very suddenly and glared down at Persie. Like the last time I'd done this, it surprised her enough to make her miss a beat in her litany, but she started again.

I slammed my hand down on the table and yelled, "Stop!" Everyone jumped, including Persie. And she stopped shouting. She stared at the table.

"I am English," I said to her, my tone soft but intense. "That might not matter to you, but it matters to me. And in England, we say 'crumble.' I'm not in England now, but I am going back, and *I* will say 'crumble.' That's my rule." I almost added, "Do you understand?" or the perennial, "Is that clear?" But I hate having those phrases thrown at me. They're dismissive and don't impart a sincere wish to be understood. So I added, "Do you have any questions about that?"

She looked towards me and quietly said, "No."

I sat down again. "Now, please, will someone pass the apple crumble, and the cream? Thank you."

Persie scowled as I spooned crumble into a bowl and poured cream over it. I set the creamer down and looked at her. In a flat monotone, I said, "Sky blue, bright red, lilac, pale yellow, bright blue, cream, lilac." I watched her face for maybe five seconds, and then she took a deep breath, which is what I'd coloured her to do. I enjoyed the rest of my breakfast in peace. So did everyone else. And the crumble was at least as good as I had expected.

Dr. Metcalf had already responded, via e-mail, about my assignment by the time I got up to my room.

Excellent work, Simon. Very well researched, nicely written. You're off to a great start. So please don't take my suggestion as criticism. You know that Oxford wants candidates who make them sit up and take notice. While this paper is very good, it needs to stand out more. Do you think you could come up with a sharper angle, a fresh perspective, or perhaps extrapolate about the progress of acceptance in society and support your position? Let me know if you'd like to discuss.

I threw my jacket on and went to sit on the roof. Traffic sounds, echoing off the buildings around me, provided white noise to my jumbled thoughts. Will everything be like this? Will everything I do, every effort I make, be *almost* good enough? Because if this is going to be the case, then I can forget about Oxford again. There's no tolerance for "almost" there.

Fresh perspective. Sharper angle. As I sat there, staring at but not seeing the sky, the buildings around me, my mind went to my paper. Extrapolate, he'd said. Where is society headed, in terms of accepting something other than normative when it comes to sex? Kay's situation came to mind.

I tried to come up with some point in time when I'd encountered a serious conflict because of being gay. Obviously, I can't ignore the legal inequalities. Even in Boston, where I could marry a man and have it legally recognised, that recognition would be in

Massachusetts and a handful of other states only. And that's just one inequality; there are lots more.

There were some idiots at Swithin who had called me names because I was obviously not interested in girls, but they were a decided minority. Ridicule on account of my "ginger" hair had been much more of a problem. Of course, I wasn't out at Swithin; things might have been worse if I had been. Even so, no one would have told me I couldn't use the boys' loo. I'll bet Kay can't use the girls'.

I suppose it's likely that in most schools, even in Boston, I would be given grief by other students, maybe even serious grief, if I were out in any obvious way. Certainly I haven't gone out of my way to announce it to anyone at St. Bony, other than to Maddy, partly because it's just not their business, but partly because I'm not quite sure what would happen. But Mum hasn't been difficult about it, and Brian has been as good as his word. Michael's grandmother thinks we're a couple and grins about it. X isn't welcoming, but they seem to enjoy making enemies of everyone, so I'm not sure how much weight to give that.

But as for Kay? What will she face?

I practically ran back to my computer to fire off a response to Dr. Metcalf. *Got your advice re my extended essay, and I need to talk to you about something that might be a good angle. When can you meet?*

Almost immediately I got back, *Is a phone convo now an option?* He included a number.

He answered on the second ring. I told him, "I have to confide in you about something. Two somethings, really. The first is about me. I'm gay."

No more than two seconds went by. "Are you planning to draw on personal experience in your essay?" His tone was neutral, like it was really just a question, nothing between the words.

"Not necessarily. I just wanted you to have that context. The second thing is about someone else." I told him about Kay, the straight girl. I described her intensity, her absolute certainty, and her goal of appearing on stage as her true self. And I described her situation with her parents. This time when I paused, Dr. Metcalf was silent for several seconds.

"I have to tell you, Simon, I had no idea. I would never have put you into this position. I wish you had told me sooner. This goes far beyond the project's scope, and you shouldn't have had to deal with something this personal in nature. How do you feel about continuing to work with Toby? Um, Kay?"

"She told me in confidence. And I'm in it now. She trusts me, and I'm almost the only one who knows. I think the only other person is a trans man named Dean whom she met in a support group chat room, who's advising her about hormone therapy. But I didn't bring this up to get out of working with her. I've been thinking about the difficulties I've faced, being gay, which have been almost nothing compared to what Kay will have to go through. I'd like to change the essay's focus. I'll build on the historical material I've already got, but the subject of the essay isn't sexual orientation, or sexual identity. It's the difficulty that society has adjusting to anything that veers from the sexual norm. And Kay's issues veer more extremely than mine. So I wouldn't downplay attitudes towards homosexuality, but I would point out the even more extreme reactions to other nonconforming ways of being."

"I see." He was quiet for a bit, but I could tell he was thinking. Then he said, "You've certainly landed on an issue of current interest, Simon. I have to say, I knew you could do it. I have to warn you, though. My own understanding of your topic is very limited. I'll need to do some research of my own. That's not a problem. It just means I'll need to come up to speed, or I won't be able to provide any guidance other than in generalities."

"So, is it all right? I need your approval, correct?"

"You do. And you have it. I would ask, though, that you submit your drafts a little more frequently than the schedule requires, just so you don't get too far ahead of me. Or, rather, so that I don't end up too far behind you."

Just before we rang off, Dr. Metcalf asked me again if I was certain I wanted to continue working with Kay. It didn't escape me that our positions have reversed; at first, I was the one looking for the out, and he had told me, "not without good reason." Now, he was practically trying to talk me out of it. I told him I'd keep on, at least for now.

"Simon, I do need to ask a potentially awkward question. You indicated that Kay is straight. Even though you're gay, might she be developing an attachment to you that could become awkward?"

I laughed. "No. In fact, she's already informed me she 'doesn't feel that way about me.'"

"Very well. But if you feel the situation is changing, let me know immediately."

I felt as though a burden had been lifted. It had been getting awkward not saying anything to him about Kay, and confidence or no, perhaps I should have mentioned it sooner.

It's also a relief to have him know about me. And he didn't bat an eye.

Boston, Sunday, 7 October

This is the third entry in a row on a Sunday with no entries since the Sunday before. School has gotten insanely busy. Reports, exams, papers have been due in almost everything, including my core IB courses (the famous extended essay, Theory of Knowledge, and of course Creativity, Action, Service, for which I'm coaching Kay). Thank the gods I remembered to keep track of all the word lists I've created; I had to include them in a report.

The City course has been as time-consuming as promised, sending me traipsing all over Boston for one thing or another.

Haven't heard from Michael. Guess he doesn't need any more guidance about English art, or maybe it was for just one paper and he's completed it by now. I'm surprised and relieved to find that I really don't care.

I have new respect for Persie. She followed my suggestion to the letter and each evening gave Brian a smile as sweet as she knows how to make it, with a gentle request to let her visit a museum "tomorrow." More impressive was that she didn't lose patience, even though it was Thursday evening before Brian capitulated. Of course, by Tuesday evening, the second request, he knew what was going on, and maybe he thought she'd give up. I think she would have gone on for years, or until he'd said "Not tomorrow, not ever." I think he nearly said that on Tuesday, because there was a long pause after she asked, her face a rigid mask of deliberate sweetness all the while. I think he considered a categorical denial, but he didn't go there.

So on Friday, Persie and Mum, accompanied by Maxine, went to the Boston Public Library. Persie had been a little difficult about the fact that I had to go to school rather than with them.

Mum told me that when they got home, Persie went right upstairs to take a nap, no doubt completely knackered. I heard them come home whilst I was upstairs in my room, deep into research about AS for my Theory of Knowledge course. Mum also said Persie had done better than had been expected, though there were a few moments—especially in the more spacious areas, like that huge, echoing staircase—where she had panicked a little.

Over dinner that evening, Persie was wide awake again. She didn't open the conversation, but when I asked her how the trip had gone, she started talking and didn't stop, except occasionally to calculate her food category portions. She didn't mention any difficulties. In his usual back-and-forth with courses, Ned looked at me several times and smiled.

The only unpleasant moment was when Persie said something about going again Monday, and Brian said, "I think one visit a week is enough, Persie. Why don't the three of you work out the best day of the week to go, and stick to that, eh?"

"No! Monday!"

I slapped my hand on the table just loudly enough to get her attention and gave her a heavy stare. She lowered her head in a pout, but she stopped protesting. I guess this impressed Brian, because he came upstairs later that evening. He sat in the reading chair, and I turned my desk chair only enough to see him; I had a lot of work to do and didn't want him staying any longer than necessary.

"I want to talk to you about Persie," he opened. "This repeated request for museum visits, and that odd smiling ploy . . . Was this your idea?" This time, his tone was not accusatory.

"Yes. That night when she asked for my help, she said that art, and museums, were very important to her, and that you'd said she couldn't go. It came up again another time, and I suggested that perhaps if she asked nicely, you might change your mind."

"That's it? That's all you said to do? Ask nicely?"

"Well . . ." I'd wanted to limit what I said about the extent of my involvement, which I expected he would see as interference. But he wasn't letting me get away with it. "I might have suggested she smile. And I said it might be better to ask only for a specific day."

He crossed his arms, nodded, and sucked his cheeks in a little. "I thought so. An insurrection, eh?"

He didn't seem angry, so I added, "I suppose I was also curious to see what she'd do with the suggestion. She doesn't smile often, and from what you've said, she wouldn't be likely to think of doing it just to get what she wants. So now," I added, thinking of how I might use this information in my TOK paper, "it will be intriguing to see if she does it for anything else."

He sat there, looking at me. It seemed as though he was thinking rather than outright staring, but I felt the need to say, "Was there something else?"

"Yes. Tonight was the third time you've slapped the table, and she's calmed down. What can you tell me about that?"

[Shakespearean aside: I've been doing some research into the Oxford admissions process, and one thing I've seen is that during the interviews, which take place in December (if one is invited), applicants are often asked questions that do not have correct or incorrect answers. The questions are intended to make the applicants reveal how they form responses, not just the depth of their knowledge. I've seen comments online from past applicants about their experiences during these interviews, and one post really stuck in my mind: "Even if you don't think you know how to answer a question, the best thing to do is to keep talking until you land on what you'd like them to take as your answer. And that might still be 'I don't know.' They actually want to hear you talk through your thought process."

Brian's question took me off guard, but not because it was unreasonable. So I pretended Brian was an Oxford tutor giving me an interview, and in my reply I used some of the language I'd already worked into my TOK draft.]

"I guess it's something I would have done if she really were a cat. You've told me she doesn't have a well-developed sense of social norms and doesn't necessarily respond to the same cues you or I might respond to. So it seemed unlikely that she'd respond to a request to, you know, 'behave.' When my cat was doing something she wasn't supposed to, I used to slap on a table, or clap my hands together loudly, to break her attention on whatever it was she was doing. Not in anger. It's just to distract. So with Persie, I didn't think about it; it was kind of automatic. But it seems to work, at least for now."

"So you're treating my daughter like a cat."

"I didn't say that, exactly."

"I'm not criticising. I'm thinking aloud. Do you think she'll learn? That she'll see patterns—when the table slaps happen—and modify her behaviour to avoid them?"

"I'll be surprised if she doesn't."

"Have you been studying AS?"

"You did tell me to look it up." I grinned at the face he made, somewhere between surprise and sarcasm. "Seriously, though, yes, I'm working it into one of my IB courses. The raw material here is too good to pass up."

He scowled, but it was a thoughtful scowl. "May I read your work at some point?"

"Certainly. I'll let you know when it's ready. I, um, I need to get back to work, now."

He stood, gave me an intense look, and said, "Thank you, Simon."

Not sure why, but as soon as Brian locked the door downstairs, Graeme sat on the edge of the bed. "You two have come a long way, haven't you?" he said, his head tilted, his smile sexy.

I got up, leaned my knees against the mattress between his

thighs, and pushed his shoulders back until he lay beneath me. "Not as far as you and I are about to go." I planted my hands on either side of his head and my mouth on his, and before long we were naked between my sheets, inhaling each other's scents, tasting each other's skin, kissing and caressing and pulling and thrusting until we were spent. And then we did it all again.

There was an odd moment when I realised that Graeme smelled like sun-warmed wool, just as Michael does. At first it felt—unfaithful, or something. But I shook that off; what was wrong with taking the one thing Michael could actually give me and making good use of it?

Boston, Sunday, 14 October

Sundays seem to be the best time for me to do these journal entries. By Sunday night most weeks, I've been working all weekend on schoolwork, and most or all of it is done; I leave nothing to the last minute, and I leave nothing to chance. Plus, I don't exactly have an active dating life. Nor do I want one. Not now, not here. I have Graeme, and that's all I need until the rest of this surreal time of my life is over and I'm home again.

Which is why I'm a little unsure about something Ned suggested. He invited me to go with him this coming Saturday night to a small party one of his friends is having.

"Don't worry, dearie," he told me. "I'm not asking you out. I just think you need a little life in your life, and one evening with this crew will give you enough to last for a month. And besides, we gotta get you outta that room before you start bonding with the wallpaper."

I'll have to work really late most nights this week to make up for the fact that I won't be able to put much time into homework Saturday night, but he's right. I could use a little diversion.

Kay still hasn't told her parents anything. She has told me about some other kids she's met online, other transgender kids. She hasn't yet gone so far as to meet any of them, but she's talking about it.

"Just be careful," I told her. "You don't know who these people are, really, just who they say they are."

"Oh, Simon, don't be silly. I'm Skyping with them. I can see who they are."

I didn't want to admit I'd never Skyped. "Still, be careful. I don't want you to get hurt."

She gave me a hug. "I like you, too, Simon."

Time to change the subject. I'd had an idea on the ride over to see her. "Kay, is there anyone at your school, someone who's friends with you, who was in the spelling competitions with you? Someone who did really well and would be willing to help you now?"

"Andrew. He was so good, I thought he might beat me."

"He's a good friend? Good enough to help you now?"

"How would he do that?"

"I'm thinking we could stage a little competition. It would be even better if you had more than just one competitor. I know you've done this before, but let's keep you in practice. I can throw words at you all day long, but the adrenaline rush you get when you're waiting your turn against someone who might outdo you can be a good thing or a bad thing. Whichever it is, I think it would be good to be as accustomed to it as possible."

"Brilliant!" Kay had recently gotten off of "fabulous." Now, everything is "brilliant." Anyway, Kay's going to see how many classmates she can talk into a couple of practice bees. She said, "You'll have to call me Toby again, you know."

"Yes. Sadly. But I will."

Dr. Metcalf was impressed, when I met with him Friday afternoon, that I'd come up with this idea. He even suggested we use the auditorium at St. Bony. "We'll publicise it, too," he said, "and have at least a bit of an audience. Great idea, Simon!"

He was also pretty taken with my letter-reading to Signora Vitale, which I'd managed to work into an interim City report.

"Simon, I have to say, you are proving to be remarkably resource-ful. From how you're handling your work with Toby—I mean, Kay—to the new focus for your essay, to this unique approach to The City, I'm very impressed. And your Theory of Knowledge course . . . What are you drawing on for the empirical portions of your draft?"

I opted against giving Michael credit for the letter-reading idea. "Brian Morgan's daughter, Persephone, has Asperger syndrome. She's eleven. She's been very sheltered so far, and she's just begin-ning to push the envelope in terms of what she's willing to try."

He nodded. "And I'm guessing you've had something to do with that."

I'm not prone to bragging, but I know that what this man says about me to Oxford will carry a lot of weight. "Actually, yes. I have."

"I think you should begin documenting your interactions with her, without names, of course. It would make an impressive ap-pendix to the report."

I didn't mention that I'm already keeping a journal; I'll let him think the appendix, when I write it, reflects how well I remem-bered everything.

"Keep up the great work, Simon. I'm already adding very com-plimentary notes in your record, and I want to keep doing that."

My walk home that afternoon was so different to the one after he'd informed me about my spelling coach assignment. This time, I was walking on air! Surely, those other school applications will be nothing but insurance. Oxford will definitely want me.

Boston, Sunday, 21 October, 2:00 a.m.

Where to start. My head's buzzing with everything that happened at the dinner party Ned took me to, but I think I'll save that and get events down here in chronological order. I'm still too hyper to sleep; maybe writing it all down will make me drowsy.

Monday, the fifteenth, was the deadline for Oxford admissions. Of course, I had submitted mine a while ago, and now I've managed to complete the other three applications as well, so all that part of the process is behind me. Over dinner I mentioned Oxford, because they'll be sending out invitations around the middle of November for December interviews.

"I'll need to plan a trip for it," I said, "though I won't know the date for a while."

Mum asked, "You can interview on the phone, or over the Internet, can't you?"

"I'm not doing that! I need to talk to them in person. It makes a huge difference."

Maxine doesn't often speak at dinner, just as Anna didn't used to; I think she's conscious of not being part of the family and is reluctant to take the liberty. And she shouldn't have spoken tonight, either, but she did.

"How can you be sure you'll go? They don't interview everyone who applies, do they?"

The room was silent for several seconds as everyone but Persie stared at her. She'd ask this, and after I'd helped out? Finally, in a tone brooking no argument, I said, "Of course they'll invite me."

Brian went next. "I'm sure they will, Simon. You have completed the applications to your other choices, though, correct?"

"Yes." I wanted the subject dropped. I couldn't afford to consider the possibility of not having an interview. And, of course, not everyone who is interviewed gets in. I have to see myself beyond the final portal. I have to take smooth passage for granted, or I won't be able to go on.

I think Mum heard this in my voice, and she changed the subject. "Where is this party you're going to on Saturday, Simon?"

"Ned's friend lives in the South End."

"Chandler Street," Ned said as he placed dinner plates around the table. "I'll make sure you have the full address before we go."

I could tell, when Ned and I had talked with Mum after school about this party, that she wasn't exactly thrilled. I think she's concerned because everyone there will be older than I am. And even if she doesn't know my "boyfriend" doesn't really exist, maybe the fact that I've never had a real date enters into the mix. She made Ned promise to watch out for me, and I decided discretion was my best course and didn't faff about her faffing about it.

Most of the rest of the week has been same-old, same-old, though Kay tells me she's lined up three friends to play pretend-bee with her. Friday Dr. Metcalf said he'd line up a couple of dates and reserve the auditorium. He suggested I put a flyer together, and he'll send an e-mail to the faculty to see if we can line up a small audience. The flyer took me less than an hour this morning, and I'll have the school make colour copies as soon as I have dates.

And there was one fun thing on Thursday. Just before dinner, my mobile rang and displayed Michael's number. I ducked into a corner of the music room.

"Hey. Sorry it's been a while," he opened. He didn't leave a pause for me to respond to that before he went on. "I'm at Spaulding with Nonna, and she wants to talk to you."

She wants to talk to me, but you don't? I waited until I heard, "Ciao, Simon!"

"Signora Vitale! *Che meraviglia.*" I wasn't sure of my choice of words to say "How marvellous," but I figured she'd get the message.

Her words were slurred but intelligible. "Your accent is very good. I love to hear you."

"I love to hear you, signora. How are you feeling?"

"Oh, good, good. I want to go home, but they say not yet."

"Soon, I hope."

"*Si, si.* I wanted to thank you for reading to me. I'm sure it helped me. And I want you to come to dinner after I'm home. You'll come, yes?"

"I will, certainly. You let me know when you're going home, and we'll work it out then. It's wonderful to hear from you."

"*Mille grazie,* Simon. Ciao."

"Ciao." I held onto the phone, thinking Michael would come back on the line, but no; it went dead. End of that chapter of my life, I figured. There was a painful jab as I thought of his beauty and, though he wouldn't acknowledge it, his tragedy. But it would be no great loss to me, or at least no loss that would set me back. I wonder if he'll be at that dinner.

And on to tales of the party.

Ned arrived to get me around seven, looked me up and down, and ushered me upstairs to see what else might be in my clothes cupboard. He found nothing he deemed appropriate other than a pair of black jeans—which he declared almost tight enough, but said they'd do—and my oxblood Italian loafers. He'd brought a canvas satchel with him, and out of it he pulled a shirt in a lively pattern of stripes and diagonal lines in various muted colours that he said made my red hair glow. I put it on, and he folded the cuffs up and pushed the sleeves a little way up my forearms. Then he gave me a sly grin and pulled a pencil out of the bag.

"Follow me, my dear." He nearly sashayed on his way to the bathroom, making me wonder what this party would be like.

I did my best to watch in the vanity mirror whilst he made tiny brown dots all around my eyes and then smudged them with the rubbery tip on the other end of the pencil. I almost protested; why on earth would I want to be made up like this? Whatever; I figured I could always wash it off. But then he turned me fully towards the mirror.

"Voilà!"

I couldn't think of anything to say. It was still me, still real, but somehow there was a transformation. Ned's dots, smudged together, seemed so natural that I was hard-pressed to detect actual makeup. My eyes seemed bluer, and my light freckles stood out in a way that I thought looked kind of charming. I'd never liked them before.

"May I see that?" I took his pencil and examined it closely.

"It's yours. I bought it for you. That colour wouldn't show on my skin."

I took another look at his face, and—sure enough—he'd treated his own eyes with something black, subtly enough that I didn't notice unless I looked closely, but it really did enhance his eyes.

"You have a jean jacket? A leather jacket? Something like that?"

I shook my head. "Of course you don't. That's why I brought one for you." The last thing in the satchel was a short, black leather jacket he said was too small for him, anyway. I put it on, and he grinned at me. "Honey, I am gonna get so much cred for bringing you! You are a sight for jaded eyes."

I was trying to contain my own grin, but I failed.

He pulled one more thing out of that bag of his. A bottle of fragrance. He sprayed a little into the air. "Do you like that? Step close but not into it, to test."

I sniffed, and the scent was completely unfamiliar to me. There was something soft about it, but it wasn't a sweet smell. "What is it?"

"It's a vetiver scent. I can't remember which one; I got several samples. What do you think?" He handed it to me, and I pointed it towards my neck. "Not that way. Take the jacket off, and then spray it into the air and walk into it." I did so. "Again." Once more, and he pronounced me complete and let me put the jacket back on. I picked up my iPhone.

"You expecting any urgent phone calls this evening?" he asked.

"No."

"Got anything super personal or super sensitive on it?" I shook my head. "Then put that thing in the jacket breast pocket, not into those jeans, and leave it there. A phone is not a fashion item and should stay hidden unless you have a particular desire to show it off."

I wanted to sneak out without having to let Mum see me in leather and jeans and eyeliner, but Ned insisted it would be better in the long run not to do that. She was in the living room anyway, which has a view of the front door, so my plan wouldn't have worked. She stood, smiled, moved towards me, and then stopped smiling.

"Simon . . ."

"What?"

"What are you wearing?"

"Oh. This is Ned's jacket, and he's lent me—"

"No, on your face. Are you—are you wearing *makeup?*"

Ned came to my rescue. "It's just a little pencil, that's all. I'm wearing more than he is."

She gave him a careful examination. "Is this typical?"

"Depends. Not everyone there will have used it, but it's kind of fun. And I thought Simon could use a little extra fun."

"And fragrance?"

I said, "Vetiver. Do you like it?"

She was shaking her head, more in puzzlement than denial. "It's just . . . I almost don't recognise you. Are you sure you want to do this?"

"Quite sure. Yes. This is already more fun than I've had in years." With a bit of a shock, I realised that this was true.

"Well . . ." She turned to Ned. "You have him home by eleven."

Ned replied, "I could do that, but I think it will put a major damper on the evening for him. What if we say before one?"

"One in the morning! Oh, I don't think so. Midnight. And not a moment later."

I filed this negotiating ploy away for future reference. We turned to go.

Ned had opened the door, and I was about to step through behind him when I heard Persie's voice.

"Good-bye."

I wheeled towards the stairs, and she was sitting almost at the bottom of them, watching me intently. "Bye, Persie. See you at breakfast." I got no other response, but when I looked at Ned I saw that he was as surprised as I was that she had initiated this greeting. He laid his arm briefly across my shoulders for a quick sideways hug, and we were off.

As we walked to Arlington Street to hail a taxi, I asked Ned if he thought Mum was really worried.

"Mothers worry. It's part of the territory. Plus, she'd never seen you look like this."

"In leather? Made up?"

"Sexy. It didn't take much to turn her son from a good-looking young man to an irresistible temptation, but she wasn't prepared for the transformation. That's to her credit, actually; I don't think mothers should be in the habit of seeing their sixteen-year-old sons as sexually inviting."

"Is that how I look?"

He gave me a sideways glance. "Now you're fishing."

I shook my head. "It's just that I'm not used to thinking of myself as attractive at all."

Both his eyebrows shot up. "Wake up and smell the pheromones, my dear." He said no more, but he didn't need to. That taxi ride felt like a magic carpet.

Ned had the driver drop us off on a main street, Tremont, I think, and he walked me around a little. It wasn't a part of town I'd been in before. There were restaurants and shops and a playhouse, and lots of people out walking around. Several times I noticed two men walking together, some of them obviously couples. It was thrilling, and I wanted to take everything in.

Which is probably how I happened to notice Mr. Lloyd, Kay's father. He had just come out of a restaurant called Hamersley's, a couple of storefronts ahead of us. In front of him, a young woman turned, smiled, and held her hand out to him. The young woman was Colleen.

I froze in my tracks, and Ned said, "Seen a ghost?"

Turning around so my back would be towards the couple, I said, "That's Kay's father. And that is *not* Kay's mother. It's their housemaid."

Carefully, not drawing attention to himself, Ned turned slightly to watch them. "You can turn around; their backs are towards us."

"I don't think they saw me."

Ned grinned. "Don't worry; they wouldn't recognise you."

"What do you suppose his wife thinks he's doing out on the town, without her, on a Saturday night?"

Ned shrugged. "Maybe she's with her own paramour." In a heavy, fake German accent he said, "Can one ever choose where the heart leads us?" I stared at him. "No? *Cabaret*? Never mind. You're just a baby, too young to know that one. But, truly, watch the film sometime. A Bob Fosse classic. Liza Minnelli is perfection as the naïvely decadent Sally Bowles." He kissed his fingers and sent the kiss towards the sky.

Chandler Street is tiny, like so many things in Boston, but it's tiny and charming. It's very narrow, with brick walkways on either side and trees planted every thirty feet or so. The townhouses are only a few stories high, but the street is so narrow they nearly block out the sky.

So much of the evening was a blur; I think I'll just try to document the highlights. First, the wine. It was Veuve Clicquot champagne, orange label. Nothing else was served, and nothing else needed to be. There were glasses of it on a side table on one side of a large, high-ceilinged room. On the other side was a long table full of finger food that kept coming from the kitchen, carried by what appeared to be caterers. There were little smoked-salmon spirals with cream cheese and chives, broccoli florets wrapped in strips of soft cheese, something Ned called q-cakes which were little quiches with no crust in cupcake papers, and maybe four other options.

Ned said, "Note the conspicuous absence of heavy carbs. Start watching your figure now, and you'll be set for life."

The flat wasn't huge, but somehow it seemed spacious. Ned introduced me to the hosts, James Miller and Roy Kennedy. It was their condo. James was maybe twenty-five, whilst Roy, I would guess, was forty. As I struggled to think of something witty to say, James told me more about the condo than I could take in, let alone remember.

"James, darling," Roy said as he hooked an arm through one of mine, "this adorable boy is too young to be concerned with real estate." To me, he said, "I'll bet you'd like nothing more than to meet some nice men. You're not 'with' Ned, are you?" He glanced at Ned and winked.

Ned held his hands up. "He's not my property. I'm just on orders to see that you don't do anything nasty with him."

Roy laughed and pulled me through the small crowd, using his champagne glass to point towards different people, giving me brief and often humorous synopses as we went, loudly enough for the men he was talking about to hear. Some had witty responses; some just rolled their eyes.

All together, there were probably fifteen people there, almost all men, almost all of whom were gay. It's not something one announces, of course, but it seemed evident. I didn't notice anyone else my age. Roy introduced one man, maybe in his mid-thirties, saying, "Tom is our token straight guy. But it's okay; he's a metro-sexual."

Tom shook my hand. "I'm the upstairs neighbour," he told me. "They have to invite me to all their parties or I call the cops about the noise." His grin told me he was being facetious. "My girlfriend is in the kitchen, I think, advising the caterers." He stressed the word "advising."

"Of course she is," Roy said. "But she might be able to improve almost anything."

Roy moved on a few steps, and suddenly there was someone standing right in front of us.

"Oh, my." Roy's voice took on a fake intensity. "It seems this one will not allow us to pass."

It seemed to me that the fellow was about twenty. He looked directly at me, his head tilted ever so slightly to one side, an almost-smile on his face. His black hair was just long enough for me to see curls. He was slender and just a little shorter than I am.

"This," Roy said in formal tones, "is Luther Pinter. Watch out for this one, Simon. He'll eat the heart out of your chest and make you ask why he can't do it again."

Luther: Bright orange, pale pink, bright blue, cream, lilac, bright red. He didn't hold a hand out, so neither did I. He said, "Simon, is it?"

I started to speak, but I found I had to clear my throat. "Simon Fitzroy-Hunt."

Luther raised one eyebrow nearly into the curl that decorated his forehead. "My word. A Brit. Roy, wherever did you find him?" His eyes didn't leave mine.

Roy had released my arm so gently that I didn't notice until I was free.

"Ned found him; not I. And you're not to hurt him." Roy smiled at me and turned to leave, his job evidently completed.

"How do you know Ned?" Luther sipped from his glass, lessening the tension a little.

"He's the cook at the house I'm living in."

"That sounds like there's a story behind it. Tell me. Please."

"I was kidnapped," I said, purely for effect, "by my mother and her new husband. This time last year I was at home in London, blissfully ignorant of my future fate." I have no idea where all this folderol was coming from; something about the place, the people, inspired me. It was fun.

"And where will you be this time next year?"

"If I have anything to say about it, at Oxford."

"You were kidnapped, you say. How old are you?"

I could not bring myself to say that I was sixteen-going-on-seventeen, and even less did I want to say that I would reach that august age on Hallowe'en. "Old enough to be here tonight. Not quite old enough to have refused to be transplanted."

"Kidnapped."

I smiled. "Ned is the cook at my stepfather's house on Marlborough Street."

Another raised eyebrow. "Nice neighbourhood. In school?"

I didn't want to say that I was still on the younger side of college, so I sipped my champagne to stall for time. Then, "Not fair. You've told me nothing about you. I'm not revealing anything else until I get some reciprocation."

He threw his head back and laughed. "You're a feisty one, aren't you?"

I barely had time to learn that he's a senior at Boston College, or BC, reading philosophy, and that he lives alone in a flat off of Commonwealth Avenue—though much farther out than Boston University and Michael's rooms—before Ned interrupted us.

He gave Luther a teasing hard stare. "I'm responsible for this young man, Luther. You'll have me to answer to if—"

"Not to worry. I've been warned already."

"Why is everyone warning everyone else about me, anyway?" I asked, trying to sound amusing, but probably coming off more sulky and immature. Ned came to my rescue.

"Let's get some food to soak up some of this Veuve, shall we? You coming, Luther?"

"In a bit." And just like that, it was over. I suppose I could have insisted that I didn't need food, but in truth I kind of did. I'd had lunch before one in the afternoon and nothing since, and I had almost drained my glass.

I didn't do a lot of talking through the evening, but I did a lot of laughing. It was intoxicating to be aware that so many of these men found me attractive; I could tell by the way they looked at me and, sometimes, by what they said. "What a darling," one fellow said. Another called me eye candy. Someone called me a fiery redhead in a way that made it sound sexy.

Luther didn't approach me again, and I didn't seek him out except a few times with my eyes. I never caught his glance, so I don't know whether he watched me at all.

I ate just enough to keep the wine from going straight to my brain and nursed the champagne so I wouldn't appear drunk when I got home, certain Mum would be waiting for me.

Ned rode back to the house with me before the taxi took him off to his own home. He didn't prod me for my reaction, just sat in companionable silence for several blocks. I opened the conversation.

"How well do you know Luther Pinter?"

"Not as well as I suspect you're going to."

This gave me a jolt of something I can describe only as pure pleasure, with a focal point at my crotch. "Do you like him?"

"Yes, qualifiedly. He's a good guy, just puts his own needs first a little more often than I would want in a partner. He's had a couple of messy breakups."

I had really enjoyed Luther's attention, and I wanted more of it without anyone worrying about me. I pulled out something Brian had once said to me. "I know that I haven't yet met anyone I want to spend the rest of my life with."

But Ned was quick with a response. "Maybe not, but any of us can be hurt by putting too many feelings in an unsafe place."

I shrugged to hide my irritation at being denied credit for wisdom. "I might never see him again, anyway." I wanted to sound like I didn't care. But I did. So Ned's next response made me feel good again.

"Oh, I think you will."

I couldn't resist. "Would you rather see me with him than with Michael?"

"Yes."

"That was quick."

"Michael's confused about who he is. That makes him a danger to you, because even if he wants to be honest, he probably can't be. And even if he managed it eventually, he'd lead you on a nasty chase first. Luther isn't what I'd call confused, and in fact I think he's pretty honest with himself, and with others, about his feelings. It's just that they're not always what you might like them to be, so just be as prepared as you can for that."

The taxi pulled onto Marlborough Street at ten minutes to twelve. "Ned," I asked, "where do you live?"

"In the South End. Not far from where we were tonight."

"But . . ."

"I had to see you home, dearie. Your mother would have had my head."

"Do you live with anyone?"

"Finally. Thought you'd never ask. His name is Manuel." He pronounced it with a proper Spanish accent. "He would have come with me tonight, except his mother's health is bad. He's with her in Santa Fe. He'll be home tomorrow night."

"So I was your substitute date?"

"You complaining?"

I grinned. "Not at all. Thanks for taking me."

Mum was waiting for me, as I had suspected. Both she and Brian were reading in the living room. I called to them, "I'm home," and started up the stairs but didn't get very far.

"Simon?" Mum called. "Where's Ned?"

Determined not to let an interrogation ruin my mood, I shuffled towards her. "He just drove off in the taxi."

"Did you have a good time?"

"I did. I met several people. It was a pretty sedate party, actually. Very sophisticated finger food."

"Alcohol?"

"I had two glasses of champagne." I'd had three. Or four . . .

"Meet anyone special?"

"Not really," I fibbed. "Nice people, though. They're all friends
with each other. Small party." Before she could ask anything else, I
said, "I'm knackered. See you tomorrow." And I escaped upstairs to
relive everything I could remember.

Boston, Sunday, 21 October, Addendum

This will be quick; just have to get a few thoughts down.

Upstairs, I had gone into the bathroom to see how Ned's handi-
work had held up. It was a little smeared, but not bad. I washed
my face and then pulled the pencil out from where I'd stored it in
a drawer. I dotted all around my eyes the way I thought Ned had
done, but when I smudged it with the soft end the effect was more
like I'd been looking into binoculars smeared with something. It
would take a little practice, I figured. I washed again, patted my
eyes with a tissue to dry the skin thoroughly, and tried once more.

This time it was better. Still not quite as good as Ned's job, but
also I was tired and a teeny bit tipsy. I put the pencil away, took a
shower, and headed to bed.

And on that bed, Graeme lay on his side, head propped on his
hand, sheet draped seductively so that it almost but not quite con-
cealed his tenderest bits. I knelt on the bed, kissed him softly,
then harder, and then harder still, and his parts—and mine—grew
decidedly less tender. We made love—had sex, really. Insistent,
powerful, male sex. The sheets were soaked and, in the morning,
would be as stiff as we'd been to get them that way.

Graeme is the light to Luther's dark, and he will always be there for me. My needs are his needs. If Luther and I start something, and he backs away to meet his own needs, I might get hurt; it's true. But Graeme will be here. He'll hold me, stroke my arm, my hip, my ass; he'll kiss my mouth, my belly, my thighs. He'll be everything I need him to be and nothing that will hurt me.

He just won't be real.

Boston, Monday, 22 October

This is going to be another short one, but I can't resist.

Luther called me tonight. I was in my room after dinner doing schoolwork (of course) when my mobile rang. I didn't recognise the number, but I answered it anyway.

"Hey there, Red. It's Luther. Remember me?"

My heart skipped a beat. Hell, it skipped several. I made sure my tone was as teasing as I could make it. "Red, is it? Let me see. . . . I don't recall anyone who uses that moniker to refer to me, no. Luther, you say? Luther who?"

He chuckled. "Pinter. As in Harold Pinter."

"The playwright?"

"Exactly, though no relation. I'm glad you know the reference. Which brings me to my point. Any interest in seeing *Betrayal* with me Saturday night? I happen to have two tickets."

I was not prepared for this. I was by no means prepared for this. Luther was asking me out on a date. I'm nearly seventeen years old, and I've never been out on a date at all. I fought for breath and finally managed, "I don't know that play. Is it any good?"

He laughed for several seconds. "Now, Simon, I know you know I'm asking you out. If you don't want to see the play, I'll find takers for these tickets and we can do something else."

I did my best to chuckle; don't know that I succeeded. But I did manage to say, "Yes, I do know. And I'm glad you called. I'd love to see the play with you."

"Pushing my luck, here . . . Dinner before? I'm thinking Brasserie Jo, just because there are so few decent restaurants near the theatre. Do you know it?"

"I'm new in town, as you might tell from my accent."

"It's casual but not too casual. Decent food, Alsatian leanings. I've been there before."

"With other dates, no doubt."

"No doubt. And would you be my 'date' there Saturday?" He stressed the word "date" oddly, as though using it facetiously; maybe gay men don't date? Maybe they—what, connect? Hook up? God, how did this happen so fast?

As our exchange had gone on, I'd performed a wild set of mental gymnastics. Ned had insisted on letting Mum see me out for that party. He hadn't argued with her about curfew; he'd negotiated. He'd made sure she had the address and his own phone number. He'd treated her with respect as someone who has authority over me. So the question I had to answer for myself was whether to dream up some story about where I would be on Saturday night, or tell her the truth, knowing she's going to want to meet the guy.

For only the second time in my life, I felt that horrible trap that most teenagers rant and rail about—of being under the thumbs of their parents whilst starting to be real people with lives of their own. The first time, of course, had been when I was kidnapped away from London.

I made a snap decision. I would go with reality. "I would love that, yes. Thanks." I was struggling with how to let him know he'd have to pick me up when he solved that problem.

"I'll come by around quarter of six. It's outrageously early for dinner, but I suspect your captors would prefer that to your getting home late after a post-theatre dinner, and I want to have dinner with you."

He wants to have dinner with me. I felt giddy. "Do you need the address, then?"

"I have it. Ned gave me your cell number as well as your address. Will I get to meet your captors, by the way?"

"I'm afraid it will be obligatory."

"Then I'll be on my very best behaviour. At least for that part of the evening."

"Very funny."

"Not what I was going for, actually, but we can explore that Saturday. See you then."

Man. Wow. Luther is only a couple of years older than Michael? Really? He seems like a man of the world. He seems . . . really, he seems too old for me. And I love it. I really love it.

I stored his number in my phone and practically danced downstairs to find Mum. She and Brian were in the den, watching television, but it was something they had recorded so I didn't hesitate to interrupt. I'm not going to catalogue here the grilling Mum gave me. I don't remember ever being so profoundly patient with anyone before, or being so strategic in my wording. I nearly lost it at one point; didn't she trust me? But we'd had no practice, trusting each other in this area. And patience did the trick; I got a qualified approval.

"This is tentative, Simon. I'm going to ask Ned about this fellow tomorrow, and if I don't like what he tells me, the date is off."

"I understand." *I understand;* I can hardly believe I said that. I can't believe those were my words, coming out of my mouth. But, although I would never have admitted this to Mum, if Ned hadn't already given me some encouragement regarding Luther, I might not have been so sure I wanted to go out with him. So I really couldn't blame her for wanting Ned's opinion. I had wanted it. And I trust Ned to put enough of Mum's fears to rest that I will, in fact, be going out with Luther on Saturday night.

Shit. I have to buy some clothes!

Boston, Sunday, 28 October

Where to start.

I'm in lust. It's definitely not love, but I'll take lust for now. I've never had either, unless you count Graeme.

Chronicling this in order will be important for posterity, so I'll start from the beginning.

After talking with Luther, I realised I would need to make a hole in my schedule someplace to buy clothes, apparel that wouldn't be a letdown after the way I had looked Saturday. Tuesdays are devoted to The City, and it's up to each student to decide what that means. Certainly commerce is one aspect of city life for cities everywhere. I wasn't sure I'd be able to work anything that transpired during a clothes shopping expedition into my City report, but I didn't see another good time to go. Saturday morning would be too late; I wouldn't wear a new shirt without laundering it, and what if I bought something that needed to be altered?

So Tuesday was it. But where to go? There were the predictable options of Saks Fifth Avenue and Neiman Marcus, but I saw them as American versions of Moss Bros in London—someplace I might go for basics, but not much there that was going to be really special. So Tuesday morning I talked with Brian after breakfast, which he takes earlier than Mum or Persie during the week, before he disappeared into his office. I didn't yet have final permission for my date, but he didn't have to know why I was asking about clothes.

"What kind of clothes are you looking for, Simon? Need something else for school?"

"Actually, no. Maybe I'm tired of looking so much like a schoolboy, I don't know, but I'm hankering for something special. My birthday's coming up next week, and this is kind of a present for myself."

"Ah, yes. Next Wednesday, isn't it?"

I was surprised he knew. "Yes. So are there any places you would recommend?"

He smiled and nodded. "I think you can't do better for some-

thing special than Louis Boston. I have an account there. In fact . . .
tell you what. I admit this is rather a tacky way to do this, and I want
you to know that I have been considering what you might want
without landing on anything. So here's a suggestion: I'll take you
shopping, and you can get whatever you want."

I was going to say no, thanks, because this was not how I had
pictured my shopping trip. But very quickly I realised that if this
worked out, I would have automatic approval from Brian for anything I bought, and too bad if Mum didn't like it. And if he proved
too judgemental, I could just get one or two things with him and
go back on my own. If it was just one store, that wouldn't take me
very long. So I said, "That might be fun. But—I was hoping to go
this week. In fact, I was going to go today, during the day."

"No school?"

"It's that City course. I have all of Tuesday to wander around
Boston and collect material for various reports."

"My only appointment today is at ten, so I could be free after
that. If you have some work you can do for the morning, I could be
ready to leave by eleven thirty, maybe earlier. Let's have an early
lunch at Sam's—that's the café they have on site—and then spend
however much time after that for this expedition. I might even
pick up a few things for myself. Sound good?"

It sounded very good. I headed upstairs to my computer and
went to the Louis Boston Web site. And it blew my mind. The
clothes I saw would be absolutely ideal. A glance at my watch told
me it was now nearly half eight, which gave me almost three hours.

I decided that, at the store, I wanted the camouflage that my
school garb would give me so I wouldn't be judged by what else I
might have on. Dressed in khakis, a blue shirt, and a regulation tie
with the knot loosened, I grabbed a jacket and a messenger bag
with a notebook and pens and headed out to the Old South Meeting House, which was central to the formation of Boston as an independent city. It was also very close to the Granary Burying
Ground, which I thought would make an interesting sidebar item.

I was home again by ten past eleven and found Brian in the kitchen
with a pot of coffee. "I thought Mum had converted you to tea."

He grinned. "It's a guilty pleasure."

A car had pulled up in front of the house by the time I'd dropped off my messenger bag upstairs. We got into the spacious backseat, and we were off. I asked, "Does Mum know we're going out? I didn't see her this morning."

"She's at the Museum of Fine Arts, laying plans for one of Persie's field trips." He was silent for a moment, and then said, "You know, I was extremely reluctant to allow these trips. I've seen her fall apart over the simplest little things, and being out in public is always a huge stressor for her. I was quite angry with you for putting me in the position of the bad cop, as it were. But I've had to change my mind."

He shifted his position so he could look at me. "Maxine tells me that Persie has had a few nasty moments, but the most amazing thing has been happening. It's as though she's realised that if she can remain calm, or as calm as possible, she'll continue to be allowed to do these outings. And she obviously loves something about them, though I haven't zeroed in on anything other than the obvious yet. I mean, the art."

"I like Maxine."

"She thinks the world of you."

That felt better than I would have expected. "Has Persie asked for any other kind of outing yet?"

He looked thoughtful, and said, "That hadn't occurred to me. I suppose I shouldn't be surprised if she does." He sat back again and asked a few general questions about school until the car pulled up in front of the store.

It was not a location I would have expected. We had driven across a sort of wide canal towards a waterfront area, nowhere near the downtown shopping district. And from the moment we got out of the car, Brian was treated like royalty, and so was I by association. Evidently, he'd called ahead, because we were greeted by a fellow named Anton who said he'd be waiting to assist us as soon as we had finished lunch.

The restaurant was very modern and looked out over the water.

We had a great table near the window, and I had a warm spinach salad and a black peppercorn burger. Brian had them put the bill on his account, and by the time we got to the exit, there was Anton.

It was everything I could do not to walk around with my jaw on my chest. The service was not surprising to me; Mum and I had sometimes shopped at upmarket places in London. But the clothes! Oh, my God.

One close look at Anton told me I could put myself in his hands. Not only was I fairly sure he was gay, but also he had chosen items for himself that I would never have put together, but they worked. Beautifully.

"I need a few outfits," I told him. "I'm especially interested in looks that are unusual without being outlandish." I was just trying to figure out how to tell Anton what I wanted for Saturday without embarrassing myself in front of Brian, when something caught Brian's eye. I can't be sure if he left us for a few minutes because he was truly interested in ties, or if he had the sensitivity to give me a moment alone with Anton. I grabbed the opportunity.

"I also want at least two pairs of trousers that would be appropriate for a fun scene, like a party. Something formfitting?"

Anton looked me up and down, and smiled. "I don't think we'll have any problem. Allow me to select a few looks for you while you browse?"

I felt like Cinderella during the good times, and Anton was my fairy godmother. Or maybe that was Brian. Whichever, I walked out of there three hours later with more bags than I'd ever seen from a single day of shopping, even though I had left three things there for alterations. There were shirts and jumpers—Anton called them sweaters—and jeans and trousers. I got a winter camel-hair coat with clean, classic lines, something I could wear for the rest of my life if I wanted to. One of my favourite items is a short jacket, a zipper-front shearling dyed to a dark moss colour with the pile cut very short so it's soft and flexible. The collar falls far out onto my shoulders, almost cape-like. I didn't need any more standard dress shoes, but I got a pair of ankle-high black shoes that lace almost like a hiking boot. And I got some black leather gloves lined in cashmere that fit like a second skin.

Brian got a tie, some gloves, some socks, and he picked up a gorgeous silk scarf for Mum with white peonies amidst dark purple grapes on vines. I never saw a price tag, but we must have spent several thousand dollars.

We were maybe halfway home when Brian said, "Do you know which items you'll wear on Saturday?"

So he knew, after all, that it was my evening with Luther that had inspired this spree. Fair enough. "I think blue jeans, that blue-and-white cotton shirt with the wide stripes on one side and narrow ones on the other and the white collar, and the dark brown leather sport coat."

"Luther will be proud to have you with him."

I glanced at Brian to see if he was having me on in some way, but he was gazing nonchalantly out the window.

Ned was at the house by the time we got back. "Dinner might be a little late. I'll just make sure the soup is on time for Miss Persie. But I have to see *everything*." And he approved. Of everything.

Later that evening, Mum somewhat reluctantly agreed to let me go out on Saturday, as I had expected would be the case, and of course she insisted on meeting Luther, but I had prepared him for that. I was sure Brian would be there as well.

My Thursday session with Kay was pretty normal; no news on her parental front. Her father didn't show up whilst I was there. I was glad for that; it was hard enough acting normal around Colleen.

I talked with Dr. Metcalf about the mock spelling bee. In fact, there were two bees planned, both on Thursday evenings, 1 and 15 November. I told Kay the fliers were all over St. Bony and gave her a handful in case she wanted to let anyone at her school know.

"Will I wear a dress?" she asked. "Kidding! But did you hear how I asked that, as though I were British? I mean, English?"

I spent most of Saturday on schoolwork. Scratch that; I spent a lot of time trying to work. Made some progress, to be sure, but I was nervous as hell. And I spent at least some time reading online about *Betrayal*, which I'd never heard of.

Around three or so my phone rang, and I was terrified it might be Luther, cancelling. But no.

"Michael?" I said in response to his "Hey." And then I asked, "Is your grandmother home yet?" I couldn't think of any reason he'd ring me unless she wanted him to set up a date for me to visit her for dinner.

"Next week, if all goes well. She asks after you."

"Please give her my best." I prayed he wasn't about to ask me to do more reading; I just didn't have that kind of time any longer. I waited a few seconds, but he said nothing more. So I prompted, "Was there something else?"

"A guy can't call to say hi?"

"He can if he also has more to say. The thing is, I'm rather short on time just now."

"And later?"

"Later . . . today?"

"I was thinking we could see a movie or something."

I nearly dropped the phone. "No, today's not really good. I—"

"Tonight, then?"

About three heartbeats went by. "I have plans for tonight."

"Really."

I wasn't going to say it, but there was something in his tone, something that had challenge or disbelief or both in it. "Dinner, and a play."

"Who with?"

What nerve. I was going to say, "No one you know," but he was irritating me on so many levels that it came out differently. "A man you don't know."

"A . . . a *man?* Going out with a *boy?*"

Now I was angry. "A man going out with me. Now, if that's all, I have tons of schoolwork to finish this afternoon. Give your grandmother a hug for me. Bye."

I had to take a walk around the block to work off my irritation before I could settle back down to trying to work.

* * *

Luther arrived at ten minutes of six: civilised; not appearing too eager. I was relieved to see that he, too, was wearing jeans. His leather jacket was black and buttery-looking, and when he took it off I noticed his green eyes for the first time; the dark green silk shirt must have made them stand out. He had loomed so large in my imagination that I had completely forgotten that he's maybe two inches shorter than I am.

There was an exchange in the living room in which Mum and Brian asked Luther questions that were polite but still obviously intended to help him understand that I am not alone in the world. Luther didn't say anything that seemed to meet with disapproval, and his demeanour was, I think deliberately, less self-assured than it had been with me, which was a strategic approach to speaking with my captors. If Mum noticed that I had used the eye pencil again, she didn't say so. I was given another midnight curfew. I draped a dusty blue muffler around my neck, and we were off.

I was quite nervous in the taxi; didn't know what to say or how to act. Luther might have picked up on this, because he talked casually about his family (in Michigan), his classes, and where he was considering going for graduate school (New York or LA). Only then did he ask about me, and he started with Oxford. I'd been thinking that he'd set the stage very carefully to help me understand that he was not looking for anything lasting, and that was fine with me.

I told him, "I've known I wanted to go to Oxford for years. I was quite put out when I was forced to leave the UK without completing my college prep where I'd been going to school."

"Quite put out, were you?" He chuckled. Then, "So . . . just finishing college prep. You're—how old?"

Ah. The question I'd avoided at the party. He had me, and I grinned at him. "I'll be seventeen next week."

"Happy birthday in advance, then."

At the restaurant, he paid the driver. Now, I want to go on record that I don't expect to be escorted by a gentleman who always picks up the bill; however, given that with Michael I had paid for everything, Luther's paying for the taxi was a refreshing change.

The place looked like fun but not overly fancy, which I liked. I didn't want to see Luther as trying too hard to impress me; that would have lowered him in my estimation, though I realise how awful that sounds—as if I'm not worth trying hard for. But it's not that. It's that trying *too* hard would have made me uncomfortable.

The menu, as Luther had said, was directly out of that odd part of Europe that's not quite Germany and not quite France. We couldn't order wine, which was really too bad, but I asked for sparkling water with lime in stemware, and Luther enjoyed that.

After we ordered, he asked, "What will you study at Oxford? Have you decided?"

"I'll be taking a fairly broad course, and it could change. I'm not aiming at any particular career yet, though I'm developing an interest in autism, and Asperger syndrome." I have no idea where that came from; it more or less fell out of me. And it felt as though it fit—at least in the absence of anything else.

"Really. That's unusual, especially in someone your age. Any particular motivation?"

My nervousness from the taxi ride was gone, and I spoke of my mother's brother and then of Persie, doing my best to highlight the inroads I've made with her without crossing that line into bragging.

"So," I concluded, "it's either that or a cat behaviourist."

Luther's laugh was hearty and gratifying. He raised his glass, and I raised mine. He said, "Here's to your noble aspirations."

We talked for a bit about the play, and I didn't let on that I'd read up about it today. "I haven't seen it," I admitted, "but I'm curious to see how the backwards time flow works. I'm not wild about plots that wreak havoc with timelines."

"No? I rather enjoy them. Maybe I like to be made to do a certain amount of guessing."

"Good to know. I'll see what I can do to accommodate."

"Only a certain amount, please note." He held my gaze as he sipped from his glass.

"And you'll get only a certain amount of accommodation."

He laughed and set the glass down. "Tell me something. Are

you representative, do you think, of British youth? I find you so much more mature and interesting than even my peers at school."

"Not British, if you please, though officially that's correct. I'm English." I gave him a quick summary of the history of England over the past millennium or so, stressing the sophistication of the Norman "invaders" over the people they pretty much conquered.

"And, of course," he said, tilting his head sideways charmingly, "you're from the Norman side of the house."

"Fitzroy. Yes. The Hunt family were nobility, just not peerage." Which led to another summary, this time about how English titles work.

"It sounds very confusing. And perhaps just understanding that convoluted hierarchy accounts for how smart you seem."

"Perhaps. Though another reason might be that most of my socialising has been with adults, not my peers." I was damned if I was going to reveal my native intelligence quotient. He was bright, but chances are he's nowhere near me. And I didn't want that to matter to him, even if I never saw him again after tonight.

We declined a sweet. Pudding. Dessert? Dessert. I said, "Will you allow me to buy you dinner?" His answer would say worlds.

He hesitated for a couple of seconds before saying, "If you like."

That was the right answer. Sort of.

I remember some of the play, which lasted just under an hour and a half. About forty-five minutes into it, Luther shifted his weight just slightly so that our shoulders and upper arms came into contact. This simple touch was enough to make me nearly unaware of anything except the roaring in my ears and the snugness at my crotch. And these jeans do not have a lot of room for . . . expansion, shall we say, so the sensations were extremely distracting. I both wanted and didn't want to move enough to adjust the seams.

It was quarter of ten by the time we were outside. "Fancy a nightcap?" he asked, and when I turned a puzzled look towards him, he laughed. "I know a great little coffee shop, just across Huntington. We could consider a bite of dessert. Maybe share something?"

"As long as they have tea."

In a horrible English accent, he said, "I wouldn't dream of suggesting it otherwise."

As we crossed the street, looking around us to avoid being run over, my eyes landed on a young man in a jean jacket, hands in his jeans pockets, standing under the awning of some store, watching us approach.

Michael.

Oh, my God. What the hell was he doing there? I didn't know whether I should say anything or not acknowledge him at all. Michael solved the problem by turning away before Luther and I got too close. If Luther noticed him staring at us, he didn't let on, and I said nothing.

Stalking me. He was still stalking me. How creepy.

Over my tea, Luther's coffee, and a shared molasses biscuit, in that funky little student hangout that could almost have been in Paris, I put Michael out of my mind. I mentioned a couple of things about the play until I felt Luther's foot, under the small table, bump gently into mine and stay there.

He said, "I have to confess, I got lost after the second or third time jump."

"You're the one who likes this format!"

"Yeah. But something was distracting me so much I had trouble paying attention."

Knowing what he was going to say, I asked, "What might that have been?"

"I think it was a certain fascinating guy who was sitting to my right."

Well, what could I say after that? I landed on this: "I'm sure I don't know whom you mean. The only fascinating guy I saw was in the other direction. On my left."

He lifted his chin. "I think we have time for a stroll by the reflecting pool."

"What's that?"

"Come with me."

I almost said, "Anywhere," but I caught myself in time.

I was glad I had brought my new gloves and muffler; it had grown rather chilly. The pool, when we got there, was divine—appropriate, since it parallels the outside wall of a huge church. Around the edges, the water flows over rounded stone, much like an infinity pool, falling quietly down into a narrow space between the pool and the walkway, making it seem as though the still water is floating on air. We walked a little way and then Luther stopped, facing the church across the water.

"You religious?" he asked.

"Not especially, no. Why?"

He pointed with his chin. "That's the Christian Science Mother Church." He pulled me gently away into a semicircle of stone, one of many along the side of the pool. "And I think they wouldn't approve of this."

His hands wrapped gently around my neck under my jaw, controlling my face, and he placed his lips on mine and his tongue in my mouth and sent me to heaven right there. I think I grabbed his hair, I'm not sure, and then something came over me. I reached one hand behind him, grabbed his ass, and pressed him against me. Maybe all that practising with Graeme had paid off. He pulled his face away just for a second, his eyes wide, and locked his mouth on mine again.

Before long it was obvious things were going to get out of hand, as it were, so we pulled apart, a little breathless, and sat on the ledge of cold stone.

He spoke first. "I have to say, you've surprised me."

"How, precisely?"

He watched whilst a man and a woman walked close by and passed. "After I met you at James and Roy's party, I was intrigued. In one way you seemed so young. But in another—I don't know, but there was something that stayed with me. I almost didn't call, but I couldn't get you out of my mind." He looked at me. "Simon, you're—I'll give you credit for seventeen. But—shit. I'm friggin' twenty-one. You're still in high school!"

I waited, but he didn't go on. So I prompted, "And the surprise?"

"I guess that would have to be the way you're acting. I mean, like, pulling me towards you just now. And picking up the dinner tab. I didn't expect that."

I nodded, remembering what Ned had told me about Luther: meeting his own needs, but honest about it. It was beginning to look like one of his needs was to be in control. "I could tell you didn't seem enthusiastic about my offer. Maybe you would have preferred me to let you treat me as though I were some old-fashioned girl?"

"Oh, now you're getting huffy. All I said was that it was surprising."

"But why? Because I'm still a child in your eyes?"

He scowled thoughtfully at me. "It's true you don't seem as young as your years."

Several seconds went by whilst I considered whether to reply to that and, if so, what to say. Did I want to call him out on his control issues, or would that be the death knell to anything else we might do together? And would that be a good thing or a bad thing?

He said, "Tell you what. Let's see where we might go from here. And let's start with something I might not have told you right away. Maybe not at all, depending." He paused briefly. "I'm bisexual."

I could tell he wanted me to be shocked. So of course, I refused to be, even though I was. "Should that matter to me?"

He laughed, really laughed. "No. But I can't tell you how many people it has mattered to very much." He ran a hand down my arm. "So this could work well for both of us. Neither of us will be here next year, and we know we're going in different directions. We can enjoy what there is to enjoy and go our separate ways. And you fascinate me. I'd like to see you again. You?"

I turned my gaze away from his face towards the church, stalling for time. I'd really, really liked kissing him. I'd like to do more than that, but I wasn't sure how much more. He seemed to be heading towards something more than a kiss-and-cuddle. Did I want that?

"I'm not sure quite how far I'd want to go." I looked back at him. "Can you live with that?"

"Why don't we see what happens? We can start low-key. How about brunch, my place, two weeks from today? I'm a pretty good cook."

His place. Well, brunch seemed unassuming enough. I decided to take the risk. "I'll bring the champagne if you provide the orange juice."

"Of course you will." He smiled at me. "I'll text you the address."

Time to take a little more control. I stood and reached a hand out. He took it, and stood, and we kissed again, with less heat this time. I pulled away. "See you in two weeks, then." And I turned and left him standing there, I hope staring after me.

I had no idea where I was, but I ended up walking north up Massachusetts Avenue, and a consultation with my iPhone—once I was sure I was out of Luther's sight—told me it wasn't far to the T stop near St. Bony. I didn't have enough time left to walk the whole way.

So yeah, I'm in lust. Because I do want to see him again. I do want to fascinate him. Will the result of that be more than I can take, though? And will I be able to control that?

Now that there's a time and place for it, I'm incredibly anxious. I'm not convinced this is how most people my age set dates up; that is, two people who barely know each other say, "Let's have sex. When's good for you?" I've heard there's a tradition, or an expectation, something, with adult straight couples, that if they're going to have sex it often happens by the third date. But I'm seventeen (for all practical purposes), and Luther isn't that much older, and we might well be skipping over two dates' worth of courtship and jumping into bed.

Is this right? Is this what I want? And how do I figure that out in two weeks?

There's this big storm headed towards the Northeast, with New York and Boston dead in its path. Sandy, a hurricane. Everyone around me has been talking about it for days. Luther and I didn't mention it; we had other things on our minds. But with my date behind me, I can sense the tension. They've even cancelled school for tomorrow. Brian had all the outdoor furniture taken in, which I gather happens every year for the winter, anyway, because of snow.

I really shouldn't have spent so much time writing about my date with Luther; if we lose power, I won't be able to get much schoolwork done.

Somehow I can't work myself into a guilty swirl over that.

Boston, Sunday, 4 November

This will have to be a short one; still haven't finished what I need to do this weekend for school, and it's after ten.

We didn't lose power in the storm, but lots of people did. It was quite exciting. At one point I went out onto my roof, which is fairly well shielded by taller buildings around it, and it was everything I could do not to get sucked into one whirlwind or another. The only bad thing for us was that it made Persie agitated, which affected everyone in the house.

My birthday was more fun than I would have expected. First, Brian had arranged for one of the housecleaners to be here and answer the door for any trick-or-treaters, so we wouldn't be disturbed. Mum and I hadn't known how much more seriously Americans take this holiday, and this was not a trivial thing. It surprised me how much I appreciated his thoughtfulness.

Ned pulled out lots of stops for dinner: beef Wellington, which I adore, creamed spinach, also a favourite, and baby red potatoes boiled and then heated in butter and crushed rosemary. The wine was a chewy St. Emilion, and Brian and I competed to see who could be more specific with tasting notes. He said I won, and I don't think it was just because it was my birthday. We both got coffee and truffle on the nose, but he didn't pick up on the liquorice until I mentioned it. The flavour notes included dark cherry and chocolate. With all the fuss, even Persie decided to try a little, but she pronounced it "awful."

The cake was a triple-layer, heavenly devil's food (if that's not an oxymoron) with the richest buttercream icing. Ned had decorated it with clumps of tiny purple dots which, when I noticed the green vines, I realised were grapes. He didn't do anything tacky like put my name or the number seventeen on it, but there were several tall, very skinny, candles clustered in the centre.

I wore one of my new outfits for dinner to acknowledge Brian's gift, but he'd done me one better. He'd bought a pair of shoes I'd tried on and loved but hadn't taken last week. They had seemed a little too flashy: a low shoe, smooth dark blue leather, with deep reddish-purple leather piping around the side panels and along the opening. The laces matched the blue. And he had remembered them.

Mum had bought me an iPad and a gift certificate for apps and material I could load onto it. You can even use it to read textbooks, so this should come in handy.

Ned gave me that leather jacket that was too small for him, the one I'd worn to the South End party. In the same box was a small bottle of Frédéric Malle Vetiver Extraordinaire.

Persie surprised everyone by asking Brian, "What did I get him?"

Brian seemed at a loss for words. So I said, "Tell you what, Persie. Over school break this winter, you can pick a place for us to go where you can show me some of your favourite art. How's that?"

She nodded and went back to her cake. I noticed Brian looking at me. I couldn't read his expression—there was amazement, but there was also some intense emotion that defied interpretation. At first I thought maybe it had to do with my suggestion to Persie, but then it hit me that Persie's question—what she might or might not have done for someone, in this case for my birthday—was not something she would ever have asked before.

I had thought this birthday would be my worst yet, other than the first one after my father died. But it was the best one since he'd taken me to get Tinker Bell. This confused me. It confused me so much that I didn't even feel like having Graeme do me any particular favours that night.

Thursday was the first of the two spelling bees at St. Bony, with Kay and her friends. I mean, Toby. I had to do a major adjustment to get back to thinking "Toby" and "him" so that I wouldn't cause any grief.

His friends Andrew, Johnny, and Janice competed with him. I was the pronouncer, and I'd reviewed the video Dr. Metcalf had sent me to be sure and do it in the official way.

I got to meet Abby Lloyd for the first time. She showed up alone, which irritated me; why couldn't Toby's father have come with her? Was he out someplace with Colleen? Or maybe "in" someplace? Mrs. Lloyd was friendly, and beautifully put together: short, dark-blond hair, stylishly cut; simple makeup; a dove grey, light wool suit, no lapels, with a pale pink blouse and a single string of creamy pearls. Simple, low-heeled black shoes. Very conservative; she'd no doubt come straight from work at her law firm.

She thanked me graciously for helping Toby prepare. We didn't talk much, but I found myself liking her a good deal. No doubt it helped that I knew she had fought with her tyrannical husband after he had had Colleen remove all Kay's girl accoutrements. And it probably helped that she told me at least twice how much it meant to Toby that I was working with him, how he thought the world of me.

The format of this bee wasn't to have anyone win or lose; all four of the kids stayed on stage the whole time. Even so, Toby didn't do as well as I had expected. He seemed anxious in a way I'd never seen. It couldn't be performance anxiety, or he wouldn't be where he is in the overall competition at this point. Which made me think it was almost certainly because Dean Furley was there, along with three other people I'm pretty sure are transgender. I made note of everything Toby missed and planned to ask a few questions next week when I saw him again.

Dr. Metcalf had done his bit; the event was pretty well attended. Even Maddy was there. We chatted for a bit before and again after—nothing terribly important, though she asked me a lot of questions about my approach with Toby. When she isn't trying to make me love her, she isn't a bad girl to talk to.

Every so often, all the nervousness about Luther I've been pushing away as much as I can comes crashing to the front of my brain. I've made a date, almost certainly to have sex. And I've never had sex. I was kissed for the first time just over a week ago.

I've been doing a lot of practising with Graeme.

Boston, Saturday, 10 November

Luther lived up to his word about texting me his address, though he waited until Friday afternoon to do it. I had to talk myself down from some psychological ledge several times, worrying that he'd forget, wondering what I should do if he did. Would it mean that he had just forgotten, which would make me feel completely unimportant? Or would it mean that he'd changed his mind and had decided this was the best way to stand me up? But, finally, a text arrived. Very direct, no frills. The address was first, followed by, *See you Sat 11*.

Saturday morning, after the most fastidious shower I've ever taken, I called a taxi to pick me up at the house; I had the champagne in a waterproof, insulated bag, and I'd thrown a little ice in. It was heavy. No T today.

Luther's flat was really half a house not far from the BC campus. I'd worn my new blue shoes, jeans, a cotton shirt pieced together artistically from large, asymmetrical pieces of different textures of white fabric, and Ned's leather jacket. The short walkway to the few steps up to the door was lined in tall yew shrubs, and I stopped there to turn my phone off; I didn't want a well-intentioned text from anyone to interrupt whatever was going to happen.

When Luther opened the door, he just stood there, looking at me. "You are always so well put together." He grinned. "Come in."

He put the champagne on the counter beside the sink and stared at it. "Okay, you non-child, you. Are you good at opening these things?"

"I am." He set two tumblers nearby. "No champagne glasses?"

"You're kidding, right?"

This was not the most expensive wine, what with the plan to mix it with orange juice, but the idea of pouring it into tumblers was almost too much for me. I barely caught myself before saying something that would have been pointless. "Where's the juice?"

"Let's just have a sip of bubbly first, shall we?"

We clinked glasses together, sipped, set the glasses down, and were in a heated embrace before ten seconds had passed. Oddly, or perhaps not oddly, we ended up on the floor. He kneaded my crotch, and it was almost enough to make me soil my new jeans. I cried out, but he smothered my mouth with his until I grabbed him the same way. He pulled away, and each of us massaged ourselves whilst we panted and laughed.

When he could speak, he asked, "There's a saying that goes, 'Life's uncertain. Eat dessert first.' Ever see that?"

"Can't say that I have. But I hope that wasn't all we're getting for dessert." Yeah; I'm ready for something more than this.

He chuckled. "No, it is not." He heaved himself up and held a hand out to me. "Let's have brunch first, eh?"

And we did. He wasn't bad in the kitchen, though either Ned or Mum could have taught Luther quite a bit. But it was fine: asparagus omelette, brioche from a bakery, mixed fruit, and of course the Buck's Fizz, using my champagne and his orange juice—a nice blending of very different substances, rather like us. He'd bought some great-looking chocolates, but I suggested we wait until later; I don't like to mix sweets with champagne.

Food consumed, we sat at his small kitchen table, swirling the last of our drinks, saying little and doing a lot of gazing at each other. Well, maybe not gazing; that implies something soft. This was not a soft feeling. It was hard, direct, and male. Maybe I don't know what the hell I'm doing when it comes to sex, but I sure know what I want to feel like.

Luther took the lead, and that was just fine with me. He stood, held a hand out, and led me to his bedroom. He undressed me slowly, and I just let him, wondering—and worrying a little, though I'm sure I could have stopped him at any time—about what he had in mind.

He stood back and admired me, his eyes falling on my erection. "And the carpet matches the drapes."

I had no idea what that meant, but I didn't really care. I reached a hand behind his neck and brought our faces together, kissing him before and after I lifted his T-shirt over his head. This felt like such a brazen act to me, but I'm sure it was appropriate in the cir-cumstances. He removed his own jeans, nothing on underneath them, and pulled me onto the bed.

He positioned me gently but deliberately so that when he was settled, we were in what I guess is the famous sixty-nine forma-tion, each of us able to grab the other's dick. I did with my hand what I hoped would feel good to him, imitating what he was doing to me—which felt out of this world—trying to avoid pulling any of the rich, dark hairs that were everywhere. And then everything changed. He'd taken me into his mouth.

Oh, my God. Oh, my God. I stopped breathing. I stopped mov-ing. My mouth opened wide, soundlessly, and stayed that way until I came, and I nearly screamed as I shot everything against the back of his throat. He swallowed but stayed on me, his mouth now very gently caressing me. I nearly fainted onto the bed and let him go on. Finally he released me, sliding gently off the end of my dick and kissing the tip of it as he let it flop onto my thigh.

And then I realised he was still hard, still in need. I roused my-self; could I do for him what he'd just done for me? I half sat up as he lay back, his beautiful, thick penis pointing to the ceiling. It curled a little to one side, which I found rather charming. There was an odd moment when I felt a certain reluctance to take it into my mouth, but I soldiered on and did my very, very best to give him the pleasure he'd given me. Within seconds I realised there was going to be a breathing issue, but it took me only one more second to figure out how to work around that problem by lifting my soft palate and breathing out as I took him in.

When he came, his shouting grunt took me by surprise, and I swallowed without having any time to think about whether I even wanted to do that. There was musk, a hint of salt, and a note of chlorine. I had to stop myself from laughing; it was a cum tasting, like fine wine. I released him as he'd done for me, and even as he lay there panting he pulled me onto his chest.

When he could speak, he said, "Oh, Red. You're a quick study."

"Always have been. But how do you know I haven't been doing this all my life?"

He chuckled. "Oh, a wild guess. I don't want you to misunderstand. You were great. Really, really great. But in my experience, people who've had a lot of sex have moves of their own. They don't tend to imitate someone else's actions. That would be mine, of course, in this case. And that's what you did. But you did it so well!"

Well, I guess that wasn't a bad review.

We kissed, and caressed, and kissed some more until I grew hard again. He pulled a small towel out from somewhere I didn't see and turned me onto my stomach, the towel under my crotch. When he pried my ass cheeks apart with his fingers I had to say, "Wait."

"Not to worry. I promise." The next sensation was such an unexpected ecstasy that I cried out. He ignored me and kept using his tongue in a way I never knew anyone would ever do. Within a few minutes I had come all over that towel. Immediately, he flipped me over again and kissed me, hard and deep. I could barely breathe.

I must have dozed for half an hour or so before I felt him get off the bed. I watched him leave the room, naked, and return with the chocolates. We lounged on the sweat-soaked sheets, tasting some of each other in the dark chocolate truffles.

"Champagne truffles," he said at one point.

I grinned and bit into another one.

There were still a couple of truffles left when he sighed and said that he had something else he needed to do today. I glanced at my watch, which was the only thing I had on: a few minutes before one. Luther didn't have a champagne stopper, so I made him promise to finish the last of the wine today. He said that would not be a problem.

Fifteen minutes later we were standing just inside his open front door, wrapped in each other's arms, kissing deeply, when I heard someone gasp.

I pulled away, my empty champagne cooler dangling by its strap from my arm, and saw a young woman at the bottom of the steps that led to Luther's door. She was around his age, a true blonde, blue eyes, and pink lipstick around the wide open mouth. The look on her face was one of horror.

All three of us were frozen like that for maybe four seconds, before Luther said, "Stephanie. You're a little early."

I pulled away from him. "What's going on?"

Stephanie said, "Yes, Luther, what's going on? What the *fuck* is going on?"

It dawned on me suddenly that Luther had arranged two dates for himself today. Me for breakfast, and Stephanie for—what, afternoon delight?

I stared at him, not quite knowing how I felt. "You said you were bisexual. You didn't say you were—I'm at a loss for words."

Stephanie was not at a loss. "You bastard!"

"Now, wait just a minute," Luther protested. "It shouldn't come as any surprise to either of you that there might be a little cross-pollination going on."

Stephanie was shrieking now. "Cross-pollination? Is that what you call this?"

It seemed unlikely that anything good was going to come of this encounter. I said, "He's all yours, Stephanie." I walked past her and out towards the street.

"Simon!"

I ignored him. I didn't have any idea what had just happened, and I wasn't sure I wanted to. It was lucky I wasn't struck by a car as I crossed Comm Ave towards the BC campus, which was the wrong way to go, anyway, if I was headed home. I wandered sight-lessly down a paved road that led into the campus and had to step to the right to avoid a large group of students coming the other way. And I found myself staring at a labyrinth.

A few years ago, my dad and mum and I had gone to France. We'd stayed in Paris, but one day we took a trip to Chartres Cathedral. Dad had particularly wanted to walk the labyrinth on the floor of that his-toric building. But when we got there, there were chairs set up all over the nave where the labyrinth was, and he couldn't walk it. We sat in the chairs, and I asked him why labyrinths were important to him.

"Lots of people confuse the labyrinth with the maze," he opened. "They're completely different. A maze deliberately sets out to confound you. There are dead ends, irregular trails that feed back on themselves, all kinds of ploys to make you lose your way. A labyrinth is exactly the opposite. And the number of circuits, and the patterns they form, are significant in both Sufi and Christ-ian traditions, so it spans East and West."

He got up and moved to a spot outside the labyrinth. "You enter here. And you follow the path, which in this style of labyrinth is extremely complex. Unless you're very, very familiar with the shape, it's impossible to anticipate when you're going to be sent in one direction or another, or when you'll be led halfway around the outside of the circle. But if you keep going, you'll eventually walk over every single spot, and you'll end up in the centre. The way out is the reverse."

As he'd spoken, I'd tried to follow the path with my eyes. The chairs made it challenging, but I quickly realised that even with-out them there I couldn't have predicted the twists and turns.

"It's like life, Simon. Unless you're looking at the pattern from overhead, you can't quite know where it's going to lead you. But if you have faith, if you put your trust in the big picture and keep putting one foot in front of the other, you'll get to where you need to be."

As I stood there on the BC campus, staring at this labyrinth shaped just like the one in Chartres, I was surprised that this description was still there in my brain. I hadn't thought about it since Dad had said it, but there it was. And it seemed as though he had just told me the same thing everyone else had been telling me for months. Put one foot in front of the other. Shift weight. Repeat.

I stepped towards the large open space and read the information that told me that the labyrinth was dedicated to the twenty-two BC alumni who had died in the attacks on September eleventh. There was no one walking it, and no one on any of the benches around the outside of it. I had the entire thing to myself. I tossed my champagne cooler on the ground, put one foot in front of the other, and moved forwards.

Somehow I knew it should be a slow walk. There should be contemplation of some kind, something to think through on the way to the six-petalled rose shape in the centre. I kept my eyes on the stone segments that made up the path at my feet and let my mind wander.

Of course, it went first to Luther, to what had happened, before and after Stephanie had arrived. Before? That was easy. Luther had been gentle, sensitive to my inexperience, and he'd made sure I enjoyed it thoroughly. It had been all about sex, but it had not been all about fucking. He'd pleasured me, and he'd taught me how to pleasure him. I could be pretty sure that almost certainly, every time Luther and I got together—if that happened again—there would be sex. And I had to expect that before long it would go beyond what had happened today to something much more invasive. Maybe it wasn't the end of the world that the sex today had been special only to me. But wouldn't I want that next important step to matter to both me and my partner?

Stephanie. What had she expected? It seemed obvious that she'd been invited for a specific time. Which means there had been something specific planned. Did he have more chocolates hidden away? And would he have offered her the remains of my champagne? Was he going to take her out someplace? Before or after they had sex? And would that act happen on the same sheets?

As for my own feelings . . . He'd told me he was bisexual, and he'd made it clear that no one should expect anything resembling love or commitment, and I had been in agreement with that. So why was I feeling so—I don't know, betrayed?

At the centre of the labyrinth, hands in my jacket pockets, I stood still and took a few slow, deep breaths. I turned slowly around, looking first at the tall, leafless trees along one side of the space and then at the stone building on the opposite side. I tried to remember anything my father had said about the centre of the shape and what it meant. The only other thing I could recall was that the outer ring, the eleventh circuit, is supposed to represent the first exhalation of the universe, of God, of The One, when he/she/it sees itself as both object and subject. I was going to have to give this some thought; I couldn't wrap my mind around it at the moment, despite the fact that the labyrinth was designed to foster exactly this kind of thinking.

And then a word flew into my mind. *Invalidated.* I felt as though my own time with Luther, my own experience, my own special-ness—even if it wasn't supposed to last in any significant way for us as a couple—had been invalidated. Luther's scheduling multi-ple partners for sex on the same day denied the importance of two individuals merging, becoming one. We're not just animals, and sex to us should have more than mere physical implications. I'm not talking about commitment, here, but sex the way I want it should blur the lines that separate two people, even for just a few moments. And there's something sacred about that, nothing to do with religion or scripture or some old man in the sky watching over us. Maybe it's the reversing of that duality, that subject-object split that happened in the universe's first exhalation. It's God breathing in again.

I shook myself; this was way, way too esoteric for me. I took an-other deep breath, released my own exhalation, and walked back through the shape. My thoughts bounced around randomly on the reverse journey; I was mostly trying to imagine what my next con-versation with Luther—if any—would be like. I ran through a number of scenarios, none of which led to anything satisfactory unless I allowed myself the luxury of telling him all those spiritual thoughts that had come to me in the rose centre. And that seemed both unlikely and ill-advised, even if he is studying philosophy.

I sat on one of the benches under the trees, feeling decidedly chilled and not really caring, when I decided to pull out my phone and turn it on again. And there was a voice message from Luther, from twenty minutes ago, probably when I was halfway into the labyrinth.

"Call me." That's all. Not "I'm sorry that happened" or "I hope you're not upset."

I put the phone into my pocket and sat back. Remembering that when Michael had changed his mind about coming to my rooftop for antipasto, I'd been very careful to give him the impression that it didn't matter to me either way. I could take that approach with Luther. But it had been dishonest then, to Michael, and it would be dishonest now. And whatever else I could accuse Luther of, dishonesty was not on the list.

I could ignore his message completely; that would be one way to let him know I didn't like being treated that way. But the fact was that I didn't like him treating Stephanie that way, either. I tried to put myself in her place. What if *she'd* been with him since eleven, and *I'd* shown up early for my date at half one, and the two of them had been standing there kissing?

Bisexuality notwithstanding, commitment-bound or not, I would have turned around and left.

I pulled my phone out and called him.

"Simon. Thanks for calling. Will you let me explain?"

"There's not much need to explain, really. It's pretty obvious what happened. The only thing I don't know, and I'm not sure it matters to me, is what your relationship is like with her. All I can know is how it makes *me* feel."

I paused, and he waited a few seconds before asking, "And how is that?"

"Invalidated."

"Simon, I never promised—"

"No. That's true. And I never expected. I wasn't looking for you to declare undying love, or any love at all. I wasn't hoping you'd dream about me for days and have to hold yourself back from begging to see me again. That's not what this was about, and I accepted that."

"Then . . . why invalidated?"

"I think you knew this was my first time. That alone made it incredibly special to me, whomever it was with. Now, if Stephanie hadn't shown up early, I'd never have known about your second date. But the fact that you were cramming two liaisons into one day cuts the importance of each of them at least in half. I can't help wondering how you thought you'd have time to shower, let alone change the sheets."

"We were going out."

"And then?"

"Then we were going over to her place. Her sheets."

I nodded, though of course he couldn't know that. "You had it all figured out, then. Well, I've figured out a few things, too. I really enjoyed this morning. Thanks for that. But I don't think I want to do this again. I appreciate your honesty; I just don't like your style."

I rang off, half expecting he'd ring me back, but after three minutes of staring at my phone I put it back into my pocket. Then I took it out again and looked up the location of the nearest T stop.

And I think that's all I want to write for now.

Boston, Sunday, 18 November

I talked with Ned about Luther as soon as I could get him to myself, which turned out to be last Tuesday afternoon. I sat at the island and he listened as he worked, occasionally asking a clarifying question but nothing else. I told him about the sex (with very little detail), about the labyrinth walk, and I stopped after describing that last phone conversation. He finished up something he was working on and wiped his hands on a towel.

"Do you remember what I told you about him?"

"I do. And you were right."

"Tell me about that epiphany again. The one in the labyrinth, about sex being the remerging of the two dualities God had divided into in the beginning of the universe."

"Is that how I put it?"

"Not quite; but isn't that what you meant?"

I shrugged. "I guess so, yes. But I wouldn't read too much into it. The ramblings of a wounded ego."

"No. That's not it at all. You're on to something important. Have you ever heard the song called "Hallelujah" by Leonard Cohen? Made famous by a number of singers, most especially Jeff Buckley?" I shook my head, and he stumbled through a few lyrics that didn't seem to gel. "Oh, hell, just go to YouTube and search for it. I think it will resonate with you."

I toyed with a few crumbs I'd dropped as I'd devoured a piece of Mum's gingerbread.

"You okay, kid?"

I lifted a shoulder. "Yeah." I grinned at him. "At least I'm not a virgin anymore."

"Oh, honey, you have no idea. But—all in good time. Now, git; I need a moment alone with some burnt sugar. It wants all my attention or it turns vicious."

Upstairs I did search YouTube, and I found the Jeff Buckley video, and I did listen to it. And then I listened to it again. And then I opened another tab and searched for the lyrics so I could follow along.

If it weren't for one particular verse, I'm not sure I would have understood what Ned had been talking about. I replayed it several times, dragging the little circle back over the progress bar. *Remember when I moved in you, and the holy dove was moving too, and every breath we drew was Hallelujah.*

I'm not fooling myself that what I had with Luther—that what I would ever have had with Luther—would even approach this. But I think I did the right thing, turning my back on a relationship that was deliberately set up to be the exact opposite, to be full of dead ends, to confound the hallelujah deliberately. I want love to be a labyrinth, not a maze. And I think sex, for me, has to at least point in that direction.

I've been so wrapped up in this situation with Luther, and so short on time generally, that I realise I've overlooked recording the fallout from the practice bee on 1 November. When I'd met with Kay on 8 November, she'd confirmed what I had suspected about her anxiety during the bee, that it was Dean and the other transgender people he'd brought with him who had thrown her off her game. She's scared to death about coming out, and her friends and even her mother were there; how could she explain who Dean was if anyone asked? I'd got Dean's phone number before I left Longwood Towers, and I'd called him that evening to ask that he not come to the next bee. He was a little put out, but I know he understood. I'm concerned that he's pushing Kay too hard. Not that there's anything I can do about that.

Neither Dean nor the others showed up for the second bee, and Toby did much better. Top of the heap, in fact. And his mother was there again, which made him very happy; this time she saw him victorious. It calmed some of my own fears, too. Because if he did really badly in March, he wouldn't go to the nationals. How much of the blame would fall on me?

I should hear from Oxford any day about my interviews—how many, which colleges, what dates. I'm all at sixes and sevens with anxiety, waiting to hear. Thank the universe for Graeme. He loves me, he pleasures me, and with him it's hallelujah every time.

Boston, Monday, 19 November

I've been sitting here staring at this screen for nearly twenty minutes. The reason I don't know where to begin is that I've wasted all my hyperbolic language, all my melodrama, all my tragedy on things that were anything but tragic, compared to today. I've run out of ways to say "life sucks and then you die."

I got a notice today. In the post. It was waiting for me when I got home from school, a true demon lying in wait to ambush me.

I can hardly bring myself to write this.

Oxford wait-listed me. No interview.

Of course, everyone in the house knew it had arrived before I even got home. And I'm sure they all expected it to say the same thing I expected it to say. That is, what I had finally convinced myself it would say. I stood in the kitchen, holding the letter, reading, with Mum and Ned looking on and ready to cheer. I read silently, and I don't think they could have said what it was that made my arms go stiff. So I had the grace of a few seconds to arrange my face, to prepare myself to say what I had to say aloud.

"Well, this is too bad," I told them, fighting to make my voice sound normal. "I'm on the waiting list." I stood there, immobilised, looking at the letter, knowing if I looked at anyone I would break down. I started to take a deep breath but quickly realised how much that would reveal that I didn't want to reveal about my true state of mind.

Mum made some motion towards me, but I shook my head ever so slightly and she froze. Desperate to keep my hands from shaking, I refolded the letter, forced it back into its envelope, and stuffed it into my school bag on the floor. As I hefted the bag I said, "Guess it's a good thing I applied to a few other schools."

"Simon?" Mum called. I stopped but didn't turn. "I'm so very sorry."

I could have said, "It's okay." I could have said, "It's not your fault." I could have said, "I think Princeton will be great for me." But I didn't believe any of it. And I couldn't think of anything to say that wasn't a brutal opposite of all of those things. So I just left her standing there.

And now I'm upstairs, too intensely stunned even to swear. Too stunned for anger at Oxford, at Mum, at Brian, at anyone. There's some kind of odd static electricity running through me. It's not energising. It's making it almost impossible for me to move. Typing is the only activity I can manage. I don't remember climbing the stairs.

I also don't remember going into the bathroom, retrieving my black leather emergency kit with the razor blades, and setting that beside me on the desk. Even if I decide to use one of them, I wouldn't do it here, so why did I fetch it?

Evidently I didn't go down for dinner. I was sitting here, staring at the screen again, still, whatever, when Ned knocked. I hadn't heard the dumbwaiter, but he'd sent my dinner up in it. He carried up a folding tray, and he set things up on it for me.

"Turn the chair, kid. I'm not leaving till you've had some dinner."

I turned my face in his direction, but I couldn't raise my eyes high enough to see his face. Couldn't muster the energy. He took hold of the chair from behind and positioned me at the tray. Then he sat in the reading chair, facing me.

I think he'd made some kind of chicken dish. There was a sauce. Maybe risotto, something with rice and mushrooms. No wine, I remember that. Maybe he figured it would only make matters worse.

"When you didn't appear for dinner, Miss Persie threw the worst tantrum I've seen since the day she nearly reamed Maxine with that notebook. Your mom's fit to be tied, ranting and forcibly stopping herself from saying unmentionable words. I think Brian's afraid to say much of anything, but there's a set to his jaw I've seen before. They're going to take some action, Simon. I don't know what. At the very least, they'll do whatever it takes to get an explanation."

I tried to nod, but nothing happened. At that moment, I didn't care. I didn't care about anything.

He stood, picked up the fork from the tray, and pointed the handle towards me. "Do I have to feed you?"

I managed to grasp the fork. I wasn't trying to be a problem. I wasn't trying to look pathetic. It's just that I couldn't feel anything, couldn't do anything. Somehow I stabbed a green bean and nibbled at one end of it.

Ned was still standing there when my phone rang from inside my school bag. I made no move to get it, so he did. He read the display. "It says Metcalf."

Suddenly I could move, but not towards the phone. In about three strides I got as far away from Ned as I could within the room, the window seat overlooking the roof. I pulled my feet up to my ass and hugged my knees hard.

I heard Ned say, "Simon's phone." In typical talk-listen pattern, he said, "He's here, but he's not feeling up to conversation. Can I give him a message? . . . Ned Salazar. I'm a friend. A close friend . . . Yes . . . What time tomorrow will you know something?"

There was more silence, then Ned looked at me and said to the phone, "She said that? . . . All right, I'll make sure he knows. Is there anything else I can tell him?" Evidently there wasn't. Ned rang off and came to sit beside me.

"He thinks something important fell through some crack or other. He's convinced this shouldn't have happened."

My words barely squeaked out. "How did he know?"

"Your mother has been raising Cain. Both Metcalf—is it Doctor?—and the headmistress are now involved. They've told your mom that their report about you was beyond glowing, and there's sure as hell nothing wrong with your grades. I guess they've sent enough kids to Oxford in the past to know how this goes, and they don't think this has gone as it should. Dr. Metcalf will phone you tomorrow after they've had a chance to speak with someone at Oxford, and your mom has already told him she'll go in with you to meet with Metcalf and Healy, both."

Suddenly there were tears. My head fell forwards onto my knees, and I sobbed. I sobbed until I couldn't breathe. If I could have spoken I might have said aloud the words that were screaming inside my head: "I'm sorry, Dad. I'm so sorry."

Ned threw an arm around my shoulders and pulled me to him. At some point I couldn't hold onto my knees any longer. I fell against Ned and let him hold me until the sobbing quieted down.

When I could speak, I said, "I don't even know what I want anymore. Nothing has gone right. Nothing has gone as it should have gone. Nothing is what it's supposed to be."

"So if you get a big, fat apology from Oxford, will you go?"

I almost laughed. "Even if they've committed the most egregious error, they won't apologise. They'll just say, 'Ah, yes. Meant to offer you a spot. Terrible mix-up, what?' "

He chuckled. I didn't. He got up, found a box of tissues and held it out towards me. "Want me to heat up your dinner?"

Blowing my nose, I shook my head. Ned laid a hand on my shoulder and more or less led me back to my chair. He handed me the fork again. I took it and made as good an effort as I could to eat. I got about halfway through everything and just couldn't manage any more. I set the fork down and looked at Ned.

"I don't know that I'd go now in any case."

"I don't blame you. But let's find out what the problem is before you make a decision." He lifted the tray out of the way.

On an impulse, I opened the folder on my computer where I keep Tink's pictures. I said, "This was my cat." The fact that I had to use the past tense made my eyes tear up all over again, and my breath caught several times as I moved through the photos. Ned made a few appropriate comments, and when I'd gone through them all he pulled me to my feet and into a tight hug.

My voice breaking, I said, "Even if I go home I can't have her back. She's Margaret's cat now."

He rocked me gently and said, "I know, sweetie. I know."

There was a knock at the door. Ned went to answer it as I told him, "I don't want to talk to anyone."

It was Mum. She told Ned, "I just want to make sure he's all right."

And suddenly, there was the anger. But I didn't shout. My voice was icy. "I'm not all right. I don't know how I'll ever be all right again. It's all gone, now—truly, all gone. And you can stop pretending that you care what happens to me. I know you didn't want me."

"Didn't want you! Oh, Simon, what on earth makes you say that?"

"You told me yourself. You said you hadn't wanted children, and you certainly didn't have any after me."

"No. Oh, no, that's not the way it was, at all! I wanted children very much."

"That's not what you said when you told me about Clive. I was an accident."

"Simon, you were no accident! I had two miscarriages before you, and another one after. I didn't plan to have children *before* I met your father. And that was because of Clive." She stepped farther into the room, towards me. "Simon, darling, how long have you been thinking these things?"

"I—I never knew. About the miscarriages."

"One doesn't like to talk about them. They're horribly painful, and I felt I'd failed your father. Simon, you were wanted. Desperately wanted. You still are."

It's difficult to articulate what I felt at that moment. Approaching it like fine wine, there were notes of shock and then disbelief in the nose; the body was dense with complex layers of grief, pain, and something that was almost but not quite joy; and the finish was numbness and confusion and an unidentifiable sense of loss.

I spun around to face the opposite wall, not wanting her to see what was happening on my face, determined not to reveal specific emotions until I'd had time to process this news. I felt rather than heard her approach me. "Don't," I said to forestall the embrace I knew she would offer. "Leave me alone. Go away."

Her voice was soft, even tender. "I will go. But first I want you to know that I'll do everything in my power to correct this wait-list situation. There's been an error, Simon. It's the only explanation. I haven't talked to you about this, because I know you haven't forgiven me and mostly avoid talking to me, but I've met several times with Dr. Metcalf and twice with Dr. Healy. All along, all through your time at St. Boniface, they've been extremely impressed with you. They've seen the effort you've made, and they've seen the results. They've seen your creativity, your resourcefulness. And they were horrified when I called them with this news. Horrified, Simon. We're all throwing our full weight behind this. You deserve Oxford, if you want it."

Without another word, she turned and left.

Ned squeezed my arm. "Anything I can get you? A glass of wine?"

I took a couple of shuddering breaths. "I'd like some brandy."

"No shortage of that in this house. Shall I bring some up?"

A picture of myself sitting up here alone, drinking brandy, seemed too depressing. Maybe it was also that I felt Oxford had betrayed me, and possibly my home was here, now. Whatever the reason, I told Ned, "I'll go down. Aren't you here rather late? Shouldn't you be home with Manuel?"

He smiled. "I'm leaving shortly. Manuel knows what's going on, and he understands why I wanted to stay for a bit. He wants to meet you, by the way. We'll have to arrange it sometime soon. I'll put your drink order in downstairs." He paused in the doorway, the folded tray under his arm. "You're gonna be fine, kid. I know it seems ugly right now, but you'll end up wherever you want to end up. Promise."

I did go downstairs for a glass of brandy. Brian and I sat in the music room and listened to Gregorian chant.

Boston, Tuesday, 20 November

We had the meeting this morning at eleven o'clock. Mum and I walked together down Marlborough, very much as we had for my placement exams so many weeks ago. We didn't talk; I don't think either of us would have known what to say.

We sat in chairs in Dr. Healy's office, whilst Dr. Metcalf stood off to the side, leaning against a wall, arms crossed on his chest. It seemed to me at first that he was trying to look casual, but before long I realised that he was trying to keep his fury in check.

Dr. Healy sat at her desk, hands folded before her. "As I'm sure you're aware, Simon, universities are not looking merely at grades, no matter how stellar they might be. They do the best they can to get a picture of the entire person. This is especially true of institutions such as Oxford. There are students there who don't have anywhere near the native intelligence you have, but they've proven themselves eager to learn and willing to grow, and they've managed to excel at something important that makes them stand out."

She shuffled a few papers, but didn't look at them. "What they told me today is that they examined your Swithin résumé and found it wanting in areas other than academics."

Mum started to say something, but Dr. Healy held up her hand.

"Hear me out, and I'll answer any questions I can. Then they looked at your St. Boniface grades, which are equally impressive. They also looked at the commentary that Dr. Metcalf and I had provided. There's your work with Toby that goes well beyond the project scope, which you've handled with sensitivity and good judgement. You've had success not only at working with your step-sister, but also in having the insight to pull what you learned from those interactions into your work. Early drafts of your papers have demonstrated not only excellent critical thinking, but also creative innovation. But because the Oxford reviewers hadn't seen anything like that from your work at Swithin, they weren't sure how much weight to give it."

She set the papers down and sat back in her chair. "Dr. Metcalf and I urged them to reconsider. We pointed out the difficulties of moving to an entirely new country, and we stressed how it would seem as though going through this fire has brought out the true metal in you. Quite frankly, we told them it will be their loss if you go anywhere else."

She smiled. "Now for the good news. You're off the waiting list."

My brain stopped working just long enough for me to nearly miss what she said after that.

"And you have interviews beginning this coming Friday at ten a.m. You'll speak with tutors from four different colleges. That's more than most students talk to, so it would seem they've taken appropriate notice now." She shuffled papers again. "I wrote them all down. . . . Here it is. Magdalen, Christ Church, Pembroke, and Trinity. That last one took me by surprise; Trinity is mostly theology, not your PPL course like the other three, but they'll have a reason. Trinity will talk with you separately; the other three tutors will speak with you at the same interview—unusual, but this is an unusual situation. I'll e-mail you the full list. The interview will be in Magdalen because of your grandfather's connection."

"Nothing from New College?" I asked.

"No. Did you hope to go there? They don't offer the aspects of your PPL course that you seem to be headed towards."

I was ashamed to say I hadn't even looked. When I'd been there years ago with Dad just to see the place, I'd known nothing about what I might study. I'd just really liked the look of it. So it was where Graeme and I were going to go together in my fantasy. And now, if it didn't offer the best course for me . . . With yet another shock, I realised this was a whole new me: I wasn't going to push this. I wasn't going to insist. I wasn't going to try and have my way, come hell or high water. I have, indeed, been through some fire. Just remains to be seen what kind of metal I am.

"No," I said quietly but firmly. "That's all right."

Dr. Healy continued, "As you know, interviews typically take place in December. They've scheduled these interviews for you this week because they've already assigned the December inter-view slots, so you'll be in there ahead of the other candidates. I told them I would ask if you're still interested."

I sat there, numb and dumbstruck, trying in vain to force my brain into gear.

"What shall I tell them? Would you be willing and able to travel to Oxford for a Friday morning interview?"

I could tell that Mum was feeling much the same way I was by this point, which was almost but not quite *Tell them to go fuck them-selves.* In her haughtiest English accent she said, "As it happens, there is a contemporary art exhibit at the Tate I'd like to see, and my husband and I are in the market for a new piece or two, so we could browse the London galleries. I believe we could possibly make that date, if Simon still wants to give them a chance." She didn't look at me, just left me space to say whatever I wanted. Which for the moment was nothing.

That was the first I'd heard of an art search. Didn't mean it wasn't true, but I'll bet they hadn't planned to go just now.

Again, I was silent a little too long. Mum turned to me, not impatient, but it was time for me to say something. "What do you think, Simon? Do you want to go home and talk about it?"

I looked at Dr. Metcalf. He was grinding his jaw, staring at something over my head. Watching his face, I said, "I'll be there Friday." He looked at me, and his face softened. Something in his eyes told me that although he was angry at Oxford on my behalf, he approved of my not standing on principle now. He wanted me to go. He'd fought for me to go. I felt overwhelmed by a rich, bittersweet feeling; it was almost like my father was fighting for me.

Dr. Healy said, "Unless you feel otherwise, I'll wait until tomorrow morning to confirm. Let them sweat just a little, eh?"

Mum stood and shook hands all around. "Thank you both, very much, for supporting Simon in this." To me, she said, "We've got some packing to do, haven't we?"

I shook Dr. Healy's hand. "Thank you. I really appreciate this."

I turned to Dr. Metcalf and held out my hand. He reached out and embraced me.

So I've got my interview. Ned was thrilled and gave me a big hug. Brian even came in from his office, beaming when Mum told him the news. And there really is a special art exhibit, and Mum and Brian really are in the market for art. So they'll stay in London whilst I take the train to Oxford for my interviews. I like that arrangement better than having them come with me.

I think.

I have to say, though, after this crisis, my attitude is radically changed. I'll go to the interviews, but they will be as much *of* Oxford as *by* Oxford. Which is to say that having them pull this on me has made me feel much less invested. They won't be able to intimidate me. And if they don't take me after the interview, if I don't get an offer in January, I'll shake the dust off my feet and move on. With the glowing report from St. Boniface, I feel confident of admission to a good school someplace else.

I sent Kay an e-mail wishing her a happy Thanksgiving and letting her know I was on my way to England, and why. I knew she'd be glad for me.

London, Thursday, 22 November

I'm just going to type that again.
London.
London!
I can't quite believe I'm on English soil again. I've been in Boston long enough so that London seems enormous, but in a good way. We arrived late last night. Brian managed to get three tickets, despite the Thanksgiving crush. The UK is not a typical destination for this holiday, so although the Boston airport was a zoo, the flight wasn't quite packed. Interestingly, Persie had asked if she might come. Instead of just saying no, Brian sat down with her and described what the trip would be like, especially the airports. And *she* decided she'd stay home.

At this moment, Mum and Brian are at the Tate Modern. I'm writing this whilst at afternoon tea in the Lanesborough, where we're staying. I'm not sure they approve completely of my working away right here, but—too bad. I have missed really good afternoon tea profoundly, I'm all by myself, and I'm not going to sit and stare blankly around me.

I visited Tink this morning. Margaret was at school, but her mother was delighted to see me.

"She's the most wonderful cat, Simon. Your mum had said, but I thought maybe it was just that she was that fond."

Tink knew me. She came right over and wound around my ankles. I stroked her gently, massaged her spine above her tail, and picked her up. She sat on my shoulder just like old times, rubbing my neck with her face and purring and purring and purring. I closed my eyes and buried my nose in her fur. She smelled just the same as she always did.

I wanted to hold her so tightly! It would have killed her for sure. I played with her some and gave her a couple of treats. She was happy and well cared for—not that I'd had any doubts, but still one wants to be sure. I left Margaret a handwritten thank-you note, gave Tink one last kiss, and headed back to the hotel.

I'm still not nervous about my interviews tomorrow. It feels so right, being here. It really is home. Actually, it feels rather peaceful.

I had a nice nap before dinner, a meal that was above excellent. The Lanesborough's Apsleys can do no wrong. Plus, now that we're back in civilisation, as long as an adult orders for me, I can have wine with dinner. I had salmon tartare, venison with wood mushrooms, and chocolate soufflé. The wine was a rich, fruity Châteauneuf-du-Pape. With pudding, I was tempted by a port, but Brian ordered Château d'Yquem for the table. I noticed he chose the least expensive vintage, but this . . . this elixir, this nectar from the gods, is costly beyond belief.

So I'm a little tipsy, but it's a pleasant buzz. I have to get up early tomorrow to travel to Oxford. I had the hotel press my interview clothes, which are strictly St. Boniface. If they didn't like what I did at Swithin, let them see me as a St. Boniface product.

I haven't let myself dwell on what I'd learned from Dr. Healy. Being a little drunk, my inhibitions are lowered, so maybe I'll go there now, and think as I type.

My marks were not in question; that much is clear. So, stretching my mind back over my Swithin career, although I was in the debate club when I was fifteen, I dropped it after that.

Why?

Thinking . . . thinking . . . As I recall, I got kind of fed up with some of the other pupils. Impatient. I didn't much like any of them, and they annoyed me.

I was in the tennis club one year, too. Same problem.

These words just flew into my brain: "You walk around with this chip on your shoulder. It doesn't take much to set you off, and when you're set off, you let everyone know it." Words spoken to me by one Michael Vitale after I lost patience with Chas and X.

This memory sent me over to a parallel but very different one, of when I had told Luther I'd had enough of him. I do see that as different in every way, including what I said, how I said it, and why I said it. Instead of judging him, I'd taken his lead—the one in which he makes sure his needs are met. He'd met one need of mine, which was to experience sex with someone. But after that, my needs and his diverged. It was as simple as that. It didn't make him wrong or me right.

If I use these two events, similar in nature but revealing different versions of me, what kind of substance was I, and what kind of metal have I become?

It's just struck me that this question is important not only to me, but also it could be something I'm asked about tomorrow. If what I'd seen on the Internet was true, they're more likely to ask me questions like this than to demand a chronology of England's monarchs.

So. Before the fire? Before Boston . . . I see that version of myself as rigid, stiff, unyielding . . . brittle. That's the right word. I was brittle. And after Boston, on this side of that fire?

The obvious place to begin, of course, is steel. But there are various kinds of steel.

An Internet search has told me that there are three good carbon steels for sword making: 1045, 1060, and 1095. Of course, my first inclination was to relate to 1095; it's the most refined and the most expensive. But examining the properties of these three, I see that 1095 is the most brittle, even though it will keep the keenest edge. That seems rather like where I used to be. It's important for me to admit this without being proud of it. I realise with a certain amount of shame that I have taken pride in exactly these aspects of my personality, and looking back I see that leaning on them—defining myself by them—is why I don't make friends. Not only has it made me unlikeable, but also it's made it hard for me to like others.

Carbon 1045 is softer and easier to work with. But no matter how much fire I'm put through, I'll never be soft or easy to work with.

Carbon 1060 is a good balance between strength and pliability. It's where I want to land, in terms of who I am. And I think I'm on the right path.

There has to be a way to work this thought process into my interviews tomorrow. And given that this transformation was the lever my mentors at St. Boniface used to open Oxford's doors, it seems very likely they'll want to know why they should consider me now, when they wouldn't have considered me at all if I'd stayed at Swithin.

. . .

I need a minute, here.

. . .

They wouldn't have considered me at all if I'd stayed at Swithin.

. . .

It occurs to me that this is the very thing they will want me to say. But—can I say it? After all the fuss I made? After nearly committing suicide *twice?* How much of a fool does this make me?

I've just spent maybe forty-five minutes sitting in a chair by the window, looking out across the relative darkness of Hyde Park. The conclusion I've come to is this: I'm not a fool, but I have been foolish. That said, my mother and Brian are not blameless. Like Luther in some ways, they put their own needs first. The question is whether a truly devoted parent would have waited for me to finish at Swithin to avoid yanking me into an unknown environment at a crucial time of my life. Mum couldn't have known that limiting my career to Swithin would have lost me my chance at Oxford, rather than assured me of it.

If she hadn't followed her own needs, though, I would have stayed at Swithin, and lost Oxford. Swithin was not going to begin my transformation into carbon 1060.

Life is complicated. And whilst I do think we can make some judgement calls on each other's behaviour, we can't ever be sure about the future, and we can't know whether an apparent blackness is only that, or if it will force us to improve ourselves so that we can create light.

Success will depend on how we manage change. Brian told me that once, and I hated him for it.

Enough. If I go round on this again, I'll be up all night.

London, Friday, 23 November

Back in Boston, they celebrated Thanksgiving yesterday. I'm celebrating it today.

After all that insistence that I wasn't nervous—well, of course I was. As I've said before, I'm fine once a test begins, but right before it I'm quite anxious. And it wasn't just the interviews. There was also the train ride to Oxford, which I'd done only once years ago with my father, and getting around Oxford. I didn't quite know what to expect: Would taxis abound, or would they be scarce? Mum offered to hire a car for me, but I really wanted to do this on my own. So I suffered through the shakes.

As it turned out, the train ride was nothing much, and although there weren't a lot of taxis about, I managed; the overall campus isn't horribly spread out, and I wasn't carrying anything heavy, just my book bag with my tablet, my mobile, a paper notebook, and a couple of pens.

I'm not going to try and rehash all my interviews. The most important things I had to say are in my last journal entry, and I made sure I said them.

Other than that, there were two things that stood out from the sessions. One was that the Pembroke tutor, Dr. Franklin, asked me the most questions—and got the best answers out of me—about the idea of working in the field of autism. Dr. Franklin was absolutely fascinated by my experiences with Persie. She knows

Persie has AS, which is different, but it's still autism. She was especially taken with my approach—to think of it like working with a cat. She was equally fascinated by the way I had used my synaesthesia in conjunction with the art that Persie already loved to communicate with her. All three of them liked that I had pulled so many aspects of my new environment into my academic work, but Dr. Franklin was the most enthusiastic.

The other thing that stood out was that Trinity wanted to talk to me at all. It turns out they'd seen quite a bit of my writing, both from Swithin and from St. Boniface, and they saw a philosophical bent that made them encourage me to consider comparative theology. Once I knew this, I realised that to take full advantage of all opportunities to get an offer from somebody at Oxford, I needed to describe my experience in the labyrinth. I was careful not to be too specific about what had driven me to walk the shape that day. Dr. Aspenwald was at least as fascinated by my metaphysical meanderings as Dr. Franklin had been about Persie.

After this interview I took myself on a little tour of Trinity. It has probably the most beautiful library I've ever seen. The grounds are lovely, and the buildings ornate and impressive.

Then I found Pembroke, which is a little farther out of town from Magdalen and Christ Church. This isn't necessarily a bad thing, and it's not like it's terribly far. Magdalen is small and pretty, and Christ Church is large. I'm leaning away from that larger size; I think I do better in smaller groups.

I was standing outside the dining hall at Pembroke, marvelling at how similar it is to other buildings all over the campus, when someone came round a corner quickly and walked right into me.

"Oh! Sorry, really." He seemed about to go on, but he looked more closely at me. "Say, are you a student here?"

"Not this year. Maybe next." He was adorable. Fresh face, lively blue eyes, blond hair going every which way.

He held out his hand. "Spencer-Nelson. Julian."

I took his hand. "Fitzroy-Hunt. Simon."

We dropped hands, but held eyes. He said, "I'm only a lowly fresher. That what you'll be next year?"

"Mmmm. What are you reading?"

"Linguistics, mostly. You?"

"More general PPL. Might study autism and related disorders."

"Brilliant. Um, are you on campus for a while?"

"No, actually, about to head back to London."

"That where you live?"

"No. Staying at the Lanesborough for a few days. We're in Boston currently."

"Lovely restaurant, Apsleys. Love to pick your brain about Boston sometime. I've visited a cousin there and can't quite make sense out of the place. Listen, if you get back here . . ." He dug into a pocket and handed me a card.

"Thanks. I'll look you up. I'm in between cards; in between countries, you know." I made a mental note to have cards made, even if they had to have the Marlborough Street address.

We nodded, in typical English fashion having sized each other up thoroughly enough to know that we have much in common: our backgrounds, our education, our social standing, our hyphenated last names, and our sexual orientation. All without fuss.

I love England.

I stood for a good five minutes staring into the front gate of New College from the street. Then I headed for the train.

I had another school visit to make today, and I didn't want to do it in school clothes. If I've had a transformation, I want to look transformed. So I went to the hotel when I got back to London and put on some of those new clothes Brian had bought me. Over the black shoes I wore my tightest jeans, a silk shirt in a terrific pattern of coloured lines, and the shearling jacket with the cape-like lapels. I made sure my new hairstyle was perfectly coiffed. And I took myself over to Swithin.

I stood across the street for a bit, marvelling at how impressive the place looks. The wrought iron front gate is formidable. When I went over and rang the bell, I recognised the guard who appeared. I smiled at him.

"Baker. Good to see you."

"I'm sorry, sir. You are—?"

I blinked. "It's me. Fitzroy-Hunt. Simon."

He blinked back. "So it is. Sorry, sir; didn't know you at first. Back for a visit?"

"Yes, please."

He opened the door, and I puzzled over whether I looked so very different out of school clothes, or whether I'd really changed substantially.

I wandered into a couple of buildings, decided against going towards any of the classrooms, and found myself outside the library. I'd seen several pupils I recognised, but even when I looked right at them they didn't respond. Could be English reserve not letting them look closely; hard to tell. I stood at the library door, debating whether to look up a couple of my old teachers, when I heard my name.

"Fitzroy-Hunt? Is that you?"

I looked to my right, directly into the eyes of Graeme Godfrey. Something about him seemed more mature—maybe just that his hair was a little shorter. In amazement, I realised he was not as handsome as my Graeme.

I found my voice. "It is. Though no one else seems to recognise me."

"Well . . . look at you. You're not the same person at all."

"No?"

He shook his head, and by the look on his face I could tell he approved of the change. "Are you back?"

"Interviewing at Oxford. Thinking seriously of Pembroke. Though Trinity gave a very good interview as well."

"Interviews? Already? Mine's not for two weeks. And . . . what do you mean, they 'gave' a good interview?"

I smiled a knowing smile. "Mine is a special case. And of course, I was interviewing them as well. It's not just me on trial, y'know."

He laughed. "You haven't changed that much, then. Still arrogant. But I always liked that about you."

It was on the tip of my tongue to say, "What else did you like? And what do you like better now?" Instead, I asked, "You still with . . . What was her name?"

"Madeleine, I think, when you were here." My mind went to red-haired Maddy in Boston, and I had to shake myself mentally. "It's Brenda now. You? Anyone special?"

"I've been seeing a couple of guys in Boston, sure. Nothing serious, of course. Knew I was coming back to England."

"What did you say?"

"Which part?" I knew very well which part. I made him ask, though.

"You said 'guys.' "

"Of course." I waited two beats. "I'm gay, you know."

"Uh, no. That is . . . no."

I reached out a hand and grasped his upper arm briefly. "Good to see you, Godfrey. Maybe we'll run into each other at Oxford." I walked away whilst he was still gawking.

Yes! That felt good. That felt so fucking good. And I don't even know why.

I like my Graeme so much better. Even so, this Graeme was right. I'm not the same person he once knew. Boston has changed me.

Boston: sky blue, terra cotta, blood red, bright blue, terra cotta, coral.

London: bright orange, terra cotta, coral, dark brown, terra cotta, coral.

Not that different, really.

London, Heathrow, Saturday, 24 November

I hate waiting to board a plane. And the airport isn't the best time or place for journalling, but I want to get something down whilst the memory is still fresh.

Our flight isn't leaving until late afternoon, so this morning I told Mum I was going to visit Dad's grave. I watched her face as she struggled over whether to come with me or not, and in truth I wasn't sure what I wanted. Finally, she said, "I'll come with you, if that's all right." So we hired a car from her old friends at London Black Cabs.

It was a drizzly day, the first wet day since we'd arrived; appropriate for a graveside visit, I suppose, but I wish it had been fair. This close to the winter solstice at this latitude, sunshine is a pale light that creates almost no contrast, but I kind of like that.

I think Mum and I were both ashamed at how long it took us to locate the grave. There had been a bit of a dilemma when he had died, because there was exactly one spot left in his family plot, a few generations clustered in there, so Mum couldn't ever have joined him. In the end she decided it would be a shame not to bury him here, in this truly lovely spot of the East Cemetery of Highgate, and of course it was just possible she might marry again. It was the right choice, as things turned out, and I'm glad he's here with his ancestors instead of waiting through eternity in half of a double site that my mother would now almost certainly not join him in. For myself, I think I want to be cremated and scattered someplace; I don't like the idea of being buried.

Mum and I gazed down at the grave, under branches mostly empty of leaves, two large umbrellas keeping us at a prescribed distance from each other. I looked at her, she at me, and on impulse I lifted my umbrella over hers and we joined arms.

My eyes were dry; hers were not, and I held her umbrella whilst she pulled out a handkerchief. As she retrieved the umbrella she said, "You take whatever time you need, Simon. I'm going back to wait in the car."

I watched her for several paces and then turned back to the grave. The deep breath I tried to take was shaky.

Softly, aloud, I said, "The thing is, one can have more than one spouse. But one never has more than one father."

I let my mind roam through the collection of memories. Our matching hair, our synaesthesia, going to church together—which was always special, even after my faith began to fade—our joint dream of Oxford for me and the visit we took to see it, Tinker Bell

. . . Each category held multiple images. I could hear his laugh, the teasing tone he often took with me.

"I'm gay, Dad. Did you know?"

I'll never have an answer to that question, but I don't for a second doubt that he loved me utterly, completely. Unconditionally. That means it wouldn't have mattered.

I wasn't aware of the first few tears, but as more followed them I heard myself say, "Why did you have to die? Why did you do that?" I doubled over with a couple of deep, gut-wrenching sobs before I managed to get myself under control.

How many times had I gone to stand across the street from where it happened? A simple chemist shop, a drugstore to Bostonians. He stopped for something, we never knew what, some incidental. Nothing critical. He was almost all the way to the back of the shop before he realised that the other customer, whose back was towards Dad, was holding a gun on the pharmacist.

The story we have comes from the pharmacist, who survived. She said that Dad saw what was happening and tried to sneak up behind the thief, but a floorboard creaked. The man whipped around, firing as he turned, and Dad was dead in a matter of minutes.

Maybe once a week for a long time, I would stand across the road from that shop, leaning against a wall, hands in my pockets, a scowl on my face, and stare. Once, a policeman approached me and asked why I was loitering there.

I glared at him. "My dad was shot in that shop. He died."

"Yes. Well. Don't you do any mischief, now."

I continued to glare as he crossed the street and went into the shop, which led me to believe they had rung the police to complain, not knowing who I was or why I was willing the place to burst into flames.

Even today, I struggle with whether I'll ever be able to forgive my father for being such a noble fool. The pharmacist was giving the guy what he wanted, he was wearing a mask so he wasn't recognisable, and he would almost certainly not have shot anyone.

"The thing is, Dad, it was not your problem."

My litany. Was it a lesson I was meant to learn, or a child's reaction to tragedy? Given another chance, would my father do the same again?

What would I do?

Boston, Monday, 26 November

Persie, who keeps surprising everyone but me, missed me. She said so over dinner last night. I assured her I had missed her, too, and she went back to her food group calculations.

This morning, back at school, I let both Dr. Healy and Dr. Metcalf know how well I thought things had gone at Oxford. I gave them highlights of the interviews and let them know why Trinity was interested.

Dr. Metcalf was delighted. "I knew it! I could tell there's a religious philosopher in you. A true freethinker, not a disciple."

He also asked what college I was hoping for. I told him Pembroke, knowing even as I said it that Julian—Spencer-Nelson—had nothing to do with that. If we met again, he would be a friend, nothing more. Dr. Metcalf smiled and nodded. "I like that school for you, Simon. It's just big enough, and it has a specialness that places like Christ Church have lost to a kind of generalness, if that's not too simplistic. Or even if it is."

At home, whilst Ned worked on dinner prep, he made me sit at the island and tell him everything, soup to nuts as he put it. His favourite bit was my running into Graeme. Of course, I had to preface that story by letting him know Graeme was the straight guy I'd mentioned when Ned had brought dinner to the roof for me, back a lifetime ago.

"I love it. And, Simon, you have changed, quite a bit. Not just your hair, and not just your clothes, no matter how gorgeous you look in them. It's the way you stand, the way you hold your head, the relaxation around your eyes. It's like before, you were trying to insist on something you expected people to doubt. Now, if they believe you, that's great. If they don't, no big deal."

I thought about this for a few seconds. Then, "How do I hold my head?"

"You stand straighter now. You used to have kind of a hunched posture, and you'd poke your chin into the air and narrow your eyes. Now you're taller than your mom, and it shows."

He was right. It had snuck up on me.

Just got off the phone with Kay. Her sky has fallen.

In my room after dinner, I was settling down with homework when my phone rang; not a number I recognised, but I answered. Kay whispered over the line.

"I waited to call you. I know how important that trip was, so I didn't want to pester you."

When she didn't go on, I said, "With what?"

"I'm kind of grounded."

"What? Why?"

"I told them. On Thanksgiving."

Oh, my God. "Are you all right?"

"I don't know."

"Did they fight?"

"They haven't stopped. Mommy wants me to get the drug therapy. Father is being awful. He called me names, Simon. I hate him." She was on the verge of tears.

What the hell could I do with this? "What does 'grounded' mean? Can I still work with you?"

And here came the tears. "Oh, Simon, please don't be mad. He was saying such awful things, and I thought he liked you. So I was trying to show him that wonderful people can be different. And now he says I can't see you anymore." The sobbing got worse.

I ground my teeth and somehow managed to bite my tongue, and blood seeped out. When I thought she could hear me, I said, "Kay, don't worry about me. I'm not mad. I'm not sure what we'll do, but this will change. Something will change. I just don't know what, yet." God, but I sounded like my mother, promising me Oxford had made an error. "You're not even supposed to be calling me, are you?"

"No. This is Mommy's phone. She said I could call you. Father took mine." More tears. Then, "I can't stand this, Simon. I want to die."

Somehow, maybe because of my own experiences, I knew she meant it.

"I'll get to you, somehow. Don't panic."

"Easy for you to say."

"Kay, don't do anything. Don't make any decisions. And I mean *any* decisions. Promise?" An American expression came to me. "Hang in there, Kay. Promise me?"

"I guess. I'll try. Please help me, Simon. Please."

Not my problem? Like hell, not my problem.

And I think I know something I can do about it.

Boston, Tuesday, 27 November

The first thing I did this morning was to ring St. Boniface to see when I could have a few minutes with Dr. Metcalf. I was told I could sneak in a brief consult at quarter of twelve.

Then I looked up the Boston administration offices for Blue Cross Blue Shield. It looked to be a fairly easy T ride from here. I rang the main number and asked for George Lloyd's office. Flattening my accent as much as possible, I told his secretary I was doing a school project about financial models for health care in the United States and asked if I could have half an hour of his time, today if at all possible. She put me on hold, and when she got back on the line she said I could have fifteen minutes at half four and asked my name. In a panic, knowing he would refuse to see Simon

Fitzroy-Hunt and not having considered this earlier, I said, "Luther Pinter."

After that, I buckled down to do some online research for my City course.

I was waiting outside Dr. Metcalf's office five minutes before my appointment, and he was four minutes late arriving. Leading the way into the office, he started speaking before I could say a word.

"I was going to call you this morning, but then I saw you'd made this appointment, and I figured it was for the same thing. Mr. Lloyd called me late yesterday afternoon and told me he's removing Toby from the project, that you're not to contact him again. He wouldn't give me a reason. Is this why you're here now?"

"Yes. Kay called me last night from her mother's phone, whispering. She told her parents about her true nature on Thanksgiving. Her mother wants her to get the drug therapy, but her father is taking this draconian approach." I told him Mr. Lloyd knows I'm gay and that he had been verbally abusive to Kay.

Dr. Metcalf sat at his desk, his fingers at his hairline, scowling. "This is such a difficult situation, Simon. We can't interfere in a family matter." He sat back. "It won't reflect badly on you, your work on the project—"

"I couldn't care less about the project. I think Kay is suicidal. She said she wants to die, and I believe her."

He stood and paced the room a few times. "I think the only thing I can do is contact his school and have a counsellor there talk to him. Her. Do you have any reason to think she's already contacted the counsellor?"

"She didn't say anything like that. I wish I'd thought to tell her to do it."

He nodded. "Leave this with me, Simon. And don't go against Mr. Lloyd's direction. *That* could cost you, and it almost certainly won't help." He sat down again. "I have a few minutes now to make that call. Did you need me for anything else?"

"No. I'm fine. Thanks for anything you can do." I shut the door behind me.

I needed someplace quiet to sit and think, or sit and not think. I thought of that green close I'd seen from my placement exam room. It was not so green now. The weather forecast was for wet snow, and it looked like that would start any second. Should mean no one else would be there. I grabbed my folding brolly and made my way out to a bench under a fir tree. I was struggling to come up with the ideal approach for when I got to Blue Cross later, not landing on anything focused, when someone else came into the close. I saw a flash of red hair and a green coat. Maddy. She didn't see me. She nearly threw herself onto a bench on the other side of the close, and I saw her face crumple. She was weeping.

I tried not to look at her, but I was afraid to get up and give her some privacy for fear she'd see me and be totally embarrassed. Carefully averting my gaze, I put my mind to Kay's problem and what I was going to do.

"Oh, my God."

I looked at Maddy, and she was looking at me. Game over. I got up and went to her. "Can I help with something? What's upset you?"

She blew her nose, and I sat beside her. "Oh, it's the same old story. No one has asked me to the holiday dinner. No one ever asks me anywhere. I've never been on a date at all. Well, maybe once, but I'm not sure it counts. It was a blind date, and it didn't go very well." She blew her nose again whilst I tried to wrap my mind around dating and dinners. I couldn't come up with what the holiday dinner even was. Should I be planning to go to it?

She sniffled. "I've tried so hard to be nice to people. And to be patient. And to be brave. I even asked two boys to the dinner. They both said no. One of them laughed." It looked like she was about to cry again.

"I, uh, I don't like admitting this, but—what holiday dinner?"

That surprised her enough that she stopped crying. "It's on December 15, at the Long Wharf Marriott. All the seniors. Some teachers will be there, but parents are pointedly not invited. How could you not know?"

It was a challenge not to say that I'd been a little busy, what with a suicidal transgender child, a bisexual almost-boyfriend, and having to make a spur-of-the-moment international trip to salvage my chance at Oxford.

"I've never been big on social events." I looked at her. "Actually, I've never had much in the way of friends. Plus, you know, there's the gay thing." I shifted on the bench to face her better. "Madeleine Westfield, would you do me the honour of accompanying me to the St. Boniface holiday dinner?"

If a girl can laugh and cry at once, she did so. "I'm sure you don't want to do that."

"When you're yourself, you're a delightful person. It's when you're trying so hard to be nice that people feel a little . . . overwhelmed, maybe? And the last two times I've had the pleasure of talking with you, you've been your delightful self. So, actually, yes. I do want to do this. The only reason not to would be if you're asked by the man of your dreams in the meantime. I would nobly step aside in that case."

"You silly goose."

"Besides, what a pair we'd make! Two redheads, brilliant both inside and outside of our heads, mingling arm in arm around the room, stunning everyone with our wit and charm. What do you say?" I got up and kneeled before her on the cold ground. "Please? Just don't wear pink." As I said this, large, wet masses of white snow began to fall from the sky.

She laughed. "It's a dance, you know. Can you dance?"

"Can I dance." I stood. "It was required at Swithin, where I attended before I moved to Boston. Waltz, my lady?" I took Maddy's hand and pulled her to her feet. In traditional Viennese stance, whilst fluffy white bits landed in our matching red hair, I led her for several steps before she collapsed in giggles, assuring me we were unlikely to be waltzing.

"You're kind of nice yourself," she said, "when you aren't doing your best to leave everyone else behind so you can do your own thing."

That hurt. But she wasn't the first to say something like it. My new, enlightened self spoke. "I suppose I deserved that." I popped my brolly and held it over her. "And now that we've identified each other's most glaring social gaps, shall we plan on the dinner?"

"Yes. Thank you. It will be fun."

I held an arm out, she put her hand through it, and sharing my umbrella we went back inside to join the rest of the school for lunch.

By the time I showed up for my meeting with Mr. Lloyd, I'd pretty much scripted what I was going to say, anticipating as best I could what his responses would be. I knew that without a specific plan, I would say things that made matters worse, or I would become tongue-tied and not say anything at all. I needed to get my message across clearly but subtly, without saying anything specific. So I needed to be very English.

The door to Mr. Lloyd's office was closed when I got to his reception area, only one minute early to avoid being seen too soon and recognised. After his secretary announced Luther's name over an intercom, I waited in a chair Mr. Lloyd would not be able to see from the office unless he stepped out of it; I wanted to be inside before he knew who I really was.

At twenty minutes to five the intercom buzzed. The secretary said, "You can go in." She got up and opened the door. With only five minutes left of my allotted fifteen, I stepped through and saw that the man was busy at his desk, writing something, no doubt trying to impress me with the importance of his job and the relative paltriness of my mission. Maybe I wouldn't have picked this up with someone else, but I already knew something about him, none of it good. I heard the door close behind me, and I didn't wait for him to acknowledge me; I moved directly to one of the two chairs facing his desk and sat down.

"Be right with you, Luther." He still didn't look up.

Allowing my accent its full bloom, I said, "By all means, take your time."

His head snapped up. His hand shot towards the phone, no doubt to get security.

"I wouldn't do that. I think you need to hear me out." My tone was friendly yet pointed; very English. Despite my heritage, I'd practised quite a bit.

He froze. "What do you mean by coming in here under false pretences?"

"Would you have seen me otherwise?"

"Certainly not."

"Asked, and answered." I hadn't planned that phrase, and I wasn't altogether sure I'd used it correctly. But it's one attorneys often use in courtrooms, if television is any indicator. Mentally I gave myself a point scored for so subtle an allusion to his wife's profession. She was now in the room with us, and I'd said nothing about her.

"What do you want?"

"I want to continue helping Toby with his spelling practice. I want him to win the March competition, and I want him on stage for the national bee." There was more, but none of it was anything I could ask for.

"I've made my position clear on that."

"Yes, you have. I'm hoping you'll reconsider."

"Why should I?"

"Whatever your opinion about what Toby is going through, this competition is something he's worked hard for, for years. He's earned it. Nothing he's done is so ghastly that he should be denied the chance to compete. And my work with him was helping."

"He has shamed me. He's been insubordinate. And I don't have to catalogue his transgressions for you. Who do you think you are, marching in here like this?"

I let several seconds go by. "I haven't been to visit Toby in a couple of weeks, now. I do miss Colleen's biscuits. How is she, by the way?" My tone was light, yet heavy with meaning.

A flash of something crossed his eyes, brief but unmistakable. "I think you'd better leave."

"Oh, I will. But I really do have a project I'm working on. It has to do with cities and the way they reinvent themselves over time." He tried to interrupt, but I ignored him. "Medicine, education, even restaurants all have their parts to play. Restaurants, though their function remains fairly constant, can vary so much over time. Some—the Union Oyster House, for one—have been around seemingly forever. Others for a mere twenty years or so. Hamersley's, in the South End, comes to mind. I'm fairly sure you've dined there." It was my script, verbatim.

We English are very good at describing things by what they're not, at using negative space to communicate what it is we want heard. It can be extremely effective, and I was playing it to the hilt. And I had him. He knew that I knew.

He nearly growled. "What do you want?"

"As I said, I want to continue visiting Toby, at his home, to help him prepare for the upcoming spelling competitions. I want to make sure *nothing* stands in his way." I paused to see if he'd say anything. He didn't, so I added, "And I wouldn't dream of doing so without your full support. Would you be willing to reconsider your position?"

He stood, stormed over to his door and nearly flung it open. "You may continue to tutor Toby. Now, get out."

"Thank you so much. I'll ring him this afternoon and tell him. Good day."

It was everything I could do not to imagine Maddy in my arms and waltz my way out of there.

Had to look up the landline at Kay's house; I'd never called it. I'd have to see about getting her mobile returned, or perhaps get a new one for her, myself. Colleen answered, and I asked to speak to Toby.

"Simon, I think you know I can't do that."

"Oh, but that's changed. I just met with Mr. Lloyd, and he's agreed to let me continue to work with Toby." My voice dripping fake sugar, I added, "I have his office number if you'd like to call him. Shall I give it to you?"

Silence. Then, "I have the number. I'll have to speak with him before I let you talk to Toby."

"Ring me back at this number, then. I happen to know he's in his office. Say, five minutes? Thanks, ever so."

She would almost certainly ring his mobile, not his office. I sat in the ground-floor lobby, grinning like a fool, whilst also praying there would be no serious repercussions to my actions, which I have to admit were pretty bold. But then, Mr. Lloyd had already known that I was smart, skilled, and full of myself. I was so full of myself at that moment, I could hardly sit still.

Within four minutes, my phone rang. Kay. "Simon! How did you do that?"

"I can be very persuasive. Shall we plan on our usual Thursday session?"

"Oh, yes! Please! I love you so much!"

"I'm rather fond of you, too, Kay. See you Thursday."

Next I rang Dr. Metcalf. He didn't answer, so I had to leave a message, just asking him to ring me back. I sat there for a few more minutes and was about to go, in case Mr. Lloyd decided to leave the building—I didn't have a script for another meeting—when my phone rang again. Dr. Metcalf. I told him as little as possible. I'm sure he suspected there was more but didn't know how to ferret it out. He'd been in touch with the counsellor at Kay's school; the matter would be carried forwards. He couldn't tell me what that would mean, but now that I have access to Kay again, I have other ways to find out.

As soon as I got home, I went upstairs, pulled out my tux and tried it on, and saw that Ned was right; I had grown taller. I'd have to get it altered for the dinner with Maddy. And . . . should I buy her a corsage? Do people still do that? I'll have to ask Dr. Metcalf.

Boston, Friday, 30 November

I was in the cafeteria at school for lunch Thursday, having an im-promptu meeting with a few of my City cohorts, when my phone vibrated. It was a number I'd seen before, but where?

"Simon. It's Mrs. Lloyd, Toby's mother." Her voice was trembling, though she was obviously trying to stay in control. "I know you have a spelling session this afternoon. I just wanted to let you know not to come today." Her voice stopped as though the breath had been cut off.

I knew something was wrong. "Is Toby all right?"

There was a long silence, and then, "No." I heard a sharp intake of breath; there was a pause, and she said, "He tried to kill himself."

I went ice-cold. "Where is he now?" Phone plastered to my ear, I reached with my free hand for my school bag.

"Deaconess."

"Is that a hospital?"

"Sorry. Yes. Emergency room area."

"Is Mr. Lloyd there?"

It was almost as though she were speaking through clenched teeth. "No. He doesn't know yet."

"I'll be there as soon as I can."

I ran down Marlborough Street until I reached Mass Ave, where I was more likely to get a taxi; good choice, and I was at the hospital in a few minutes that seemed to take forever.

Mrs. Lloyd was pacing the emergency room waiting area. She said, "He won't speak to me. Will you see if you can do anything?"

Time for a reality adjustment. I switched pronouns. "Has she seen a counsellor?"

There was a blank stare. "She . . . Oh. Not yet. They've called someone. No one I know."

"What did she do?"

"Ran in front of a car. His . . . her injuries aren't bad, just a sprained ankle and some bruised ribs. Thank God the car wasn't going fast, and the driver was able to stop quickly."

I went into the bay Mrs. Lloyd indicated, and in a wheelchair with her bare left foot propped on an extended shelf was a girl. Kay had on a bright pink dress with white lace across the bodice, and there was a pink fake-fur jacket on the floor. Her face, blotchy with makeup badly applied, was turned a little to one side, and her eyes were closed. I took the hand nearest me.

"Kay. It's Simon."

She opened her eyes and immediately started crying. "I'm sorry. I'm sorry. I just couldn't do it anymore."

"Do what, Kay?" I was vaguely aware that Mrs. Lloyd had moved forwards to listen.

"If I can't be a girl, I don't want to live. My father won't let me get the treatments. I hate him! I hate him!" She nearly screamed with the sobs.

I leaned over and wrapped my arms around her as best I could. She cried and cried until my back was aching from holding that position, and as I stood up she clasped my hands so tightly it hurt.

Mrs. Lloyd had moved to the other side of the chair. To her, I said, "I think she wouldn't talk to you because you were calling her Toby. That's not her name anymore. Did you know her name is Kay?"

Mrs. Lloyd shook her head, one hand clutching a tissue to her mouth.

"I take it Mr. Lloyd laid down the law?"

She took a shuddering breath and nodded. "There was a discussion last night."

A "discussion," was it? And I thought the English were masters of understatement.

Almost immediately an orderly appeared and wheeled Kay's chair out of the bay, and Mrs. Lloyd and I followed around corridors and up to a private room. We sat with her until the counsellor, a Dr. Schaeffer, arrived and asked us to wait outside. Mrs. Lloyd and I found a waiting area and sat, side by side, silent and tense, until I couldn't take it any longer.

"Um, look, you can tell me this is none of my business, but what's going to happen now?"

She gazed across the room for a bit. Then, "I don't think I would ever tell you this is none of your business, Simon. Toby . . . Kay obviously trusts you. How long have you known?"

"She told me she was a girl the first time I came by. It was the second visit when she told me her girl's name. It means 'rejoiced in' in Welsh. She made me promise not to tell anyone. And at the time, there was no apparent danger. Nothing like this." I clamped my mouth shut before I could say more; I wasn't convinced I'd done the right thing, keeping that confidence.

"I'm not blaming you, Simon. I don't think you could have predicted this." She heaved a breath. "Well, she—I'm going to have to get used to that, but I will—has already done all the research about this course of drug treatments. I confess I had a hard time taking it seriously; it seems so radical, and of course after a certain point it's irreversible. And the fact that it must be done when the child is so young—before puberty. I just . . . I just couldn't believe we had to face it, I guess. But Kay has convinced me."

"And her father?"

Mrs. Lloyd's jaw hardened. "He will not have anything to say about it." Her tone was so final; I didn't dare ask anything more.

We were silent again. It felt as though this woman beside me was a different person to the one who'd come to the two bees at St. Boniface. That woman had looked like the professional counsellor she is, but her demeanour had been tempered by love for her child and pride in "his" achievements. This woman, today, was somewhere between killer attorney and an enraged mother tiger protecting her cub.

"Thank you, Simon. For all you've done." She reached out and took my hand in hers. "This is so unfair to you, pulling you into the middle of this mess. But I allow it because it's for the sake of my baby." She shook her head gently and smiled. "My daughter. And I would do anything for her."

"Well, as soon as she's feeling better, I think you might take her out and get her some decent clothes."

She looked at me, puzzled, and then threw back her head and laughed. "You are so right! That dress is hideous, isn't it? And that jacket! That's a brilliant idea. I can't think of a better way to cheer her up than to take her on a shopping spree."

I waited with Kay whilst Dr. Schaeffer spoke with Mrs. Lloyd in the hall, and when Mrs. Lloyd came in she was all smiles.

"Kay, darling, they're going to let me take you home Saturday morning. I know that seems like a long time"—and she held up a hand to discourage Kay's protests—"but you were hit by a car. They need to be really sure there's nothing wrong they haven't found yet. Dr. Schaeffer will come and talk with you a few more times. And, sweetheart, I'm going to see about that treatment. We'll look into it together. How does that sound?"

"Really? You really mean it?" Kay didn't look like she quite dared to believe it. "What about Father?"

"You leave your father to me. And here's more good news. To help cheer you up while you're recovering from this sprained ankle, I'm going out to buy you some new clothes. Girl clothes. And then, when you're up and about, we'll go on a real shopping spree. How does that sound?"

Kay's face broke into a huge smile, and although her eyes dripped tears it was obvious they were from joy. Then Mrs. Lloyd said, "Simon, can you stay for a little while longer?"

"It's Thursday afternoon. This is my time with Kay." And I wanted some time alone with her, anyway. As soon as Mrs. Lloyd was gone, I pulled a chair closer to the bed. "Kay, in confidence, did you really intend to kill yourself by stepping in front of that car, or was it more that you were trying to prove how serious you are about this problem with your father?"

"I wanted to die, Simon." Her voice was soft, no histrionics to it, which made me believe her. "I even left you my dictionary. There's a note on my desk."

Oh, child . . . "Then I need you to promise me you won't ever do that again."

"If Mommy can't really fix things with Father, I can't promise anything. I can't be a boy anymore, Simon. I can't. I just can't!"

"Listen to me now, because I know what I'm talking about. It will get better. Your mother will help you, and even if it gets bad again, you're going to be all right. You'll get through it, and you'll still be you. This is a very difficult time; I know that. But it won't last. It's just a short span in the long line of the rest of your life." Where have I heard *that* before?

"How can you say it will be all right?" Now there was some anger, a challenge.

"Because things can change so quickly, in ways we can't predict. Look, our first session was 30 August. If anyone had asked me on 28 August if I'd be working on spelling with an eleven-year-old transgender girl before the week was out, what do you think I would have said? I didn't even know then that I'd be working with *anyone* on spelling. And if that same person had told *you* on 28 August that before the week was out you would tell a complete stranger that you were really a girl, what would *you* have said?" I was warming to my subject. "And before that day I told you there were lots of other transgender people, you thought you were the only one! How long did it take you to feel vastly different, once you knew you weren't alone?"

She looked hard at me for a moment. "That doesn't mean things will keep getting better."

"No, but sometimes when they get worse, there's a reaction to that and everything swings back in the right direction. Last night, your father took a firm stand and denied you exactly what you need. Until that point, your mother had argued with him, but she hadn't taken a firm stand. As of today, *she's* taking a firm stand, too, and she's fully on your side. Didn't she just tell you you'll be getting a new wardrobe? One that fits who you are?"

"You don't know what it's like, Simon! Having your whole world fall apart before your eyes!"

I clenched and unclenched my hands, closed my eyes, took a deep breath, and looked at Kay. I'd never told anyone what I was about to say. "You're wrong. I do know. Because I tried to kill myself. Like you, I felt as though my whole world had crashed and burned. There was no reason to go on, and all kinds of reasons to end things. And, Kay, I am so glad I failed. I can't even tell you how glad. You are a wonderful, wonderful girl who's going to have a wonderful life. Don't you want to know what you're going to look like as a woman? Don't you want to go to college, maybe pledge a sorority, have boyfriends? Maybe learn to put on makeup well?"

She glared at me, annoyed. That was good; annoyed was good. Annoyed people aren't likely to kill themselves.

I laughed. "Don't look at me like that. Everybody needs lessons in that kind of thing. I had to have people tell me how to style my hair, and that was just a few months ago. And then I had to have someone tell me what clothes look good on me." Which made me think of a good way to change the subject. "Do you want to hear about my trip to Oxford?"

"All right." She sounded a little sulky. But then, "Was it wonderful?"

"It was. It was brilliant." I winked at her and gave her every detail I could remember. She ate it up.

I stayed with her until Mrs. Lloyd appeared again at around ten after six. To Kay, she said, "You're looking more cheerful! Simon is good for you, isn't he?" Then she asked me out into the hall.

"Just so I don't leave you hanging, my husband and I have come to an agreement. He will be moving out. In fact, I need to leave to be there while he packs, and I have a locksmith coming, but I'll be back. Why don't you go home, now? It's way past your scheduled time with her. She should probably rest, anyway."

I was just thinking how quickly the lady was making use of female pronouns towards a child she'd always considered her son when she added, "In case you'd like to know, I've fired Colleen." So she'd known. She watched my face, and she must have seen something. "George asked me if you had told me anything. I assured him you had not. Sometime I'd like to know what that's all about."

I caught a taxi at the front entrance, and it seemed to take forever to get home. Once there, I slid into my chair with about three seconds to spare. Persie was watching for me. She said, "You're not late. But it's all right if you are."

I blinked stupidly at her. So did everyone else. "Thank you." It was all I could think of to say.

Halfway through her food calculations, Persie set her silverware down. In my memory, she had never done this before finishing what was on her plate. She turned towards Brian.

"Would it be all right if I get a cat tomorrow?"

Everyone set their silverware down.

Brian said, "A cat?"

"Yes. Please." She smiled as sweetly as she knew how.

I covered my mouth with my napkin and burst into laughter. Maxine was next, giggling nearly silently into her own napkin. Before long, Mum was nearly helpless, and I could tell Brian was trying to smother laughter. Only Persie was unmoved by the humour of what she'd said. Ned came to the door, nothing in his hands, and stared into the room. The perplexed look on his face sent me into new gales of belly-deep laughter. Maxine laughed so hard she snorted.

Slowly, person by person, the laughter abated, with the occasional upsurge of giggles and snorts. Persie must have been waiting for things to quiet down, because as soon as they did she smiled at Brian again. "Please?"

Brian had to cough and clear his throat before he could reply. "Not tomorrow, no."

Persie looked at me for a microsecond, her eyes telling me that she knew just what to do. She would ask again Monday.

After dinner, when Persie headed up to her rooms, I followed and knocked on the open door. "May I come in for a few minutes?"

Without a word, she sat on a chair, and I sat on a nearby one after turning it to face her. "Sorry this is out of position. I'll move it back before I leave." No response. Persie wasn't likely to benefit from preamble, so I plunged in. "You asked your father for a cat. Can you tell me why?"

"Of course I can." Silence.

Right. Literal. If I were to ask her if she knew what the time was, she'd say either yes or no and leave it at that. "Will you tell me why you want a cat, please?"

"Cats obey rules. They make rules based on their environment, and they follow them. When the environment changes, they make new rules. I understand cats. I always wanted a dog, but Daddy always said no. They need to be walked. They bark. They need to be bathed. They're big enough to knock things over."

"Where did you find that information about cats?"

"On the Internet. And in my book about cat behaviour."

"You have a book about cat behaviour?"

"*Understanding Cat Behavior.* Roger Tabor. David & Charles, April 30, 2003. One hundred forty-four pages. Roger Tabor lives in Cressing, Essex. Northeast of London. I looked it up."

I did my best not to look shocked, or flattered, or any of the other emotions she might not understand. "What are you going to do if the cat acts in a way you don't like?"

"I'll figure out what rule it thinks it's following."

I was not expecting that level of insight, or of understanding, or something. "And if you can't, or if you can't arrange things so the cat changes its behaviour?"

"I'll keep trying to understand why it made the rule it made and look for ways to influence the rules. I might change the environment a little."

There was no way to poke holes in that plan. "What kind of a cat do you want?"

"One nobody else wants. I want you to take me to MSPCA-Angell. Kindness and care for animals."

That sounded like their slogan. And yet another job for me. "Well, keep in mind that your father still might say no, Persie. You need to be prepared for that. This isn't like asking him to allow you to go to museums. A cat would change his environment, too, not just yours. So this isn't just about you, and you'll have to accept his decision. Any questions?"

"No."

I stood and returned the chair to its proper position. "Good night, then."

"Good night, then."

I chuckled all the way upstairs.

Boston, Sunday, 2 December

I'm just realising that I neglected to record something that happened at my last session with Dr. Metcalf, on Friday. There was so much to write about in the last entry that it wasn't top-of-mind.

First, I gave him an update on what was happening with Kay, adding that I'd resume coaching sessions as soon as she was ready. He was suitably horrified to hear about the incident, but seemed satisfied that Kay was being seen to appropriately.

Next I also told him something I'd been terrified to admit to myself, and even more terrified to admit to him. "With everything that's been happening, I'm concerned that I won't be able to meet the due dates for reports that are coming up *and* study for exams."

Before I could get as far as asking what leniency I might beg for, Dr. Metcalf agreed that there had been sufficient extenuating circumstances to warrant granting me an extension on the drafts. It's going to mean working more over the Christmas holiday than I might otherwise have done, but what else would I do with my time?

Just before lunch today I was in my room, doing schoolwork (as usual), when my mobile rang. It was Brian, and he asked me to join him in his office. He needed my opinion about something.

Well, that was mysterious. I barely know where his office is, and I've never been inside it.

The door stood open, and as I walked through Brian said, "Please close the door behind you, Simon." He was in there with Maxine. And this was Sunday, part of her standard weekends-off arrangement. Curiouser and curiouser.

They sat on the other side of the room from the desk, she on one end of a short couch and he on a chair across from her. Brian indicated a chair between them for me. "Maxine," he said, "would you tell Simon what you've told me?" I could tell nothing from his tone of voice.

Her posture—back straight, head erect—made it look as though she was determined about something. "I think Persie should be allowed to have a cat."

As though expecting contradiction, she went on, words tumbling over each other. "I've been in touch with Anna Tourneau, and it seems to both of us that Persie has made significant progress in terms of her ability to adjust to her environment. She's less rigid, she speaks more often and more easily, and she's shown herself to be able to consider others to a much greater degree than in the past. Going out into the world, even in the controlled way she's been doing, has helped even more. And while continuing these outings should result in more improvement, I think that having another creature to care for, one that is at least to some degree dependent on her, will allow her to take a very large step forwards."

She paused for breath, and when no one contradicted her or asked any questions, she continued. "I'm not altogether sure what started this progress. Anna thinks Persie's interactions with Simon have had a lot to do with it, and then of course having Anna leave and a new person come in forced some adjustment. But many of Persie's adjustments have been voluntary. And the fact that she *asked* for this change, *asked* for something to care for, and the fact that she's taken it seriously enough to do quite a bit of research into it, makes me think it would be very good for her."

Brian turned to me. "Simon?"

He'd said he wanted my opinion. So I gave it. "I agree."

"Can you provide a little justification? Something Maxine hasn't said?"

"Persie told me she understands about cats forming rules. She's already laid a plan, one that shows she understands cats, for what to do in the event the cat behaves in a way she doesn't want it to." I shrugged. "I have to say, it seems to me that working with a cat could give her insight into her own thought process."

I'm sure it helped that all morning I'd been writing about Persie and cats for my TOK paper.

I added, "When we teach someone something, we learn more about it ourselves. If Persie can teach a cat—that is, influence how it forms rules—she might be able to teach herself about herself. Meta learning, if you will."

"Meta learning?"

"Learning about learning would be the best way to think of it.

Another thing. She told me she wants a cat no one else wants. So I think she identifies with a creature on the fringe. And one thing I know about being on the fringe is that it can be a lonely place. I think she's asking to be less lonely."

Brian sat back and scowled, thinking, peaking the fingers of his hands together. Maxine and I sat still. We'd done all we could.

Then he said to me, "If we do this, what does it mean to have a cat no one else wants? What kind of cat would you recommend?"

"My guess is it would be something that puts the cat outside the norm. It might be ugly; it might be missing part of an ear or the tail, something like that. So that probably means a cat, not a kitten; almost all kittens are adorable. And, besides, kittens haven't formed rules yet, so Persie would be looking for something that wasn't there. I'd go with an adult."

"And you'd be willing to guide her?"

"Yes, as long as we all understand that it's a major responsibility to own a cat, and a bigger one to choose one for someone else. I'll do the best I can, and I'll help get the place ready. What to buy, where to put things, how to comb it, that sort of thing."

He exhaled audibly. "I need to think about this. Maxine, thank you for your insight, and for taking so much initiative."

Maxine and I took this for our dismissal, and we stood and moved towards the door. I opened it and waited for her to exit, but I turned back to Brian before I walked through. "It seems to me you chose very well with Maxine." I didn't wait for a reply.

Brian was waiting for me at the bottom of the stairs when I came down for dinner. Persie had already gone by.

"Simon, would you have time on Tuesday afternoon to go to Angell with Maxine and Persie? I know Tuesdays are fairly open for you."

I was ahead of him. "Not only that, but I've given some thought about how to work animal care into my City course. The way a society treats its animals parallels many other aspects of its development. So I was already planning to go over there. If it's for Persie's cat, I'll just identify the best person to talk to and set up an appointment to go back."

He closed his eyes for a second as though holding emotion in. "Thank you."

"Maybe Mum could go shopping for supplies and things?"

He smiled. "I'll go with her. I wish I could go on Tuesday, but I trust you."

At dinner, he asked Persie if she'd like to go meet some cats on Tuesday. I don't think I've ever seen her face light up the way it did just then. She actually looked right at her father, then at me, and back to Brian. "Yes, please."

Brian reached for a handkerchief to blow his nose, and Mum had to excuse herself for a moment. I only wished Maxine could be here right now. I would make sure to tell her about this scene tomorrow.

Boston, Tuesday, 4 December

We have a cat. Well, Persie has a cat. It's not here, yet; they're careful at Angell about who adopts pets, and because neither Brian nor Mum was with us, they need more information, and more formal authority. But they're holding Arria for Persie. Mum will pick her up tomorrow.

Brian had a car drive us over there this afternoon, and the driver was to wait. But as soon as we entered the building, the smells and sounds and general unfamiliarity were too much for Persie.

"I need to leave. I need to leave. I need to leave."

Maxine wrapped a protective arm around her shoulders and turned back towards the door. To me, she said, "I was afraid this might happen."

"Persie?" I said. She stopped, but wouldn't look up from the floor. "Do you want to wait in the car and I can pick out a cat for you, or do you want to reconsider getting one at all?"

"You do it. You pick my cat. One no one else wants."

I got the name of someone who could meet with me next week

for my City research and went to look for Persie's cat. Not many people were in the adoption rooms. There were several cages with kittens, but we had agreed on an adult. I went from cage to cage, wanting to hold every one of them, even the ones that cowered in the backs of their cages and hissed at me. But when I saw Persie's cat, I knew it immediately.

The tortoiseshell calico shorthair, probably three years old, had been found in an alley, although she was not feral; she was spayed and had obviously been someone's pet. But during her days on the street something horrible had happened to her front left paw. It had healed fairly well, but it was obviously mangled. She hobbled a little when she walked, the attendant told me, but she was a good-natured cat. They'd been calling her Callie for want of a better name.

With that paw, she'd be more sedate, less of a jumper. Perfect. She allowed me to hold her, scratch gently under her chin and around her ears, and within a few minutes she was purring. It was a delightful purr, more musical even than Tink's, almost as though she were singing.

And this is how she got her name. When I described the cat and showed Persie the photos I'd taken with my phone, she approved of my choice. And when I mentioned the singing purr, Persie told me she'd been researching names and said that one she'd considered was Arria.

"It's a woman's name from ancient Rome. It's like *aria,* from an opera. It reminds me of *arrhostia,* because it has two *r*s."

I scowled, stretched my mind, and finally landed on the word I'd nearly missed in my placement exams at St. Boniface. Arrhostia. More red in it when spelled correctly. Arrhostia, which had prompted Persie to ask me to colour her name out for her. Arrhostia, which had led to the Clyfford Still art. I had to explain it to Brian and Mum, of course. Brian shook his head, amazed, and I'm sure it was because here was yet more proof of how much his daughter has grown, how much more she considers other people than she used to do.

I'll have to be careful not to get too attached to Arria.

Boston, Friday, 7 December

Michael rang me last night. At first I was sure it would have something to do with his grandmother, but no. Not exactly.

"You never did get that dinner at Nonna's," he opened. "And you read those letters anyway. She really enjoyed that. So, I was wondering if maybe I could thank you with dinner, even if it's not at Nonna's."

I took a few seconds to try and wrap my brain around that. Was he asking me out on a date? "You mean, a dinner out? At a restaurant?"

"It won't be really fancy or anything. But there's a nice family-style Italian place out my way. Good food, atmosphere's not bad. Tomorrow night, maybe?"

What did I want to do? I'd pretty much left Michael behind. Graeme hadn't had to distract me from thinking about him for a while, now. Luther, yes; Graeme was still helping to distract me from Luther. But not Michael. So, should I accept because it wouldn't mean anything in particular? Or should I turn it down for the same reason?

Before I could stop my voice, it said, "Sure. Where do you want to meet?" There was no way he was picking me up.

He gave me the name and address of the restaurant, and we agreed on seven o'clock.

I was maybe five minutes late. I'd dithered with what to wear; I was determined to make him see what he had lost out on by not admitting he was gay and therefore not getting me, without making it appear as though I wanted him to do anything about it. It was a fine line. I did not use my eye pencil, but I did spray on just a bit of fragrance, more for me than for him.

He was right about the restaurant. It was pretty unremarkable, but the food was decent. They used canned mushrooms in my chicken marsala, but the uncooked tomato sauce on my appetizer, wafer-thin eggplant rolled around a thick ricotta filling with nutmeg and pepper, was fresh and delightful. And the tiramisu, per-fection.

We chatted about his grandmother's health for a bit, and he said he'd picked up where I'd left off, reading letters, starting the day he'd appeared on my doorstep after the apple-picking outing. "I figured, you know, my Italian wasn't up to yours, but she knows Italian, and it was supposed to be good for her. I do think it helped her recover."

I was feeling generous. "It might have been even more helpful; if the Italian sounded a little off, she'd have to work harder to wrap her brain around what was being said."

"The thing is, though, she still needs a lot of help. I don't know when she might be able to cook again. I'm not sure you're going to get that dinner."

He talked about his classes, about some art he was working on. I told him a little about my Oxford trip. Then he asked about Luther. "I know you saw me that night, when you went to see that play with that guy. You probably thought I was stalking you again." Deciding on discretion, I took a mouthful of tiramisu and didn't respond. "Are you, y'know, still seeing him?"

I didn't see any point in lying. "Probably not. We have different styles." Let Michael wonder what that means.

As we left the restaurant, he said, "My place isn't far from here. And there's . . . well, there's something I'd like to ask your opinion about."

"Etchings?" I asked playfully, but he didn't seem to get the old joke about asking someone in to see your etchings. "Never mind. Sure. I can't stay too long, though. I'm behind in a lot of my schoolwork."

"Still with the schoolwork."

"Yes. Michael, I have a very demanding course load. And I have to have excellent marks for the rest of the year, even if I get an offer from Oxford."

"Fine. Don't get so defensive."

I nearly told him to go fuck himself, but I was kind of curious about what he wanted to show me, ask me, whatever. So we walked together in something less than companionable silence to his place on Aberdeen. As we climbed the stairs, he said, "My roommate's gone for the weekend."

I almost asked after Chas and Dick, but thought better of it.

He closed the door behind me and took my leather jacket. "This is a nice piece," he said. "You've changed."

"How so?"

"I'm not sure. You're just different. I mean, partly it's the clothes; you look really good."

Uncharitably, I was thinking that maybe the difference was that I couldn't care less about him as romantic potential. Though I had to admit that I still found him extremely attractive.

Michael gestured for me to sit on the small couch in the corner of the front room, and from a small fridge on the other side of the room he fetched two bottles of beer and offered one to me. I stared at the thing in my hand, wondering how long anything between us would have lasted if Michael had been willing to start something with me. He sat beside me and took a swig. I sipped some of the cold, tasteless stuff and waited.

"The thing is," he opened, and then paused. "Hell, I'm just going to say it. I think I was wrong. That is, I was right before, and then I was wrong."

"About?"

"About being gay." I'm sure I gaped at him. "You don't agree?"

"Oh, it's not that. I've never believed you were straight." Shaking off the astonishment, I asked, "What caused the turnaround?"

"I can't stop thinking about you."

Oh, my God. Options flew through my brain, lightning fast. His timing couldn't be worse, of course. Before Luther, Michael might have had a chance. But now? He seemed a child to me now. A sweet, gorgeous child, but still . . . And my heart was once again so full of getting home that I couldn't imagine starting something like what I thought he'd want this to be. I was sure Michael would throw at least some of his heart into it; I would not.

I said, "What did you want my opinion about?"

"Whether I still have a chance. With you. I think I might have, once."

Christ! Feast or famine! "Oh, Michael . . ." My voice must have given away my regret.

"I waited too long, didn't I?"

I wanted to tell him that wasn't it, but the fact was that maybe he had. He'd waited until I'd had time to experience Luther, to see Michael for the sweet but unsophisticated person he is, to find my heart again and let it lead me home.

He turned his head to look at the floor. "Nonna told me not to be an idiot. That if I wanted you, I'd have to let you know. But now we'll never be that love knot Nonna showed me."

"Michael, you need to understand. I'm not staying in Boston. I'm expecting at least two offers from Oxford, and that's where I'll be just as soon as I've graduated St. Boniface."

He looked up at me. "Okay, but until then—"

"Until then I don't know what else might happen. Who else might not be able to stop thinking about me, or me about him. And I don't think you'd be comfortable with that." I paused, watching his face grow rigid, seeing that my assessment was correct; he wouldn't want to allow me the autonomy I would insist upon. "Michael, I think you're terrific, and gorgeous, and talented, and sweet—"

"And there's no hope for us, is there?"

Softly, sadly, I told him, "No."

He nodded. He nearly whispered, "I've never kissed another guy. I want to kiss you. Will you let me do that before you walk away?"

I stood, taking his hand and pulling him up, and as he leaned towards me, I closed my eyes and let his scent of sun-warmed wool wash over me. The kiss was bittersweet, poignant. Then there was another, less sweet, and another, and there would have been more than kisses if I hadn't pulled away. I wouldn't do that to him.

I touched his face lightly. "*Addio*, Michael." I picked up my jacket and left.

Boston, Friday, 21 December

Two weeks. It's been two whole weeks since my last journal entry. I'm not sure whether exams at St. Boniface seem more horrendous than they ever did at Swithin because this is my last year before uni, or because it's a more rigorous programme. I'm unbelievably glad I got extensions on those papers that I'll need to work on over the Christmas holiday.

I had an acceptance letter this morning from Princeton. It's good news, of course, though my hope is that I'll be in England again in a matter of months. I truly feel that's where I belong.

Arria is a pet in every way she can be. Everyone loves her, although she seems not to be terribly fond of the housecleaners and hides from them whenever they appear. She's a sweet cat, and on some level she knows how good she has it now. Persie is lots of fun to watch as she approaches cat stewardship so earnestly. I have to say, she can offer a cat the one thing it values most after food and comfortable shelter: consistency. They're great together.

I called Kay every day after her suicide attempt, until I'd seen her again and was convinced she was out of the woods. Her mother was as good as her word, and Kay's been very nicely dressed in gender-appropriate clothing each time I've seen her. Her hair is getting longer, and yesterday she informed me she'd been to a "real" stylist. The cut looked great on her.

Her mom hired a replacement for Colleen, a formidable woman in her fifties who wants to be called Mrs. Fife. She's not the friendliest person, but she treats Kay well and seems to accept Kay's situation completely, which makes her just fine in my book.

Last week when I went to work with Kay, she was far from her usual bouncy self, and she was doing so badly at spelling that I finally asked her what was wrong.

"I might have to change schools."

"Why is that?"

"The other kids are being really awful. They're teasing me, and they won't call me by my right name. Even Andrew won't talk to me anymore."

"Your teacher doesn't protect you?"

"No one can protect me, Simon. No one! There's even a problem over which bathroom I can use. They told me to use the boys', but when I try the boys push me and tear my clothes."

I could see tears welling up in her eyes. "What if you use the girls' room?"

"I tried. But the other girls screamed, and I got in trouble and had to stay after school. They made Mommy come and get me."

"But—doesn't the girls' room have booths? No one actually sees anything, do they?"

"It doesn't matter. They still won't let me in."

Honestly, this seemed to me like much ado about nothing. What on earth were they afraid Kay would do in the girls' room, break down the door of an occupied booth? And then what?

"Mommy's trying to get them to designate one of the restrooms for transgender kids, but no one else there is like me. I don't think they'll do it. And it won't help anything else."

Visions of the boys taunting Kay on the playground, and of the girls forming a militant cadre to keep her out, jostled for attention in my brain.

"So if you went to another school, how would that help?"

"At least they wouldn't ever have known me as Toby. I could use the girls' room, and no one would know."

"Have you talked with Dean or anyone from one of the support groups?"

"Mommy's talking to people."

"What's the status of the hormone-treatment route?"

She brightened visibly. "Mommy set up an appointment for January ninth. I can't wait!"

"And they'll be able to tell you when you might start, and what the process will look like? How long it will take, that sort of thing?"

"Well, first they make you talk to a psychologist. I've been reading about it. They want to make sure you know what you want before they start the treatments. And they start with reversible things first. It's going to take a while."

What was going through my mind, and what I didn't dare say aloud, was to wonder how the hell this could happen to someone. How could nature have gotten it so screwed up? Why should anyone have to go through this just to be who they are?

I know that my own biology supports my sexual orientation. I can't force a natural sexual response to women any more than straight guys can force themselves to be attracted to me. Doesn't mean I couldn't have sex with a girl if I wanted to, but it would be completely unnatural for me.

Once again, I tried imagining myself trapped in a female body and just couldn't get there. The thought of not having a cock and balls, the idea of a hole where there shouldn't be one, the feeling of having breasts where my chest is flat—it made me shudder. My mind refused to let me go there, even in my imagination. What must this profound disconnect be like for Kay?

It made me want to throttle anyone who would ridicule her, who would make this horrible, horrible situation even worse. And all I could do was pray that this process would be complete enough for Kay in time for her to take physical ed for girls when she got a little older, where she'd likely have to deal with open changing rooms and gang showers. Though I had no idea what the surgical options were like. Whether she'd lose her male equipment that soon.

Before I left, we exchanged Christmas gifts. She gave me a book on Scottish fold cats, beautifully photographed. I gave her something that sent her positively over the moon: a single strand of black pearls. She shrieked; she cried; she bounced; she nearly swooned. I think the pearls were a hit.

Maddy and I had a great time at the holiday dinner. She wore a simple, elegant, steel-blue gown that was perfection on her, and I'd bought her a huge white orchid wrist corsage. Her hair was piled on her head in an apparently casual style that I know was fussed over by someone who knew what they were about; it looked amazing. We danced a lot, and maybe it was because she was having a great time and just being genuinely herself, but a couple of other guys asked her to dance as well. Watching her during one of these dances, I considered what I might do starting in January to be at least a little more friendly, to at least a few of the other students. But then girls started asking me to dance. The only times I've danced with anyone were during enforced lessons at school, so this was a new experience for me.

And then something truly astonishing happened. Daren Bateman, a boy I'd noticed and admired from a distance, asked me to dance. It had never occurred to me he was anything but straight as a lance—which is why I haven't mentioned him. I refuse to fall for another Graeme.

Daren took my hand and led me onto the dance floor. I think my face must have been flushed the whole time, and we did get a few surprised looks, but no one gave us any grief. The first dance was a fast rhythm. The second was slow, and he held me close.

Maddy was a dear about it. She could have been cheesed off, and not unreasonably, but I'm sure it helped that one of the boys who had asked her to dance is someone she would love to see more of.

As I saw her home, she said, "Did you know Daren was gay?"

"He might be bisexual. But no; didn't have a clue."

"He might ask you out. Or I suppose you could ask him!"

"Perhaps." I changed the subject, and she took the hint. All in all, it was a great evening. And but for Maddy, I would have overlooked it.

Luther called this past Monday night. It was an interesting conversation, which opened with an apology to me. "You were right, Simon. It was tacky of me to set up two dates the same day. Not even day and night. The same day. Thanks for calling me on it."

"You're welcome, I guess. Has Stephanie forgiven you?"

He sighed. "No. Pity, too; we had some good times together. And I'm not talking about sex. Which brings me to the other reason for my call. Would you let me take you to a holiday party?"

My brain froze. But he waited until I said, "What kind of a holiday party?"

"It would be a little like the one where I met you, only not as elegant. Someone at school is having one in his apartment. I promise to be on my best behaviour."

"So harking back to your earlier comment, this would be a good time but no sex?"

He let a couple of beats go by. "It can be whatever you want it to be. I'm not expecting sex. If you want it, you feisty redhead, it's yours. I'm happy just having you go to the party with me."

"I guess you can't be much more reasonable than that."

"You inspire me to be reasonable. Open to suggestion, but reasonable."

I tried to stop grinning so he wouldn't hear that in my tone. "When is this sexless party?"

He laughed. "This Saturday. It's not a dinner party, though there will be finger food."

"No Veuve, though, probably."

"No. Though I am bringing wine so I don't have to drink beer."

"Ah. That kind of party."

"Yes, but good people. You'll come?"

I decided to give him another chance. There's a lot to be said for honesty.

St. Boniface closed for Christmas break yesterday, and this afternoon Persie and Maxine took me to the Boston Public Library, the fulfilment of Persie's birthday present to me. She had identified several favourite art pieces, some paintings and some sculptures. The library has become her favourite place for an outing, because it has so many places where she can hunker down and hide for a bit if the need arises.

Back to work, now; those papers will not write themselves.

Boston, Tuesday, 1 January

This entry is going to be all about Luther, I think. Because he's back in the picture for me, in a big way. The parameters haven't changed; still no commitment, no expectations, no exclusivity required. But the content . . .

The holiday party on Saturday, 22 December was pretty much as he had described it. I met him at a pizza place, we had a couple of slices, and then we walked to the flat where the party was taking place. It was quite a mixed crowd, nowhere near as gay-slanted as the one in the South End had been. But then, Luther is bisexual. I had decided against eyeliner and was glad of it; that kind of expression would have made me feel awkward here, where only the girls wore makeup. I wore the same clothes I'd worn to Luther's flat, except for my jacket, which was the shearling this time. Not only is it warmer, but also it seemed more appropriate for this crowd.

I got a lot of attention, partially because of my accent, but even more because of being with Luther; he seemed quite a favourite. I'd expected he'd drift about a bit and I'd be left to fend for myself part of the time, but he stayed with me almost every minute. There was some marijuana, and Luther smoked, but I didn't. The wine he'd brought was drinkable; nothing special. The real reason to be there was the crowd—full of fun, lots of witty exchanges, the occasional discussion of anything from the state of performance dance to Nietzsche's concept of the eternal recurrence of the universe to the best local rock band. I can't say that there seemed to be anything especially holiday-oriented about the party, though there was a decorated evergreen in one corner, and someone had provided a disgusting (to me, anyway) version of wassail.

Luther waited with me whilst I hailed a taxi to get home, standing so close to me that I could feel his body's warmth. We kissed a few times, never passionately, and this had the effect I think he wanted: It made me want him.

At home, after Graeme helped relieve me of the tension Luther had inspired, I sat in my window seat, lights off, gazing into the

Boston night and thinking of Luther. He's honest, as Ned had told me. He's intelligent, thoughtful, and sexy as hell. If I wanted to have someone in my life to a limited extent, someone I could part from in a few months with some sadness but no regret, someone who would forever occupy a special place in my memory without any bitterness or any sense of "if only," I probably couldn't do any better than Luther. The question is whether I want that or not. And then there's the question of sex.

Assuming we take things as far as they could go, does it matter to me that my first experiences will be with someone I like very much but don't love? Someone who likes but doesn't love me? Is the imbalance of his experience over my naïveté a good thing, or would I prefer to learn things with a partner who's my sexual peer?

And who would wear the condom?

I suppose it's a given that he would, the first time. After that? I'm not so sure.

After that party, I kept myself very busy getting through the assignments I'd been allowed to postpone, trying to deny to myself that I was starting to feel really anxious again about Oxford. Would I get even one offer?

Although I certainly thought about Luther from time to time, I didn't moon over him or wonder, "Will he call me?" It also didn't really occur to me to call him. So it was a pleasant surprise, nothing more, when he called on Thursday last week.

"You know, Red, you're allowed to call me sometime, if you like."

I laughed. "Trust me, it's not fear of appearing forward that's kept me from it. It's all this bloody schoolwork. I've been swamped."

"Well, do you think you could tear yourself away for a real treat?"

"Such as?"

"I've been invited to a New Year's Eve dinner dance. I'd been planning to go stag, but I thought since we both had so much fun last weekend I'd see if you were interested. It's formal; you'd need a tux."

"I have a tux, as it happens. Just had it altered for a recent formal event. What colour gown are you wearing? I ask only so I can procure an appropriate corsage."

His turn to laugh. "Is that a yes? Please say it is."

"Let me just check my schedule. . . . Well, I do have something earlier in the evening. Maybe I could squeeze in two dates. What time would you—"

"Ha, ha. I know that's not your style, remember. I'll be in the taxi that picks you up at eight on Monday. I'll have a white carnation for you, to match the one I'll have. See you then."

He rang off without saying anything one way or the other about sex. Would this be a similar arrangement to the one last weekend? Or might there be room in the evening for something more intimate? If we were still at the party for the midnight hoopla, it seemed unlikely I'd have time to go anywhere else and make it home in time; I'm sure I'll have a curfew. Maybe I could get it stretched a little?

Pretty sure that Ned was still cleaning up in the kitchen, I headed down the two flights of stairs. Persie was in her rooms, and she and Maxine were playing with Arria, rolling something back and forth on the floor between them. Mum and Brian were watching the telly in the den; perfect.

I positioned myself at the island and waited for Ned to acknowledge me. "Something you need, wunderkind?"

"Advice. Or at least opinion." He put down the bowl he'd been drying and sat on the stool next to mine. "I went to a party last weekend with Luther," I opened. "He apologised for the double-booking fiasco, took all the blame, so I forgave him. Even though the girl hasn't. Anyway, this party was all BC students, and he was a perfect gentleman."

"Does that mean no sex, or just nothing you didn't want?"

"No sex. But I think I'd like some more."

He laughed. "Of course you would, silly. And I'll bet he would, too."

"He just rang and invited me to another party. A formal affair, New Year's Eve."

"The Black Party? Are you serious?" His eyes were huge.

"I don't know. He didn't say."

"Where is it?"

"No idea." He made a motion with his hand for me to continue. "I expect we'll be ringing in the New Year at midnight with everyone else. But ... well ..."

"You'd like to ring a few more intimate bells?"

"That's it. If that's to happen, I'd have to stretch my curfew. But more important, I think I'd need to be ready for ... well, for a little more than happened last time."

He nodded. "And you want to know if I think you should?"

"Yeah."

"Simon, no one can answer that question for you. But here are some things to consider. First, no one gets inside you without protection, and you don't get into someone else, either. Period, end of story. Full stop, as I think you Brits say. Second, if this is your first time—which I'm assuming it is—give some thought to whether this is the guy you want in your head for the rest of your life. Because your first time should be something you always remember. Something you always want to remember."

He paused, but I didn't know what to say, so he added, "Was he gentle with you before?"

"Yes. Very."

"Then, would you want him to be the guy you always remember?"

"I guess that's what I need to decide."

"Having it happen on New Year's is kind of special."

I nodded. "It would depend on the curfew, too."

"Or you could leave the party early. Play it by ear. I wouldn't go with your mind made up, though; he might be intending to be a perfect gentleman again. Is that making you want him more?"

I grinned. "It is, I admit."

"You could do a lot worse, Simon. But I'm not encouraging you. If you don't have this experience for four more years, that's just fine. There's no rush."

He was right. There is no rush. I did spend some of the rest of my time before bed on schoolwork, but I also did some online research about sex between men. Not porn; honest research. Not sure why it had never occurred to me to do this before. I also looked into Massachusetts law regarding sex with minors, and it seems that as long as Luther has my full cooperation, at my age it's not considered statutory rape.

When I finally closed my laptop, I hadn't made up my mind. I decided to take Ned's advice and play it by ear.

This next bit isn't about Luther, but I need to make note. It kind of harks back to the day we arrived in Boston, that hot, steamy day in August, when it didn't seem to me that it would ever be cool here.

Well, it snowed on Saturday. Six inches! I've never seen so much snow. Persie, it seems, likes snow, so we bundled up and went out onto the patio and made a snowman. That wasn't enough for her, though. She started in on some other shape I couldn't figure out.

"Persie, what are you making?"

She stood up from her bent position near the ground. "It's a cat. For the snowman."

A cat. Persie made a snowcat. Well, the least I could do was contribute the whiskers. I brushed snow off of one of the potted evergreens, broke off some needles, and gave them to Persie, who positioned them as carefully as if the cat were alive.

Because of the Happy New Year timing, I got Mum to allow a curfew of one in the morning, though this wouldn't leave much time if the ear I'm playing by decides it wants some alone time with Luther. We'd just have to see.

If I thought Luther looked good before, well . . . in a tux? The guy is drop-dead gorgeous. On the ride over, I asked if this was the "Black Party" Ned had referred to. It was, so I asked what that meant.

"It's a Boston tradition in the gay community. Justin Dall and his partner, Lawrence McDonald, are fabulously wealthy. They own a townhouse here in the Back Bay, with a ballroom on the top floor, and each year they invite some of the same and some new people to a New Year's Eve party. I think part of it is that the only way gay men get to dance together is if we throw our own parties. But also they like to meet new people, and they get a kick out of the fact that a lot of couples have had their start at this party. It's a kind of mixer."

I decided against mentioning Daren Bateman's courage. "Is that why you were going to go stag?"

"Sure. But then I realised I'd already met someone new, someone I like very much." He took my hand. "Just so you know, I expect to dance with other men, and you should do the same. But we arrive together, and we leave together, unless one of us misbehaves horribly."

"If I do any misbehaving tonight, I hope it will be with you."

He gave me an intense look. "I was hoping you'd say that."

So much for playing it by ear. Or maybe that's what had just happened.

The entire evening for me was coloured by what we'd said in the taxi, knowing at least to some extent what would happen later. There was champagne, and I had enough to get a pleasant buzz, but not so much that I was tipsy. At one point, Luther advised me not to drink too much, and I could tell he wasn't merely being solicitous; he had something planned.

Of course, just being in that environment was heady. I'd never ever been anywhere like it, and there was the distinct possibility that I never would again unless, someday, I could host a party like this, myself. Everywhere I looked, gay men. It was incredible and exciting and validating.

Validating: the opposite of what I'd felt seeing Stephanie on Luther's doorstep. So not only had he neutralised that feeling by apologising, but also he'd reversed it by giving me this amazing experience. Several times I wondered what was out there that would be anything like this for Kay. Surely trans individuals would benefit from this kind of validation, too.

Around quarter of eleven, Luther cut into a dance I was having with a tall, Nordic-looking fellow. Into my ear, he said, "You turn into a pumpkin at one, correct?" I nodded. "How set are you on watching the ball drop with these folks?"

"Isn't it expected?"

"There are nearly a hundred people here. Do you think they would miss us?"

I held my breath for a few seconds as if that would help me decide. As if I needed to decide. "Let's find out."

I wouldn't say we rushed out, but I will say we wasted no time. We kissed and groped in the backseat of the taxi all the way to Luther's, but once inside he slowed things down.

"I have a surprise for you," he said. I followed him into the kitchen, where he'd already set out two champagne glasses (evidently newly purchased), a cotton towel, and a champagne stopper. "Hope you haven't had too much to drink yet." He opened his refrigerator and pulled out a bottle of La Grande Dame.

This touched me so much it was everything I could do not to throw my arms around his neck. But I knew that would be exactly the wrong move. I held out my hand for the bottle, and he gave it to me to open. That gentle pop when champagne is opened correctly is music to my ears. I poured some into each glass, then stoppered the bottle and put it back in the fridge. I was about to reach for my glass when Luther picked up both of them.

"You know what I've never done, but I've always wanted to?" I smiled and shook my head. "I've always wanted to drink champagne in bed with someone terrific, naked as the day we were born, and then have really nice sex. And then have more champagne. And then maybe more sex. And then—"

I led the way to his bedroom, where I found another surprise. I turned towards him as he came through the door. "What's all this?"

He shrugged. "I've also always wanted to drink champagne naked in bed in candlelight."

There were candles everywhere. He set the glasses down and walked from one candle to the next, lighting them, smiling at me. Then he wrapped his arms around my waist.

"I've been wanting to say this all night," he said. "You are absolutely stunning in a tux. Just the sight of you turns me on so much." He let go and stepped back, touching only my arm with an outstretched finger. Slowly, he walked all the way around me, trailing his finger over my body as he moved. He stopped in front of me and, the touch so light I almost couldn't feel it, he ran his finger from my lips to my chin, down the centre of my chest, without stopping until he touched my crotch. Still barely touching me, holding my eyes with his, he caressed me until I thought I would explode in my trousers. I closed my eyes and groaned.

Suddenly he was all over me, fingers digging into my back, tongue on my jaw and then in my mouth. He undid my belt and waistband and pushed me onto my back on the bed. Cupping my balls with one hand, he took my dick in his mouth and did wondrous things to me. I yelled as I came and sank against the bed.

When I opened my eyes he was naked. He removed the rest of my clothes, threw the covers back, and fetched the glasses.

"Happy New Year," he said. We clinked and drank, and I reached for his dick. But he lifted my hand away. "I have a suggestion I hope you'll like."

Here it was. I had expected it. But suddenly I was nervous as hell. It must have showed.

"I know it will be your first time. And I don't want to brag, exactly, but I'm really great when it comes to sex with a virgin. If you need to, you can stop me at any point, and we can do what we did last time. But I hope you're ready to try. Are you?"

I watched his face for about three seconds, lifted my glass, drained it, handed it to him, and threw myself back down onto the bed. He drained his glass, set both of them on the bedside table, and reached for two things in a drawer: lubricant, and a condom.

He kissed me and kissed me—my face, my mouth, my neck, my tits, my belly, my balls, my thighs, until I was hard all over again. He turned me gently and kissed everywhere he could reach. Everywhere.

He wasn't just bragging. He knew what he was doing, and he was very gentle with me. My research had not quite prepared me for this experience, for either the good or the not-so-good parts. But I had reason to believe that the good parts would get even better while the rest would matter less and less.

When we'd recovered enough to sit up again, Luther refreshed our glasses. We sat silently for several minutes, sipping those marvellous bubbles, basking in the afterglow. Then he leaned towards me and gave me a sweet kiss. "Thank you, Red."

"Thank me?"

"Yes. For being brave. And sexy. For being you." He clinked his glass against mine.

I sipped and leaned back against the pillows. "Can I tell you something?"

"Something secret?"

I laughed. "Not exactly." I took another sip. "I was stark raving furious with my mother when she married Brian Morgan and moved both of us, lock, stock, and barrel, to Boston. Furious!" Another sip. "My litany, in my rant at her, was that she was ruining my chances for getting into Oxford, where my father had really wanted me to go. Where I had really wanted to go. I was at Swithin in London, a school famous for prepping students for OxCam, as we refer to Oxford and Cambridge together, as though they were Siamese twins instead of siblings locked in rivalry. I was sure that my fabulous marks, and the fact that my grandfather had been at Magdalen College, would get me in for sure, but only if I finished at Swithin. But since then, I've found out that if I hadn't been kidnapped, if I hadn't been forced into St. Boniface school in Boston, if I hadn't been forced to expand my outlook in several ways, Oxford would not have wanted me."

I took another sip, and Luther said, "So you're glad you were kidnapped?"

"Well, what I was really going to say was that Oxford would not have been the only thing I'd have missed out on." I waved my glass for emphasis. "Don't worry that I'm going to get all clingy on you, but—this, you, would never have happened in London."

"Why not?"

"I had no intro into the gay community there. I had no Ned. I knew a couple of other kids at school who were probably gay, but I wasn't chums with them. So I would have lost out on Oxford, *and* I would have lost out on great sex."

"And do you know that you haven't lost out on Oxford?"

I wasn't sure where to start. He didn't know very much about this oh, so important part of my life. "We haven't really talked, have we? Not about important things. I guess that's mostly okay. But Oxford is really important to me. As it happens, they wait-listed me because they weren't impressed with my work at Swithin. It wasn't until people at St. Boniface raised a ruckus that they capitulated and gave me interviews with four tutors, which is a lot. The interviews went really well, but—I'm still pretty nervous about getting in. But if I do, it's all due to having come here. Against my will. Profoundly against my will. I was horrid to my mother."

We let that sit for a minute. Then Luther said, "Can I tell *you* something?" He resettled himself a little closer to me. "I really, truly wish that I could see you again in a few years, to see what you're like then. To see what else you've learned, about yourself, about life. You are going to be one amazing gay guy."

I laughed. "You never know. Perhaps you'll take a trip to England, or I'll come back to visit, and we could meet up again. I'd kind of like to see where you go from here, too."

We didn't finish the champagne; I would have been positively ill otherwise. Luther called a taxi and threw on some jeans and a jumper, and I donned my formal attire again. He walked me out to the taxi, opened the door, and kissed me.

"Let's wait a few weeks before we connect again," he said. "Do you mind?"

I smiled; he was still Luther, and that was fine. "I'll give you a call when I hear from Oxford. Should be a few weeks, tops. How's that?"

"Perfect."

And without another word, he turned back towards the house.

On the ride home, I grinned like a fool. I wasn't in love; that much I was sure of. And if I never saw Luther again, tonight had been a great way to end it. But I'm fairly sure I will see him. And if so, it just might be that the condom is on the other dick.

Boston, Sunday, 13 January

I've neglected my journal lately. It's funny, really; when I had nothing but complaints, I wrote all the time—in the beginning of my time in Boston, it was every day for a while. But now that I'm feeling less angry with the universe, I'm not feeling the same need, unless I have some sexploits to write about. Of course, it's also that schoolwork didn't let up for me despite the Christmas holiday. I got everything done I needed to, and done well, I think. And since 7 January, it's been back to classes, with new assignments and more work.

After my evening with Luther I didn't see Ned alone until Wednesday evening. I went into the kitchen after dinner, ostensibly to help Ned, but really wanting to talk with him about my adventure. When I told him how we had left things, he chuckled. "Good old Luther. Don't let him get caught admitting that someone got under his skin."

"Did I do that?"

"Honey, does the sun rise in the east?"

"Well, it doesn't matter. I'm in no rush to see him again, though I hope I will at some point."

"Don't call him. That's the surest way to get him to call you."

I knew he was right. I had promised to ring Luther when I heard from Oxford. Maybe I'd wait and see if he rang me first.

Speaking of Oxford, it's not exactly late for offer letters, but I don't think it's too early, either, and I haven't seen any. At least I haven't seen a rejection, either. Every day, on my way home from school, I make a huge effort not to feel anxious, in case anything has arrived. Dr. Metcalf is carefully not asking me; he knows I'll tell him as soon as there's something to tell.

Boston, Thursday, 17 January

Still nothing from Oxford. On tenterhooks, now.

Kay and I have stepped up her prep; the March bee isn't far off. And she has lots of time now, because her mother has decided to stop sending her to that school. There was a fist fight; Kay slugged a boy who wouldn't let her into the boys' room. I think it surprised the hell out of her that she had that in her, but her determination to be who she is, as she once put it, has not flagged.

Maddy and I have become best buddies. I was a little worried about it at first. I said to her, "What if a boy is interested and doesn't know I'm gay? He'll think you're with me."

She grinned. "As a matter of fact, another boy is interested. I'm going out on my first date! Other than the dance with you, of course, but that doesn't really count, does it?"

"No." I smiled at her. "That's terrific. I want to hear all about it."

"And anyway, everyone saw you and Daren dance. It's been quite the topic of discussion."

"Are they freaking out?"

She shook her head. "No; just wondering if you're a couple."

How cool is that? They don't care that it's two guys. Or if they do, it's not rising to the surface in a threatening way. I truly hope it won't be too much longer until this is how it is for Kay.

Boston, Sunday, 20 January

Kay's had her first two sessions with the psychologist. She saw her alone for the first one and with her mother for the second. There will be a few more before Kay moves on to medical experts and the first stages of the treatments, but so far it doesn't look as though there will be a snag anyplace.

Friday I talked with Dr. Metcalf about setting up another practice bee for Kay. This time it wouldn't be with her school chums. This time it would be with volunteers from St. Boniface. And this time, there would be eliminations, and a winner.

He loved it. He said he'd poll the other students on his roster and work with the other counsellors to drum up some stiff competition. He was pretty sure there were one or two past Scripps contestants in the student body. We set a date for the evening of 7 February.

He never asked about Oxford. The question was conspicuous in its absence.

Boston, Wednesday, 23 January

This afternoon when I got home from school, there was a kitchen chair positioned just inside the front door. On it were two envelopes from the UK. Oxford.

My ears rang, and my breathing grew odd. It felt as though my stomach was determined to see daylight by leaping out through my throat.

No one else was about. Or if they were, they were keeping out of my way. I stepped towards the chair and had to will myself to reach out. The contents of these envelopes would determine the rest of my life. A career at Oxford is not something one leaves behind; it sets one up in a way almost nothing else can do. Either of them, or both of them, could contain an acceptance or a rejection. Each was from a different college. My hand hovered a foot over them until I forced it down. Grabbing both at once, I headed for the stairs. I wanted to be in the privacy of my room when I discovered what was in these missives.

I shut the door and threw my school bag on the floor by my desk. The envelopes I dropped on the bed. I pulled my desk chair over and sat there, staring at them.

What would I do if they were both rejections? Of course, one or both of the two that had not yet arrived might contain an acceptance; I'd had four interviews. But this first volley seemed all-important.

There was Princeton. I could go there. I would leave Boston and start a whole new life in New Jersey, a place I knew nothing about, really, except as the butt of jokes. I might be accepted at Yale. I'd never visited either place, but the online photos of Yale had left me with the impression that it was attempting to replicate Cambridge University here in the States, and I wasn't sure I'd feel right. I might still get into Stanford, too. California seems like another world, and maybe that would be a good thing.

I walked around the bed and sat on the window seat, looking into the afternoon dusk. I felt light-headed, my stomach still churning. I wouldn't open either envelope until I was calmer; if it was bad news, I wanted to start from a place of relative calm or I might go over some edge. I breathed in for two beats, out for four. In for two, out for four. In for two . . .

Twenty minutes later, I felt calm enough to face whatever Oxford had to say to me. I had decided on Princeton as my alternate; they had been the first to accept me, and one could hardly go wrong there.

Blindly I picked one envelope up and opened it. It was from Trinity.

They wanted me. Comparative theology.

My knees buckled, and I landed rather hard on the floor. All my breathing exercises forgotten, I was nearly panting with emotions I couldn't identify. Could I read this subject seriously enough for a degree? What would I do with it? Probably teach. Did I want to do that? Alternatively I could travel, research world religions, write books, speak at conferences. Did I want to do that?

I managed to get up onto my knees and reach the other envelope. I sat down fully on the floor again; no more falling. I held it in my hands, willing myself to accept that what should happen, will happen. Hadn't this move to Boston been a really good thing for me, after all? Hadn't I changed for the better in so many ways?

Didn't I like myself so much better now? Didn't other people like me when almost no one had before?

Boston had been a big win for me. Whatever else happened, nothing could take that away. I am my own person now. The spell? The one I'd told Ned had been cast upon me? The spell was broken. And now that I know who I am, I'm ready to *be* who I am.

I opened the envelope. Pembroke. Black, lilac, brick red, sky blue, bright red, terra cotta, hot pink, lilac.

They accepted me.

I kneeled by the side of the bed, leaned my arms on the mattress, and wept for joy. I was going home.

Boston, Friday, 25 January

This will be short. Just want to record that I got two more letters from Oxford today. It was validating (there's that word again) that Magdalen accepted me. And I'd never really wanted Christ Church, so when they didn't, there was no serious pain. I'll be responding to the three acceptances next week; just wanted the whole collection first.

Brian is taking Mum and me out to L'Espalier Saturday to celebrate. Supposedly it's a world-class restaurant. It will have to go some distance to compete with Apsleys, but I'm sure I'll enjoy it. I asked if Ned could come, too, and so not only was he invited, but also Manuel is coming. I can't wait to meet him.

Mum's disappointed, I can tell, that I'm choosing Pembroke over Magdalen. But I'm convinced Magdalen gave me an offer more on the strength of my grandfather's connection than because they especially want me, and I really liked Dr. Franklin.

When I told Mum, she cried and hugged me and cried some more. And I thanked her for standing by me, for pushing for me. For believing in me. Then I called Dr. Metcalf.

My father would be so thrilled.

Boston, Sunday, 3 February

Over a week since my last entry. Truth be told, this journalling thingy is beginning to feel a little old, and more like an obligation than like something I want to do, or that I need to do. Maybe soon I'll put it aside and see if it calls to me. But I'll keep on for now.

Quite a bit has happened. L'Espalier on the twenty-sixth was actually very nice. Fantastic service, haute cuisine, and no question about it. Still couldn't have any wine, which was a bit of a bummer.

Manuel is adorable. He's as short as Ned is tall, with just a hint of a lilt to his accent. His parents moved to the US from Mexico when he was a baby. He laughs all the time, and it's obvious Ned is head over heels in love with him.

During dinner, I decided it was time to tell Mum and Brian about Kay. So many other things had captured my attention, my energy, that it had never occurred to me that the stamp of confidentiality was no longer sitting on top of this information, though I didn't mention the suicide attempt. Ned had not told Manuel, which made me respect Ned even more. Mum was near tears when I talked about the difficulties Kay had at school. When I'd said about all I could, Mum suggested that she and Brian and I should get together with Kay and her mother sometime. I was a little surprised at how much I liked that idea.

Towards the end of the meal, Brian asked Ned and Manuel if they could make use of some tickets he was holding for a concert, Renée Fleming and Susan Graham at Symphony Hall. He and Mum have to go to some event a major client of his is hosting.

When Ned and Manuel didn't take them, I said, "If they're going begging, I might be able to use them." There were a number of people I could invite: Maddy, Luther, Daren. . . .

Sunday, the day after that dinner, tickets to the concert in hand, I sat staring at them. I was supposed to ring Luther with my Oxford results, but Ned had said not to do that if I wanted him to ring me. Did that matter to me? I guess really what mattered was that Luther never get the impression that I'm expecting something from him that he's not going to give me. Something I don't want, anyway.

Maddy? Maybe in a pinch; I didn't want to send the wrong message.

I dug out my school directory, picked up my phone, and rang Daren.

We chatted for a minute about school, both of us knowing that wasn't why I had called, and finally I said, "I happen to have two free tickets to see Renée Fleming and Susan Graham at Symphony Hall on Sunday, 3 March. Any interest?"

"Wow. For real? I'd love that."

Easy as that. We made arrangements to meet there. And because I'd told him the tickets were free, there was no awkwardness about who was paying for what.

Luther rang me on Monday evening. I had to chuckle as I saw his number appear on my mobile.

"Hey, Red," he opened. "How are things?"

"Going really well, actually. You?"

"Don't be coy, Simon. How well? Did you hear from Oxford?"

I laughed. "I did. All's well. I'll be attending the college of my dreams."

There was a slight change in his voice, a sense of—I don't know, relief or something, like he'd been worried for me. "Which college would that be?"

"Pembroke. I got in at two others, but that's where I want to be."

"Two others. You little . . . Does anyone ever get more than one offer from Oxford?"

"Sure they do! Lots."

"Prove it. Name one person."

What did I know? "I don't think I will. Maybe I'd like you to go on thinking of me as truly special."

"No question about that, Red."

We chatted for a bit, nothing in particular, and rang off. There was no suggestion of getting together, which I think was his way of keeping just enough distance for comfort—a necessary precaution if he had, in fact, been worried about me. I'm pretty sure I'll be seeing him again.

So today was the concert. Daren was waiting in the lobby of Symphony Hall when I arrived. There was a little awkwardness at first: Shake hands? Embrace? Nod? We settled on the nod, found our seats, and I opened conversation by saying this was the first time I'd been in the hall. Which gave him a chance to talk about other concerts he'd been to there. He said one of his favourite times was coming to see David Sedaris. I didn't know who that was, but before he could enlighten me, the concert began.

After the concert, I asked if he'd like to get a coffee or something, and we went to that little place Luther had introduced me to, that student hangout that was a few steps up from most of the places right on Comm Ave. It wasn't too far from Symphony Hall. Daren had never been there, so that was a coup for me.

He told me about David Sedaris over coffee for him, tea for me. Evidently the fellow is some kind of raconteur and author, hysterically funny, and gay.

"He'll be here in April," Daren said. "I have tickets already. Um, would you like to go?"

"Sounds like fun." Another date. Who would have guessed?

We walked together to the T stop at Mass Ave. There was another slightly awkward moment as we parted. He was headed outbound for Newton, and I was going into town. Plus, there we were in public. Daren solved it; maybe he's had a few more dates than I have.

He held his hand out, and I gave him mine, but because of the way he held it, instead of a true handshake, it was more of a hand embrace.

"I really enjoyed this, Simon. Thanks for asking me."

"Me too. Really glad you could come."

I think we might do something else together before April. Maybe he'll ring me next time.

Boston, Thursday, 7 February

Kay's St. Boniface bee was tonight. She showed up with her mother, both dressed elegantly like the ladies they are.

"I'm really nervous, Simon. What if I don't win?"

"If you don't make mistakes, how will we know how to improve your performance?"

"Right. I'll try to think of it like that."

"Even so, Kay . . . knock 'em dead!"

I was a little nervous, myself. After all, these weren't kids I was pronouncing for this time, not kids for whom I'd had to prepare sentences demonstrating how the words would be used, not kids for whom I'd chosen the words themselves. These were my peers, and my own performance would be under a more rigorous scrutiny and had to be letter-perfect. I had access to lists from the Scripps Web site, but still . . . And it had been so difficult not to work with Kay on the words I'd selected, not to give her that edge. Because what if she didn't do well?

The room was pretty full. Eighteen St. Boniface students had volunteered, including Maddy. So there were parents and siblings and teachers and who knew who else out there watching. Daren wasn't spelling, but he was in the audience. We spoke briefly before the bee began, and I couldn't help seeing that a number of other students noticed this; I guess Maddy was right, and there is some speculation. I kind of like it.

Mum, Brian, Ned, and Manuel were all there as well, which I thought was pretty great.

Three St. Boniface students fell after the first round. The next round saw two fall. Then no one fouled, and then four. Nine of them left, plus Kay.

Five went in the next round; the words were getting harder with each round. So five people were left now, including Kay, who looked nervous but excited in a good way. She smiled a lot and kept cracking jokes, including once when she pulled the same stunt she'd pulled in my very first session with her.

"*Guilloche,*" I called out.

"*Guilloche*. May I have the language of origin, please?"

"French."

"May I have the part of speech, please?"

"Noun."

"May I have the definition, please?"

"An ornamental border formed of two or more curved bands that interlace to repeat a circular design."

"May I have the spelling, please?"

To be honest, she nearly got me; I stuttered before actually saying the first letter, but it had been right there. Kay giggled, and behind me came a riot of laughter from the audience.

"Will you use it in a sentence, please?"

"The architect was at pains to convince his clients that guilloche trimming in their contemporary home would be extremely out of place."

"Are there any other pronunciations?"

"There is one other." I gave it to her, knowing she didn't need any of this information. And she spelled it perfectly, smiled at the audience (who laughed again), took a curtsey (to a smattering of applause), and sat in her chair.

The last three contestants, Kay and Maddy and Phil (who'd come in fifth when he had competed at the national bee several years ago), were tough, and we went three rounds with no errors. Then Maddy tripped up over *lymphopoiesis*, and it was Kay and Phil for four more rounds. Phil finally tripped on *aoristic* when he put an *h* after the *r*. If Kay spelled the next word correctly, she won; if not, Phil had another chance, and so did she.

Kay spelled *oecus* "*a-e-a-c-u-s*," and I had to hit the bell. The entire audience groaned, and Kay's eyes went wide with horror. It was an effort to remain calm, myself, or at least to appear so. Still, I couldn't help but think this would be good for her humility. She'd done exceptionally well, and if she lost tonight she'd work that much harder.

Still . . .

Phil's next word, which I was so very tempted to skip, was *calo*.

In my heart of hearts, of course, I wanted Kay to win. And this word looked just too easy. But Phil put two *l*s into it.

Back to Kay. The next word was *bombycinus*.

She must have asked for the language of origin three times. I knew she was not listening to that same answer; she was thinking, picturing the word, and a finger on her right hand was scribbling furiously on her left palm. This is one of those words for which a number of different spellings could make sense, and unfortunately it did not appear to me that Kay knew the word itself. Or, if she did, she couldn't be sure she remembered the spelling quite correctly.

I had to call thirty seconds.

She closed her eyes, pronounced the word once more, and began to spell. She never paused. She got all the way through to the *s*, pronounced the word again as she was required to do by the bee's rules, and opened her eyes on my face.

My smile told her everything she needed to know. She raised her arms, gave a little scream, and danced back and forth whilst the audience clapped, cheered, stood, then clapped and cheered some more. Mrs. Lloyd joined her on stage, Phil stepped forwards, rather gallantly, I thought, and shook her hand, and Dr. Metcalf surprised the heck out of me by coming out of the wings with a trophy.

Once the hoopla had quieted down a little, Mum and Brian stepped forwards for an introduction, and it seemed so odd to me that these two groups of people, who had been so crucial—so central—to my life, had never met. Mum and Abby Lloyd hit it off immediately and agreed they'd be in touch about getting together. Kay, shy in a way I'd never seen her, cozied up to Brian in a big way, and he seemed very paternal. Solicitous, even. Ned picked Kay up bodily and gave her a big hug, which made her squeal with delight. In so many ways, she's younger than her eleven years. And in so many ways, she's a very old soul.

We're expecting a massive snowstorm—a true blizzard, they're saying—this weekend. Glad I'll get to have that experience before going home, where we don't have blizzards.

Boston, Sunday, 31 March

Ye gods. Nearly two months since my last entry? That kind of says it all, doesn't it? When I'd started, I really needed to "talk" about things; no friends, crisis after crisis (real or manufactured), and some odd combination of unfulfilled romance and fulfilling sex. Now my life is mostly about that one-foot-in-front-of-the-other labyrinth pattern with very few things to trip me up. Though, of course, schoolwork is a constant demand; I have to keep my marks up or lose Oxford again, and I will not let that happen.

The March bee is behind us. I say "us," because it really is both of us: Kay and me. We're a team. Man, I never would have thought I would say that. And I never would have thought that, sitting there next to Abby (which is what she's asked me to call her), I would be so fucking nervous! Watching past years' videos of the final competition, I'd seen the camera land on the faces of parents who were covering their mouths with their hands, and the commentator would say something like, "Their son will be disqualified if anyone in the audience is seen to be mouthing letters." I almost had to cover my own mouth. And the pride I felt at hearing her name—Kay Lloyd—called as the winner . . . My eyes are tearing up just to write about it. And it wasn't just that she'd won. It was that Kay's name, not Toby's, had been called, and an ecstatic girl dressed in a pink and white polka-dot dress had beamed at the crowd as she accepted the praise.

I almost felt bad for Toby, but he had never really existed, anyway.

So in May off she goes to the national bee. And Abby and I will go with her.

I have to say, I loved the blizzard (back on the first weekend in February). I did feel sorry for people who lost power for days or whose seaside homes were swept away. We lost power overnight on that Friday, but it was back before sundown on Saturday. Even so, we huddled in the living room in front of the fireplace. Ned, bless his heart, had made sure we had some firewood on hand, and he'd left us with lots of food we could eat without cooking it: boiled eggs, cheese, bread, crackers, lots of options. Plus gallons of water.

The wind howled and howled and sometimes blew smoke back down the chimney. Arria was very unsettled, and I think Persie would have been worse than she was, except that she was focusing so hard on taking care of Arria. They make a great team.

The city, after the storm, was a winter wonderland. There was a traffic ban through the entire weekend, and Mum and I braved the snowy streets on foot a few times, just for the sake of it, not getting very far and getting quite wet in the process. It was something I might never experience again, though of course Mum is likely to see real snow every winter now.

Boston, Tuesday, 30 April

I sat down to write about the bombings three, maybe four times? Just couldn't quite form thoughts around it. I didn't exactly know anyone who was there, but Maddy's mother is a doctor, and she was in the tents that day, ready to tend to runners who needed medical attention. I wouldn't have known this, not being especially interested in the marathon, if it hadn't been for what happened that day.

There was no school on Monday, 15 April. Something called Patriot's Day in Massachusetts is when the marathon takes place. Schools and lots of businesses close, especially if they're anywhere near the route the runners take. The finish line is on Boylston Street, a few blocks to the southwest of us, right about at the library. And that's where the first bomb went off.

I was on the roof, a pot of tea and biscuits beside me, working on the presentation I'll have to give for my City course. Suddenly my eardrums felt pressure from something low and explosive, my teacup rattled on its saucer, and my heart stood still. I sat there, frozen, trying to reason out whether there was anything in the house that could cause a noise like that, when the second one— almost as loud—bounced off of buildings and windows all around me, a dull, thudding sound that felt completely wrong.

Maxine stood in Persie's open door as I flew past, but I couldn't have told her what had happened so I kept going. By the time I got to the ground floor, Ned and Mum were at the open front door, and I wasn't sure whether that was better or worse than, say, the stove blowing up. If it had been in the house and no one was hurt, then it would have been limited. But if it was outside, it must have been massive.

Brian came running into the house from his office, alone; no appointments today, because no one would have wanted to come anywhere near this area on marathon day even without explosions. He stepped out onto the front steps, but there was nothing to see, so he told us all to stay in the house and then raced back into his office, me on his heels; I knew he was going on the Internet to see what was happening. He opened a news site, found a live feed, and we watched as chaos spread across the screen. Sirens blared, some of the sound coming from Brian's computer and some from outside. Ned came in, and Brian looked up at him.

"Persie?" Brian asked.

"Emma's gone to her."

Manuel called the landline to check on Ned; he said the police were asking people not to use mobile phones, because bombs could be rigged to explode that way. I reached for mine and turned it off.

It was several minutes before we knew enough for Brian to head upstairs with at least a little news, no doubt wanting to avoid making Persie any more anxious than could be helped. Because even after it seemed unlikely that anything else was going to explode nearby, we still didn't know very much. That it was some kind of terrorist attack seemed obvious; but would there be more to it? Or would two explosions be the end?

Maxine and Mum took turns staying upstairs with Persie, while the rest of us—Ned popping in and out of the kitchen to tend to things—hung out in the den, watching things unfold on television. Someone from St. Boniface called the landline to check on me and let me know school was cancelled for Tuesday. Then I tried to think of anyone else from school who lived close by and was appalled to realise that I had no idea. For all I had intended to get to know my classmates better, I knew where only a very few of them lived.

Dinner was a tense affair, with everyone trying to act normally and avoid upsetting Persie, who knew only that something on Boylston Street had exploded. We wanted her to believe it was all over, and maybe it was. At least, the explosions were over. But the air was thick with the fog of not knowing.

I brought my laptop down to the music room after dinner. Somehow I didn't want to be alone. There was a panicked e-mail from Kay, who hadn't been able to reach my mobile, and the landline here is ex-directory, so she couldn't look it up. Around nine I got an e-mail from Maddy telling me about her mother's role. Dr. Westfield hadn't been one of those who rushed towards the explosion sites to pull people away and tie emergency tourniquets and carry bloody, screaming children to relative safety. Dr. Westfield had stayed in the tent where she'd been expecting to treat dehydration and cramped muscles, and instead found herself piecing people back together as best she could, performing battlefield triage in the hopes of saving as many lives and limbs as possible. Maddy said her mother was now at Brigham and Women's Hospital and would be there for some indeterminate amount of time, and that huge numbers of people had been injured, some horribly. The bombs had exploded from somewhere near the ground and had sent shards and nasty metallic bits into people's legs. There had been lots of amputations already, with more almost certain to come.

I couldn't wrap my mind around this. Who would do this, and why? The event wasn't something I had been interested in—and very glad I was of that, at this point—but it was a festivity, a celebration of astounding physical prowess and of determination and of commitment. It was supposed to be a happy event.

And maybe that's what it was about. Someone who was miserable, for whatever reason, maybe not even knowing that was at the heart of their motivation, couldn't abide the joy, the feeling of connectedness that created happiness and assuaged defeat.

While I would never have committed violence on anyone other than myself, I had some idea what that place of misery was like. But I can't, and probably never will be able to, get to a place in my head where any amount of misery would drive me to do something like this. And that makes me feel very lucky. Very lucky, indeed.

By late Tuesday, the authorities had figured out enough of what had happened that St. Boniface decided to open on Wednesday, only to close once more on Friday as the surviving perpetrator was reported to be on the run to nobody-knew-where, though he had been spotted in a place called Watertown. On Friday the authorities issued some order called "shelter in place" for Boston and a few suburbs while a massive manhunt took place. Brian cancelled an appointment with a new client, we didn't leave the house, and Ned didn't come to us. Mum cooked dinner, and a very good one at that. No one had wine; not sure why, but even I didn't want any.

By bedtime we'd heard the news about the capture of the final terrorist, a boy, really. The image of the boat where he had hidden, behind a house, shot full of holes, haunted my dreams. Imagine having it be your boat . . . That's just not something one can prepare for, you know? Having troops of law enforcement shooting up one's back garden.

For reasons that weren't clear right away, Persie had begun to follow the story in detail by Tuesday morning. It didn't seem to upset her; it was more like she was trying to puzzle something out.

By the weekend, the news stories began to focus more and more on the memorial items people had been leaving near the finish line. Quite a variety of things: running shoes, of course; teddy bears, which I don't understand; messages, some personal and some from groups such as a third-grade school class someplace.

For the second week in a row, Persie wasn't allowed to go on any outings, and I thought perhaps that could explain why she began to fixate on this pile of stuff. By the end of the second week, though, it was clear that she wanted an outing very badly, and it had to be to the memorial site. Over Thursday dinner she announced to Brian that she was going there on Friday.

"Why do you want to see that?" he asked.

"I just do. I need to."

Trying to keep his voice even and calm, Brian told her, "Persie, there are so many reasons why that won't work. Not the least of which is that there will be lots of people crowded around a relatively small space, all pressing together and trying to see the items and read the messages. It would make you react very badly."

"It won't. I will stay in control. I'm going tomorrow, not on the weekend. There will be fewer people."

He tried again, but she merely replied, quietly but firmly, that she would go tomorrow. He began to grow irritated, but she didn't, and she stuck to her guns. I don't know whether he noticed, as I did, that this was not a request. She did not fall back on her tactic of asking if she might go "tomorrow" with the intent to repeat the request like water torture, which had worked for other things. This told me how important this mission was to her.

I admit, I had a certain curiosity about the collection, myself. "Brian," I said, "what if Maxine, Mum, and I all go with her on Tuesday? I'll have a mostly open school day, and maybe by then the crowds will have diminished somewhat."

His face grew tense, and I'm sure he was about to raise his voice in denial, but Mum laid a hand on his arm. "Let's you and I talk about this later, what do you say?"

So now, *she* was calming *him* down. I stifled a smile so as not to be misinterpreted as impertinent, but it occurred to me that they really are a good couple. And I was pretty sure she'd convince him.

She did. So early this morning, hoping to avoid crowds as much as we could, we all—including Brian—walked quietly and purposefully to Copley Square, that open area surrounded by ancient Trinity Church, the huge glass John Hancock Tower, and the Boston Public Library across Dartmouth Street. Our approach brought us along Boylston past Trinity to the memorial area. There were lots of people already there, and as I walked behind Persie I saw her stiffen, I hoped in resolve rather than fear. Brian was in front of her, Mum and Maxine on either side.

As we drew close, Brian stopped and turned to ask Persie if she was sure. She was. She locked arms with Mum and Maxine, and as we moved forwards I wondered for the umpteenth time why this was so important to Persie. I'd asked her once, but she'd just shaken her head and said she had to.

Not a large space, the site was cordoned off on three sides by those dull metallic gates often used for crowd control, open only on the sidewalk side. Tied all the way around to the metal gates were pairs and pairs of running shoes, some with messages written or taped on them. There were colourful handprints made by children, a large piece of black slate with chalk messages scribbled all over it, piles of stuffed animals with messages on some of them, and there were hats.

I was moderately unmoved until I saw the hats. Set on the ground, so close together that you couldn't see between them, most were baseball hats with stylized B initials, but there were also hard hats worn by construction workers, something that looked like a policeman's hat, all manner of hats, really. And I couldn't tell you what it was about them, except that each represented someone's head. Someone's brain. Someone's face. All connected, all close together, all pulling together and sharing whatever there was to share.

My eyes watered as I stood there, transfixed. To break the spell, I lifted my head and looked to my right, past Persie and towards the library. An involuntary shudder went through me.

That beautiful building! What if it had been damaged? Wouldn't that have been the worst possible thing?

Then I looked back at the hats. And no, the library would not have been the greatest loss. People conceived of that library. People built it. People created what went into it, from knowledge to art. People visit it, admire it, take advantage of its resources. People maintain it.

If I need any proof about how much I've changed these past months, it's this: I know, finally, that it's people who matter here.

When we got back to the house, Persie ran to her room. Maxine followed, no doubt assuming the same thing I was, which was that the experience had been a lot for Persie to bear. But as I started up the stairs, headed for my room, I heard Persie's door slam, and I knew Maxine would not have done that.

Sure enough, Maxine stood outside the closed door, knocking, trying to open it, calling to Persie. If I remembered right, there was no lock on Persie's door; why couldn't Maxine open it?

Maxine looked at me as I drew close. "I think she's propped a chair under the doorknob."

"Oh, my."

We stood there, staring at the door as though trying to see through it, when we heard Persie say, "Simon. Only Simon." Something shifted in the room, and when I tried the handle, the door swung in.

Maxine nodded at me and stood back.

Persie had assumed the position, the one she'd taken before, where she sits in a wooden chair facing the one she wants me in, even though she won't quite look me in the eye. I closed the door behind me and sat. And waited.

Finally, she said, "I need to know how to do it. How to feel what they feel. Tell me."

And it dawned on me what she'd tried to do. "You mean, like at the memorial. You want to feel moved, to feel connection with people who are sad about what happened. Is that it?"

"Yes. I've watched you, because I think you don't care about other people very much. So I need you to tell me how you can feel. I saw your eyes water."

It was as though she'd hit my chest with something sharp enough to pierce into my heart. I took a shaky breath, opened my mouth, and no words came out. I took another shaky breath, reminding myself that if there was one thing that was true of Persie, it was that she didn't say that to hurt me. She just calls it as she sees it. I would try to do the same.

"As a matter of fact, I care about people a lot more now than I used to do. I wish I could tell you how or why it changed. I really do, because I understand why you're asking. But I didn't know my eyes were going to water. I didn't know how moved I would be by what we saw. All I can say is that it wasn't what we saw that moved me. It was what it meant. And I don't know how to tell you where that comes from. I'm sorry."

"It was just a pile of hats."

True enough. "But they represented people. Individual people, and people all together. It made me feel connected to the people who were hurt and to the people who care about them, but beyond that I felt connected to everyone. Because it's something universal, caring about each other. And that caring, that connection, defined what happened that day so much more than the bombs themselves. So for me, that's what the hats meant."

Her face crumpled. "It's not universal. I don't know what that feels like." She sat there and cried, not even trying to cover her face or turn away. It was everything I could do not to weep, myself. I felt an urge to reach out to her, but that felt wrong for her. I got up and fetched a box of facial tissues; it was the only thing I knew to do, other than to repeat, "I'm sorry I can't tell you more."

And then something else occurred to me. "But I will tell you this. I think the fact that you cry for wanting to feel is important."

"You do?"

"I do. I think it's very important."

She nodded and blew her nose. "You can go now."

I can't sleep. My brain keeps bouncing between that dart Persie shot at me, about not caring about other people, and the realisation I came to at the memorial. I've come to the conclusion that I have no excuse for ever falling back into that way of thinking, of feeling—the way that Persie can't escape. Maybe she will one day; I don't know enough about AS. Yet.

And now I think that this escape from not caring that she wants and doesn't know how to find might be the area that I want to concentrate on when I get to Oxford.

Boston, Sunday, 5 May

I've just browsed back through my journal, picking a spot here or there to reread, surprised that I haven't done more rereading than I have up to now.

There's so much of me in here. I mean, of course, that should be obvious. It is obvious. But my point is . . . What *is* my point?

My point is that this journal paints a picture of me that's painful for me to see, in places. Some places it makes me ashamed, or it makes me laugh, or it makes me cry, and sometimes it makes me proud. And always, it makes me wonder what will come next. What will I be like in five, ten, twenty years? Will I be that Oxford don Mum has in her mental picture of me? Will I marry some handsome fellow, and will we have children? For sure, we'll have cats. Will Kay come and visit me in England? Will she be at Oxford, perhaps?

I had a dream about Michael the other night. We were a couple, and we were at school together someplace. We walked around campus holding hands. And we made love. Tender, sweet love.

Michael. What will become of him? What *has* become of him? We haven't been in touch since that night in his rooms when he'd told me he really is gay, and I never did go to his *nonna*'s for dinner. Did I leave him in the lurch? I don't think so. I've searched my soul a few times to consider what I might have done to help him. And each time I found myself on the verge of contacting him, it felt like a fool's errand. What could I say to him? If we could have been friends, perhaps I could have offered support. But I'd wanted him, and even after that was no longer true, he had wanted me. Nothing good could come of that. Still, perhaps I'll at least let him know I'm truly off for home in a few months.

Persie has changed so much since that first dinner when I'd shown up a few unforgivable minutes late. Will she be able to live on her own someday? That might be too much to hope for, but I'm fairly sure she'll be more independent than Brian ever thought she could be. He was very impressed with my Theory of Knowledge paper, and I'm pretty sure he'll keep giving her chances to stretch herself.

I want her to see the Clyfford Still Museum in Denver.

And I want Mum and Brian to be happy together.

And I want Kay to win!

Daren and I are considered an item at school, though we see our connection as much looser than that. Even so, we have done a few more things together, including a serious make-out session once when I visited him at his parents' home in Newton. He knows I'm headed for Oxford, and he'll be at Harvard next year. So, as with Luther (whom I'm also still seeing occasionally), it's for the simple pleasure of being with someone. No strings. No expectations. Just a lot of fun.

Almost forgot. I threw out my razor blades.

Part III

A Whole New Chapter

Oxford, Thursday, 4 July (Independence Day in Boston)

Oxford. Oxford! I'm over the moon. I don't have the mental focus to document the trip over or the logistics of renting a furnished flat until I can move into my Pembroke rooms. I'm looking forward to digging into the things Mum and I put into storage nearly a year ago and pulling out what I'll use at Pembroke.

Mum wanted me to stay in Boston through the summer, of course, until the fall sessions begin. But I wanted to go home. Staying in Boston felt like so much time being killed.

I will devote some space here to Miss Kay Lloyd, second runner-up in the Scripps National Spelling Bee. I went with her and her mother to the competition in May. She was magnificent. Being one of the final three contestants meant she had all the time she could have asked for on stage. Abby and I had gone with her earlier in the month to shop for clothes, and she looked beautiful up there in a white blouse with a lace collar and a pale blue skirt. She was so confident, so adorable, and her bubbly personality sent the audience into laughter so often that she was dubbed Kay the Comedienne.

I thought she might be unhappy about coming in third. I should have known better. "I'll win next year. And my hair will be longer!"

Her hormone treatments began as soon as she got home. She's starting in a new school in the fall, and she'll be able to present herself as who she really is.

Parting with Luther had gone about as I had expected. We'd seen each other several times after that special, wonderful New

Year's evening together. We didn't have sex every time, and when we did he didn't always play top. Usually, though. He's so good at it.

We took a walk through the Boston Public Garden, sat on a bench for a bit, talked about where we'd be this time next year. He's been accepted into Columbia for the next phase of his academic studies in philosophy, so he's going to New York City. Might be a good place to visit someday.

When we got up from that bench we embraced, kissed, and walked in different directions.

I rang Michael up a few weeks before I left. It was an odd conversation, and it left me feeling I had been right; I couldn't really have helped him. He's gone back to X, back to pretending he's straight. It makes me very sad. I just don't know what to do about it. And I can't help wondering if friends of addicts feel at least a little like this: I want to help, but the change has to come from inside him. I also can't help wondering how badly things would have gone if I'd responded differently, if we'd started a relationship.

Not all love is meant to be, I guess. Still, this is one problem that isn't mine that I really wish I could have helped resolve.

I've been putting off writing about what it was like to leave my family behind. And that is what they've become. My relationship with my mother will never be roses and candy, but it's a hell of a lot better than it was a year ago. We treat each other with respect and affection now; I think we've both learned a lot about each other—and about ourselves.

I would never in a million years have thought I'd miss Brian. But I do. We developed a camaraderie that matured over evenings in the music room, trying different brandies and cognacs, critiquing different performances of music we both know and love. He has quite an acerbic side to his personality, too, when he lets it out, and some evenings we tried to outdo each other, neither willing to reveal how brilliant he thought the other's last comment was, both often fighting laughter that would reveal exactly that. And often we lost that fight.

Persie gave me a going-away present. *Clyfford Still: The Artist's*

Museum, by Sandra Still Campbell. It's full of glorious colour plates of his work and describes his life and the creation of the museum in Denver. I was quite moved. I gave her my iPad; it's a great way to display art, and I knew I'd need something different at home anyway because of the different power supply. Besides, it was a good excuse to get a new one. As I was leaving the house for the airport, with Mum and Brian, Persie threw herself at me bodily. My arms went around her, and I realised with a shock that we had never touched before.

I've left Ned till last because of the connection we had. And also because of a certain shame I feel. As wonderful and sensitive as he'd been to me, and as much help as he'd given me, it wasn't until the night of that party in October that I had asked about him, about his life, other than that challenge I'd thrown at him about maybe needing a push (when he told me he'd finished his master's degree in food science). And although I met Manuel eventually, I didn't ask much of anything else.

So the Saturday before I left, when he sent iced tea and biscuits up in the dumbwaiter for our last rooftop repast and handed me his going-away present, I was stunned. It's a watercolour drawing he did himself. It's beautiful and poignant, full of love and tenderness. The near ground is a tangle of brambles, black and reddish brown, thorny and massive. But on the left side, a passage has been torn through them. Leading away from them is a faint path over soft green grasses, winding diagonally up to the right under a soft blue sky. Barely on the paper, where the path disappears, the blue of the sky gently feeds into faint rainbow colours. Not a rainbow, nothing that obvious—just the colours. It's titled *The Colour of Life*. And "colour" is spelled just like that—the UK English way.

I cried, and it wasn't only because it was so beautiful and so perfect and so "us." It wasn't just because I expected never to have another connection like this one. It was also because I hadn't even known he could draw. A talent like this, and I hadn't known.

If he realised what I was feeling, he said nothing about it. He did tell me his plans, though, despite the fact that I'd never asked again.

"You asked me once, when I told you that you needed a push, if

I might need one, too." He took a sip of tea. "You were right. I did. And you, Simon, you pushed me."

"I did?"

"Yup. Because all that great advice I was giving you? I needed to take it, myself. My brambles were different. They had more to do with lack of confidence. With fear, even, that I wasn't good enough to follow my own path. I've watched you clearing away bramble after bramble and making baskets out of them where you've packed everything you want to take with you. It's inspired me." He leaned back in his chair and grinned. "I'm going to art school in the fall."

"Ned! That's—oh, my God, that's so wonderful! Where?"

"RISD. Rhode Island School of Design. So I'll cook for Brian through most of the summer and then head to Providence."

"And . . . Manuel?"

"Oh, he's coming with me. His company has a branch there. He works from home half the time, anyway. And I have more news."

"Yes?"

"We're getting married in August."

I couldn't sit there any longer. I jumped out of my chair and pulled him to his feet for a long, long embrace. As I sat down again, I asked when, and if there would be guests.

"August tenth. It will be small, but yes, a few guests. Brian and your mom will be invited. I'm not expecting you to come back for it, though."

"If I want to, am I invited?"

"Of course."

"Then I'll be there. With bells on."

So the final lesson I take from Ned is that I have it in me to let the sweetness, the connection of a wonderful relationship be one-sided. To let it be all about me. That won't happen again.

I took a tourist bus around the city today, in the open top of a double-decker. Great way for me to get the lay of the land, as it were, and start to feel at home in my new home.

Graeme sat beside me on the bus, smiling with me, at me, helping me remember everything we were seeing. It felt bittersweet. I'm not sure, but it was almost as though he were letting me know that it's close to the end for us, that he'd seen me safely here, carried me through my exile, and soon we won't be together any longer. I will miss him so much. But if that's the way it has to be, I can take it.

Because I'm here. I'm home.

Bright yellow

Bright orange, terra cotta, Kelly green, lilac

Brick red, periwinkle

Bright orange, bright yellow, pale green, lilac.

Appendix: Letter Colours			
A	pale yellow	N	coral
B	sky blue	O	terra cotta
C	pale brown	P	black
D	dark brown	Q	forest green
E	lilac	R	bright red
F	pale green	S	blood red
G	fuchsia	T	bright blue
H	cream	U	pale pink
I	bright yellow	V	Kelly green
J	maroon	W	navy
K	hot pink	X	dove grey
L	bright orange	Y	periwinkle
M	brick red	Z	dark purple

EDUCATING SIMON

Robin Reardon

ABOUT THIS GUIDE

The suggested questions are included to enhance
your group's reading of Robin Reardon's
Educating Simon.

DISCUSSION QUESTIONS

1. As the story opens, Simon is not a very likable person and, in fact, essentially has no friends. He acts as though not only does this not trouble him, but also that it's actually the way he likes things. By the end of the story, do you think he has changed into someone capable of real friendship? If so, do you think he could be friends with someone he didn't consider to be at least close to his intellectual equal?

2. In the beginning of the story, Simon is furious with his mother for uprooting him at a critical juncture in his academic career. He comes to the conclusion that he doesn't matter very much to her, that her guilt over a childhood event and the absolution he thinks she wants are more important to her than the rest of his life. Do you think he's correct? Toward the end of the story, as he looks back over what happened as a result of his mother's decision, do you think the results exonerate the selfishness that Simon saw in her?

3. Simon's very early take on Persie is that she's a cat who needs an attitude adjustment. What characteristics has he noted that bring him to this conclusion? Who else in the story has similar character traits?

4. Do you think Michael Vitale is gay? If so, do you think Straight Edge can change that? If he's not gay, what is the source of his attraction to Simon?

5. When Kay tells Simon her secret, Simon finds it confusing and has at least some trouble taking it seriously. If you don't identify as transgender, how does what she tells Simon feel to you? Is it real, or in her imagination? Should she be encouraged or discouraged? If you do identify as transgender, what do you think would help those who

don't understand how real and how undeniable the situation is for you?

6. According to Ned Salazar, Luther Pinter "puts his own needs first a little more often than I would want in a partner." Based on how Luther handles his time with Simon, do you agree, or would you describe Luther differently?

7. Simon's meditation in the Boston College labyrinth leads him to understand that he wants the "Hallelujah" referred to in the Leonard Cohen song by the same name. What do you think he means by that? What would a relationship based on the Hallelujah look like to you?

8. After the bombings, Persie insists on seeing the memorial items near the marathon finish line. As she watches Simon react to the display of hats, she is troubled by her own inability to feel strongly about what happened on April 15. Can you put yourself in her shoes? Will your own capacity for empathy make that possible?

9. Consider Simon's relationship with the imaginary Gorgeous Graeme throughout the story. When Simon returns to London and visits Swithin Academy, he encounters the real Graeme Godfrey for the first time in several months. As you watch this encounter, how disconcerting do you find the difference between the two GGs? Do you think Simon will be able, finally, to leave Graeme behind? Can you imagine having a lover who isn't real but who would always be there for you, who would understand your needs and troubles, who would love you as you need to be loved and make no conflicting demands? If you can, how difficult would it be to end that relationship? What would have to happen for you to be able to let it go?

10. When Simon learns about Oxford's initial decision regarding granting him an interview, he goes through a transfor-

mation, or he believes he does. And when the decision is reversed, he believes himself to be less invested in his father's dream. Do you believe him? And after he returns to Boston and finds Kay in trouble, is his response to her problem—and the degree to which he involves himself—another transformation, or the only true one?